DANCE WHILE YOU CAN

SUSAN LEWIS

HarperCollinsPublishers

To Dad and Gary, with love

Acknowledgments

My sincere thanks to G.V. Hardyman and Christopher Dale of
Clifton College, Bristol. To Victoria Walcough of Christie's,
South Kensington. Lindsay and Bob Hall. My friend Fanny,
who not only introduced me to Sark but gave unstinting
support throughout the book. A very special thank you to
Patrick Early of the British Council in Cairo, and John
Kelsey-Fry. And, of course, Laura and Toby.

FROM THE MOMENT I MET HER, there was never any doubt in my mind that one day I would have to kill her. Perhaps it was a genuine vision of the future, though I recall no images, not even the vividness of the fire that was to consume so much. I felt only the overwhelming need to protect myself, and all that was mine.

Elizabeth Sorrill. She was blessed with the kind of beauty I had only dreamed about, bringing love and laughter to my brothers, while all the time she nursed the pain of a love she had lost—a love she would never give up.

And what right had she to that love? I am a woman, I have known love, I have known the pain of loss. Have I spent my life making others suffer for it?

But I know now that I have never experienced anything like the love that bound Elizabeth and Alexander. It was a love that not only bridged the gulf of class, but survived years of parting, the agony of rejection, and that most destructive of emotions, guilt. Do I envy her that love? No, I pity her. A love of that depth, that strength, extracts its own price. I was the one to call in the debt, and I have no regrets. Why should she have had it all? What was her suffering compared to mine? My brother gave her the world—but it was my world too, and I lied, cheated and murdered to get it back. Yet all the time my enemy—my invincible enemy—was not Elizabeth, nor Alexander, but the love they shared.

Why was their love so indestructible?

I rest my head against the wall. There is nothing to see here, only darkness, but my nostrils flare at the cloying stench of my surroundings. Among the few, almost indistinguishable sounds, I can hear myself laughing. Laughing and laughing. The bitter irony of it is, if anyone could answer me that last question, then here, at the end, they would hand me the key to life itself.

As it is, it is they who hold the key—Elizabeth and Alexander.

Elizabeth

1

A SCHOOLBOY! You're telling me you're in love with a *schoolboy?*"

Already wishing I hadn't said anything, I met Janice's incredulous gaze. "I didn't say I was in love with him, I only said . . ."

"Yes, I know what you said. You said you can't stop thinking about him. And the way you've been moping around here, well, I can't believe how dense I've been. But a schoolboy, Elizabeth. Do you know what you're doing? Do you realize what it means?"

"I'm not doing anything, and it means you're getting everything out of proportion, as usual."

"You've been stuck down there at that school for too long, it's turned your mind. Christ, I could understand if it were one of the masters. But a boy!"

"If you saw him you wouldn't call him a boy."

"Well, how old is he? Fifteen, sixteen?"

"Nearly seventeen."

"And you're twenty-one. And this is 1964, and you're probably one of the most beautiful women I've ever seen in my life. You've got to get away from that place, Elizabeth, and fast. Junior matron at a boys' public school, I ask you! I never understood why you went there in the first place. So what's happened between the two of you? You haven't . . ."

"Of course not. We danced together at the end of the term, that's all."

"Danced! I can hardly get a word out of you because you danced with a schoolboy? There really is something wrong with you, Elizabeth Sorrill. I'm going to have to find you a man, and fast."

Janice liked her "and fast"s, but just at that moment they irritated me. I'd come to spend the summer holidays with her, in the studio we used to share in Putney when, like her, I'd been a nurse at the Meadford Clinic. But I'd only been there a few months when a vacancy had come up for a junior matron at Foxton's Boys' School, down in the west country. I'd lied about my age, collected my references from Mrs. Carey at the Meadford, and gone. I'm not quite sure why I did it, except it seemed like a challenge and I'd never really felt at home in London. That was six months ago.

"I take it you do want to find a *man?*" Janice said, when she realized I wasn't going to say anything.

"You don't have to say it like that, and as a matter of fact, I don't."

"Elizabeth, think about it! This relationship can't go anywhere, and you'll land yourself in a whole heap of trouble."

"Stop moralizing. I danced with him, that's all, and I like him. He's . . ."

"Spare me. You're going to tell me he's tall, dark and handsome, and he's got a winning smile."

"As a matter of fact he is tall, dark and handsome. And as for his smile, one of his teeth is crooked. What I *was* going to say was that he's made me feel as if I belong at the school—not easy in a place like that. I have a lot of fun there now, more than I ever did flitting round pubs in the Kings Road. I'm happy, Janice. I feel as if I belong there, as if I have a place there—and it's all due to him."

"Due to *him?*" She looked at me and I could feel one of her "and fast"s coming. "Don't you realize the effect you have on people, Elizabeth. No, you don't, do you, you never did. Look at yourself. You're all the things the rest of us dream about: sensuous, longlegged, voluptuous; you've only got to move and something happens to a man. Jesus, there are things about you . . ."

"Janice . . ."

"Like the way you make someone feel they're the most special person alive. What's the name of that song, 'From a Jack to a
King.' Even the bloody sun comes out when you laugh. And it's
not just men, you have that effect on women too, so God only
knows what you're doing to those poor little buggers down there,
locked away in that school. Try looking at yourself through their
eyes. One day you just appear in their lives; you don't speak like
them, you don't act like them, nobody knows anything about you.
You're a mystery . . ."

"Stop talking rubbish. I'm just an ordinary person, Janice, like
anyone else. I don't talk about my past because it's too painful. But
you know what happened, how my parents were killed, then I came
to London and trained—with you—as a nurse, so why don't you
drop all this nonsense about a mystery?"

She sighed. "You really don't know what I'm talking about, do
you? You say things in that funny, rich, accented voice of yours and
everyone stops to listen. I'll bet he's smitten. I'll bet they all are.
Well, I'm going to get you out of there, and fast. It's time you came
back to the real world. What's his name, anyway?"

"Alexander. Alexander Belmayne."

If her eyes had been any rounder they'd have burst out of her
head. "Alexander Belmayne! The one you wrote to me about? The
one you couldn't stand, who made your life a misery?" She covered
her face with her hands. "Jesus, you're in bigger trouble than I
thought."

"You always dramatize everything, Janice. OK, so I didn't like
him at first, but only because I hadn't got to know him. That's all."

"*That's all!* You nearly left at Easter because of him, remember?"

"I wish I'd never told you now. And I'm going back to Foxton's at the beginning of next term, so you can forget about finding
me another man, another job or another anything."

"Then all I can say is, don't come crying to me when he gets
over his schoolboy crush. Except he won't, will he? Men never get
over women like you. It's just left for the likes of me to pick up the
pieces."

She flounced out, but I knew she'd be back. We'd quarreled
before and it usually ended with one or the other of us storming off.

It gave us time to reflect on who was right and who was wrong.

But of course, Janice was right: I was ignorant of the way I looked, the way I was. And if I'd left the school then, as she suggested, got away, who can calculate how much pain might have been avoided? But all that seemed important to me then was that Foxton's, a school of just over two hundred boys, should remain the center of my world. I couldn't see what I might be doing to Alexander, or he to me. Naturally there were others there, like Miss Angrid the senior matron, whom I'd come to care for a great deal, but it was Alexander who'd made me feel . . .

But I'm getting ahead of myself. Things moved so fast, and so much happened, that sometimes I have to think quite hard before I can remember how it all started. Then I laugh, because it is madness to think for one moment that I might really have forgotten.

2

IT WAS JUST AFTER LUNCH on a cold spring day when Miss Angrid, the senior matron, picked up her well-thumbed volume of Shelley and turned her chair to face the fire. "Well, at least that's over for another six months," she said, referring to the medicals that had been going on for the past two and a half days. "Why don't you treat yourself to the afternoon off, go and explore the village? There's no point in hanging around here, unless you want me to read to you, that is."

She peered up at me from under her whiskery eyebrows, knowing full well I'd do anything rather than sit through a recital of *Prometheus Unbound*. She laughed as I grabbed at my starched cap and shook out my hair. "Beautiful," she said. "Too beautiful. I wonder if I've done the right thing, taking you on. Still, wouldn't be without you now, even if you do run at the mention of Shelley."

I was on the point of making good my escape when Christopher Beadling, a spotty, skinny little thing from the second year, knocked and came in. "Left my blazer behind, Miss," he said, and looking at me he blushed and started to snigger—along with the boys who were huddled around the "grub" cupboard outside.

"Next door in Miss Sorrill's surgery," Miss Angrid answered,

9

then looked at me. "No idea what they're planning?" she said, after he'd closed the door behind him.

"Not a clue." But they were up to something, that was clear. Some kind of initiation ceremony Miss Angrid had called it, when she'd warned me that the boys would be bound to take advantage of my first night duty alone. "Insufferable beasts!" she said now, and went back to her book.

I'd been at the school almost two months by then, and was settling in quite well, although I still felt quite overawed by my surroundings sometimes, and had to pinch myself to make sure I wasn't dreaming. The whole place was much grander than I could have imagined, with its endless gilt script lists of honored old boys and its portraits of Foxton's achievers. The corridors were dark and dank and smelt of beeswax and boiled cabbage. The boys were such a contrast to their gloomy surroundings that I was still sometimes surprised when I heard them stamping around and shouting and laughing. And the way everyone spoke made me wish I could be rid of my rounded, half west country, half London accent, and become one of them. But I was working away quietly on that, along with everything else. Ever since I'd arrived I'd felt a kind of excitement bubbling away inside me. It was as if I was waiting for something to happen; like a chrysalis almost ready to burst.

When I got outside, because the sun was shining and I'd seize on any excuse not to have the embarrassment of using Tonto, I decided to walk back to the cottage.

Tonto was the nickname the boys had given the golf cart that Miss Angrid used to ferry herself to and from the cottage where both she and I lived, she on the bottom floor, I on the top. "Quite self-contained, quite separate," as she had told me when she'd first shown me round. It was on the edge of the school grounds, closing the only gap in the thick hedge on the south side of the field beyond the rugby pitch, and sandwiched between Foxton's copse—five trees, some bushes and a pond—and the farmland behind. From my bedroom window I could see the statue of Arthur Foxton, the school's founder, far in the distance, standing in the courtyard in front of the school like a general in front of his army.

As I passed the sixth form common room Godfrey Barnes opened a window, gave a long wolf-whistle and asked if I'd like to go in for tea. I said I might pop back later, provided they didn't make me take part in another debate on the economic and trade whatsits of Britain joining Europe. Last time, I'd said I thought England was already in Europe, and they'd all laughed so much that I'd had to get out the atlas next day to reassure myself that I was right.

"How about telling us what you thought of *Lady Chatterley's Lover*," Richard Lock called out. "You have read it, I take it?"

"Bits of it," I admitted.

"No prizes for guessing which bits. Did you know there are thirty fucks or fuckings, fourteen . . ."

Time to walk on, I thought, suppressing a giggle. I'd got as far as the front entrance when the main door opened.

"Miss!"

"Yes, what is it?" I said, trying out my haughtiest voice. I was never like that with anyone else, but for some reason with Alexander Belmayne I couldn't help myself. He was in the fifth form, one of the most popular boys at the school, and without a doubt the best looking.

"Er, it's nothing, Miss, only that, well . . ." He looked up at the sky as he sauntered towards me. "Isn't it good to see the sun, Miss? Been jolly beastly weather lately, it's much better here in the summer. Can get outdoors more."

I looked at him, knowing I was blushing, and unable to think of anything to say.

"I was just wondering, Miss." He was looking straight into my eyes. "If you're not intending to take Tonto back to the cottage, then me and a couple of the others were thinking about taking in a few holes on the golf course. Miss Angrid would never know, she'd think Tonto was with you. We'd take good care of it."

I took a step back, shaking my head. "I'm sorry, if it was mine it might be different, but . . ."

He held up his hands for me to stop. "It's OK, Miss, I understand. I shouldn't even have asked." Then, smiling to himself, he turned back inside.

I was glad he'd given in so easily as I didn't know how long I could have held out against him, and it wasn't until I started back down the drive that it suddenly dawned on me: there was nothing to stop them taking the cart anyway. And if it got damaged . . . It would be better all round if I took Tonto with me, and at the same time I'd show Alexander Belmayne I wasn't quite the idiot he took me for.

Reversing Tonto out of its space, I flicked the switch that shot out the little orange indicator arms at the side. The third form had installed them about a month ago, but unfortunately they either came out together or not at all. I shifted the gear lever to go forward. It must have been two or three seconds before I realized I was still going backwards. I pressed my foot on the brake. Nothing happened. I turned round to see if anything was in my path only just in time to avoid a collision with the Headmaster's brand new Rover. It was a narrow miss, and I was still on the move. Then suddenly the machine roared and I was hurtling round the parking lot.

Just missing the ha-ha, I shot round—and to my horror saw Mr. Lear's red Ford Popular coming towards me. I yanked the wheel but it was too late. Tonto gouged itself right along the fender of the car. After that, things happened so fast I didn't know where I was until I shot out of the seat and skidded across the gravel, tearing my stockings and scattering the contents of my bag. Tonto, tipping on its side, groaned to a stop. I covered my face with my hands, taking deep breaths to try and steady myself.

A loud tapping brought me to my senses. Two floors up a cluster of faces was pressed against a window, every one of them laughing fit to burst. Someone waved, and suddenly I was so angry I wanted to scream.

As I ran into the school, tears streaming down my face, I bumped straight into Alexander Belmayne. "You!" I screeched. "It was you, wasn't it? You didn't want to borrow the cart at all, you just wanted to make a fool of me. Well, you're going to pay for this. Now get out of my way!"

"Look . . ."

"Don't touch me! It's too late for apologies."

Miss Angrid's face turned white with anger when I told her what had happened, and how I had been tricked into using the golf cart. "Yes, that's Belmayne's style all right. Come with me," she barked and marched me straight off to the Headmaster.

Mr. Lorimer's first concern was for his Rover. When he found I'd managed to avoid it, he was sympathy itself—at least, as far as I was concerned. "Get Belmayne here," he snapped. Miss Angrid bustled out of the study, and all of a sudden I felt hot and dizzy, and started to shake.

"Sit down, Miss Sorrill." He waved me to the brown leather Chesterfield. "It must have been quite a shock for you. Can I get you something?"

"No, no," I muttered, trying to pull my skirt down over my grazed knees and cover the holes in my stockings.

He picked up the phone and buzzed through to his secretary. "Find Mr. Lear and have him come to my study as soon as he can. He should be sitting prep for the fourth form."

We waited in silence. Mr. Lorimer, in his gown and grey suit, stood with his back to me, staring out of the window. I was acutely aware that my hair was loose around my shoulders, and tried to tuck it into the collar of my coat.

At last Miss Angrid came in with Alexander Belmayne.

"Thank you, Miss Angrid," Mr. Lorimer said, walking around his desk, "that will be all." Miss Angrid looked disappointed, but no one argued with the Head, so she turned and closed the door behind her.

"Belmayne," Mr. Lorimer looked the boy straight in the eye, "you know why you have been summoned here?"

Alexander's face was white. "No, sir."

"Were you responsible for Miss Sorrill's mishap in the golf cart, Belmayne?"

"No, sir."

"Miss Sorrill seems to think you were."

Alexander's eyes were fixed on the floor.

"As a prefect of this school you don't need me to tell you that the punishment for this irresponsible display and the resulting damage could be expulsion?"

I gasped, and Alexander's head snapped up. He dashed the dark curls out of his eyes and glared back at the Head. The threat had only roused him. I could see that the Head would have no easy victory.

And so it proved. Alexander was ordered to name names, but he refused, and consistently denied he'd had anything to do with the golf cart. It was clear the Head didn't believe him, and the interrogation started all over again when Mr. Lear came in. All the time my eyes were riveted on Alexander's face. He didn't look at me once as his grey eyes flashed and the shadow on his chin seemed to get darker as he fought to control his temper.

I don't know how long we were in there, but it felt like hours. Alexander handed over his prefect's badge and Mr. Lear laid a cane on the desk. In their eyes Alexander might be just a boy, but he was taller than both of them, and already filling out into the man he would soon become. My heart went out to him as I realized what this was doing to his pride.

In the end Mr. Lorimer drove me back to the cottage. "I shall speak to Lord Belmayne before I make a decision about what to do with the boy," he said, when I asked what would happen to Alexander. "In the meantime Mr. Lear will take charge."

The next time I saw Alexander he was on his way to bed with the rest of the fifth form. I stood on the surgery landing watching them pass. He didn't look at me, and neither did anyone else.

"Pity it had to be Belmayne," Mrs. Jenkins said, as she turned over a page of the newspaper.

I looked up from the crossword puzzle I was doing. The Latin teacher was between lessons and had come to my surgery for a cup of tea. "Why?" I asked. "I'd say it's a pity it had to be anyone at all. I mean, it *was* dangerous."

"True, but more of a pity it was Belmayne." She pushed her empty cup across the table. "Of course, it's your own fault. All this silent treatment, I mean. You let the boys think you were their friend, didn't you? Shouldn't wonder if you don't actually encourage them to misbehave sometimes—what about that snowball fight you became embroiled in three weeks ago, most undignified. I know you're young, Elizabeth, but you have a position to maintain—and buying the boys Brylcreem when you go to the village so's they can look like Elvis Presley is ridiculous. Lucky Miss Angrid put a stop to it before Mr. Lorimer found out. You can't pretend to be one of them and then go and report the very one they all idolize. They'll never forgive you, you know, at least not until Alexander does. I saw him earlier, on his way out to the rugby pitch. Must have been quite a thrashing Mr. Lear gave him, I could still see the marks."

"But it was almost a week ago!" I said.

"Precisely. Mr. Lear is very fond of that car of his. Unfortunately the Lord Chief Justice seems to have rather a lot on his plate right now, if this article is anything to go by," she went on.

"What's the Lord Chief Justice got to do with it?"

She looked down her nose at me. "Surely you know the Lord Chief Justice is Alexander's father." She went back to the paper. "Those damned gypsy types! Here," she passed the newspaper as she got to her feet, "read that. It might give you some insight into what kind of man Lord Belmayne is—and his son is going to be."

I wasn't going to show her I was interested. I waited for her to leave before I picked up the newspaper.

The Lord Chief Justice, Lord Belmayne, is again locked in bitter conflict with the family of gypsy murderer Alfred Ince. The family has always claimed that Ince, sentenced to death for the notorious "farm murder" in 1954, was innocent. Lord Belmayne, who presided over the long and much-publicized trial, at which several members of the Ince family were arrested for contempt of court, has since been the victim of continuing harassment.

This is not the first time the Ince family has taken up residence on the Belmayne estate. Some weeks ago there were violent scenes when Lord Belmayne had them evicted from his land. More recently, Belmayne property, in London and Suffolk, has been subjected to acts of vandalism, and Lady Belmayne is said to be suffering from shock following an incident in which a brick was hurled through the window of her Belgrave Square home.

According to local sources, the gypsies arrived back on the Suffolk estate in the early hours of yesterday morning. Lord Belmayne, whose outspoken comments on the trial in South Africa of African National Congress leader Nelson Mandela have recently won him considerable publicity, spoke to me shortly afterwards. "These people are causing anguish to my family and my staff. I will do everything in my power to have them removed." It has been suggested by his estate manager that acts of perversion involving underage girls and boys, are being practiced at the gypsy

camp, but Lord Belmayne refused to comment. In a
heated speech in the House of Lords on Thursday he
once again . . .

There was a knock on the door. "Sorry to bother you." It was
Mr. Ellery, the chemistry master. "A bit of a burn to the old fingers
in the lab. Should be wise to it by now, of course, but they all think
they're the first. Loathsome little creatures they can be at times, third
formers. They heat up a glass, you see, and leave it on my desk for
me to pick up."

I led him over to the sink and put his hand under the running
cold water then went to the medicine chest to find a cotton bandage.
"It'll be a bit painful for a while," I said, as I dried his fingers.

"No matter. I'll live." He looked down at my desk and with
his other hand pulled the newspaper round to read the article about
Lord Belmayne. "Unlucky," he said after a couple of minutes. "Still,
the press is usually much harder on him than this."

"Have you met him?" I asked.

"Several times. His son is here at the school." He looked at my
face. "But, of course, you already know that. I gather he's coming
down on Sunday, after chapel."

"Oh."

"Cheer up. Young Belmayne will get no more than he deserves.
He could have caused a very nasty accident."

"But he didn't," I said, "and now I just wish the whole thing
would go away. I was getting off to a good start before all this
happened."

"Mmm, shame," he said, making me feel worse. "Just a pity it
was Belmayne."

"That's what Mrs. Jenkins said," I muttered.

"Well, boys will be boys. I'm afraid you're going to have to get
used to it if you want to survive at Foxton's. Now, I'd better be
getting back. Heaven only knows what havoc they've wreaked in
my absence."

Absentmindedly I watched him go. The door was almost
closed behind him when suddenly he came back in. "I've been
meaning to ask. Do you play bridge, Miss Sorrill?"

I looked up. "Bridge?"

"Just a thought," he shrugged, then left.

The following Sunday was an exeat, so straight after chapel most of the boys went off to spend the day with their parents. After lunch Miss Angrid and I roamed the empty dormitories looking for sweets and comics before she went back to the cottage, leaving me alone in my surgery. I'd been trying for days to think of a way I could approach Alexander and see if we could put the Tonto incident behind us, but he looked so hostile whenever I saw him that I couldn't seem to pluck up the courage. Mr. Ellery, whom I'd been to the Bistro with the night before, had reminded me that I was a member of the staff, and as such could call him into my surgery any time I liked—but it wasn't as easy as that. I'd been nervous of Alexander ever since I'd arrived, even though during my first week he'd gone out of his way to make me feel welcome. After that he'd left me to my own devices, and secretly I'd been glad. There was something about him that made me feel self-conscious and awkward.

I was going over all this in my mind when suddenly the door opened and he came in. "Alexander!" I felt myself blush to the roots of my hair.

It was plain that he was in a filthy mood. "Mr. Lorimer would like to see you in his study," he said, and without waiting, he turned and walked out.

I knew who the grand-looking gentleman was the instant I walked in, and felt myself shrinking inside. "Please sit down, Miss Sorrill," said Mr Lorimer. "Lord Belmayne has asked to speak to you, so I shall leave you together."

Lord Belmayne was a handsome man, older than he appeared, I guessed, but with a magnificent head of grey hair, and piercing grey eyes. I could see straight away where Alexander got his looks from—in this case, angry ones.

"I believe I owe you an apology for the childish and irresponsible behavior of my son," he said, barely looking at me. "I am only thankful that you sustained no injury."

His presence was so overpowering, his manner so cold, that when I opened my mouth to speak, nothing came out.

When he was satisfied that I wasn't going to say anything, he went on. "Rest assured that Alexander has been sufficiently punished, both by the school and by myself, and I trust nothing like this will happen again." He glanced towards the door, then, clutching his hands behind his back, he walked to the window. I had been dismissed.

3

*A*S THE TERM WENT ON my life became more and more of a misery. Apart from tasteless practical jokes involving dead mice and spiders and the stealing of my underwear from the laundry room—later found wrapped around Arthur Foxton's head—none of the boys took any notice of me. They just filed past on their way to bed, and at mealtimes they were respectful but silent. All sickness was reported to Miss Angrid, while I sat in my surgery hoping someone would come in; but apart from Mr. Ellery, no one did.

It was he who told me that Alexander's punishment from his father was to miss his skiing holiday with the family at Easter. As the walls of the room Alexander shared with Henry Clive were plastered with posters of skiers, I could see how severe a punishment that was for him. Well, good, was all I could say—it was less than he deserved! That was how I felt when Mr. Ellery told me, but my mood swung without warning, and instead of the outraged, injured party, I became again the junior matron who remembered how kind Alexander had been when she'd first arrived and known no one . . .

By the end of the term I was so unhappy I decided I had better leave. I would go away for the Easter holiday, and simply not come back. But on the last day I knew I couldn't walk out on Miss Angrid without telling her.

She listened while I explained how my friend Janice kept writing to me about the great time she was having in London, how she was combining nursing with a bit of part time modeling and had hundreds of boyfriends—I blushed when I admitted that I'd never even had one. "You see," I said, "I keep reading in all the magazines what people my age are doing, and I'm not doing any of it. The only thing I've got that shows I'm a bit up-to-date is the poster of George Harrison on my bedroom wall, and a Mary Quant minidress I sent away for. I know I should have given you more notice, and if you like, I'll come back until you find someone else. Janice's cousin has got a shop on Carnaby Street, I might be able to work there. It's not because I don't like it here, or anything like that, everyone's been really nice to me, it's just, well, I don't think I can stay any longer. I miss London, you see."

"But really," Miss Angrid said, "you're going because of the boys?"

I looked away. I should have known she'd see through all that.

She gave my hand a squeeze. "Would you believe me if I told you all this will blow over?"

I shook my head.

"It will, you know. They're behaving childishly, of course they are, but you have to remember that's exactly what they are—children. And as for Alexander, well, he's a popular boy with a lot of pride, but he'll get over it."

"He won't! He hates me!"

"Now you're sounding like one of the juniors! Speaking for myself, young lady, I'd miss you a great deal if you went. You've brightened this place up more than you realize, even Mr. Lorimer's commented on it. Oh, you're a bit of a handful sometimes, I'll admit that—especially when you take it into your head to defend yourself from catapults with a catapult of your own!—but there's no harm done, and you've won as big a place in most of our hearts as I happen to know we have in yours. And now you're blushing again, goodness you do blush easily, don't you? Well, maybe you're right, you should be up there in London modeling or working in a fashionable shop. But unless I've got you completely wrong, I don't think that's really your scene, as they say. So come along with you now, you don't strike me as someone who gives up that easily."

I fished around in my sleeve for a hanky, keeping my head lowered so she wouldn't see I was crying. "Now, how about giving it until the end of the summer term?" she said, passing me a tissue. "And I think you'll find that if you try talking to Alexander, he'll listen. He's far too decent a chap to bear a grudge for long."

"Is he?" It was pathetic how much I wanted that to be true.

"You take my word for it. So are you going to stay?"

I nodded. I wasn't brave enough to put my arms around her, but I wanted to.

"That's my girl. And now there's something I have to tell you. Mark Devenish, the little boy in the first year who suffers with homesickness? Well, his aunt came to the school early this morning. Mark's mother died last night. He's in Mr. Lorimer's apartment now, they're waiting for you."

I don't know why Mark's aunt left him behind at the school, I didn't like to ask, but I'd never seen a child look so lost and unhappy. He ran into my arms when I walked into the room, and I kept his face buried in my shoulder so he wouldn't see that I was crying too. Poor little mite, he was only eleven and had hardly any friends. How could everyone have deserted him?

I took him back to the cottage so that he didn't have to watch the other boys getting ready to go away for the holiday. He had a pack of cards in his pocket and taught me how to play Trumps. I gave him some lemonade and cakes, but he didn't eat anything and he didn't say much either. But every now and then I saw his eyes fill with tears, and I put my arms around him while he clung to me like the frightened little child he was.

When Mr. Lorimer knocked on the door later that afternoon I was touched by the way his face softened when he looked at Mark. He ruffled his hair and listened while the boy told him how he'd beaten me at seven games of Trumps, and I winced when he added that he'd won three-and-six off me.

Luckily Mr. Lorimer laughed, then he turned to me. "I'm afraid it seems we've got another casualty on our hands, Miss Sorrill. Miss Angrid's taken a tumble down the stairs. Mr. Parkhouse has taken her to the hospital, though she insists it's no more than a sprain." He glanced at Mark, who for the moment was happily engaged in looking through my records. "Perhaps you wouldn't mind walking down to my car with me a moment."

He waited until we got outside before he spoke again. "I'm glad of this chance to talk to you, Miss Sorrill, because I want you to know that I am aware things haven't been easy for you lately, and I'm sorry for it. However, Miss Angrid tells me that you wish to stay on at the school, and I want you to know how grateful I am. You have a naturalness in dealing with the boys that makes me very glad of the contact they have with you; your lack of pretension is good for them. I'm sorry if I've embarrassed you, but your contribution to the welfare of the boys has been much appreciated."

All these compliments in one day, I'd have to offer to resign more often . . . "Thank you," I said graciously, thinking how grown-up and dignified I seemed to have become lately.

"There is another matter, Miss Sorrill. In light of Mark's fondness for you, and the fact that Miss Angrid will not be mobile for a week or two, I was wondering if I could impose upon you to remain at the school over the Easter break? You will, of course, receive suitable remuneration."

"Oh, that's all right, I'll be fine in the cottage."

He gave me a strange look, then said, "If you would be so kind as to bring Mark to my apartment around six, after he's collected his belongings from the dormitory, I'll talk to him about going to the funeral."

Poor little Mark. It looked as if his guardians were only too glad to pass all responsibility for him over to the school. If that was the case, it was probably better for him to be with us; I'd been lonely enough after my own parents died to know how awful it was to be with grown-ups who didn't want you.

As it turned out, I didn't see very much of him. He stayed in Mr. Lorimer's apartment and the two of them only joined us for meals. Sometimes I saw them going off in the Rover or strolling about the grounds, but every night I went to say goodnight to Mark, and stayed with him until he fell asleep.

For the rest of the time there was Miss Angrid, who qualified— leaving all competition standing—as the world's worst patient. I wheeled her round the grounds and watched television with her, but apart from that, and her Shelley readings, there wasn't very much to do with all the boys away. So when Mr. Ellery popped in during the week he was nearly bowled over by the welcome he got. Mark was at the cottage with us that day and his face lit up when he saw that Mr. Ellery had brought his Monopoly set. I'll bet the four of us made more noise over those games of Monopoly than any of the boys did on the rugby field—mainly because Miss Angrid kept trying to cheat.

It was on Easter Sunday that Mark showed me a letter he'd been nursing for days. I'd thought it must be from his aunt, but I could hardly believe it when I saw it was from Alexander Belmayne. He'd written to Mark to say how sorry he was to hear about his mother. Miss Angrid beamed all over with pleasure when I told her.

"Alexander is Mark's house captain, that's why he wrote. It will make a world of difference to the lad. The others won't dare to be unkind to him once they find out Alexander's written to him." She looked at me. "You see, he's not such a bad sort, is he?"

When all I did was look back at her she shook her head and handed me the letter. "You've got too much pride, young lady, and you know what that comes before."

Two days before the holiday was over, Mr. Ellery and I were strolling along the sixth form corridor on our way out to the kitchen garden. I was laughing so hard at something he was saying that I didn't hear the voices coming from inside the common room.

"No sixth formers here, are there?" Mr. Ellery asked, even though he already knew the answer. "Intruders! Burglars!" He started an exaggerated tiptoe towards the door. "Get ready to run for help."

I covered my mouth, trying not to giggle, and waited while he pushed the door open.

"Gotcha!" he cried. I heard a scuffle, and then Mr. Ellery said: "Belmayne! What are you doing here?"

My heart turned over.

"Watching TV, sir," came the reply.

"This is the sixth form common room," Mr. Ellery pointed out, as if Alexander didn't know.

"Yes, sir. But I thought as they weren't here, sir . . ."

Mr. Ellery waved his hands. "Never mind about that, why are *you* here? You're not due back until Wednesday."

"My grandmother is going on holiday, sir. She'd forgotten to tell my father. Mr. Lorimer knows all about it, sir."

"Did you know anything about this?" Mr. Ellery turned to me. I shook my head. "Well," he said to Alexander, "what are you going to do with yourself?"

I stepped inside the door in time to see Alexander shrug. His face reddened as he saw me, something Mr. Ellery must have noticed too. "Well, I'm sure we'll find something to keep you occupied," he said. "What are you watching, boy?"

"Football, sir."

"Don't forget to turn off the set when you leave. I'll speak to you later."

"He's a strange boy, isn't he?" I commented, as we strolled out into the garden.

"Who, Belmayne?" He sighed. "Academically speaking, he's near brilliant. And he's a great kid, you know. Too much charm, too much wit, and too good-looking by half—but you can't help liking the boy."

"You can't?"

He laughed. "Come on, enough about him," and grabbing my hand, he pulled me up over the hill.

At the top there was a swing that the boys had made in a tree. I sat in it while Mr. Ellery pushed. He was flirting with me, but when I pretended not to notice he pushed me higher and higher until I was screaming out for him to stop. In the end I managed to throw myself off, fell over, rolled down the hill and knocked over the bins full of dead leaves.

He came running after me, obviously scared stiff I'd injured myself, but when he saw I was laughing, he reached out to pull me to my feet. "You're far-out, do you know that?" he puffed. "And come to that, so are your legs."

"You shouldn't have been looking!" I cried, as I picked the leaves from my uniform.

At that moment I happened to glance up and saw Alexander standing at the window of the music room, watching us. I don't know why, but it suddenly seemed as though the sun had gone in and I shivered.

"Cold?" said Mr Ellery. "Come on, let's go back inside. I'll get someone to come and clear this lot up."

We walked round to the front and went in through the main door just as Alexander was coming out of the music room. "Go and clear up the leaves outside the walled garden, boy, will you?" Mr Ellery said.

Alexander glared at me so fiercely I nearly took a step back, then he brushed past us. Mr. Ellery called after him. "I don't care much for your attitude, Belmayne. You can come back here and apologize to Miss Sorrill. Now!"

Alexander turned round, but didn't come back. "I apologize," he said.

Mr. Ellery and I parted company at the bottom of the stairs—where I waited until he'd disappeared into the staff room before turning to follow Alexander.

I found him refilling the bins as he'd been told. The gathering of dead leaves was normally a punishment, and one reserved for the younger boys, so I understood why he was mad at having to do it. He looked up, but when he saw it was me he went back to work.

"Can I help?" I offered.

"No thanks."

I stood there for a while, watching him. Slowly I became aware of a kind of churning inside, and felt so jittery that I was glad he didn't look up. Eventually I said: "I've come out here so we can have a chat. Will you listen to what I've got to say?"

He stopped what he was doing and stood up, looking straight ahead.

"Look, I don't mind saying I'm sorry, or that I'm really un-happy about all that's happened. And I thought that as we have to live under the same roof, it might be better if we tried to get along together. How about starting by looking at me when I'm speaking to you?"

To my surprise, he did—and the dreaded color started to creep into my face.

"That's better," I said. "Now, I don't want to go over what's led to all this, and I don't expect you do either. All I will say is that if you had thought about what might happen before you doctored that stupid golf cart, then you would have known that . . ."

"And what makes you so damned sure it was me who doctored the golf cart?" he snapped. "Did you see me do it? No. Let's face it, you've had it in for me ever since you started here. You . . ."

"Don't you shout at me, Alexander Belmayne. You tricked me and you know you did."

"I did not trick you, you stupid woman!"

"How dare you! I'll have you know . . . No, don't you interrupt me, I'm not listening to another word from you."

"Why? Afraid of what you might hear?"

"I'm not afraid of you!"

"*No?*" He stepped towards me—and I stepped back. "Look at you!" he shouted. "Not quite so stuck-up now, are you? Now you can listen to me for a change. I liked you, did you know that? I thought you were all right. I bothered to welcome you into this school, and what did you do in return? Ignored me. Whenever you saw me coming you walked the other way. If I spoke to you, you put on that hoity-toity voice of yours, though with everyone else you were as nice as pie. As I said, I don't know what I'm supposed to have done, but you must have got your own back by now. So why don't you leave me alone!"

"I never ignored you. After my first week it was you who ignored . . ."

"Did you know, it was me, *me* who told everyone it didn't matter if you weren't quite like the rest of us. *Me* . . ."

"I'm common! Is that what you mean?"

"Yes, common!" He glared at me. "And now tell me this. Did it ever occur to you that the golf-cart might have had a genuine fault? No. You were adamant that someone had played you a trick. Well, they had, as it happens, but it wasn't me! You've lost me my prefect's badge, got me a caning and lost me my holiday too. So if you came out here trying to beg forgiveness, forget it, it's too late."

"Beg forgiveness! From you! You conceited little . . ."

"So why did you follow me out here?"

"I was played a trick by someone and I'm suffering for it. And if it wasn't you, why did you say it was?"

He answered through clenched teeth. "In case you didn't notice, I didn't say it was me." He started to walk away.

My mind was in a spin. "But you took the blame," I shouted after him. "Why did you do that if it wasn't you?"

He turned to look at me, his eyes filled with contempt. "I should have sneaked? Is that what you're saying? Sneaked on some-one else?" He was spitting the words, and his face was white. But as he turned away from me again, I saw that he had begun to smile. It was a bitter, contemptuous smile, and before I knew what I was doing I had caught hold of him and started pummeling his shoulders.

He put his arms up to protect himself, but I didn't stop. "You nasty, small-minded, arrogant little creep! You think you're really smart, don't you. Well, here's what *I* think of you!" And I slapped him sharply round the cheek. Immediately, he grabbed my hands. Then, looking down into my face, he snarled, "Why don't you just leave here? Go away somewhere, as far as you can get, with your own sort. You don't belong here."

I tore my hands free, and turned quickly before he could see there were tears in my eyes. I stood with my back to him, for some reason unable to walk away. He was the first to speak.

"I'm sorry. I had no right to talk to you like that."

I didn't answer, so he came towards me. "Please don't cry. I'm sorry, really I am. I don't know why I said that." He put his hand on my shoulder. "I didn't mean it."

I shrugged, and then I was able to walk away.

Later, when I was alone in my surgery, I tried to remember everything we'd said, but all I could really think about was how everything inside me kept going hot and then cold, and how sick I felt. I stood up and sat down, made tea and didn't drink it, opened a book and couldn't read, started to leave the room and came back.

I knew I shouldn't have hit him, but then he shouldn't have spoken to me the way he did. And he shouldn't have apologized to me like that either—I didn't know why, he just shouldn't have!

The day before the term was due to begin, Henry Clive, Alexander's roommate, arrived back at the school. His face was nut brown after his skiing holiday, which I don't suppose cheered Alexander up much. I'd kept out of Alexander's way since I'd hit him, but it was obvious he'd told Henry about it, because when I saw them they started laughing. It seemed that every time I turned a corner they were there. I wanted to shrivel up, I was so embarrassed.

And there they were again, coming out of the pool house as I wheeled Miss Angrid past in her chair.

She was still chuckling away at something she'd said, when

Henry yelled out and came sauntering over to ask how she was. She was delighted. Alexander followed and stood to one side as Henry and Miss Angrid joked with each other. I knew he was watching me, but I wasn't going to give him the satisfaction of making me blush.

"Well, Belmayne," Miss Angrid said, turning to look at him, "you're too old to have wet your pants, so why are you standing there like a dog with a guilty secret?"

He grinned. "How are you, Miss Angrid?"

"Better, better. Now what's all this I've been hearing about you two putting on a play next term?"

"It was supposed to be a secret," Henry groaned.

"Nothing is secret from me," Miss Angrid answered, "you should know that by now. Come on, out with it, what is it?"

"Actually, it's something Alexander's written," Henry answered. Of course, it would be! I continued my study of the sky. "And Mr. Lear," Alexander put in.

"Don't let him take any of the credit," Henry objected, "he's only helped you with the research."

"More respect from you, Henry Clive!" Miss Angrid barked. "So, what's it about, this play of yours?"

"You'll have to wait and see," Alexander teased. I knew he still had his eyes on me and was laughing quietly to himself, so I smiled at Henry—who wasn't even looking at me.

"How long shall I have to wait?" Miss Angrid asked.

He shrugged and looked at Henry, who looked back at him. "Oh, sorry, thought you'd said something," Alexander grinned, as he shot a look at me. "How long? Couple of weeks, I suppose."

"Who's in it?"

"Us."

"Surprise, surprise. Is there room for anyone else? I suppose not, with two such overgrown egos."

Alexander and Henry laughed. "I told you, you're just going to have to wait and find out," Alexander said.

"Well, off you go, then," said Miss Angrid, "dry your hair, the two of you, before you catch cold. And reserve me a good seat for the play!"

"Things any better between you and Belmayne?" Miss Angrid

asked, as the boys stalked off and I started to wheel her back to the cottage.

"I told you, he hates me."

"And I suppose you hate him too?" she chuckled.

"Yes."

Later that evening I was in my surgery listening to the radio and getting ready for the start of the new term, when there was a knock on the door and Henry Clive came in.

"Can I have a word, Miss?" he asked.

I reached out to switch off the radio. "Of course. Come and sit down." And struggling not to show how pleased, or how surprised I was to see him, I waved him towards the chair at the other side of my desk. "Nothing the matter with you, is there?"

"Oh no. No, fighting fit."

I raised my eyebrows and looked him over. "I don't suppose I can argue with that."

He laughed. "No, it's nothing to do with being ill. It's, well, it's something that I'm not really sure whether I'm allowed to ask."

"I've never known that to stop any of you before."

"You won't be offended?"

"I don't know, do I?"

He shrugged. "Fair point. It's only that, Alexander and I, we were wondering . . . You know Miss Angrid mentioned our play this afternoon? Well, afterwards when we were talking about it, we had a brilliant idea. You see, there are only three characters in it, and we need a woman for one of them. We were going to use one of the other boys and dress him up, but as, well, you're a, you know, woman . . ." The blush that had been steadily creeping up over his cheeks suddenly rushed into full blossom. He waved his hand in the air as if to say, Oh what the hell. "Well, we thought that maybe you would play the part." He sat back, obviously glad that was off his chest.

I looked at him in amazement, I think my mouth even fell open. "You want *me* to be in your play?" I said. He nodded. "I don't . . . I mean, are you sure about this? What about Alexander, won't . . ."

"Oh, don't worry about him," Henry interrupted. "Anyway,

it was his idea. Call it an olive branch, if you like. Look, the fact is, after what happened, you know, when you hit him, and he said sorry to you, and you cried . . . Well, he feels bad about it, and we really do need someone in our play, so what do you think?"

He waited while I thought. "And you say it was Alexander's idea?" I said finally.

"Yes. So, will you do it?"

"I don't know. I mean, I've never acted before."

"Well, you've only got to learn the lines and move about the stage where necessary. Alexander's directing it, he'll show you what's to be done."

"What sort of part is it?"

"You'll be playing my wife." He announced it with such pride that I could hardly keep myself from laughing.

"All right," I said, "I'll do it, on condition that my role involves nothing dangerous."

"Now what could be dangerous about being my wife?" He grinned and got up. "First rehearsal tomorrow morning at eleven, in the history room, before everyone gets back."

4

WITH MY INVITATION TO PLAY the part of Beth Wonderful, wife of Heeso Wonderful, everything changed. It didn't surprise me one bit to discover that Alexander Belmayne, the director, was a tyrant and a bully. He propelled me round the history room like I was an Aunt Sally—but I told him that if he pushed his luck too far, I'd beat him up again. His answer, because he thought it was witty, was: "Oh beat me, beat me!" Still, I showed him. Not only could I act, but when we needed flowers for the set I made chrysanthemums out of wood shavings from the carpentry room, which I painted with my nail polish; and when we needed curtains for the stage, I borrowed them from the Headmaster's drawing room. Well, he was the only master who had really big windows, and we did take care of them . . .

There might have been quite an awkward moment when Alexander told me I was going to have to learn to "speak posh." I overreacted, I admit it, but it was a sore point with me.

"Oh, there goes the prima donna again, tossing her head and stomping out. Just like a woman," he called after me.

"That's why we cast her," Henry said. "And tact is not your strongest point."

"Don't worry, she'll be back," I heard Alexander say, just before I slammed the door. That was it! Nothing would get me back now! That was, until he came and knocked on my door . . .

"All right, I'll beg if I must," he said. "Please, please will you come back?"

"No!"

"You're a stubborn, high-minded . . ."

"I suppose you'll be calling me common next!"

He burst out laughing, and so did I.

We put on our play at the end of the third week of the term. It was called *The Wonderfuls*, a comedy about an old man—played by Alexander—who (to quote Alexander's uninspired program notes) tried to show the Wonderfuls—a prosperous, self-seeking twosome—how superficial and meaningless was their way of life. The old man never quite succeeded, as the Wonderfuls were too stupid and too pompous to understand, but the outrageous dialogue—most of which even I knew owed more to Bernard Shaw and Oscar Wilde than to Alexander Belmayne—had the staff, as well as the boys, corpsed with laughter.

When the play was over the three of us stepped forward to take our bows. Then Henry and Alexander presented me with an enormous bouquet, and to great whoops and cheers from the entire school, I wept like a waterfall.

Mr. Ellery seemed as pleased as Miss Angrid that the war between Alexander and me was over. In fact the only person who wasn't obviously delighted was Mrs. Jenkins; she thought us too frivolous for words—though I noticed it didn't stop her coming to my surgery for cups of tea. I didn't mind that so much, I just wished she'd stop reading to me from the newspapers. Anyone would have thought she was the only person in the world who had a husband on Fleet Street.

"I can't get over the change in you," Mr. Ellery said one evening a week or so later, when we were dining at the local bistro. "You're so happy. The boys adore you, you know. I've never known anything like it. Everywhere I go these days I come across boys talking about you. Yesterday I found a touching ditty by one of our first year poets, describing you as a changeling."

"A what!"

"A princess sneaked from her cradle by elves."

I burst out laughing, but Mr. Ellery said, "Well, he might have a point. None of us knows anything about you, where you come from. Is there a mystery?"

"No. I just don't like talking about myself. Anyway, there's nothing much to tell."

"There must be something."

"Even if there was, I wouldn't tell you because you're teasing me."

"Me!"

I threw my napkin at him. "Yes, you!"

"Then I suppose I'll just have to join your fan club and theorize along with the rest of them. Do you know, every notebook I come across in the lower school these days has got Bobby Moore's name scrubbed out and yours plastered right across it?"

"Not the upper school?" I complained.

"Ah, the upper school take themselves much more seriously, so they're a little more, shall we say, subtle about it."

"Oh yes? In what way?"

"In that they don't dare let me see because they know I'll get jealous."

I could have kicked myself for falling into that one.

"Have I embarrassed you?" he asked, without a trace of embarrassment.

"Yes."

"Good. Then perhaps I'm getting through to you at long last. I mean I've hardly seen you these last weeks—I have to fight my way through a throng of adoring adolescents just to get to you."

Later, we strolled back up the hill to the school. "Cup of tea wouldn't go amiss," he said, when we reached the door of my surgery.

Recognizing the look in his eyes, I smiled. "I'm right out of tea, I'm afraid."

He rested his hands against the wall on either side of me, and looked down into my face. "Two minutes," he pressed.

I heard a movement at the top of the stairs and looked up. It was Henry Clive. "Sorry, Miss," he stammered, "I was looking for . . ."

"Yes?" said Mr. Ellery. "What were you looking for?"

"Nothing, sir."

"Spying, were you?" said Mr. Ellery, sounding unusually sharp for him. "Back to bed, boy. I'll speak to you in the morning."

"What's all the noise out here?" said Miss Angrid, coming out of her surgery. "Be quiet, the pair of you, you'll wake the boys."

"Sorry, Miss Angrid," Mr. Ellery said, sounding for all the world like one of his smaller pupils.

She turned to me. "Come in here a moment, will you, Elizabeth."

I pushed my way past Mr. Ellery, throwing him what I hoped was an apologetic look. Miss Angrid closed the door behind me. "That saw him off, eh?" She might as well have shouted it. I burst out laughing.

"Shame Henry Clive saw you, it'll be all round the school tomorrow."

"We weren't doing anything," I pointed out.

"Don't have to, the boys will fill in the missing spaces. Anyway, I must get back to the cottage in time for Billy Cotton. You'll be all right, will you?"

"Fine." For someone who claimed she couldn't bear TV, her devotion to *Billy Cotton's Band Show* was amazing. And *Coronation Street*, and *Peyton Place*.

"Oh, by the way," she said, popping her head back round the door, "the second form are planning a midnight feast in the Hardy bathrooms. Keep an eye out, will you?"

"How on earth did you find that out?"

"I know everything there is to know around here," she answered, then tapped her nose. "You'd do well to remember it." And chuckling to herself, she closed the door behind her.

Although I was still smiling as I went into my own surgery, I couldn't help but feel a bit disturbed by what she'd said. For some reason it sounded like a warning.

It took no time at all for the rumors to start. Miss Sorrill and Mr. Ellery. Anonymous notes started to appear under my door, with outrageous sketches of what the boys assumed us to be up to. I had to give them credit for imagination, even though I was shocked by how much they knew about sex. Mr. Ellery was getting the same treatment, but he found it funny.

"It won't be long before Mr. Lorimer finds out, you know." Mrs. Jenkins eyed me with hostility as she sat sipping tea in my surgery.

"There's nothing to find out."

"The boys are very astute, Elizabeth; they miss nothing. And I'll tell you, I've noticed myself, the way you've been throwing yourself at Richard Ellery. It won't do, you know. Anyone can see he's embarrassed by the situation. I suggest you keep yourself to yourself a little more."

The old cow! How dare she! "How can I keep myself to myself," I snapped, "when Mr. Ellery keeps fawning after me like some puppy dog!"

"Miss Sorrill!" she gasped. "You're talking about one of the masters of this school!" She pulled herself up from the chair and strode towards the door. "Your conceit has obviously grown to preposterous proportions. Perhaps you are not such suitable material for Foxton's after all."

"You've got no right to talk to me like that," I cried, and jumped at the violence with which she slammed the door.

Her attack was so unexpected, not to mention unjustified, that it was several minutes before I could pull myself together. It was unusual for me to stand up to one of the staff like that—but she deserved it. I'd been edgy ever since the rumors had started; there were some boys who obviously saw them as much more than a bit of fun—Alexander and Henry, for example, had really cooled off towards me. I'd hardly seen them lately.

I went off to the dormitories to make sure the boys had cleaned under their beds and tucked in their hospital corners. My mind was only half on what I was doing, but I made an attempt to note who had not performed his duties correctly, ready to chalk them up on the board. If their number appeared, they had to report to the matron.

When I got to the Lawrence fifth form room which Henry and Alexander shared, my heart sank. It was in a terrible state. I decided to tidy it myself, at least that would avoid a confrontation. The drawers were half open, with clothes hanging out, so I took them out one by one, folded them neatly and put them away. It was as I was closing the last drawer that I noticed the blue suede winklepickers in Alexander's shoe rack. He had special permission for the shoes, but was only allowed to wear them when he was performing in the school pop group—they should not have been in his room, but downstairs in the clothes cupboard outside Miss Angrid's surgery. As I pulled the shoes out, a small red book fell on the floor. I opened it to the first page, and found in beautifully proportioned calligraphy the name Beth. I closed the book quickly, but my heart was already beating faster. No, I told myself. Just because I had played the part of Beth Wonderful in his play . . . No, it couldn't be.

"What the hell are you doing?"

I dropped the book and spun round. "Alexander!" I gasped.

He snatched the book from the floor and turned back to me, his face white. "I'm sorry," I mumbled. "It fell out of the shoe rack, I was just . . ."

"Go round snooping in everyone's diaries, do you? Or is it just mine?"

"I told you, it fell out and I opened it to see what it was. I didn't read any of it, so don't worry, your secrets are safe." I tried to laugh.

He stared down at me, and for a minute I thought he was in pain. Then he flung his hand through his hair, sweeping it away from his face before he turned and thumped the wall. "Just go," he said.

"I'm sorry, Alexander, really, I'm . . ."

"I said go!"

"Alexander, please . . ."

"Please what?" He swung round.

"Look Alexander, I know I shouldn't have looked in the book, but I told you, I didn't read any of it, only the inside cover."

"Well, that was enough, wasn't it?" And before I could stop him, he had stormed out of the room.

5

MISS ANGRID LOOKED at the thermometer, shook it, and walked off across the room. "Nothing wrong with you, young lady."

"But I keep going all hot, and then I feel queasy. I've been like it for weeks. And my heartbeat keeps going up and down as well, it's really peculiar."

She came back out from behind the screen. "Good heavens, what on earth are you crying for? I told you, there's nothing wrong with you."

"I don't know why I'm crying."

She folded her arms over her chest and smiled. "Well, I think I do. It's very likely a combination of the time of the month and the heat. You'll be all right in a couple of days. Off you go now, or you'll be late for the film."

"What film?"

"That James Bond film the upper sixth have all been dying to see."

"All right, I'm going." I blew my nose and got up from the chair.

"Elizabeth!" Miss Angrid called as I got to the door. "Aren't you going to take your bag? Dear me, I don't know what's got into you these days. You'll forget your head next."

It was Commem. weekend, and I was wandering across the lawns with some of the junior boys, stopping while they introduced me to their parents—and trying to ignore Mr. Ellery as he pulled faces at me through the crowd. I heard a voice I vaguely recognized, looked up and saw the Lord Chief Justice walking across the lawn towards me, with the Headmaster. I caught his eye and smiled. I might just as well have smiled at one of the cherubs over the doorway; he looked right through me and held his hand out to someone pushing past me. I watched him for a while, then realizing that Mr. Lorimer was scowling at me, I turned to work my way back into the crowd.

Alexander and Henry were rather overdoing their enthusiasm for the school band, and I giggled as several parents swung round at the sound of Darren Goodchild blasting his trumpet into Henry's face. Though he gave no sign of it, I knew Alexander was aware of me watching him. I wished I could just go up to him and say something—the trouble was, I didn't know what. Ever since that day in his room, he'd changed towards me.

I looked around for my faithful followers, and found that for the moment I had been deserted. Suddenly I knew I had to go inside or I would disgrace myself by crying in public. Just why I wanted to cry I didn't know, but I'd been doing a lot of crying for no reason lately.

I let myself in through the music room just in time, and groped for my handkerchief. I sat down at the piano. Then I got up and walked around the room. I didn't want to go back to my surgery because Miss Angrid would be bound to come and turf me out again. But the music room proved to be no refuge. Mr. Ellery came in so quietly that I almost leapt out of my skin when he spoke.

He laughed, and asked me why I wasn't outside on this bright and beautiful summer's day. I told him I'd come inside to cool off.

"And the tears?"

I looked up, and to my horror they started again.

"Don't tell me it's the condom," he said, referring to the little package I had received that morning. "I think you're losing your sense of humor, you know."

"My sense of humor!" I cried. "Just tell me what was funny about that filthy object, or what was inside it."

"But it was only glue." He grinned. "Perhaps someone's trying to tell you they're stuck on you."

"That's not even funny."

"No, perhaps not. And you think Belmayne had something to do with it?"

I shrugged. "No, not really. But . . . oh, I don't know."

We both looked out of the window to where Alexander was standing with his father. "You two haven't fallen out again, have you?"

"No. Well, at least, I don't think so."

He grinned. "Tell you what, I'll have a word, put him straight about a few things, that should do it. Now, how about some coffee?" And he started to usher me towards the open French windows.

"No, I can't go out there looking like this," I said. "I'll go and freshen up first."

As I got to the door he called out, "I take it you know what Alexander's problem is, Elizabeth?" He winked, then went off to join the party.

The next day was my twenty-first birthday. Not that I could tell anyone at Foxton's that, having lied about my age to get there; as far as Miss Angrid was concerned, I was twenty-three. It was also the day of the summer ball at St. Winifred's Girls' School, and Alexander's pop group had been rehearsing in the music room all day.

I busied myself in the surgery while I listened to them playing, and at some point I must have drifted into a world of my own, because I only realized the music had stopped when there was a knock on the door and Alexander came in.

He watched me from the door, moving his hand across his forehead to sweep the hair out of his eyes. "I—" he glanced over his shoulder, and I saw Henry outside, leaning over the banister to talk to someone below—"that is, we, would like to invite you to the dance tonight."

I didn't seem to be able to do anything except stand there and stare at him. Then Henry turned round. "Haven't you asked her yet?" he said.

Alexander spread his hand over Henry's face and pushed him out of the way. He was still looking serious when he turned back, but when he saw I was laughing, he laughed too.

"You mean the dance at St. Winifred's?" I said.

"Yes. Everyone's dressing up and Mr. Ellery said he'd take you in his car."

"It's either that or Tonto," Henry chipped in.

Alexander rolled his eyes, and I said, "Then it'll have to be Mr. Ellery's car."

Mr. Ellery picked me up at seven o'clock sharp and wolf-whistled so loudly I nearly ran back inside. "You're sure going to knock them off their feet in that," he said, watching my hem-line wriggle further up my thighs as I settled into the car.

"You don't think it's too short?"

"Are you kidding? It looks terrific!"

But just walking in through the door of the school hall told me that I was all wrong. The girls from St. Winifred's all had long dresses—real ball dresses—and in my tight-fitting Mary Quant mini-dress, I felt like a totem pole. But it was too late to turn back, so I just told myself that I was older than them, so allowed to wear what I wanted. And with Alexander singing on the stage, I clapped my hands and tapped my feet, and laughed at all the boys as they tried doing the Locomotion. The Headmaster kept glowering at me, but I was having too good a time to care. "Up and down and round and round we go again," Alexander sang, and everyone kicked off their shoes, let down their hair and twisted themselves silly. The boys, looking very different and almost grown up in their black polo sweaters and grey slacks, spun the girls off their feet to "Rock Around the Clock," and even lined up to have a go at the Madison.

Alexander sang the first line of "Doo Wah Diddy Diddy," and everyone cheered as Mr. Ellery spun me out into the middle of the floor.

"Everything all right?" he shouted, as he twirled me round.

"Perfect. By the way, what did you say to Alexander?"

"Let's just say I put him right about a few things."

"Like what?"

"Me and you."

"Was that what was bothering him?"

"You know it was," he shouted—and Henry Clive caught my hand and turned me round to dance with him while someone else took over the drums.

It seemed no time at all before the band took their bows, and after that the lights went down for the final record of the evening. The end of the summer ball, the end of the summer term. It was one of my favorites, "Sealed With a Kiss" by Brian Hyland.

I picked up a Coke and smiled as Mr. Ellery invited the St. Winifred's Headmistress to dance; then turning round, I saw Alexander leave the stage. As he started to walk towards me my heart began to pound and suddenly I was hit by panic. I reached out for a bottle to refill my glass, but his hand closed over mine, and without looking at him I put the glass down and followed him out onto the floor.

I hardly dared to move, I was so aware of his arms round me. I could feel his breath on my cheek as he sang the words to the song:

> I don't want to say goodbye for the summer,
> Knowing what love we will miss,
> Let's make a pledge to meet in September,
> And seal it with a kiss.

His legs were moving against mine and I knew he was holding me too close, but I couldn't break away. I kept my head lowered against his shoulder and my hands rigid on his back. After a time I realized I was shaking—and that he was, too. Mr. Ellery caught my eye, but I looked away. I was so full of feeling, I thought I would suffocate, and the panic I'd felt earlier sprang into life again. And then the music faded and he pulled away. I looked up and saw that his face had the same look it had worn that day in his room when I found the diary; and then his expression softened and his eyes seemed to sink into mine. I looked at his mouth, and as he started to lean towards me the lights suddenly came up.

The Headmistress clapped her hands and started to shoo her girls out of harm's way. Alexander was still watching me as I searched the room frantically for Mr. Ellery. I found him waiting for me at the door and ran over to join him.

All the way back to Foxton's in the car, Mr. Ellery chattered on—and all I could do was smile and nod. I couldn't speak, I couldn't think, even. I just wanted to be alone. When I got back to the cottage, I ran straight to the mirror in my bedroom. My eyes looked bigger than normal, my skin was flushed, and then I realized I was hot, too hot. And I wanted to be back on the dance floor. I wanted to hear him sing those words again, I wanted the lights to be down, I wanted him to . . .

I clapped my hands over my face. I wanted him to kiss me.

6

So THAT WAS HOW IT STARTED. A silly prank, a play and a dance. Janice and I didn't discuss it again, but when she drove me to Paddington on the last day of the holiday she said: "You're heading for a fall, Elizabeth. It's all wrong and you know it."

But it was she who was wrong. I'd had six weeks in which to get things into perspective, and I'd already made up my mind that when term started I would keep out of his way. Now that he was in the lower sixth and his room was in the stable annex, that shouldn't be difficult . . . And it wouldn't have been difficult if, despite my resolutions, I hadn't found myself taking the weirdest routes around the building just on the off chance of bumping into him. And it seemed that every day there was something he had to pop into the surgery for, or a reason why I had go to to the sixth form common room. Nothing was ever said, but sometimes I would catch him looking at me and know he was remembering the night of the dance. Mostly I avoided his eyes, though, because I too couldn't forget that night.

Then I went down with a bout of flu. Miss Angrid flatly refused to let anyone near the cottage until I was out of bed and brought up the get well cards, fruit and flowers herself. After six days I ventured out as far as Foxton's copse which was little more than ten paces from the front door. Once it was known I had left the cottage, I was bombarded by boys wanting to accompany me on my walks, and one evening Alexander and Henry arrived in Tonto to take me for a drive round the grounds. After that, even when I was better, the three of us met every evening for a walk if the weather was fine, or a chat in the common room if it wasn't. Sometimes, of course, Alexander was too busy or had to go somewhere with one of the masters. Those evenings always seemed empty.

Before long I was beginning to find I couldn't sleep for thinking about him. I wanted him to kiss me so much that sometimes I had to bury my face in the pillow to stop myself from screaming his name. I took to standing naked in front of the mirror, looking at myself. I'd never taken much notice of my body before, but now it seemed the most important thing in the world. I hated my breasts for being too big, but when I touched them I cried tears at the way it made me feel.

By Christmas I was looking at him, wondering about him in a way that shocked me. When I saw him playing rugby it was as if everything inside me was aching. I looked at his legs and his shoulders, and the way he moved; his hair, how it fell over his eyes; the way he'd rest his hands on his knees, getting his breath back. And then I'd wait for his smile when he looked at me, and my heart would flip over to see that silly old crooked tooth.

The day before the end of term I invited some of the boys over to the cottage for mince pies and hot punch. I did it purposely in the hope that Alexander and Henry would stay on later, and they did. They were sitting on my battered old sofa listening to records when Henry suddenly said, "I know! Why don't you come and stay with us for Christmas?"

At first I thought he was speaking to Alexander, but he was looking at me. I laughed. "I don't think your parents would reckon much to that. Anyway, I'm already going somewhere."

Alexander got up and went to stack more logs on the fire. I watched him as he squatted in front of it, resting his elbows on his knees and staring into the flames. Henry's eyes met mine and I shrugged. It wasn't at all like Alexander to be this quiet.

I turned back to finish wrapping a present for Miss Angrid, and my pen shot straight across the gift tag when Henry suddenly clapped his hand to his forehead and cried, "Oh hell, I've got a present for you, Elizabeth, I forgot to bring it with me." He looked at Alexander.

I knew immediately what they were up to, and even though there was nothing in the world I wanted more than to be alone with Alexander, I was suddenly afraid. "You don't have to get it now," I said. "Give it to me in the morning, before you go off." I picked up the small parcels I'd wrapped for them and handed them over. "Not to be opened until Christmas Day."

"Not allowed," Henry objected. "We've got to open them now. We can have our own Christmas, the three of us. I'll go and fetch your present." And he was gone before I could stop him.

Alexander sat down on the chair next to the fire. "You're quiet this evening," I said.

He stood up, stuffing his hands in his pockets, and began to pace the room. His back was towards me as he stopped. "What *are* you doing at Christmas?" he asked.

I was taken aback by the angry tone of his voice. "I told you, I've got plans," I answered steadily.

He turned to face to me. "You're spending the time alone, aren't you?" he said, fixing my eyes with his.

I swallowed hard. He was right. Janice had gone to the Caribbean with her parents, so I had booked myself into a small hotel in London where I was planning to read Edna O'Brien through the holiday, until I could come back to Foxton's again. "No, of course I'm not. Honestly, Alexander, I don't know what's got into you."

Suddenly he was beside me. "If you must know, I don't much like the idea of you being on your own over Christmas," he growled. "That's what's got into me!"

"But it's nothing to get angry about, and anyway, I told you, I'm not going to be on my own."

"Then who are you spending it with? I know you haven't got any family, so who . . ."

"That's none of your business," I retorted. He looked hurt, and immediately I was sorry. "I'm going to London, I'm staying with some friends."

"What friends? You never talk about them."

"That's because they're not part of my life here at Foxton's. Come on," I said, trying to sound bright, "what are you doing over Christmas?"

"You know what I'm doing." Suddenly he leaned towards me and my heart turned over at the look in his eyes. "Elizabeth, let me come with you. I can tell my parents I'm staying with Henry."

"Alexander, you can't! It's ridiculous even to think of it. Your parents will want to see you, and you'll want to see them too."

"I don't. I want to be with you."

His cheeks were red with embarrassment and anger, and I didn't know what to say. He sat down beside me, and took my hand. I tried to pull away, but his grip was too strong. "Alexander," I gulped. "Stop it, please. Look, I think you'd better go before you say something you regret."

"I won't regret it. Damn it! Stop treating me like a child! You know how I feel about you."

"Alexander!" I jumped up from the settee. "Don't say any more. Boys—young men, young men still at school, you're bound to have crushes, I understand that. But, Alexander, you're taking it too far. You're making a fool of yourself."

I could see I had hurt him deeply. "Do you know how it feels?" he said. "Do you know what I've been going through these past months, since that night at the dance? If you didn't care, then why?"

"Oh Alexander, I do care." What was I saying? "I like you. I enjoy your company and I thought you enjoyed mine. It was no more than that, Alexander, honestly, no more than that."

"You're a liar!" he yelled. "You led me on. You made me think you felt about me the same way I feel about you—and all the time it was just a pretense. Now I can see you for what you really are. You're nothing but a lonely old spinster, pampering your ego at my expense."

"Stop it! Stop it! I wasn't leading you on, I . . ." I started to reach out to him, but wrenched myself away and went to stand behind the sofa, using it as a barrier between us.

"You've been laughing at me all the time, haven't you?" he shouted. "I can see you now, telling Mr. Ellery everything, and laughing at the way I haven't been able to do my work, the way I haven't been able to do anything for thinking about you. I was nothing more than a figure of fun, was I?"

I pushed my hands up to my face. "You're wrong, Alexander, believe me. I wanted, you were . . . oh please, please go."

"I'm going, and don't expect either of us back. You see, you even had Henry fooled. Even he saw the way you were with me. But that's it from now on, Elizabeth, it's over for all of us." He reached into his pocket. "And here! Here's your Christmas present. Merry Christmas!" He flung it down in front of me.

The door slammed behind him, and suddenly I knew I couldn't let him go like that. He was at the bottom of the stairs when I tore open the door. He looked up as I called out his name. Then almost before I knew it was happening, I was in his arms. I knew it was wrong, but I couldn't let him go.

He led me back into the sitting room and pulled me onto my knees in front of the fire. "I'm sorry," he whispered, reaching up to wipe away my tears. "I'm sorry for everything I said."

"Me too." I lowered my head, but he lifted my face and kissed me. At first his lips were gentle, but as his hands closed around my face I clung to him, needing to feel him closer.

"Tell me you love me, Elizabeth. Please, tell me," he murmured.

He kissed me again, and this time I felt his tongue move against mine. I twisted my fingers through his hair and was saying the words before I even realized it.

"Now will you let me come with you?" he asked.

I shook my head. "Please, look at it sensibly, Alexander. You can't come, you mustn't. Just because we've admitted to the way we feel doesn't make it right. You have to go home to your parents, and I'll go to London. Then after Christmas . . . well, who knows? I think it would be better if we don't spend any time alone together after this."

He put his hand over my mouth. "Don't say that. Don't ever say that again. I'll agree to go home for the holiday, but only if you agree that you'll see me afterwards, only if you promise that you'll still love me when I come back. Elizabeth. Please, promise me, Elizabeth."

In the end I was too weak to refuse. I loved him too much already.

7

COULDN'T HAVE MADE A BIGGER MISTAKE than to go to Mr. Billings's little hotel off the Bayswater Road. He was a kind and jovial man who told me with pride that I had the only room with a bath, but the wallpaper and curtains were drab and, feeling the way I did, once the door had closed behind him it was a struggle to hold back the tears. The big armchair under the standard lamp was just right for sitting and reading in, but I never got any further than the first few lines of *Girl with Green Eyes*.

I went for walks round the shops or in Hyde Park, and tried as hard as I could not to think about Alexander—but I thought about nothing else. At night, listening to the sounds from the street, I sat by the mirror and ran my fingers over my lips, remembering what it was like when he kissed me. And always I'd end up wrapping my arms around myself, wanting to cry out with the need to touch him.

On Christmas morning I opened the present he'd given me. I'd said once, when we'd all been talking about what we would buy if we had lots of money, that I'd buy some expensive French perfume called *Y*. He'd remembered. I wished so much that he was there then that I was almost stifled by the longing. And because I was shaking when I opened the parcel, I dropped it, and the bottle smashed. All Christmas Day I sobbed into my pillow, and most of Boxing Day too. I couldn't bear to think of losing him, not yet.

It was two days after Christmas, late in the afternoon, when Mr. Billings knocked on my door. I must have been asleep because there seemed to be a fuss going on in the corridor, and I heard someone call that she thought she'd seen me going out. I pulled myself up from the bed, my book thudding to the floor. As I opened the door and flicked on the light I could see Mr. Billings at the top of the stairs.

His face lit up when he saw me and he started to speak, but I was looking past him. It couldn't be. I was dreaming. He didn't know where I was . . .

". . . nice to have visitors, especially at Christmas," Mr. Billings was saying. He clapped Alexander on the shoulder and pushed him towards me. Then I heard Alexander refusing the tea Mr. Billings was offering, and in a daze I let him take my arm and pull me inside the room. When the door was closed he turned to look at me, lifting his hand and pulling the scarf away from his mouth.

"Merry Christmas," he said quietly.

My voice seemed to come from somewhere far away inside me. It shook as I said, "How did you know . . . ? What are you do-ing . . . ?" He put his hand on my face and I moved into the circle of his arms, and his mouth, still cold from the wind, was against mine, and his arms were holding me tight. He let me go and my eyes flew open.

"Alexander . . ."

"Just tell me you love me, Elizabeth. Please."

Cupping my face with his hands, he kissed my eyes and my nose and my cheeks, and then my mouth again. "I couldn't think, I couldn't sleep, I couldn't eat. I had to come. Tell me it's been the same for you too. Tell me you love me as much as I love you."

"I love you," I whispered, my voice breaking as I tried not to cry.

He took off his coat and put it on the chair. I looked away, but he put his fingers under my chin and turned me back again.

I tried to smile. "I don't want to wait any longer," I whispered.

He kissed me slowly, and his fingers were shaking as he started to unbutton my dress. After a while he lifted my hands and nodded for me to undress myself while he took off his own clothes. Most of the time I kept my eyes on the wall opposite because I was afraid to look at him, and afraid he might be disappointed in me. And then he was standing next to me, running his hands over my arms and I buried my face in his neck.

He undid the catch at the back of my bra, then gently pushed me away from him. As he pulled the straps down over my arms and my breasts fell free, I heard the breath catch in his throat. I tried to cover myself, embarrassed by the way my nipples were standing out. He took my hands away and drew them to him. "Look at me, Elizabeth," he whispered. "Look at me here."

I looked down, mesmerized by the way my hands were moving over him, and then as he took my nipples between his fingers, my hand tightened around him. I looked up as the sound came from the back of his throat, as if he were choking. And then my hand and my arm were suddenly wet.

"Oh my God!" His voice was thick with fury and disgust. He turned away, burying his face in his hands.

I stood there, not knowing what to do, and then he pushed past me and escaped into the bathroom.

He was standing in front of the washbasin when I went in, one hand on each side, staring down into the sink. "Alexander," I whispered.

"Don't," he growled. "I don't want your pity."

I walked over and leaned my head on his shoulder. "I love you," I said. "Don't be angry. Sometimes these things happen the first time."

"How do you know?" he snapped.

I slipped my arms around him and started to kiss his shoulder. He turned round and crushed me hard in his arms. "I just couldn't stop it," he whispered.

"I understand," I said.

Picking up a towel he wrapped it round his waist, then sat down on the edge of the bath. I cradled his head in my arms, running my fingers through his hair. He had tried to be so brave for both of us, and now I knew that it was my turn.

"Will you come back in now?" I said eventually. He nodded, so I took his hand and led him to the bed, where we lay down together.

"Elizabeth," he whispered into the silence. "What you said

just now, that these things sometimes happen the first time . . ." He lifted himself onto one elbow and looked down into my face. "I wish I could find the words to tell you how much you mean to me." I closed my eyes and pulled him down to kiss me. After a while I pushed my tongue into his mouth, and it wasn't long before I could feel the passion rising in him.

His voice was gruff as he spoke. "Do you think we could try again?"

I nodded, then found I had to swallow hard as he lowered his mouth to my breasts. When he lifted his head again, he pulled me against the length of his body, and I could feel him hard against my belly. I was afraid, and closed my eyes as he slipped my pants down over my legs. And then he began to tease me with his fingers. I had never felt anything like it before. I stiffened, clamping my thighs against his hand, and then I looked up into his face and tried to say his name.

He took his hand away, and easing my legs apart, he lay down on top of me. Then very slowly I felt myself opening to him, pulling him towards me, until with one gentle push we were together. He touched his lips against mine, then pushed again. I gasped at the pain, and he stopped.

"Are you all right?" he whispered, looking down into my face.

I nodded, and my whole body swelled with love as we started to move together. He pushed his hands underneath me and lifted me closer to him. And as I wound my legs around his, he started to move faster until his breathing became labored and heavy, and then he called out my name as with one final push he fell against me.

I wrapped my arms around him, holding him still. Our bodies were sticky and damp, and his heart was thudding against mine, but I didn't want him to pull away yet. He lifted his head to kiss me, and I felt his tears against my cheeks.

Finally he moved away. I knew immediately that something was wrong, and I was terrified that he regretted what we had done. I had given myself to him so easily, what if he despised me for it now? I wanted to speak as I watched him sitting there on the edge of the bed, his head in his hands, but my tongue was paralyzed with fear.

"Tell me what I have to do," he whispered. "Tell me what it is you want."

When I didn't answer, he turned to look at me. "You're so beautiful, Elizabeth, and what you have just given me . . . But it must be the same for you."

I closed my eyes against the surge of relief, and reached out my arms to him. "Just be here," I whispered, "all you have to do is be here."

"But I can give you more," he insisted. "I know I can. Tell me, show me how to do it."

"I don't know," I answered.

He looked into my eyes and I saw the doubt in his. "Can I try?" he said.

I nodded, and as he started to stroke my body and then push his fingers between my legs, I suddenly knew what it was he had to do. So taking his hand, shyly, I held it where it was. "There," I said. "Just there." And as he touched me, and began to stroke me again, I experienced something so beautiful I could never even begin to describe it. We slept for a while and when I woke up his fingers were tracing tiny circles around my nipples. He was frowning, as if he couldn't really believe what was happening to my body, then he smiled when he realized I was watching him.

"Can I make love to you again?" he whispered.

Later, after I'd been downstairs to fetch tea and sandwiches, we talked, and I tried to pretend I was angry when he told me he'd looked in my diary before leaving school, and that was how he'd known where to find me.

"It's no use you frowning at me like that, Elizabeth," he said, sitting naked on the end of the bed and ripping apart a turkey sandwich with his teeth. "I know you were glad to see me. You were, weren't you?" he added when I didn't answer.

I shrugged. "Sort of."

"Sort of?" he choked. "Then I'd hate to think what physical state I'd be in now if you'd been really glad to see me. And stop looking at me down there, you know what it does to me."

"I'm not looking at you anywhere," I objected. "Now tell me, what about your parents, where do they think you are?"

He shrugged. "In London."

"Doing what?"

"Well, not sleeping with the junior matron of Foxton's, that's for sure."

I stopped smiling. "Don't, Alexander, please don't say that."

"I'm sorry. They think I've come down to see a show with some of the other boys."

"Are you only staying one night?" I tried to keep the desperation from my voice, but already my heart was beating so hard that I tried to cover it with my hands.

He must have sensed how I was feeling because he came across to my chair and knelt down in front of me. "I'm not leaving you now, Elizabeth, I can't."

He looked so young, so brave. What was to become of us?

It was two days later when we finally ventured out to the theater. We went to see a matinée of *Happy Days,* the Beckett play that, despite a really morbid theme, had us gripping our sides with laughter, as Winnie, buried to her waist in earth, tried to fill her days by filing her nails and rummaging around in her handbag.

All through the play Alexander held my hand, and every now and again he leaned over to kiss me, just as he did when he thought I was asleep. I kissed him when he was asleep too, because he looked so young then, and vulnerable, and I knew that despite his outward confidence he was as afraid as I was that something might destroy our happiness. There were times, too, when he couldn't hide his bewilderment at what was happening to him, and he would gaze at me for minutes at a time, then beg me to tell him how much I loved him—and I'd laugh and say silly, romantic things until he laughed too.

When the show was over we decided that as we were having such a good time, we would splash out and find a noisy restaurant somewhere in Covent Garden. And we were just heading for The Bistro, tucked behind the market, when the unthinkable happened and Alexander spotted Mrs. Jenkins walking down the street on the arm of her husband. Quickly Alexander pulled me into a shop doorway, took me in his arms and buried my face in his neck.

Mrs. Jenkins sailed by and didn't even look in our direction, but we stayed in the doorway for several minutes after she had gone, numbed by how close we had come to discovery. We looked at each other. This, we knew, was only the beginning. In the privacy of our little room in Bayswater, it had been easy for us to tell each other how bravely we would face the world. The reality was different.

The evening ruined, we walked back to the hotel in silence. By the time we arrived I had made up my mind what I was going to do. Seeing Mrs. Jenkins had made me almost sick with shame: I, like her, was supposed to be a responsible member of the school staff. Suddenly I could imagine the accusing eyes of Alexander's parents, Miss Angrid, Mr. Lorimer, Mr. Ellery, and the rest of the boys who had placed their trust in me. I had been crazy to allow things to go this far. Had I ever really, in the past few days, thought about what I was doing to Alexander, stopped to consider what effect all this might have on him? He was too young to know his own mind, he was headstrong, determined and spoiled. He might look and behave older than he was, but that didn't change the fact that he wasn't yet seventeen. Our relationship had to stop now, no matter what pain it might cause me, because that was nothing compared to the damage I would cause him if I let it go on.

Before he could push open the door of the hotel, I stopped him and made him turn round to face me. "Alexander," I said, softly, "I want you to go inside now and collect your things. No. No. Please don't say anything, don't let's argue, I couldn't bear it. We've got to say good-bye, my darling, so let it be now, before the outside world can spoil what we have had together. I've decided that it would be for the best if I don't come back to Foxton's in the new year . . ."

"Elizabeth." He put his hand over my mouth. "I'm staying here with you. Come inside, please. We have to talk, I know we do, but don't try to push me away like this."

My voice was constricted by the loss I was already feeling. "It's easier this way, Alexander. If we talk it'll only make it more difficult. I'm going for a walk. Please, take your things . . ."

"You said you loved me, Elizabeth."

Almost choking on my tears, I shook my head. "I do, Alexander, but I can't. I can't . . ." And tearing my hand away from his, I ran off down the street.

I expected him to follow, and when he didn't I had to bite my lips hard to stop myself from screaming out in an effort to fill the emptiness. I walked about for over an hour, hardly knowing what I was thinking or where I was going. I was terrified of going back, but knew I had to. It was the first step I had to take in facing my life without him. I steeled myself as I walked in the door of my room—and he was there, sitting on the bed, waiting for me.

I closed the door, quietly watching him through sore and swollen eyes. He stood up, reaching out for my hand, and led me across to the bed.

"Sit down," he said, "I want you to listen. I don't want you to interrupt, will you promise me?"

I nodded dumbly.

He went to sit in the old tapestry chair, and with his dark head on one side, he looked across the room at me, in the half-light, holding on to me with his eyes. "I know everyone will think that I can't know my mind at my age, that I'm ruining my life—and all the other things they'll say. But it doesn't matter what other people think, Elizabeth, because none of it will change the way I feel about you. Of course it isn't going to be easy, especially when I know that even you think I'm too young for what we have between us. All I can say is that in all the books and films I care about and in all the life I've witnessed—even though I've only seen such a little of it—love has never recognized age. I love you, and I want you to go on being the most important part of my life. I don't care about anything else. I know there will be times in the future when other things will be important to me, too—but always, no matter what, it will be you that I love. Nothing will change that, Elizabeth. I can't put into words what it is that you've done to my life; all I know is that it won't mean anything without you. And if you leave me now, you'll be hurting us both, more perhaps than either of us can understand.

"What I'm trying to say is very simple really. Not only do I love you now, I know already that I'm going to love you forever. And if you don't believe me, then maybe we'll have to wait forever for you to find out. Either way, it won't change the way I feel. So please, don't shut me out of your life."

It was now almost completely dark, and I could hardly see him across the room. It was a long time before I stood up and walked over to him. He held out his arms, and sitting down on his lap, I held him, rocking him back and forth and wiping the tears from his cheeks.

"Like you, I don't know what the future will hold, but let's hope our love is strong enough to face it."

8

I WOULD NEVER HAVE THOUGHT IT POSSIBLE, but as time went on I grew to love Alexander more and more. Once we were back at Foxton's the agony of being so close, yet not able to touch, was so intense that the only way to control it was to try and laugh about it. The way Alexander deliberately went around looking as if he was in the worst kind of physical torment made me laugh till I cried. "But this is the way I really feel," he said, when I told him he was overdoing it.

In between lessons he'd dash up to the surgery, close the door behind him and kiss me so hard and so quickly that I hardly knew he was there before he was gone. And at the end of each day we'd always manage to go for a walk, or if it was raining I'd slip down to the common room for a cup of coffee, just as I had with last year's sixth form. Even though there weren't many times when we could be on our own, we still managed to make love twice during the first weeks of the term.

The first time was in a barn that was a two-mile hike from the school. But I didn't mind about my muddy shoes and wind-torn hair when I got there—still holding the note he'd left inside his pillowcase that morning, asking me to meet him at four, when the sixth form were normally in their rooms studying, or playing records in the common room. Afterwards, when our bodies were bruised and tender, I giggled at the way I'd thrown off my matron's uniform and tumbled into the hay with him—at the way we'd laughed and frolicked together like two lambs in a field.

As several of the boys regularly visited both Miss Angrid and me in the cottage, no suspicions were aroused by Henry and Alexander coming too—though it caused some heated arguments between us when I wouldn't let Alexander come more often, and alone. But there was one occasion, early in the evening, when he did come, just as I was about to get in the bath. The inevitable happened, and it was only a matter of seconds after we'd finished dressing that Miss Angrid knocked on my door and walked straight in.

She eyed us suspiciously, and afterwards I was so shaken by the narrowness of our escape that it caused the first serious rift between us. I was stunned by the fact that Alexander didn't seem to care, and yelled at him for being immature enough to think that Miss Angrid would be on our side. He hated being reminded that he was younger than me, so he hit back by saying that I was using my position to hide the fact that I was ashamed of him.

"Well, I'm not exactly proud of what we're doing," I said.

His face turned white. "So, you are ashamed. I'm nothing more than a randy little schoolboy who suits your . . ."

"Don't speak to me like that! I wouldn't be doing this if I didn't love you, but this kind of stupid irresponsible behavior of yours sometimes makes me wonder how much longer we can go on. You're not to come here again, do you hear me?"

"Agreed! And don't even think about slipping notes inside my pillowcase, I'll burn them before I even read them."

We smoldered in silence for two days, until his resolve weakened and I found a note pushed under my surgery door. He wanted me to know that he hadn't meant anything he'd said, that he didn't mean to be cavalier, it was only that he loved me so much that he wanted the whole world to know. He could see now how childish that was, so would I forgive him and meet him later in the woods? I ignored it. There was another note the following day, and two more the day after that. Still I ignored them. The last note was delivered to the cottage, and told me to go to hell.

Which is where I stayed, until he caught my eye at dinner and made me laugh. But that still didn't stop me from getting into a state. I was so worried about what we were doing, so afraid of it all and how it would end that I just didn't know what to do. That was how he found me one afternoon, alone in my surgery, sobbing my heart out.

He looked at me, his face saying nothing as he reached out his hand and pulled me up into his arms. I tried to turn away.

"No! Don't!" he said, angrily. "For God's sake, why are you making us suffer like this?"

"I don't know what to do," I said. "I love you, I do, but Alexander . . ."

"Look, we both knew this wasn't going to be easy, so don't let's make it any worse. Now come on, just let me hold you."

And I let him hold me, because just at that moment I didn't care who might walk in and find us. I loved him, and that was all that mattered.

"They're back!" Alexander cried. "The bloody gypsies are back!"

Henry looked up from his newspaper and Alexander winked as he saw me coming towards them. It was late in the afternoon, and they were sitting next to the tennis courts, reading that morning's papers and calling out the odd rude remark to the boys who were playing tennis.

"Thank God I'm not at home," Alexander said. "I can see my father now, his face will be an ugly shade of purple and that snakey vein in his neck will be throbbing away. Nobody's life will be worth living."

Grinning, Henry took the paper from Alexander and handed it to me.

"Did you read that bit about them being vermin?" Alexander said, looking up at me. "As my mother says, we're never going to get rid of them if father doesn't cut out the vitriol. Still, it's true what he's saying. I saw them when I was there at Christmas, filthy beggars. I wonder if it's true that they're running a child prostitution ring. The local rag said it was."

"Not only the local one," said Henry. "There's something about it here."

"Henry, dear boy, what on earth are you doing reading *that?*"

I laughed. "You're such a snob, Alexander Belmayne."

"Couldn't agree more," said Miss Angrid, coming up behind us.

Alexander pulled a face, then turned back to Henry. "What does it say?" he asked.

"Headline stuff. As you say, all about the child prostitution thing. Your father is quoted as saying something about calling in Rentokil to deal with it."

Alexander gave a yell of laughter. "Renta who?" I said.

"Rentokil. The pest control people," Miss Angrid enlightened me.

"Sounds like my father," said Alexander. "No doubt he's pissing himself with excitement at the forthcoming battle."

"Alexander!"

"Sorry, Matron, momentarily forgot myself." And as he threw her a kiss, I had to turn away before she saw me laughing.

"Anyway," I continued, as Miss Angrid strolled off, "what are you two doing here? I thought you were going to the theater this afternoon."

"Mr. Lear's gone sick," Henry answered, draining a can of shandy. "Titus Andronicus leftus in the lurchus."

Alexander held his can out for me to drink. "All I can say is, I'm glad I'm not at home now. Just having those people in the vicinity makes a chap itch in his bed at night." He stood up and came to put his arms around me, kissing the back of my neck.

"Alexander!" I cried, jumping away from him. "For God's sake, someone might see!" He laughed and I glared at him, but at the same time heard myself telling him to come to my surgery after supper.

Henry stretched and yawned. "You know, I've been thinking," he said. "We ought to try and find a way to take you up to Oxford with us, Elizabeth."

A smile stretched painfully across my face as I watched Alexander sit down again and pick up a paper. It was something I didn't allow myself to think about—the time when they would have to leave.

"Hope the females at Oxford are a bit more desirable than the ones at St. Winifred's," Henry mused. "I can just see it now. Orgies and more orgies. Maybe I ought to be getting in a bit of practice.

Can't have you running off with every available female in the place, Alexander."

As I started to walk away I heard Alexander say, "Henry, old chap, what's happened to your brain?"

There was a pause, then Henry said, "I didn't mean anything. Just wasn't thinking. Tell her I'm sorry, will you?"

A few minutes later, hearing my surgery door close, I walked out from behind the screen. "You don't have to say anything," I said, before he could speak. "But we're going to have to face it, you know. When you leave here, well . . ."

"It's a long time away yet, Elizabeth. Besides, me being at Oxford won't change anything. We'll still see each other, all the time."

He kissed me, and not for the first time I felt myself beginning to fall apart. I would lose him, I knew I would.

He was grinning as he let me go. "And what's so funny?" I said.

"You."

"Me! Why?"

He shrugged. "I don't know, you just are. I love your hair," he said, taking off my cap and pulling out the hairpins. "Ebony hair and ebony eyes. Lift up your skirt, I want to look at your legs."

"Can you come to the cottage later tonight, after ten?" I said, as he ran his fingers under my suspenders. "I want you to make love to me."

His face was suddenly serious. "I'll be there," he said.

I'd bought us some wine, and put out some crisps and peanuts, but when he arrived all that was forgotten. Later, when we were sitting in front of the fire with our clothes all over the room, he started to talk about what we had done. It had been the first time we'd had oral sex. I don't know why—probably because I'd been feeling insecure all day—but suddenly I burst into tears.

He stopped what he was saying straightaway, and moved round to sit next to me. "What is it?" he said. "I thought you'd like it. I'm sorry, we won't do it again."

I laughed then. "Of course I liked it," I said. "That's why I'm crying."

He gave me one of his lopsided looks. "And I suppose I've got to work that one out for myself."

I sighed and leaned my head back on his shoulder. He picked

up his wine and held it to my mouth, then, taking a sip himself, he pulled the chair round so he could rest against it.

"What are you thinking?" he asked.

"I'm thinking that one day I hope you'll look back on all this and remember it the way it was. You know, how much we loved each other, how much we taught each other . . ."

"I don't like the sound of what you're saying. We'll be looking back together, won't we?"

"All I'm trying to say is that, if for some reason that doesn't happen, I hope we'll always be a very special memory for each other."

"Stop it, Elizabeth. Stop saying things like that. It's what Henry said this afternoon, isn't it. Well, I might as well tell you now, I won't be going up to Oxford. I've decided it will be easier for us if I don't."

I smiled at that. "You will go to Oxford. If you don't, then I really will leave you. Anyway, I'm just being morbid, Alexander—ignore me. Where's the wine?"

He got up to get the bottle, and when he came back I watched him as he poured. "Smile, Alexander. I want to see your crooked tooth."

He laughed and then sat forward, bringing his mouth to mine. And all my insecurities went away, because every time we were together we became more a part of one another.

A few mornings later I was sitting with Miss Angrid, packing up first-aid boxes for the Easter Outward Bound course, and idly chatting about the current experiment of introducing St. Winifred's girls into the sixth form lectures at Foxton's. Deciding that the girls were, without a doubt, an unnecessary distraction for boys who were trying to achieve a decent grade in A levels, she went off to make a cup of tea—but when she came back and settled herself in her chair, instead of picking up her cup she took a long, hard look at me.

I felt uncomfortable, and tried to laugh. "It's me, Elizabeth," I said. "You look as though you're seeing me for the first time."

She shook her head. "Oh no," she said, "not the first time. I've seen you plenty of times, my dear."

"What a strange thing to say."

She sighed heavily, and reached out for her tea. I waited for her to go on, trying to ignore the alarm bells that were already ringing inside my head.

It was a while before she spoke again. "All that chitchat just now about the girls . . ." she began. "Well, I suppose there's no point in beating about the bush. You know what I was leading up to." She stared at me, waiting for me to answer. "Do you know what you're doing?" she asked bluntly.

"Packing the first-aid boxes," I quipped.

"Elizabeth."

I felt myself color, and looked away.

"I saw him leaving the cottage the other night," she said.

When I looked into her face I understood the silent request for no lies, and though I wanted to deny it, tell her she was imagining things, I found I couldn't. I got up from my chair and went to stand by the window. "I don't know what to say."

"There's nothing to say. It's what you have to do that matters."

I swallowed hard. I wanted to shout at her, call her a nosy, interfering old woman who should mind her own business. But in my heart I knew she was right.

"His work is falling behind," Miss Angrid went on. "He's failed his end of term Latin. Did you know that? No, I thought not. He's taking English today, yes?" I nodded. "Mr. Lear thinks he's going to flunk that too."

"Does Mr. Lear know?" I gasped.

"No. But questions are being asked. He's always been ahead of the others, way ahead. He's been called in by Mr. Lorimer, did you know? The boy is besotted with you, Elizabeth. He can't see straight or think straight. If he fails his A levels next year, well, you don't need me to spell out what that will mean."

I shook my head. She was telling me, in as kind a way as she knew how, something I already knew. I was ruining his life.

"Do you think I should leave?" I said, after a while.

"No." She was emphatic: if I left he would be even more distracted than he was now. What I had to do was to speak to him myself, try and make him see sense.

"Are you going to tell anyone what you know?" I asked her.

She smiled, and it was the first time I had seen that strange, whiskery old face close to tears. "No," she said. "I think I know the way you feel about him, Elizabeth. Others will think you have led him on, that you're playing with him. But I know. I've seen it from the very beginning."

My heart turned over. "I tried not to," I said.

"I daresay you did. But it's too late now, it's done. Just get him through his A levels, that's all I ask. Once he's at Oxford then the whole thing will fizzle out. He's too young for all this, and the same goes for you. You should be out with people your own age."

"They say the truth always hurts," I smiled.

She took my hand. "I'm very fond of you, Elizabeth. The last thing I want is to see you hurt. But I think you know in your heart what it is you have to do."

That night I asked Henry if he would come for a walk with us. We'd stay in sight of the school, then no one need have any cause for suspicion.

Alexander shouted and raved when I told him what Miss Angrid had said. At first he was intent on storming back to the school and telling her just what he thought of her, but among us Henry and I managed to stop him. Finally, after he had calmed down and we'd talked it over among the three of us, Alexander and I struck a bargain. If I would agree to go away with him, just the two of us, at Easter, then he would knuckle down to some serious studying the following term.

As Alexander's parents were traveling to France to see his sister and her husband, they weren't too put out when he told them he was going to help supervise one of the junior Outward Bound courses. We took separate trains to Penzance station, where I hired a car, and then we went off to a cottage we'd rented just outside Zennor.

During that two and a half weeks I tried a thousand times to tell him it was over but I couldn't do it. It was as if everything he did had the sole purpose of making me happy, and he was so happy himself that the idea of spoiling things was too painful even to contemplate. I knew he was pretending we were married from the way he tried to help in the kitchen, or fought with the carpet sweeper, or walked up to the bar in the local pub to order my drink without asking what I wanted. It was the first time we had been free just to be ourselves, the first time we hadn't had to look over our shoulders and worry that someone might see us. He was a different person, even more confident, so grown-up, so protective—though of course we had our share of rows. It was a wonderful taste of what our life together could be like—and that made it all the harder for me to tell him that at the end of the holiday I didn't want to see him again . . . For I'd decided that was the only way to do it. If he thought I was ending it because someone else had told me it was the right thing to do, he wouldn't accept it; but if I could somehow persuade him I didn't love him anymore, then he would have to let me go.

I waited until our last day. We'd run out of milk so I walked down to the village to get some while he stayed at the cottage. I was surprised when he said he wasn't coming with me, because we'd hardly been apart for a moment the whole holiday. At least it gave me time to prepare what I was going to say. I was gone a long time, walking round the churchyard, staring out over the bleak moors, telling myself that I was doing this because I loved him, because it was the best thing for him—and trying not to think about how much I was going to hurt him.

He was looking out of the window when I opened the garden gate, and I could see he'd been worried by my long absence. My heart went out to him, and I had to fight to stop myself from smiling and waving.

I took a deep breath as I went in through the door. He was still standing by the window, watching me come in, and I could tell straightaway that he was up to something. Then I saw what it was. Hanging from one of the oak beams was a banner, and on it was written: *Please will you be my wife?*

He was obviously nervous—and yet I'd never seen so much love in his eyes. "I didn't know whether to put Please will you marry me, or whether you would like the word wife," he explained. "I can do another saying whatever you like, only the . . ."

I broke down and cried then, and immediately he was holding me, and I was clinging to him, begging him always to love me, never to leave me . . . In the end he managed to calm me down and went to make some tea. I started to laugh when he brought it back, and then I couldn't stop laughing. It was as if I had lost him, and now he'd come back to me. He laughed too, but I knew he was confused.

"I'm laughing because you're an idiot, and because I love the word wife, and because I love you so much I think I'm going to burst with it," I said.

"Does that mean you will marry me, then?" he asked, searching my face.

"It means I'd marry you now, this minute, if we could . . ."

"Please don't give me a list of reasons why we can't. I only want to hear you say yes, then we'll talk about when."

"Ask me again."

"Will you marry me?"

"Yes."

It wasn't until later in the day that we were able to discuss it sensibly. By then, even though I couldn't let him go, I had made him agree that we wouldn't talk about marriage again until he came down from Oxford.

"I'll still want to, you know," he whispered.

"I'll pray to God every night that you will."

9

ECAUSE WE REALIZED now what would happen if anyone found out about us, we both behaved more responsibly when we got back to Foxton's for the summer term. All the same, Alexander obviously found it very hard to be discreet, so on my free evenings I went to the pub so that he wouldn't be tempted to come to me at the cottage or the surgery. The rest of the time wasn't so bad, except that there were always other people around; but at least we did see each other, and we left notes for one another inside his pillowcase every day.

Then—predictably, perhaps—Alexander found a way round our difficulties: he discovered an abandoned railwaymen's hut a mile or so from the school . . . We met there at least once a week, and were so careful that we didn't even tell Henry about it. Alexander approached it from the railway tunnel, a hundred yards along the track, while I, after a quick lunch-time drink, wandered behind the pub, climbed a stile, made a mad dash across a field full of cows, then picked a path through the remains of the station, to find him waiting—once with a railwayman's hat on, a flag, a whistle, and a toy train on the track.

I never told him, perhaps because I thought he might be unhappy about it, that I'd made a friend at the pub. Her name was Ruth. Her family lived in the village, she told me. She talked a lot about herself and made me laugh when she told me about all the boyfriends she had and the way she kept them dangling.

"You'll have to meet Peter," she said one day, after she'd told me in detail what the two of them had been up to the night before. And the next time I went to the pub, Peter was there too.

One day, very casually, I mentioned Ruth and Peter to Alexander. He was jealous, just as I'd thought he might be, so I didn't refer to them again.

Towards the end of the term Alexander's parents came to the school to find out from Mr. Lorimer how he was doing. The report they received wasn't brilliant, but it was better than either of us had expected. Of course, Alexander's father wasn't too happy about it, and he let Alexander know it. He grilled him all day, then took him and Henry down to the village for dinner.

I had arranged to meet Ruth in the pub at seven-thirty. Peter had been in London on business for the past couple of weeks, so I was rather surprised to find him there too. We settled down in the corner of the bar with our drinks, and while Ruth and Peter talked about London I wondered what Alexander was doing at that moment.

"You seem a bit quiet this evening, Elizabeth," Ruth said. "Nothing the matter, is there?"

I looked up. "Sorry, I was miles away."

"Miles? Or a few hundred yards up the hill at Foxton's?"

"If you ask me, she's hiding a secret lover up there somewhere," Peter chipped in. "Come on now, who is it? The Latin master? The English master? I know, it's the Head!"

"That's typical of you," Ruth said. "Everything's got to come down to the same thing in the end, sex." She turned back to me. "Ignore him."

I liked them so much. I wished I could introduce them to Alexander.

"Tell me," Ruth said, "don't you ever miss London? That was where you were before you came here, wasn't it?"

We chatted about where I used to work in London, and the places I used to go. Lord Belmayne's visit to the school had unsettled me, and my mind was only half on what I was saying, but neither Ruth nor Peter seemed to notice.

When I got back to the cottage at about half past ten, Alexander was waiting for me. I knew straightaway he'd been drinking; he was hiding in the bushes of the copse, and was making very heavy weather of getting out of them.

"Where've you been?" he said, as I tried to pull him up.

"You shouldn't be here. Where's Henry?"

"Gone to sign us in," he slurred. "Always good to see the old parents, you know, but they do go on. Any chance of some coffee?"

When we got inside the cottage he insisted on making the coffee himself, then crashed over the arm of the sofa on his way to the kitchen. "Just how much wine did you have?" I asked.

"Not much. Must have been the brandy that did it."

I eased him onto a kitchen chair, and he sat patiently watching me until I went to the fridge for the milk, when he came and put his arms around me.

"I wish we were married," he said, lifting my hair and kissing the back of my neck. "We will be, won't we? One day, you will marry me?"

"Yes," I said. "Yes, I will."

"I nearly told them about you today."

I tensed. "You didn't though, did you?"

"No. But I'm going to. During the summer break. I'll go home for a few days, tell them then . . ."

I was shaking my head. "No, no, you mustn't. Not yet."

" . . . then we'll go away somewhere, just the two of us. Where do you want to go?"

I started to protest. "Just answer the question," he said. "Where shall we go?"

I could see there was no point in trying to reason with him now. "You suggest somewhere," I said.

"Sark. It's a little island just off Guernsey. Very romantic."

"Are we taking Henry with us?"

"Are we hell!"

I pushed him away and he followed me back into the sitting room. "I don't suppose I could persuade you into making it a honeymoon, could I?" he said, weaving his way round the sofa.

"You could not."

"Thought you might say that. Still, we can always pretend. I'll book it in the name of Mr. and Mrs. Belmayne, how does that sound?"

I smiled as my heart turned over just to hear the words.

"Ah, I almost forgot. Damn! I must have left it in the bushes. Now stay right there, and don't move."

When he came back again he went to the record player, and put on the record he'd brought in with him. As the music began to play he pulled me to my feet and wrapped me in his arms. "Remember?"

How could I forget? It was "Sealed With a Kiss."

"Happy birthday, and happy anniversary, darling," he said, as we started to dance.

"Anniversary?"

"It was a year ago tonight that I held you for the first time, and we danced to this record."

I looked up into his face, and wondered what I had done to deserve someone so hopelessly romantic.

"Now close your eyes, I've got another surprise for you."

I did, and as his lips pressed against mine I felt him fumbling with my left hand. It was an eternity ring.

"With my love, my heart, and my life," he whispered.

When I went up to London for a couple of days, just before the end of term, I gave Alexander the excuse that I had to help Janice out of some trouble. He wasn't very keen on my staying away overnight, but I pointed out that as he was due to play cricket at a school in Dorset, then he wouldn't actually miss me too much.

Miss Angrid was waiting for me when I got back, she was holding open the door to her surgery. "Elizabeth, come in, will you?" The moment I saw her face I knew something was wrong; despite the heat my hands turned to ice. All I could think was that something had happened to Alexander.

She closed the door behind me and walked over to her desk. "What is it?" I asked, and was shocked by the deadened sound of my voice. I tried again. "Paul Raven, wasn't it measles?"

"No, Elizabeth," she said gravely, "it's not Paul Raven." She

69

looked down at the newspaper on her desk, then turned it to face me.

I looked down at the page and at that moment I knew what it was like to feel the whole world fall out from under me. "EXCLUSIVE: LORD CHIEF JUSTICE'S SON IN LOVE NEST WITH GYPSY." For an instant I thought I was going to faint as the walls of the surgery seemed to close in around me.

I had never dreamt, not even in my worst nightmares, of anything like this. Front page, glaring out for all the world to see. Huge black letters, and a picture of Foxton's. A smaller picture in the bottom right hand corner showed the gypsy camp on Lord Belmayne's estate. I read the first few lines of the article. "Following the allegations of gypsy child prostitution on the Suffolk estate of Lord Belmayne, the Lord Chief Justice, our reporters can now reveal that Lord Belmayne's son, the Hon. Alexander Belmayne, has been pursuing a life of debauchery at the elite Foxton's Boys' School with a gypsy love of his own . . ." The words became a blur and I had to grip the edge of the desk to steady myself. Miss Angrid pulled up a chair for me, then handed me a glass of brandy.

"Alexander," I said, trying to get up. "Where is he? Has he seen it?"

Miss Angrid reached out to stop me. "He's in the Headmaster's study. With his father."

I closed my eyes and felt my hands begin to shake again. My stomach was churning, and I thought I was going to be sick. Miss Angrid pulled up a chair and sat next to me. She took my hands and started to rub them. "Elizabeth," she said, "look at me."

I dragged my eyes to her face.

"I know you grew up on the fair, child, Mrs. Carey told me when she gave me your references. There's nothing to be ashamed of in that. But you've got to tell me, dear, are you anything to do with the Ince family?"

I shook my head. "No."

"Then why does the newspaper say you are?"

I swallowed hard, trying to control my voice, but it was coming in short gasps. "I don't know," I said. "The fairground, they must think . . ." I looked at her. "I'm not a gypsy, not the way they mean it."

Miss Angrid squeezed my hand, then in her gruff, deep voice, she said, "Does Alexander know where you grew up?"

"No. It never seemed important." I looked up at her again. "I knew that one day our relationship would have to end, and I've tried, honestly I have. But oh, don't let it be like this. Please, Miss Angrid . . ."

I jumped as the buzzer sounded on her phone. She patted my hand and went to answer it. "Yes," she said. "Yes. I will." Her face was grim as she put the receiver down. "It was the Head. Lord Belmayne wants to see you."

I couldn't face him. My eyes, my face, my whole body ached. "They're wrong! Please, Miss Angrid, you've got to tell them, they've made a mistake."

Miss Angrid placed her hands on my shoulders. "It's too late, child. I tried to help you before, but now there's nothing I can do." Suddenly I was in her arms, and she was rocking me back and forth like a baby. When she let me go I saw tears wending their way through the strange pattern of lines on her face. "I'm going to miss you, Elizabeth," she said. "Probably more than you'll ever know."

I held my breath, trying to take it in.

"I'll walk down with you," she said, and led me to the Headmaster's study.

Lord Belmayne waited for the door to close behind the Head, then, keeping his hands clutched behind his back, he turned away from the window to face me. "So," he said, "you have succeeded in making fools of us all. I hope you are satisfied." He glared at me, but when I tried to speak my voice had disappeared.

He leaned forward and put his hands on the desk. "You do realize you could have ruined my son's life? But that's what they put you here for, isn't it? To make a laughingstock out of me—and out of my son, a seventeen-year-old boy. You failed the first time, didn't you? Over that golf-cart business? He might have been expelled then, but for the fact that I happened to believe in his innocence. But he still took what punishment was going, because *you* insisted. And now it's you again—*you* who have managed to get his name spread across this filthy rag. Except that your dirty little trick has misfired again, because he won't be expelled this time either. Oh no! No, it's you who are going, Miss Sorrill. But before you walk out of that door I want to know exactly who you are. Ince's grand-daughter, are you, or his niece? Or are you just an obliging friend?"

"I'm nothing to do with the Ince family," I cried. "I'm not a gypsy. I didn't . . ."

"Listen to me, young lady. I did everything in my power last night to stop this going to press. In the end I failed, and do you know why? Because they'd done their research. They had the facts, and the facts speak for themselves. So I'll ask you again, who are you?"

"My dad was a showman. I grew up on the fairground, but . . ."

"Fairgrounds! Gypsies! It's all the same thing!"

"No! It's not! Please listen to me. I love your son, and he loves . . ."

He slammed his fist down on the table. "Don't waste your lies on me! You are nothing to my son, do you hear me, nothing! If you ever go near him again . . ."

"I'd never do anything to hurt him, I swear it. Never!"

"Names! I want the names of the people who put you up to this."

My hands were over my face. "It's all a mistake. Ask Miss Angrid, she'll tell you!"

But he wouldn't listen. He was determined to find a connection between me and Alfred Ince. And if there was no connection, as I insisted, then he wanted to know why I hadn't told the truth about my past when I'd first come to the school. Why, of all the schools in England, I had chosen Foxton's? And of all the boys in the sixth form, why I had chosen his son? The questions were coming at me so fast that my mind was spinning and anything I tried to say came out wrong. Why had I gone to London the day before? he wanted to know. How much were the journalists paying me for my story? What further filth were they going to print? How much longer was this vendetta going to carry on? Was there no human decency in people like me?

"I want you out of this school within the hour," he finished, "do you hear me? Out! And I am personally going to see to it that you never set foot inside a decent school again."

‡

Miss Angrid drove me back to the cottage in Tonto. I knew the boys were watching us from the windows, but I couldn't bring myself to look up. As we got out of the cart Miss Angrid stopped me. "I think you should know who is responsible for this, Elizabeth. It was Mrs. Jenkins. I gather she saw you in London at Christmas? Well, she's been keeping an eye on you ever since. And with her contacts in Fleet Street . . . You made some friends at the local pub?" I nodded. "Reporters."

It was a nightmare.

Miss Angrid walked me up the cottage stairs to my sitting-room. Alexander was there. Miss Angrid looked from one to the other of us, and left.

I could see the strain on his face and guessed that his interview with his father had been no easier than my own. He had a copy of the newspaper in his hand. "You shouldn't be here," I whispered.

His voice was cold and sarcastic. "I've come to say good-bye."

"Oh."

"How could you, Elizabeth?" he yelled suddenly. "You've made a fool of me, and of my family. Why did you do it?"

"I didn't," I said. "You've got it wrong, you all have. Please listen to . . ."

"Stop lying!" he shouted. "Why else did you go to London yesterday if it wasn't to do some deal with this filthy rag. I want to kill you, do you know that?"

"Please, Alexander . . ."

"It's too much of a coincidence, Elizabeth. There they are on my father's land, and you're here at the school. My father's right, isn't he? It's a setup. Well, here's what you've achieved. Go on, pick the filthy rag up. Keep it with you. Then whenever you're feeling down you can gloat over what a fool you, Elizabeth Sorrill, made of the Belmayne family." He looked at me with loathing. "And to think I believed you when you said you loved me."

Miss Angrid came in. "Alexander," she said quietly, "I think that's enough."

He snatched up the box that he'd stuffed with the books and records he'd lent me and walked to the door. As his hand hit the handle he turned to look at me, and the hatred and pain I saw in his eyes I knew I would never forget.

Miss Angrid came to stand beside me at the window, and together we watched him walk across the field to the school. I looked down at the ring he'd given me, only two days before. Now I would never have the chance to tell him why I went to London. I was carrying his baby.

Alexander

10

IT HAS TAKEN ME A LONG TIME to come to terms with my behavior in the years that followed Elizabeth's departure from Foxton's—and from my life. Now, with the benefit of age and experience, I know why I did what I did. But still it is with shame that I recount these years, and the considerable pain I caused not only myself, but others too. At a time when every student's mission in life was to make the world a better place, I went up to Oxford, consumed by anger—an anger that burned more fiercely with every passing year as my struggle to deny the void Elizabeth had left in my life grew ever more desperate.

For though she had lied to me and made a fool of my family, I couldn't forget her. Because of her my first year at Oxford is mostly lost now, dispersed, along with the sweet-smelling smoke of the marijuana that provided my only respite from the confusion and resentment that burned in my heart. And yet, on the surface, I behaved much like any other student. Now and again, if it took our fancy, Henry and I might make our way to the occasional lecture, but mostly we spent our time indulging in intellectual debate on how we, as students, should assume responsibility for world peace. Peace was the watchword of the times—though, ironically, despite our long hair and our fashionable socialism, there was very little that

77

was peaceful, or indeed socialist, about our behavior. We roared around Oxford in the new Mercedes 230 SL my grandmother had equipped me with on my eighteenth birthday, we threw outrageous, extemporized parties, raged against the establishment, and took aggressive advantage of the trend for making love not war. Sex was made easy for me by the succession of girls flocking to my door as though I were the reincarnation of Giacomo Casanova himself: the scandal of the "gypsy love affair" lived on. All I had to do was crook a finger and they would all but fall at my feet. I relished the way I could use them, then just walk away.

It was sometime during my second year that the boredom of easy conquest was alleviated by a new turn in events. Students in Paris struck out at the Gaullist government, creating an unprecedented furor among students worldwide. My participation in sit-ins, boycotts and rallies was both vigorous and vociferous. We felt the time had finally come to make ourselves heard, to condemn the forsaking of revolutionary vocation for capitalist comfort, and to make known our disgust at the atrocities that were being committed all over the world. Along with thousands of others Henry and I marched on London to demonstrate against the war in Vietnam, against the Russian invasion of Czechoslovakia, and against UDI and the oppression of blacks in Rhodesia. Demonstrations and protests became as much a part of the times as Janis Joplin, hippies and pop concerts . . . And pop concerts offered yet another opportunity for rolling up a joint, taking off your clothes and making love in the grass. After a concert everything was peace and harmony and everyone loved the world.

It was after a concert—The Festival of the Flower Children—that I first met Jessica. A crowd of us had gone back to Henry's and my rooms at Brackenbury Buildings to listen to more music, but I was bored, only half stoned, and in need of a new woman. The superior-looking chick who sauntered into the room late in the evening—so strikingly out of place among the spaced-out flower children with her silent, condescending scrutiny of her surroundings and her obvious awareness of her own sexuality—fitted my bill perfectly.

At first I only watched her, as she stood alone, taking in the scattered bodies through a blue haze of pot and incense. She didn't seem to be looking for anyone in particular, nor did she seem to care that she was the only woman in the room who wasn't in kaftan and plaits. In fact, looking at her, petite as she was, was like watching the pages of *Vogue* flutter into animation.

"Far out," Henry muttered in my ear.

"Who is she?"

He shrugged. "Never seen her before. Ask your friend." And with a grin he nodded to someone behind me.

I turned to find a girl whose name I had forgotten glaring up at me in doped paranoia. I recognized the look immediately: I had screwed her three times—which, in her book, gave her some sort of territorial rights on me. Clutching my arm, she dragged me outside, and since there were several people on the landing freaking out to Cream, she pulled me down the stairs. "Her name's Jessica Poynter," she hissed.

"Really?" I drawled, stuffing my hands into my pockets and leaning back against the wall. "Wouldn't care to introduce me, would you?"

She slapped my face, harder than they usually did, and stormed off. I looked after her, rubbing my jaw and grinning, then turned back up the stairs and pressed my way back into the party.

When I found Jessica Poynter she was studying the obscene faces of Ensor's *Intrigue,* something I had stuck on the wall to brighten the place up.

"I find it beats looking in the mirror," I said.

She gave me an unhurried once-over, then turned back to the painting.

I watched her, amused by her deliberate indifference, and let my eyes wander slowly from the thick penciled lines that sloped from the inside corners of her eyes towards her temples, to the knee-high white socks that finished at least nine inches below her hemline. Her dress was crocheted, and as far as I could tell she wore nothing underneath.

"So, it's the famous, or should I say infamous, Alexander Belmayne."

I smirked, and lifted my eyes from her barely concealed breasts to rest on her whitened lips.

"Is it true what they say about you?" she said, without looking at me.

"Depends what you've heard."

She took a step back and put her head on one side, still studying the grotesque faces on the wall. At last she lifted her eyes to mine, using her lack of height to perfection. "They say you despise women."

I wasn't unaware of this popular myth, spread mainly by the rabid feminists who were sprouting up all over Oxford, most of whom had availed themselves of my services on more than one occasion. But this was the first time someone had actually come right out with it—or at least come out with it before I laid them rather than afterwards.

I laughed. "And how would you like me to answer that?" I said.

"Whichever way you choose."

"I choose to get you a drink," I said, taking her empty glass.

I was gone for some time, and half expected her to have disappeared by the time I returned, but she was still waiting. Why were they all so predictable?

"Thank you." She smiled up at me as she took the drink, and I couldn't fail to notice the challenge in her eyes. "You didn't answer my question. Do you despise women?"

I sighed, feeling suddenly bored. "I despise women," I said, and turned to go.

She caught my arm. "I won't do anything to change that."

"You couldn't."

"I couldn't?" She laughed softly, and I was arrested by her condescension, or maybe it was aggression.

"I haven't seen you before," I said.

"Somerville. I study hard." She shrugged when I didn't answer. "Isn't that why we're here?"

"It could be."

She smiled slowly. "Just as long as we come out with what we want at the end of it."

"And what do you want?"

She cast her cool gaze over me again. It was answer enough.

I held the silence between us, keeping my eyes on hers. Then I said: "Sleep with me tonight."

"Is that what you want?"

"Yes."

"Do you always get what you want?"

"Usually."

"But not always?"

I shook my head. "Can I see you again?"

"I shall be around."

I laughed, and for a fleeting second she looked unsure of herself. "I'll take you for a drive tomorrow," I said.

"In the famous Mercedes? Not tomorrow. Make it the day after. My parents are coming tomorrow."

"Can't I meet them?"

She seemed surprised, and this time her eyes were mocking me. "OK. Come for tea. Four-thirty." She looked across the room, then smiled. "If you're desperate for some company in your bed tonight, it looks as if your friend Henry has finished with Rosalind Purbright. I'm sure she'll be more than willing, she usually is."

I raised an eyebrow at that. "And if I did take Rosalind Purbright to bed tonight, would you mind?"

"Why should I?"

"Maybe because I want you to."

"OK, then, I'll mind. Should I also slap her face tomorrow, or would you prefer me to slap yours?"

"I've already had mine slapped twice this week."

"It's a very slappable face."

"Thank you," I said. "So is yours."

She laughed and raised her face in invitation. I caught it in my hand, and eased her back against the wall, feeling her skin through the holes in her dress. She looked up at me, her lips slightly parted, and suddenly I wanted to enter her, there, in the middle of the party. From the way she was looking at me, I knew she wanted it too.

As I bent my head to kiss her she slipped her hand between us, and began to caress me through my jeans. I groaned into her open mouth, and caught her hair in my hands. In response she pressed her hand harder against me, and for one horrifying moment I thought I was going to come.

Then, abruptly, she pushed me away. "Ciao," she said, and dropping her empty glass into my hand, she left.

I didn't meet Jessica's parents the following day, as for some reason they couldn't make it—which was just as well as I had a rugger match I'd forgotten about. I invited Jessica to come along and watch, but she wasn't interested.

I saw her a few times over the next month or so, but almost always in the company of the party types she mixed with, and if we did spend any time alone and I raised the subject of sex, she simply sighed, "Is that all you ever think about? There's so much more to life, you know." And when she wasn't dabbling around with the History of Art, she'd take off for Hull or somewhere, to organize the fishermen's wives or Dagenham to join the sewing machinists in their strike for equal pay. She was teasing me, I knew, and for the time being it amused me to let her. But before much longer I'd put a stop to it and give her a session she'd never forget—before moving on to someone else . . . Meanwhile, I concentrated rather more than I was used to on things like lectures and tutorials and put Jessica and her art and feminism out of my mind. She'd find out soon enough that Alexander Belmayne never went crawling after a woman.

Then Henry told me she was screwing Guy Hibbert, one of our group. I fell straight into the trap, and my fury knew no bounds when she coolly responded to my dinner invitation with a note informing me that she would be otherwise engaged. However, she went on to say that her parents were arriving the next day, and as I had expressed a desire to meet them once before, if I was still of a similar mind they would be arriving around four-thirty.

I screwed up the note and hurled it against the wall. And to demonstrate just what I thought of her, I set out in search of Rosalind Purbright and promptly humped seven bells out of her.

Four-thirty the following day found me at Somerville College. I had taken the trouble to root out a pair of my least torn jeans, and I'd got a nurse from the Radcliffe Infirmary, whom I'd been seeing on and off, to iron me up a decent shirt. I was annoyed with myself for making an effort, and even more annoyed by Henry's amusement.

Jessica and her family were waiting when I arrived. Her mother had planned a picnic, so we piled into her father's Bentley and set off for the countryside. We stopped somewhere on the road to Stratford and found a "nice, shady little spot," as Mrs. Poynter became faint in direct sunlight.

We looked ridiculous, the four of us sitting there on the side of the road, but I was the only one who seemed to feel it. Mr. Poynter soon fell into a heated argument with Jessica on whether or not women should be allowed to join the Stock Exchange.

"Never heard anything so ridiculous in all my life," he grunted. "Women! On the floor! What nonsense will you come out with next?" He stuffed another chicken leg in his mouth. Mrs. Poynter took out a little battery-operated fan which hummed a monotonous circle about her face. Jessica looked at her with contempt, but to my relief she dropped the argument with her father and poured me some more wine. I tried not to look at my watch. It could be a reasonably pleasant afternoon, I thought, if only the old man would shut up; and even better if Jessica and I could be alone.

"So," said Mr. Poynter, delving into his teeth to remove a piece of chicken, "what are you reading, my boy?"

"Law," I answered.

"Yes, of course, law. Met your father once. Can't remember where now, probably at the House. How is he?"

"Very well the last time I spoke to him, thank you, sir."

"Oh, it's so hot," Mrs Poynter complained. "Fetch my parasol from the car, darling, will you?" She blinked at Jessica. "She's such a good girl," she said, when Jessica had gone. "Have you known each other long?"

"Not really," I answered. She nodded, and batting away the flies that seemed dementedly attracted to her, she appeared to lose interest in me.

Jessica came back with the parasol, then lay down on the grass beside me. Her braless nipples were very evident beneath the thin cotton of her T-shirt, and my jeans became uncomfortably tight as she trailed her fingertips over her breasts before letting her hands fall to the grass.

"Ever get rid of those blasted gypsies, did he?" Mr. Poynter asked.

I tensed, but before I had to answer Jessica said, "Have either of you heard from Lizzie recently? I haven't had a letter for ages."

"She's somewhere in Turkey," her mother answered. "Heaven alone knows why she should want to go there. I just hope she doesn't bring back anything nasty."

"Lizzie's my sister," Jessica explained. "She dropped out of the university and went off round the world to find herself. Two years ago, haven't seen her since."

"Very enterprising of her," I remarked.

"Enterprising, you say," Mr. Poynter jumped in. "Downright irresponsible, I call it."

"Yes, that too," I said, and heard Jessica giggle.

"Have you known each other long?" Mrs. Poynter said. She leaned against a tree and closed her eyes, blissfully unaware that she'd already asked once.

"Not very," Jessica answered, stretching and yawning. "Alexander wants me to sleep with him. What do you think I should do, Mummy?"

I choked.

"Oh heavens, I don't know, dear. Is it necessary?" Her mother was smiling pleasantly, eyes still closed. Mr. Poynter was ripping apart another chicken leg, and looking bored.

Jessica flung herself back in the grass and laughed. "I'm not sure really," she said. Then abruptly she jumped to her feet and held her hand out to me. "Let's go for a walk."

I got up, and mumbling something to her parents, followed her across the field. "Did you have to say that?" I said, when we were out of earshot.

"No, I don't suppose I did. But it was worth it to see your face."

"Don't they mind? I mean, you sleeping with men?"

"They've never seemed to."

"Unusual parents. Especially with a daughter."

"But it's all right for a son?"

"I didn't make the rules," I said, holding up my hands in defense.

She pulled me to a halt and turned me to face her. "And I'm changing the rules, Alexander."

She looked beautiful. Her blonde hair, piled carelessly on top of her head, was curling in wisps around her neck, and her intelligent eyes studied me, waiting for my response. When I didn't answer she shrugged and started to gaze around her. After a while she lifted her arms to the sky and let her head fall back. When she spoke it was as if she were reciting poetry, and slowly she brought her eyes back to mine. "Tell me, Alexander, because I need to know. Who do you really think I am? What is my purpose in this world?"

It wasn't the first time I'd heard her ask these questions, and I knew just how serious she was. I looked at her. She was a mystery to me. Her search for meaning and value to her life took her further from me than any earthly distance could. In a way it made her more desirable—I wanted to possess her and make myself her only purpose.

"Is purpose just another word for fate?" I asked. "Or are you using it to evaluate your movement through life?"

She stared back at me, surprised and intrigued—surprised because I had never taken her seriously before, and intrigued because I had managed to say something that she considered worthy of thought. "I can see your intention is to penetrate my psyche," she said, eventually, and then started to walk slowly on across the field.

Relieved that the pondering of life's little complexities seemed to be over and not a little pleased with my own stimulating but unanswerable contribution, I started after her. It was a sleepy summer's day, and these lovely Oxfordshire cornfields were wasted as a setting for a discussion on the meaning of life.

When we reached the stile to the next field Jessica climbed over. As I made to follow she stopped me, putting the stile between us. "Would there be a purpose to us consummating our relationship?" she said.

Only just managing not to groan, I looked around, trying desperately to dredge up another piece of mind-boggling profundity. When I looked back at her she was still watching me. The moisture on her lips caught the sunlight, and she had unclipped her hair.

"I think there would be," she said, and smiled. "I want to be naked. I want you to be naked."

I felt my penis swell at her words, and reached out to touch her. Her mouth was already open, and as I pushed my tongue deep inside, she took my hand and placed it on the small mound of her breast. "Harder," she groaned, as I began to rotate her nipple between my finger and thumb. "Harder."

Quickly I leapt over the stile. Her hands slipped down to my waist and she was unzipping my fly. I was solid by now, and could feel the blood pulsating through me. She pushed at my trousers, dragging them down over my thighs, then reached up to slip off her

T-shirt. I fumbled with the zipper on her jeans, but she pushed me away. "I'll do it," she said. "Undress with me."

Naked, we walked into the field beyond. The corn came to our waist, but there was no one around to see us. After a while she stopped, and sank to her knees. Her face was on a level with my penis, and lifting it away from my belly, she covered it with her mouth. I held her head and moved with her, feeling her teeth rub against me. After a while she let me go and looked up into my face. I pushed her back and lay down beside her, maneuvering myself to kiss her behind the clutch of blonde pubic hair.

I waited until I felt her muscles start to contract, then sat up quickly, holding her legs apart, ready to enter her. She licked my lips, sinking her teeth gently into them, and clawed her nails across my buttocks. I positioned myself above her, then making her look into my eyes, I thrust into her with all my might. She screamed out. I thrust again, paused, then again. I knew I was hurting her, but she cried out for more. I was going to come soon, but she wasn't there yet, and I wanted to make her scream out again—scream and scream. She looked up at me and I saw she was laughing. "Think of your life, Alexander. Think of everything in it and use it, push it into me. I want it all."

I lowered my head and kissed her savagely on the mouth, then grabbed her legs and pushed them up, so high her knees were almost on her shoulders. "That's it, oh yes," she groaned. "I can feel you coming to me. All of you. Use it, Alexander! Use it to fuck me!" I was looking down into her face; it was contorted with lust. "Was she as good as this?" she snarled. "Your gypsy?"

I stopped dead.

She laughed. "Is that who you're thinking of now?" she said, writhing beneath me and twisting her fingers through my hair. "The gypsy slut?"

My hands slipped round her throat, almost strangling her, then with all the strength I had left I hammered into her, so hard that she cried out for me to stop. But I kept on going, thrust after thrust, driving her into the ground, crushing her beneath me, and not looking at her once. Let her scream, let her struggle, she was going to pay for that mistake. And then my climax was upon me, crushing me, blinding me, choking me, and it was my voice that cried out—a single name—as my body exploded into hers.

She was trapped beneath me. When she tried to move, I felt sickened and rolled over onto my back. I could hear her breathing, and after a while she started to move again. Finally she pulled my face round to hers. She was masturbating.

"Watch me," she whispered.

I felt only disgust. She saw it, and laughed. Then her back arched from the ground, and she moaned as waves of orgasm surged through her body. I watched her, hating her.

"So her name's Elizabeth, is it?" she said, as we stood at the stile putting our clothes on. She was pulling on her jeans, and seeing her slight body writhe its way into them, I had to fight the urge to crush her with my hands.

"You're still angry," she said, when I didn't answer. "Just think for a moment, Alexander, and you will see that your anger was the purpose to our lovemaking. You needed to face up to your pain."

"What pain? You don't know what the hell you're talking about, so just shut up!"

"You're angry inside, Alexander, it's why you're the way you are. You need to face it, and I want to help you. I told the Federation I could, and I think I have, though maybe you don't realize it yet."

"Federation! Do you mean to say you've been discussing me at your lesbian orgies! You're sick, do you know that?"

"No, Alexander, it's you who are sick. In the way you abuse women, you're sick. And by abusing us you're abusing yourself. I was right, it's because you still yearn for the gypsy. Does it hurt terribly?"

I turned away. "Poor Alexander," she cooed.

"Shall we change the subject," I snapped.

"Sure. But if I can face it, and handle it, why can't you? After all, if we're going to get married I'm going to have to live with her too, aren't I?"

I spun round. "If we're what!"

She was laughing, and I'd never hated anyone so much since the day I found out the truth about Elizabeth.

She started to climb the stile and I grabbed her arm. "You'd better get this into your head now, Jessica. I've no intention of marrying you, or anyone else for that matter. So—"

"OK," she said, and dropping a kiss on my cheek, she skipped over the stile and began running back across the field.

11

I HATED HER, yet I was obsessed by her. The harder I tried to stay away the more I found myself going to her. It was as if she had spun a web and trapped me; when she felt like it she crept out of her lair, sated her lust on me, and then discarded me. Weeks turned into months and still I was seeing her. Her independence and elusiveness almost drove me out of my mind. Her quest to find a purpose in life continued and she made it clear that this was something more than I could supply. Her need for identity, recognition, a status, was the source of endless fights between us, but she could no more stay away from me than I could from her.

Henry despised her, but that only served to make her more acceptable to me. When she and I decided to move from our respective colleges and find ourselves a small house on the outskirts of Oxford I thought it was going to be the end of my friendship with him.

"You're insane," he yelled at me, standing in the doorway of my room as I packed.

"Maybe," I said, taking the Ensor from the wall and grimacing as I remembered the first night I had met Jessica.

"She's no good, Alexander. She's sleeping with other men, you know that, don't you?"

I nodded. "Yep, I know that."

He punched his fist against the wall. "How can you just shrug it off? Jesus, I don't think I know you anymore."

I laughed at that. "This is beginning to sound like a lover's tiff, Henry."

He didn't even smile. His eyes were brilliant and I could see that he was struggling with himself. I turned away and began stuffing my shaving equipment into a bag.

"It's Elizabeth, isn't it?" he suddenly burst out.

I turned back to him, my razor still in my hand. This was a forbidden subject between us, and had been since before we left Foxton's.

"It's Elizabeth. Jessica's told me all about it. She lets you think of Elizabeth when you're screwing her, doesn't she?"

I felt the blood draining from my face. "You're out of your mind—"

"No! It's you who's out of your mind. Listen, do you know why she does it? Why she lets you carry on this insane delusion? It's so that you will never completely own her. So that she can walk out on you whenever she feels like it. She's using you, Alexander. You're her cause, her challenge. If she can conquer you, break you even, she'll have scored *the* great victory for womankind."

"You don't know what you're talking about."

"I bloody do. I'm Not Fodder for the Male Chauvinist Pig! Christ, it's emblazoned all over her T-shirt! She's made you a laughingstock, Alexander, the way you go running around after her. And you don't really think you're going to get Elizabeth out of your system by—"

"Out of my system! What in hell's name are you talking about? So I made a mistake when I was a kid—why can't you do as I did years ago, and forget it? And as for all that crap about—"

"It's not crap. Jessica told me herself, she's told everybody. What is it she does for you, Alexander? Put on a nurse's uniform?"

"For Christ's sake!" I yelled.

Henry's face was white. His eyes fell to the razor I was still holding. "Why don't you use it now?" he said. "Slit your wrists and be done with it, before Jessica does it for you. Because take it from me, Alexander, she'll destroy you."

Before I could answer he had stalked out of the room, slamming the door behind him.

I didn't see him for several weeks after that, but I was so busy with Jessica I had no time to think about him. Intellectually my life took a new turn as I entered her bohemian world of artists and writers, and languished away the days posing nude while she stood at her easel creating unrecognizable portraits of me. This was her surrealist period.

The novelty of living together soon wore off though, as Jessica started to introduce her feminist friends—the lesbian brigade, as I irreverently called them—into our house, and returned to her old habit of attending women's rallies in far flung corners of the country. At that time the Women's Liberal Federation, the organization she belonged to, was trying to bring about government legislation for equal pay. They had plenty of other causes too, such as free contraception, maternity rights for working mothers, laws against sexual harassment in the workplace, Jessica's old favorite about allowing women to join the Stock Exchange—in fact so many that I often lost track of what Jessica was doing, and got fed up with the endless political wrangling that I seemed to get caught up in whenever she was at home. It wasn't that I didn't believe in what she was trying to do, it was just that I was growing a little weary of helping her cope with the basic contradictions in her behavior. On the one hand she believed passionately in every one of the Federation's feminist ideals, but on the other, she was not only living with one of the common enemy, she was actually falling in love with him. She could not come to terms with this—nor could I. It wasn't as if I expected her to cook for me, wash up after me, iron for me, they were all tasks I could and did perform for myself; but sometimes, when she was feeling particularly warm towards me, Jessica insisted on doing these things. She did them because she loved me, because she wanted to do them, that was what she said at the time—but afterwards she would fly into a terrible rage and nothing I could do or say would convince her that she hadn't drastically diminished her status as a modern, liberated woman. All men wanted women for was to slave for them, she'd yell at me; they wanted to parade them as status symbols, and then drive them home and father children on them in their own image. There was nothing to compare with the arrogance and stupidity of the male ego! And all this because she had darned a hole in one of my socks, so small that I hadn't even noticed it was there.

After an altercation that very nearly came to blows just because I asked her to post a letter for me, I walked out of the house. I was sorely in need of male company. I sought out Henry and in no time at all we were slapping each other on the back as if our quarrel had never taken place. Robert Lyttleton, a chap who had come up from Eton a year after us, and knew Henry's family, was now occupying my old room. The three of us began to spend a lot of time together, mostly at Brown's or the King's Arms. And Parson's Pleasure was a convenient male-only retreat that I frequented because I knew it annoyed Jessica.

This isn't to say that I stopped living with Jessica, of course. Our erratic and eccentric relationship continued along its rocky path, painfully cemented by a compelling mix of hatred and lust. I thrived on the way I could torment her because she loved me; she tried desperately not to mind about the other women I had—and hit back by taking lovers herself. I, at least, was happy with the way we were, and didn't intend to change it.

So when, after finals, I had the idea of inviting Miss Angrid up to Oxford for the weekend, no one was more surprised by the suggestion than me. From the look on his face, Henry was pretty flabbergasted too.

"Just think of the old dragon," I said, before he could say anything, "waddling her way round college telling everyone to stop biting their nails and tuck their shirts in. It'll be a kill."

"Where will she stay?"

I shrugged. "Why not with me and Jessica?"

Henry's eyes widened, and I realized that perhaps that wasn't such a good idea. This was confirmed later when Jessica rounded on me and demanded to know how she was expected to cope with a morbid old bag of a matron hanging round her all day. Why on earth had I invited her in the first place—or was I just kinky about matrons?

In fact I had been having second thoughts about the invitation, but after that jibe I went ahead and composed a letter to Miss Angrid the same night. The following week I received a reply saying she'd love to come, and could I book her into that nice Eastgate hotel—the Ruskin suite if I could manage it—where she had stayed the last time she had been up.

On our four-hundred-and-twenty-pounds-a-year grant, plus the six hundred pounds allowance we each received from our fathers, Henry and I managed to stretch to the Ruskin suite, and I was at the station to meet Miss Angrid on the designated Saturday. I was annoyed to find how nervous I was at the prospect of seeing her again, and silently berated Jessica for forcing me into it. And the fact that my heart gave an Olympic-style somersault as Miss Angrid stepped off the train annoyed me even further. However, the situation was saved by the Mercedes. She made no comment, except to purse her lips and glance at me over the top of her new spectacles, but it was a look I remembered so well that I very nearly threw my arms around her and danced her round the parking lot.

Henry was waiting at the hotel and leapt from his seat when he saw us come in. He then proceeded very nearly to buckle his back by trying to sweep her off her feet. Her face was beaming so hard it looked painful.

When lunch was over, she produced a well-thumbed guide of the city and took us on a tour, dragging us from monument to museum, college to library, impressing us like mad with her vast knowledge of the place, until at last we arrived at Balliol where she insisted Henry show her his room.

I almost choked when I saw Henry's face; it was as if we had stepped back in time. Miss Angrid was duly horrified at the state of Henry's room and demanded to know who was responsible for letting him get away with it. Henry whispered to me that his scout was away, and we both heaved a sigh of relief at the narrow avoidance of past and present worlds colliding . . .

We dined with her that evening. I stayed longer than I'd intended, mainly because with Miss Angrid there, Jessica suddenly seemed an intrusion in my life, an irrelevance. But I had to face her wrath sooner or later, so leaving Miss Angrid and Henry to their brandies and reminiscences, I went home. Jessica wasn't there. Her wardrobe was empty and there was a note on the bed. I didn't even bother to read it. I knew she'd be back.

The following day Henry was taking part in the Eights Week races, so I took Miss Angrid for a stroll over to Magdalen to see the deer park.

"So you'll be going down at the end of the month," she remarked, as we wandered past the tower and on to the bridge.

"Mmm," I waved to a couple of friends emerging from beneath the bridge in a punt.

"What do you intend to do with yourself then?"

"Bar school."

"And Henry?"

"Same."

"And are you still determined to practice criminal law?" she asked, leaning against the side of the bridge.

"Yes."

"Is your father any happier about it? I thought after all that business—"

"Not really, but we don't row about it anymore."

"How is he? I read in the paper he'd not been well. Heart, wasn't it?"

"He's better, I think. Apparently the doctor's told him he's got to take things a bit easier, but you know what he's like."

"And your mother?"

"Oh, she's fine. Gave her a bit of a fright, naturally, but now Lucinda's had the baby she's got something else to occupy her mind."

"Of course. I was forgetting you had a sister. She married a Frenchman, didn't she?"

"Etienne. And now they've got a son. And before you ask, I'm sure they'll be putting him down for Foxton's—unless Etienne insists he has a French education!"

She laughed. "Now, what about you? Who's this Jessica Henry was telling me about last night?"

"Henry told you about Jessica?"

"He did. But I had already guessed there must be someone, otherwise you and Henry would be sharing digs together. So, what's she like? Why haven't I been introduced?"

"She's gone to keep her grandmother company for the weekend."

She eyed me suspiciously. "Mmm. Serious, is it, between you two?"

I answered with a shrug, then deftly maneuvered her round to telling me the news of Foxton's. Mr. Lear was now the Deputy Head, I was suprised to hear, and Mr. Ellery had married a new English mistress who had joined the school just after I left. Foxton's had been slaughtered at rugby by Monkforth Abbey for three years running, she added with disgust. "Seems they forgot how to play the wretched game after you'd gone. You got a blue, I hear?"

"You hear a great deal down there at Foxton's," I laughed, and pushed myself away from the walk to walk on. She followed, a pace or two behind. "And the other matron?" I asked, after a short silence. "I've forgotten her name now. Is she still there?"

"Miss Austen. Yes, she's still with us."

When we came to the other side of the bridge, we wandered down the steps to the riverbank. It was several minutes before I realized Miss Angrid was no longer walking beside me. When I turned round I found her watching me, her hands bulging the pockets of her cardigan and her blue rinse tilted to one side.

"Is something the matter?" I asked. And when she didn't answer I looked at my watch. "I know! It's time for tea. There's a great tea shop not far from here. No hot buttered toast, I'm afraid, but they do a terrific scone with homemade jam and fresh . . ."

"Why don't you ask, Alexander?" She waited, her eyes steadfastly holding mine. "It's why you invited me here, isn't it?"

I stared out across the river. I hadn't been conscious of any motive, but maybe that was because I hadn't allowed myself to be. It was all so long ago now—I couldn't even picture her face anymore. So why was my heart beating faster? Why did the palms of my hands feel damp?

I looked back to Miss Angrid. She was still watching me. "I can return to Foxton's without mentioning her name if that's what you want," she said. "It's up to you."

I sat down on the grass and rested my elbows on my knees. After a while she came and sat beside me. I couldn't meet her eyes as I spoke. "Have you heard from her?"

"A postcard." She fumbled in her handbag. "Here, I brought it in case you wanted to see it."

94

I looked at it for a long time, but didn't take it from her. "When did she send it?" I asked finally.

"Just over a year ago."

"Do you know where she is?"

"No."

"She doesn't say on the card?"

"No."

I laughed, and knew it sounded bitter. "Well, that's it then, isn't it," I said, getting to my feet. "She could be dead by now for all we know."

Miss Angrid said nothing. "Well, what am I supposed to say?" I shouted angrily. "She went out of our lives four years ago. She knows where we are, if she wanted to get in touch she would. I gave up losing sleep over her a long time ago." It wasn't what I'd meant to say, but somehow the right words wouldn't come.

Miss Angrid sighed, and held out her hand for me to help her to her feet. "It's no good, Alexander," she said, "I can see it in your eyes, even after all this time. I thought maybe you'd have got over it by now, but common sense tells me I wouldn't be here if you had." I turned away so she couldn't see my face, and she sighed again as she looked out over the river. "She was very special, wasn't she? I don't suppose any of us really knew how much you two meant to each other. You were both so young. All I can say to you now is, stop punishing yourself and—from what Henry tells me—everyone around you too. It's been a long time, Alexander, time enough for you to come to terms with what happened. That's the only way you're going to stop hurting, you know—and when you stop hurting, then it really will be over."

I swung round to face her. "It is over! For God's sake, what do I have to do to prove it? Yes, she did mean something to me, but you said it yourself, it was a long time ago. I was a schoolboy. Things are different now. Things, *I*, have changed."

She sighed and hitched her bag across her elbow. When she looked at me again her eyes were sad, and she shook her head slowly.

I glared at her, and in that instant I felt such rage well up in me that I wanted to strike out at her. Why wouldn't they all stop tormenting me? Why wouldn't they believe me when I told them it didn't matter to me any more? There was another woman in my life—there had been for more than a year. Damn it, surely that must mean something!

I was glad when Henry joined us for tea at the Eastgate and sensing the tension between Miss Angrid and me, immediately set about breaking it. He almost succeeded, but I refused to be drawn completely; knowing that he thought the same as Miss Angrid angered me.

Later I drove Miss Angrid to the station and waited with her until her train was ready to leave. As I was closing the door of her carriage she turned quickly and pushed a note into my hand. The sudden lurch of my heart must have shown on my face, because she shook her head.

I waited until I got back to the car before I unfolded the note, then smiled as I saw it was a verse from Shelley. I read it slowly.

> Life may change, but it may fly not,
> Hope may vanish, but can die not,
> Truth be veiled, but still it burneth;
> Love repulsed—but it returneth.

I banged my hand hard against the steering wheel. Damn! Damn her! What did it take to convince her that not only was I no longer in love with Elizabeth, I was in love with someone else? Jessica was a bitch, but I couldn't live without her; we were made for each other, Jessica and I, and the rest of the world could go to hell. And what was more, I now knew exactly what I would do to show the rest of the world that Elizabeth meant nothing to me anymore—absolutely nothing.

"What do you mean, no?" I stormed. "You mean you're refusing?"

"That's precisely what I mean." Henry walked slowly across the room to refill his glass, then sauntered back to his chair and sat down.

"Then I'll have to ask Robert Lyttleton, I suppose," I said.

"You can always ask."

I swung round to face him. "Look here, Henry, I'm getting married. It's supposed to be one of the most important days in a man's life. I'm asking you to be there, with me."

"And I'm saying that I don't want to be. In fact I don't want to be there at all. I refuse to sit and watch my best friend make a fool of himself. The whole thing's a sham, Alexander, as you well know."

"A sham! Good God, man—"

But Henry interrupted me. "Look, it's been ever since Old Anger came to visit. She got under your skin, didn't she, about Elizabeth? OK, OK, it's all over, I've heard you say it a thousand times. I believe you, all right? You don't have to marry Jessica to prove it."

That took the wind clean out of my sails.

"You see, I'm right," he went on. "Practically everything you've done in the last four years has been because of Elizabeth. Your reputation as a stud and a heartbreaker was such a legend that the biggest feminist in Oxford came gunning for you. The only trouble was, she fell for you too. They all do, Alexander, because you're a bastard. Because you don't give a shit about any of them, except to make them pay for the fact that you feel you've been 'betrayed' by one of their sex—a girl you *claim* you don't even love anymore. Well, if you don't love her anymore then why not stop behaving like this? Stop now, before you make one of the biggest mistakes of your life."

"Impossible," I said.

"It's not!"

"I mean, it's impossible for it to be the biggest mistake of my life. I've already made the biggest."

"When you were no more than a kid. And you're still behaving like one."

"I've already asked her," I said.

"Tell her you've changed your mind."

"Why should I do that? I haven't."

He gave an exasperated sigh. "Oh, to hell with it. If you want to ruin your life, then go ahead and do it. I can see that nothing I've got to say is going to stop you."

We sat through a long silence before either of us spoke again. Finally I caught his eye and grinned. Reluctantly, he grinned too. "Have you fixed the date?" he asked.

"June nineteenth."

"Why does it have to be so soon?"

"Why not?"

He shrugged. "And if Elizabeth were to walk through that door now, what then?"

I jumped up from my chair. "For God's sake, Henry!" Then I gave a half-hearted grin. "If she did, I could invite her to the wedding."

He laughed. "You really are a bastard."

"It's why Jessica's marrying me, or so you would have me believe."

"I can think of no other reason. Apart from the title, I suppose."

It was my turn to laugh. "Let her have her title, what the hell? We understand each other, Jessica and I. She's just the sort of wife I need. If you didn't hate her so much, you'd see it too. She's a perfect barrister's wife. For one thing she's great at dinner parties. She's witty, intelligent, and she's got her art which gives her something to do besides making my life a misery with the lesbian brigade."

Henry looked at me aghast. "I take it you've never said that to her."

"Would I be alive to tell the tale? Anyway, shall I go on? She's got an independent, though I admit, sometimes warped mind. She's beautiful. Good child-bearing hips with which to produce the Belmayne heirs. What more could a man ask?"

Henry's look was sardonic as he said, "I thought you of all people would know the answer to that."

12

"*I* JUST CAN'T THINK where they've got to." Jessica stood back from the mirror, eyeing herself critically. Around her our bedroom was in its almost permanent state of chaos. Damp towels lay where they'd been dropped, shoes spilled from the wardrobe, the contents of Jessica's handbag were strewn across the bed that only an hour before had been rumpled by our lovemaking, and the clothes we'd been wearing that day were draped in an untidy heap over the chaise longue. I kicked a towel out of the way before she tripped on it, then stood behind her, watching her in the mirror. Her fingers hovered around the pearls at her throat, then adjusted the thin halter strap of the dress that had cost me eighty-three guineas the week before because I had turned up over an hour late for an exhibition where two of her paintings were being shown. She was beautiful. Her fine blonde hair was swept up from her neck in a cluster of curls and held in place by a sapphire and diamond hairpin, the family heirloom my mother had given her almost a year ago on our wedding day. It matched her dress perfectly.

"Probably just delayed in traffic," I said, still watching her.

She leaned towards the mirror and peered at herself through

narrowed eyes. "What do you think of this eye shadow? Do you think it's too heavy? I've got a lighter one."

I shrugged, and carried on tying my tie. "Personally speaking, I think you look ravishing in anything." I looked at my watch.

"Now you're trying to rush me," she complained. "Well, I shan't be moved until you express a preference."

"I like the one you're wearing," I said, and she laughed. "Come here." And taking me by the arm, she turned me round for inspection. "Mmm, yes, you'll do," she decided, flicking invisible specks from my DJ. "Have you got the tickets?"

I patted my pocket to make sure they were there, then caught her by the hand before she sailed back to the mirror again. She turned in my arms and I brushed my lips against her bare shoulders. She smelt good.

"One kiss?" I said, my mouth very nearly on hers.

"No, you'll smudge my lip . . . Oh Alexander, now look what you've done," she grumbled as I let her go, but her eyes were bright and I kissed her again.

"I wish someone had warned me what a trial it would be to have a husband around when one is trying to get ready for a ball," she laughed, picking up her lipstick. "Oh God, where can they have got to? Why aren't they here yet?"

"Maybe Lizzie's flight was delayed," I suggested. "Shall I ring the airport?"

"Yes, yes. Good idea."

But British Airways confirmed that the flight from Melbourne, due in at six-thirty, had arrived on schedule.

"Well, what do we do now?" I noticed the warning blotches of color rising on her cheeks, as they always did when things weren't going according to plan.

"We go without them," I said. "Henry's got their tickets. Anyway, it's a long flight, Jess, maybe she's tired."

"You don't know Lizzie."

"Then maybe they've gone straight there."

"Oh, don't be ridiculous, Lizzie has to get ready first. No, they must be on their way. Let's wait another five minutes. Did you pour me a gin and tonic?"

We went downstairs to the drawing room where we waited for five minutes, and then a further five, while Jessica paced up and down the room, her heavy skirts swishing around her ankles. My earlier surge of affection had by now diminished, and I was watching her with increasing irritation. Sometimes her behavior so resembled that of a spoiled brat that I was tempted to put her over my knee and spank her, hard. In fact I had done it once, but predictably, Jessica had become so aroused by my aggression that we ended up writhing madly on the kitchen floor. Ever since I had wondered if she misbehaved purposely in order to get me to do it again. But, watching her face become almost ugly with ill humor, I doubted if sex was on her mind just at this moment.

Marriage to Jessica was everything I might have expected, had I only stopped to think. We never stopped competing with each other. Jessica feigned disinterest in almost everything I did, and declaring she wasn't some bovine creature content to sit at home and chew the cud of her husband's success, forced her artistic triumphs down my throat—along with her resentments, her jealousies and her feminism. I was repeatedly unfaithful, but the strange thing was that even though my feelings for her were so ambivalent, I was always sorry for what I'd done when I saw how hurt she was.

But as time went on, and despite all my efforts, our incompatibility out of bed became more and more destructive. I couldn't help imagining how my life could have been, should have been, if only . . . Elizabeth . . . In the end everything came back to her. I couldn't understand it. It was more than five years ago.

Jessica tutted, and I looked up as she began to pace the room again. I sighed. How different it would all be if I were married to Elizabeth. There would have been none of the rage that had almost crippled me at Oxford. None of the resentment that made me want to hurt any and every woman, even now, who crossed my path. Dear God, I'd been only a boy then, why hadn't she understood? I hadn't meant to be cruel, to turn my back on her the way I did. I knew she'd loved me—what was it that had made her stay away?

Damn! I jerked myself to my feet. Why was I still suffering like this? And even if she did come back into my life, what the hell could I do? I was married now. Just think about that, Alexander Belmayne. Married—when you swore to her that you would always love her. Married to Jessica, and why? To prove that you didn't love her anymore, when all the time, if you'd been man enough to face the truth . . .

"Damn! Damn, damn and damn!" Jessica slammed her glass down on the table and went to look out of the window. I swallowed my irritation and went to pour myself another drink—I knew better than to get into a fight with Jessica before we went out—but I was finding it increasingly difficult to hold my tongue. I hadn't wanted to go to the Berkeley Square ball in the first place, but Jessica had found a possible new patron for her paintings in George Mannering, who owned a small gallery in Knightsbridge, and as he was going to the ball Jessica saw it as another opportunity to court him.

It had been my idea to invite Henry, saying he could escort Jessica's sister Lizzie, who was returning to London "for several months, but possibly forever, who knows?" Henry had leapt at the idea, and the stirrings of conscience I had felt on behalf of Caroline, whom he'd been seeing a little more regularly than his other girl-friends, were eased. Henry was without a doubt the current Deb's Delight, and had even been listed in *Harpers & Queen* as one of the country's most eligible bachelors—something that had made us both yell with laughter.

We now had four more dinners to go at the Inns of Court, one last batch of exams, and then, hopefully, we would be called to the bar. My determination to practice criminal law had wavered not at all, and my father no longer raised any objections—with hanging now firmly abolished, any anxieties he had about my being involved in a repeat of the Ince affair were laid to rest. So, providing I gained the results required, I would enter chambers at the Inner Temple where Lord Green was one of the benchers. It would be said that my father had put in a word for me, but I could shrug that off. Since my father had become Lord Chancellor, no matter where I went people would accuse me of being "the protégé of the woolsack."

The clock on the mantelshelf began to strike nine. "Right, that's it! We've waited long enough," Jessica announced. "They'll just have to get themselves there."

Obediently I put my drink down and walked across the room to fetch her cloak. Suddenly I felt sorry for her. I knew she had been looking forward to seeing her sister, and the Berkeley Square Ball was the perfect opportunity for welcoming her home in style. "Cheer up, darling," I said, putting her cloak around her shoulders and fastening it at her neck, "after all, you've still got me to keep you company."

Immediately her face softened—but I found myself turning away.

Everyone from our set was at the ball, half of them already three sheets to the wind, and the other half struggling to catch up. As Jessica and I walked into the marquee I heard her swear under her breath as her heel sank in the mud, and took her by the elbow to help her along. It proved to be a rocky journey over to the champagne, as her high heels were sucked and plucked from the ground.

"If you dare to say you told me so," she hissed under her breath, "I swear I'll kick you."

Robert Lyttleton was in the middle of the crowd, wearing an extremely attractive middle-aged woman on his arm. Robert was second only to Henry in the playboy stakes these days, and, if my information was correct, he was poised for a takeover: his rise at the Foreign Office had been meteoric, and he was undoubtedly bound for foreign climes in the very near future—but word had it he needed to acquire a wife first.

He introduced his companion as Rachel, then immediately turned his attention to Jessica. Jessica rose to his flattery as she always did, and I felt a stab of jealousy as I wondered, not for the first time, if they had ever been to bed together at Oxford.

"So you're Alexander Belmayne," Rachel was saying. "I've met your mother once or twice. How is she?"

I tore my eyes away from Jessica as she threw back her head and laughed at something Robert had whispered in her ear—and found myself looking into Rachel's rather bewitching green eyes. They held mine in an openly seductive gaze while her lips, full and smiling, parted to reveal a set of perfect white teeth. Probably because of my sudden surge of jealousy, I was almost overwhelmed by the impulse to lean forward and kiss her, brutally, but I was saved by someone knocking against her and spilling champagne over her hands. She laughed softly, but didn't take her eyes from mine as she ran her tongue over the tips of her fingers.

"How is she?" she repeated, when I didn't answer.

"Who? Oh, my mother. She's very well, thank you." I glanced quickly at Jessica, but she had joined a group of friends and looked as though she had all but forgotten me.

I danced with Rachel, remembering to look up occasionally to see if Henry had arrived, but there was no sign of him. So I concentrated on Rachel. I had known, since the moment I'd taken her in my arms to dance, where things were leading. Normally I was bored by women who threw themselves at me, but with Rachel's soft, mature, slightly overweight body moving seductively against mine, I felt myself responding handsomely to the promise of something new.

She held her glass out for more champagne and I went off to oblige. On my way I looked around for Jessica, but she seemed to have disappeared, and for a fleeting moment I felt wildly free—but the feeling was quickly followed by the fear that Robert Lyttleton might have taken her off somewhere. I'd never felt jealous of any other man, but for some reason it was different with Robert Lyttleton. He was so damned smooth, so damned good at everything. As far as I was concerned Jessica could screw whoever she liked just as long as it wasn't him—although these days Jessica never seemed to screw anyone except me.

I had several more dances with Rachel; I took her to supper; and after supper I danced with her again. By this time it was almost one in the morning. Still there was no sign of Jessica. And I knew from the way Rachel was looking at me that she was ready to do something about the erection that had been pushing its way between us for the best part of the evening. Taking her somewhat roughly by the arm, I started to steer her towards the nearest exit.

"Oh darling, there you are!"

I froze. Beside me I heard Rachel mutter an expletive, and several seconds must have elapsed before I was sufficiently in control of myself to turn round. Jessica's hair had slipped anchor and was cascading about her face. Her lipstick was smudged and there was a bow tie round her neck, its ends dangling between her breasts.

"I've been looking for you everywhere, Alexander. Isn't it the most perfectly wonderful ball? Aren't you glad you came now? I told you you'd love it."

With that she blinked several times, before fixing Rachel with one of her cold stares. Then, taking me by the arm, she said to her: "Sorry, I didn't catch your name, but I'm sure you won't mind if I take my *husband* away for a dance, will you?"

I glanced apologetically at Rachel, but she only smiled, and inclining her head vaguely in Jessica's direction, she disappeared into the crowd.

"There was no need to be so rude," I said, attempting to hold Jessica upright as we bumped our way through a fox-trot.

"So sorry, darling," she hiccoughed. "Oh, look at you, you're angry with me. Maybe you would have liked my blessing on your little liaison instead. You were about to go and fuck her, weren't you?"

"You have a vivid imagination," I said, "and you're drunk."

"Ah, but not too drunk to catch my husband in the act. Or at least, very nearly in the act. Tell me, out of interest, where were you planning to do it?"

I looked at her for a moment, trying to gauge her mood before I answered. "In our bed," I said, finally.

"Oh, very naughty." She threw back her head and laughed uproariously. "You always get ratty when you're found out. I suppose she looks like Elizabeth, they usually do, don't they." She screeched with laughter again. "It's about time you learned that I know everything about you, Alexander, everything."

"Then you'll know that I'm tired of this conversation, and I think it's time I took you home. Get your cloak."

"Get it for me."

"I said get your cloak."

She usually knew when she'd gone too far, and more often than not it was a reference to Elizabeth that did it. She walked off, leaving me in the middle of the dance floor as she weaved her way through the crowd. I wasn't sure whether or not she was intending to come back again, but nevertheless I looked round for Rachel. She was in the midst of a group of people I'd never met, and caught my eye before I reached her. It was clear she didn't want to provoke a scene with Jessica, so she quickly gave me her address and told me to meet her there the following afternoon at five.

Jessica did come back, together with her cloak and naughty-little-girl look. She giggled most of the way home in the taxi, and kept trying to open my trousers, but I wasn't in the mood. In the end she gave up and started to suck her thumb, knowing it annoyed me.

When we pulled up in front of the house, the lights were on in the drawing room. "It'll be Lizzie!" Jessica cried, and I felt a wave of relief. My first thought had been that it was burglars.

We let ourselves in quietly and Jessica crept along the hall to the sitting room. When she got outside the door, she stopped and turned round. "Do you hear anything?" she whispered.

"She might be asleep," I said.

Jessica looked undecided for a moment, then turning the handle, she pushed the door open and burst into the room. "Lizzie!" she cried.

I walked in behind her, and as Lizzie and Henry looked up from the sofa I felt a grin spread across my face. The timing of our interruption was immaculate—though, catching a glimpse of Henry's expression, I guessed he might want to contest that. Jessica appeared quite unperturbed, though she couldn't have missed Henry's surreptitious attempt at doing up his fly. He threw me a look, then got to his feet and stood back as Jessica and Lizzie embraced each other. "You might have given us a bit more warning," he muttered.

"From the look of you, old chap, it was too late for that. By the way, those yours?" I nodded towards a pair of white silk panties that were lying on the floor beside the sofa.

"Alexander, come and meet Lizzie. Isn't she simply divine?" I gave Henry one last grin, then turned to greet Lizzie. Until that moment I hadn't really been able to get a good look at her, so lifting my eyes from her discarded panties and preparing to embrace her in a brotherly way, I was caught completely unaware. She wasn't quite as small as Jessica, nor quite so beautiful, but she had something, something that defied words and oozed sex appeal in unimaginable quantities.

"Well, come along," Jessica urged, "give her a kiss."

I don't know if I imagined the brief press of her body against mine when I put my arms about Lizzie, but just her touch was enough to make me pull back as if an electric current had shot through me. She laughed, and her eyes swept over my face. "Well, Jess, he's every bit as handsome as you said he was. I'm sorry I missed the wedding now, Alexander. I might have been able to persuade you to change the bride."

Jessica laughed, and putting her arm around her sister, ushered her out of the room and upstairs, eager to show her the bedroom that had been prepared for her.

I turned to Henry. "Jesus Christ!" I exploded, as soon as I gauged them safely out of earshot.

Henry burst out laughing. "Too much for you to handle, my friend. She'll have you for breakfast. And if Jessica gets to find out about it, she'll carve you up for dinner."

I shuddered. "Well, you sure as hell didn't waste any time," I remarked.

He held up his hands in defense. "Don't look at me, old chap. It was her. From the minute I picked her up at the airport she was all over me like a rash."

Laughing, I walked over to the bar and poured us both a brandy. Upstairs I could hear Lizzie shrieking with delight as Jessica showed her around. Henry sat in an armchair looking like the cat that got the cream, as he described, in minutest detail, the incomparable body he had been taking advantage of all night and fully intended to take advantage of again. One look at Lizzie was enough to tell anyone that she would have been the one taking advantage, but I refrained from saying so.

Eventually Jessica called out that it was getting late, and Henry got up to go. At the door he clapped his arm round my shoulders. "See you in the morning, old chap. Try not to overdo it tonight, more exams tomorrow don't forget. Oh, and tell Jess I won't be staying for dinner tomorrow night, I'm taking your ravishing sister-in-law out instead."

"Tell you what, give her one from me next time, eh?" I grinned.

"Oh but, Alexander, surely you can do that for yourself."

Henry and I swung round together—to find Lizzie standing on the stairs. She was wearing a transparent pink lacy affair, and was starkers underneath. My eyes were transfixed as she sauntered down the last few stairs and came to stand between us. Her lips were wet and her nipples stood out firmly against the gossamer-thin fabric.

"Good night, Henry," she purred, sliding her arms around his neck and opening her mouth. I saw their tongues meet. Her eyes never wavered from mine.

I was surprised, a couple of weeks later, when I arrived home one afternoon to find Caroline Truman, Henry's ex, waiting outside the house for me. With an admirable effort at holding back the tears, she asked me what she had done wrong. Why didn't Henry call her anymore? Couldn't I talk to him, please, get him to say he'd meet her, if only for an hour? Though I'd always liked Caroline, I was annoyed that she had managed to corner me. Even if I was partly responsible for the split between her and Henry, it wasn't as though I'd forced him into Lizzie's arms. Rejected women were all the same, crying and sniffling, and all but begging a man to go back to them, even when it was quite clear he didn't want to. And what the hell could I do about it? I suggested a good shopping session and a few more cocktail parties, and if she still felt lonely after that, well there was always me. She walked off in disgust.

And as the invitations continued to stream through the mailbox—opening nights, concerts, exhibitions—I, like Henry, soon forgot about her. Almost every night there were parties or clubs to be attended, places to be seen at, bottles of champagne to be drunk and new games to be played. Our own wild parties became the talk of the town as windows and doors were thrown open to the world, and the dignified quiet of Belgrave Square was rocked to its foundations. Somehow, during this orgy of frivolity, Henry and I managed to accomplish the dining of four more dinners, and having mysteriously achieved our finals, were called to the Bar.

I couldn't help noticing during this time that it wasn't only Caroline's company Henry was denying himself; every female who threw herself his way—and plenty did—was rejected, so that he could concentrate his inimitable charms on Lizzie. And the more Henry saw of Lizzie, the more I saw of Rachel. I knew that all too often when I made love to Rachel I was fantasizing about Lizzie, but it was the safest way of trying to work my sister-in-law through my system. I had told Jessica time after time to speak to Lizzie about walking round the house naked, but Jessica was too busy with her own life to worry much about what Lizzie's magnificent breasts were doing to mine. As far as Rachel was concerned, I eased my conscience by assuring myself that, attractive though she was, she was still rather lucky to have someone of my age interested her. Besides, she was my companion in another kind of fun that I had been growing rather attached to of late—gambling.

Jessica I saw little of. Since Lizzie's arrival she had redoubled her efforts on behalf of the Women's Movement, showing off to her sister and trying her damnedest to enlist her in their war against men. Lizzie was as bored by it all as I was, though she managed to hide it a little better. But dedicated as Jessica was to her cause, she wasn't one to let it get in the way of her own personal glory. When she wasn't holding meetings in the parlor at Belgrave Square, which she had commandeered for the use of the lesbian brigade, she was either in her studio at the top of the house or at George Mannering's gallery in Knightsbridge.

And things were coming along "frightfully well" with her art, she assured me whenever I remembered to ask. George thought it showed "unusual potential," and was sure she would be ready for an exhibition of her own within the year. I couldn't stop my eyes from flicking to the paintings that adorned the walls in Belgrave Square when she told me that, and wondered what my mother would say. There had been an uneasy truce between my mother and Jessica ever since my mother had descended upon the house, having heard that Jessica was hanging her paintings alongside the master-pieces my mother, and my grandmother before her, had worked so hard to acquire. Secretly I thought my mother very restrained when she merely remarked that she felt Jessica's *chefs d'oeuvre* looked somewhat incongruous beside the buhl, the ormolu and the passe-menterie. Jessica sulked for three days after my mother's visit, and claimed I'd given her no support whatever in what was a matter of fundamental importance to her. Rather flummoxed, I objected that I was being thoroughly supportive, in that I was prepared to suffer the paintings without complaint. Not a wise choice of words, and the price I paid was a new dinner service.

But there was no getting away from it, Jessica's paintings were, to put it mildly, extreme. The only thing I had ever recognized in any one of them—and they were coming off the easel by the dozen—was a rabbit, which had been tucked away—"rather clev-erly," I remarked—in the corner of a painting she called "The Warren." Of course the title had given it away, but I had been rather pleased with myself all the same—until Jessica's wrath descended upon me with all the subtlety of the erupting volcano the painting was supposed to depict . . . I never did manage to find out the reason for the rabbit. Nor did I venture to guess her subjects again after that, but meekly accepted my role as one of the uninitiated and waited until she was ready to explain precisely the feeling she had tried to capture in the painting, and then assured her that indeed she was getting it across. She never believed me, of course, but it was a little charade that satisfied us both.

In fact, it was through her art that I first began to notice a change in Jessica. We'd been talking on and off for some time about starting a family. Jessica's first reaction, when she realized I was serious, was one of horror.

"*You* want a baby! Don't make me laugh, Alexander. What would your friends say? I mean, it's hardly the macho image you try so hard to cultivate, is it? With your ridiculous male pride, I'm astonished you even have the guts to say it."

"Jess, I said it because you're my wife. If I can't tell you, then who the hell can I tell? And as for the macho image, *you* astonish *me!* I'd have thought you'd be more likely to accuse me of vanity in wanting to reproduce myself."

She laughed. "Yes, there is that, too. Anyway, it's out of the question. I'm sorry if you're feeling broody, darling, but I'm not."

I wasn't going to give up that easily, and she knew it. Nevertheless I was surprised when she listened, without ridicule, to my case. Afterwards I listened to her explanations of why it was a bad idea. They started with the fact that she was too young and ended with the totally predictable statement that she was *not* my brood mare.

But eventually, and without a detailed feminist analysis of what this might do to her as a person—which I had expected and indeed prepared myself for—she agreed to stop taking the pill. I should have been warned then, for Jessica never gave in easily on anything, particularly where the "exploitation of her womanhood" was concerned. But my reaction was so positive that it surprised even me; I hadn't realized until then how very much I really did want a child. I was even slightly embarrassed by it. Jessica couldn't resist teasing me, but it was an affectionate teasing, and for a while we were closer than we had been for a long time.

Even Lizzie got caught up in the spirit of it all, and was already treating her sister as though she were pregnant. Jessica lapped up the attention, and our lovemaking took on a tenderness that had been alien to us until then. Oddly enough, though, contented as I felt at the way things were going, I was still finding it impossible to stay faithful. If I didn't see Rachel, or someone else, for three or four days, then I became jumpy and irritable. I never stopped to question why, I guess I just assumed that this was a natural state of affairs for someone like me. The only thing that mattered was that Jessica should not find out, so I took her on trips to Paris, bombarded her with flowers and did everything I could to make her happy. That lasted for about three months, and then things began to change.

Up to this time, Jessica's paintings had always been bright and over-filled with color; garish even, some might say—not me, of course. But now a kind of morbidity was creeping into them. There were only two or three of them at first, that had found their way onto the walls of our bedroom. As this was an essentially feminine room, full of chintz and lace, the paintings created an almost ghoulish contrast, and their greys and blacks, smudged over with violent streaks of reddish brown, made me uncomfortable. But when I ventured to suggest to Jessica that perhaps they might be a little more at home in the garden shed, instead of flying at me in a rage she merely looked at me with what I can only describe as sightless eyes, and smiled into the distance.

I mentioned it to Lizzie one evening, but she only shrugged. "Oh, you know what artists are," she said, "they're all a little insane, couldn't do it if they weren't. And Jess is a genius, you know." I thought that was taking sisterly devotion a little too far, and decided to drop the subject.

"Where's Henry tonight?" I asked. We were having dinner, just the two of us; Jessica had gone off to an exhibition in Fulham with George Mannering. That was another thing. Before she always used to invite me to go with her to art exhibitions, but now, despite the fact we were getting along so well, she was almost secretive about where she was going.

"Henry? Henry's sulking because I told him we were seeing far too much of each other."

"I thought you were becoming rather attached to him," I said.

She shrugged. "Maybe."

Sensing she didn't want to talk about it, I sat back to finish my wine. I noticed that another of Jessica's morbid paintings had appeared on the dining-room wall, this one directly opposite the chair I always occupied. I stared at it for some time, not liking it any more than I had any of the others. Then I realized that she must have hung it there on purpose, and for no accountable reason I felt the hair prickle at the back of my neck.

"Something the matter?" Lizzie asked. Her voice startled me, and it must have showed. "You seem very edgy tonight," she said.

I laughed. "Deep in thought. Devilling for a particularly unpleasant murder trial at the moment, it's probably getting to me a bit."

Mrs. Dixon had stayed on that night to fix the meal, so when we had finished I helped her clear the table before going to find Lizzie in the drawing room. She was sitting on the floor, reading a magazine, and barely looked up as I walked in.

I sat down on the sofa and stretched my legs out in front of me. It was a warm night and the windows were open. There were no sounds coming from outside and I lay back to enjoy the peace, for once free of the restlessness that normally plagued me. I watched Lizzie's hair as it fluttered in the breeze, and her small hands as she flicked over the pages of the magazine. My mind wandered back to the hour or so I had spent with Rachel that afternoon, when I knew that once again, in my mind, I had been making love to Lizzie. But I would make it up to Rachel when I saw her later at the Clermont . . . My eyes snapped shut, and I was immediately aware of feeling restive again: I'd lost a lot of money last time I was there, more than my quarterly allowance, and I was only going again tonight in an attempt to win it back. I glanced over at the clock. I'd have to be leaving in half an hour.

"It's so hot in here, don't you think?" Lizzie stretched, and I noticed that the top two buttons of her blouse were undone. She leaned forward and at the same time threw her hair back over her shoulder. Her right breast was almost completely exposed. Then tossing her magazine to one side, she uncurled her legs and lay down on the floor. Her short skirt wriggled up around her hips and I caught a glimpse of white panties as she lifted one knee.

Slowly her eyes came round to meet mine, and I watched as she dampened her lips with her tongue. She was smiling and I didn't dare to move, the suddenness of sexual tension was shooting through the air like currents of electricity. She's your wife's sister, I kept telling myself. Anyone, you can have anyone, but leave her alone. My eyes were still on hers. She's Henry's, you can't do it, it's not worth losing a friend for. I clenched my teeth, and my fingers were biting into the arms of the sofa, but I was all too aware of the ache in my groin that was making a mockery of my resistance.

"I do love these warm nights, don't you, Alexander?" she purred, running her hands down over her breasts and letting them fall to the floor on either side of her. "They always make me feel, mmm, so . . . good."

"Lizzie, do you think Jessica's having an affair with George Mannering?" I blurted out. Suddenly the air was clear. Lizzie's knee went back to the floor and she sat up.

Her eyes flashed at me for a second before she spoke. "Are you serious?" she said. "George Mannering?"

Of course I wasn't serious. Jessica's devotion to me these days was more than evident, and George was a pretty poor specimen of manhood by anyone's standards, let alone Jessica's. I shrugged, "Well, haven't you noticed how strangely she's been behaving lately?"

"You said that earlier," she very nearly snapped. "Strange? In what way?"

"Her god-awful paintings for one thing."

That seemed to annoy her. Apparently she was prepared to bed her sister's husband, but was not prepared to have the said husband speak detrimentally of her sister's art. I watched her face, sensing the inward struggle. The question she was asking herself, I knew, was, how desperately did she want me in the sack? If we argued over Jessica she'd never regain the earlier mood. In the end she shrugged, and I was aware of Jessica's art sliding neatly into second place as she said, "She seems perfectly normal to me."

I couldn't ignore the brief feeling of victory, but had myself fully under control by now. "Henry said he saw her in Harley Street yesterday."

"Is there something strange about Harley Street?"

"Of course not. It's only strange that Jessica was there when she told me she was going to Bristol for some meeting or other."

Lizzie yawned loudly, making it clear she was becoming bored by the subject of her sister. "All I can say is, a girl's got to have some secrets, even from her husband." She stopped as if something had suddenly occurred to her, then turned to look at me. "You're not jealous, are you?"

"Jealous! What of?"

"I don't know. Her art?"

I looked through to the dining room, at the painting that was hanging there. "Not jealous, no," I said.

She got to her feet and ambled over to look in the mirror. The silence hung heavily in the air, and I knew she hadn't given up on me yet. "I think I'll go and take a shower," she said, looking at my reflection. "Care to join me?"

I laughed. "Thanks, but I have to go out."

She gave a long and enigmatic smile before she turned round. "Rachel waiting, is she?"

"Rachel?" I said, surprising myself at the innocence in my voice.

"Rachel Armstrong. The woman you go to see most afternoons, in Lennox Gardens."

I closed my eyes, feeling suddenly very tired. When I opened them again she was still watching me. "How do you know about Rachel?"

She tapped the side of her nose. "Now that would be telling, wouldn't it?" she said.

"Does Jessica know? Is that what all this is about?" I waved my hand towards the painting.

"Jessica? Oh no, I don't think Jessica knows. And I won't tell her if you won't."

My breath escaped in a long, drawn-out sigh. "Why do I get the feeling that there are going to be conditions attached to that?"

She gave a low, throaty laugh. "Because there are. Shall we begin by taking that shower?"

I closed my eyes and tried to pray that Mrs. Dixon had already gone home. I tried to pray that Jessica wouldn't walk through the door, and last of all I tried to pray for resistance. But all I could hear was the sound of Lizzie taking off her clothes, until there was no sound anymore. When I opened my eyes she was standing naked in front of me, holding out her hand.

What could I do? I had no choice.

13

I T WAS PAST MIDNIGHT when I walked upstairs to the gaming room of the Clermont. The cashier greeted me in a friendly manner and I wondered what he would say if I pushed over the bank statement that had fallen through my door that morning.

A low murmur erupted from the roulette table as I reached it, and I saw three towers of black chips being added to Rachel's substantial collection. Her slanting eyes flickered in my direction, but she gave no other sign of having registered my presence. I guessed she was angry with me, and in turn I was angry with her. OK, I was late, but her reaction to it stifled me. Deciding I had no desire to witness her further success, I went to watch Robert Lyttleton trying his hand at chemmy, before taking my place at a blackjack table.

From the start I played recklessly, doubling and splitting wherever I could, and I raised the table to a thousand in the first hour. The inspector recorded my drop as I won almost every hand, and I had nearly twenty thousand pounds worth of chips at my elbow by the time Rachel joined the crowd that had grouped around me.

She ran her hands over my shoulders and stooped to whisper

something in my ear, but I wasn't listening. This time I had pushed ten thousand pounds to the center of the table and the dealer had just peeled a second three from the shoe. Her eyes moved across the short distance between us.

"Split," I murmured, and placed my cards side by side to make two hands. The entire twenty thousand was at stake.

The six of spades landed beside the three of diamonds. "Nine." The dealer's voice was the only sound in the room. "Seven," she said, as the four of hearts joined the three of hearts on my second hand.

With the next card my first hand totaled sixteen. The king of diamonds slipped and spun as it came to rest on my second hand. "Seventeen."

I didn't have to look at the old woman who was playing beside me to know that she was holding her breath. Surely I would stop now, no one in their right mind would carry on. My heart was thudding so hard against my ribs, I thought I could hear it through the hush that had engulfed us. I knew everyone was watching me, fascinated and horrified to see whether I would go on.

"What!" It was Robert Lyttleton's voice that hissed through his teeth as I nodded. Several people shuffled and strained to come closer.

I waited as the next card was turned over. The voice of the dealer was matter-of-fact. "Twenty-one," she pronounced. The woman beside me totaled nineteen. And then I turned to the dealer.

"Stand-off." And the dealer calmly pushed ten thousand pounds in my direction, followed by another ten.

I sensed that the old lady wanted to leave, that the presence of the crowd had unnerved her. But my crazy bravado had captured the entire casino and she too stayed to watch.

"Ten." I felt Rachel's thighs pressing against my arm.

"Double," I said immediately. Once again my stake was twenty thousand. The dealer wasted no time in revealing the next card.

"Blackjack," she pronounced the word quietly, as if she herself couldn't believe it. The tension must have filtered through to her because her hand trembled as she turned over her final card. The hum that threaded through the crowd was one of incredulity and excitement.

I had won fifty thousand pounds.

I stared up at the faces that bobbed over me. Everyone was smiling, reaching out hands to congratulate me. Fifty thousand pounds wasn't a large amount to most of them; what had impressed them was my nerve—the nerve that had not stuck at seventeen, and the devil's own luck that had delivered blackjack on a stand-off.

"Champagne," Robert said, clapping me on the back. "Your treat."

I felt Rachel's hand slide into my trouser pocket and at the same time was aware of someone tugging on my arm. Removing Rachel's hand, I turned stiffly to see who was trying to attract my attention. It was the woman who had been playing beside me all evening.

My lofty expression dissolved as she smiled. She reminded me of my grandmother. She too had that paradoxical air of reckless safety about her, leaving you in no doubt that an hour in her company would be worth three with most other people. "Won't you join us downstairs?" I offered.

She shook her head. "Thank you, but no. Time I was in my bed." She had a deep, commanding voice that was surprising, coming from such a frail body. "I just wanted to offer my congratulations. There aren't many who would have taken a card again on seventeen." She was looking searchingly into my eyes, as if seeking something that only she might be able to find. Then her face broke into a smile again. "You know, if the old adage is true—lucky at cards, unlucky in love—then I fear for your heart, young man." And laughing at her little joke, she bade us all goodnight.

Robert grinned. "And yet another conquest with which to swell the Belmayne harem," he quipped. "Now, are we going downstairs or aren't we?"

"Why don't you be a darling and go find us a table?" Rachel jumped in before I could answer.

Robert saluted her. "At your service, ma'am. What'll it be?"

"The best they have, of course," Rachel answered, and chucking him under the chin, she turned him round and gave him a gentle push in the direction of the stairs.

The second she turned back I knew we would not be joining Robert. Her expression was one of naked desire—and it was only then that I realized I had an erection. How long I had had it I didn't know, but I knew that winning had acted like an aphrodisiac on us both. We needed to fuck, and couldn't wait.

Outside in the car my fly was open before I could get the engine started. I dropped the keys, and as I stooped to retrieve them I felt her fingers circle my penis. I cried out as the juice began to surge from my body, and tearing her hand away I pushed her back in her seat. "Wait!" I snapped, and starting the car I drove out of the square, only narrowly missing a police car.

When we reached Lennox Gardens I reversed up against the railings and turned the engine off. Rachel started to get out, but I pulled the door shut again. The power I felt swelled in my chest, almost choking me. "You want to fuck," I said, "then you do it my way."

Her mouth trembled, and leaning over I crushed it with my own. "Get into the back seat." She started to protest, but I ripped open the front of her dress and scooped her breasts free. "Do you want it?"

"Yes. Oh God, yes," she groaned, her head rolling back against the seat.

"Then get in the back."

For a moment she looked at me, then as her eyes dropped to the erection she had lifted free of my trousers, she turned to do as I told her. I waited until I heard the back door close, then, almost exploding with the need to humiliate her, I got out of the car. When I made no move to join her in the back seat she pushed open the door, watching my face as I gave her my brief instructions.

Obediently she turned away and lifted her legs onto the seat. And forcing her onto her hands and knees, I ripped her underwear and penetrated her from behind.

That night was the first time I had truly fucked Rachel. I couldn't say we made love, because there was nothing tender about the act that took place in the back of the car; but now, having possessed Lizzie, I could concentrate on Rachel and all that I wanted to do to her. I was drunk with the power of my success. From now on this was how it would be with me and Rachel, I would make her a slave to my lust, just as I was a slave to Lizzie's.

When I finally returned home the sun was threatening to break the horizon. I looked up at the bleached façade of the house in Belgrave Square and thought of my wife lying in bed, obediently waiting for me to come home. And my sister-in-law in the next room, who only hours before had panted beneath me, begging for more as I thrust into her. And then I thought of the fifty thousand pounds I carried in my pocket.

My blood began to move faster, charging me with the same surge of sexual arousal I had felt when I'd won at the Clermont. I was ready for more. I wanted to win again. I'd go to Lizzie. I'd show her who called the shots around here. And I'd do it while Jessica was under the same roof.

I crept up the stairs, and passed the door to Jessica's and my bedroom without even stopping to look in. At the end of the landing I stopped at Lizzie's door and pushed it open.

In the dim light that filtered through the curtains I could see that another head lay on the pillow beside hers. The sheets were in a tangle around the two bodies and for a moment I felt an insane jealousy, wanting to kill him, whoever he was. Then realizing that it must be Henry, I closed the door.

My own bed was empty.

Almost bursting with rage, I went downstairs to see if Jessica had waited up for me, but there wasn't even a note. I made myself some coffee and slumped into an armchair to wait. If Jessica had walked in at that moment I might have tried to kill her: everyone did as I said, everyone wanted me and I controlled everyone—with the exception of my own wife.

I must have dozed, because I noticed by the clock that it was ten minutes past seven when I heard a noise at the bottom of the stairs. Heaving myself up from the chair, I swore as my half-drunk cup of coffee tumbled to the ground, spreading a dark stain across the carpet. I stared down at it, wondering what to do. Then I heard the front door close and footsteps outside.

Quickly I ran to the front door, wanting to tell Henry about my win. But as I looked out into the grey London dawn it wasn't Henry I saw, getting into his BMW, but Robert Lyttleton starting up the engine of the E-type Jaguar he'd brought round to show off the week before.

As he drove away, I stood trying to sort out the thoughts that were spreading through my head.

I didn't hear anything, it was more an awareness of the presence of someone else that made me turn and look back through the open door.

Lizzie stood halfway down the stairs. Her hair was tousled, her mouth a deep, savagely kissed red. Her eyes were watching me, taunting me into speech, but I wasn't looking at her. I was looking at the woman standing beside her, one arm draped over the banister, her bare foot beating a tattoo on the floor. Their smiles reached me in waves of triumph, leaving me in no doubt as to what it was that had been happening in the room at the end of the landing.

"Hello, darling," Jessica murmured. And as I moved towards the bottom of the stairs, she threw back her head and let out a screech of laughter.

I have no clear recollection of what happened after that. All I knew was a blur of colors, crashing around me, blinding my sight, blinding my reason. Sounds of manic laughter, and then screams, deafening me, piercing my brain. And blood. Blood on my hands, blood on the walls. And all around me pain and chaos and destruction.

I looked around at the paintings on the wall. I'd never noticed them before. They were very like the paintings that adorned the walls of Belmayne House in Suffolk. I shifted my eyes restlessly from one to another, until yet again I was confronted by Monet's "Roche-Blond at Sunset." Normally I enjoyed looking at Impressionist paintings, but now, different though they were from Jessica's doom-laden canvases, they somehow reminded me of her, and heightened my guilt.

I stirred in my chair and turned back to the newspaper. A report on page two outlined the background of the forthcoming Haley Weinberg fraud case, and again I felt guilt. Jeremy Corbyn had been handed the brief two months ago, and I'd been deviling for him. I should ring chambers and at least let him know where I was. But I didn't.

I'd been with Rachel for four days—four days during which I had alternately slaked my fury on her body and gambled like a lunatic at the Clermont, where I was now in debt to the tune of eighty-five thousand pounds. I blamed Jessica. Thinking about her, I could feel my fingers digging into the palms of my hands, the unholy images crowding into my mind as I remembered the early hours of that morning. If only she hadn't laughed.

The door opened and Rachel came in. She was wearing the

sable coat she had purchased with her roulette winnings the week before, and just the sight of it made me want to lash out at her.

"You still here?" she said, dropping her bag onto a chair.

"As you can see."

She went to hang up her coat. Coming back into the room, she said, "That's a Morant," and nodded towards the table that was propping up my feet. I removed them. "And now you can do the same with those cartons," she said, indicating the remains of the Chinese take-out I had had sent round earlier. I scooped them up and stuffed them into the waste-paper basket next to my chair. Rachel sighed and went to get herself a drink.

"Scotch for me," I said, and went back to the newspaper.

"Get it yourself."

"For Christ's sake, I'm only asking you to get me a drink."

She spun round to face me. "Alexander, I'm getting a little tired of you lately. Isn't it about time—"

"Forget it! Just forget it!" I yelled. "I'll get my own."

We smoldered through the silence that followed; turning pages, and ice clinking against glasses, made the only sound.

It was Rachel who spoke first. "You didn't tell me you destroyed her paintings."

I shot a glance at her, but she was still flicking through the magazine. When she realized I was going to say nothing, she looked up. "Why did you do it?"

"Why did I do it? You can sit there and ask me why I did it?"

"She went to bed with another man. She was unfaithful. Is the whole of your life built on double standards, Alexander?"

"We were supposed to be trying for a baby, for God's sake! What if I hadn't come in when I did and then found out in two months time she was pregnant? The child might not have been mine—and I wouldn't even have known! And let's not forget, she wasn't the only one in the bed with Robert Lyttleton that night. Her sister was there too, her own fucking sister! And in *my* house! She's—"

"Oh shut up, Alexander. I'm tired of your tantrums. And I still say no matter what happened you shouldn't have destroyed her paintings."

"Have you seen them? They gave me the spooks. I couldn't stand them any longer. Anyway, she was asking for it."

"It's you who are asking for it, Alexander. You think you can do whatever takes your fancy, don't you, and be damned to how anyone else feels about it. Well, it's time you woke up to the fact that the world wasn't created for the sole purpose of satisfying the bottomless appetite of Alexander Belmayne's ego. Your life is a mess, and you've only yourself to blame. Look at you! What you've done to yourself God only knows, but what you've done to your wife is unforgivable. And who are you, anyway, to sit in judgment on her art? Just who the hell do you think you are?"

I opened my mouth to speak, but she stopped me. "You're nobody, that's who you are. You're not fit to sit in the same room as decent people. You think those good looks of yours give you the right to behave just as you please. You don't care who you hurt or what you might be doing to those who love you, like your wife. Do you know why she did what she did? Because she knew you were coming round here. She knew that all the time you were telling her you loved her, you were lying to her, cheating on her—and what she's done is to show you that two people can play at that game, and you don't like it. They're none of my business the dangerous games the two of you play with each other, but I'm telling you, Alexander, your pretty face means nothing. It's what's underneath that's important, and you've got nothing underneath. You're shallow and empty, and a waste of space."

She got up to refill her glass. Her voice was calmer as she turned round, but her eyes were still cool and hard. "I want you to leave, Alexander. Now. Go back to your wife, if she'll have you. Go anywhere. I don't want you here anymore."

I leapt up from my chair then, and bunching my fist, I thrust it between her legs. "How about here, Rachel? Don't you want me here any more either?"

She glared at me and I laughed. "You can't live without it, Rachel. You'll be begging me for it within a week. Well, here's one last one to be going on with." I started to fumble with my fly.

"You touch me, and so help me, Alexander, I'll kill you."

I laughed again. "You want me to rape you, is that it? You want me to rough you up again. What'll it be this time, Rachel? Shall I tie you up? Or shall I just beat you?" My hand was still between her legs and she made no move to back away.

Suddenly she slumped forward, pushing her glass onto the table. "Alexander, stop it," she pleaded. "Just stop. This anger, this violence, it's destroying you. Look at yourself—what's happening to you?"

Slowly she removed my hand. She held it between her own two hands, and uncurled my fingers, looking down at them as she did so. "Oh, Alexander," she sighed, "I'm so sorry for you, though God knows why. Her paintings, Alexander, how could you have done it?"

I turned away, feeling small and loathsome in the suffocating well of my guilt. "How did you find out?" I asked.

"Robert told me."

I felt myself beginning to tense. "Robert Lyttleton? That must mean Jessica's seen him again."

"No. It means Henry is looking for you."

"Does Robert know I'm here?"

She nodded. "He does now. I saw him this afternoon."

"In his bed?"

She smiled. "No, Alexander, not in his bed. Incest never did hold any appeal for me."

My head snapped up. "Incest?"

"Robert's my son. Don't tell me you didn't know."

I wrenched my hand away from hers. Her face was soft and smiling, but all I could see were the lines that fanned at the corners of her eyes, the broken smoothness of her neck—and for a brief moment my eyes glazed and I thought I was looking into the face of my own mother. My stomach churned. Rachel was Robert Lyttleton's mother. And while I fucked his mother, he fucked my wife. He fucked my wife's sister. And my wife and her sister . . .

"Jesus Christ," I choked. "Jesus Christ."

She turned away and went to pick up her drink. I watched her, hating her, and as she looked back at me my hatred turned to disgust, all-consuming disgust that sucked at my insides, making me want to rip out my guts, tear at my skin, anything to exorcise myself of this obscenity. For it was I who had dragged them all into this sordid gutter. Jessica, Rachel, Lizzie, and countless others I had abused along the way—they had all been nothing more than pawns in my own sick game of misogynistic power. All I'd ever wanted to do was hurt them, humiliate them, and then walk away, leaving my contempt entrenched in their souls.

My head dropped as my shoulders began to heave. Dear God in heaven, when would it all end? How much longer could I go on living with this pain? Where was she? Dear God, where was she?

Elizabeth

14

EVERYONE WAS LAUGHING. Bright lights flashed, children screamed, "Sugar, Sugar" blared out of the speakers, and somewhere in the distance a siren brought the dodgems to a standstill. People wandered about with their goldfish and colored balloons, hugging themselves into scarves and hats to keep out the bitter wind that cut across the common. I tucked the scrap of newspaper back in my pocket and waited while a little boy rummaged in my basket for a ticket. His cheeks flushed with excitement as he pulled one out and tore it open. No prize. The child's face fell and his father, who had earlier returned my smile, now gave me a look I knew only too well.

I turned away, withdrawing into myself, needing to escape, if only for a moment, this prison of festivity.

My uncle was watching me as he handed out darts, shouting to the crowds to come and try their skill. He didn't trust me, I knew that, but he had taken me back because they had been short-handed that summer, and I'd had nowhere else to go. That was five years ago now. I leaned against the side of my stall and closed my eyes. Oh, when would it stop hurting?

Someone called my name. It was Edwina, the old hag whose

husband ran the big wheel. I could never look at the big wheel without thinking about my parents. It had been theirs, before the storms blew it over, killing them both. If things had been different, and they'd lived, then maybe I'd never have left in the first place.

"You're right to be getting on with things, girl," my uncle had said the day I told him I was going to leave the fair. Violet May, the fortune-teller, had been looking after me until then, but I was a constant reminder to my uncle that he was shirking his duty by not taking me in himself. "You've got your education, your mother saw to that, so off you go." As he opened the door of the London train for me, I wanted to tell him I'd changed my mind, but by the time I'd turned round he was already walking away.

I'd been fourteen then but sometimes it seemed like yesterday . . .

Edwina yelled at me again, indicating the little line of children waiting to buy tickets from me. I gritted my teeth and looked away from her. Edwina had always hated my mother, and after she'd died, had turned her resentment on me. And as soon as I'd walked back into the fair, only hours after I'd watched Alexander walk out of my life, Edwina had been there screaming at me, telling me she knew what I'd done, she'd read the newspapers—I was a trollop, and they didn't want my sort here. My uncle, along with the others, had stood by and watched. In the end I'd picked up my bag and started to walk away, but Violet May came after me. She would hear none of my going to Janice; the fair was my home, she said, it was where I belonged, never mind Edwina. And I'd stayed because I couldn't face Janice trying to find me another man, another job, or anything that might end the way things had ended at Foxton's . . .

"I've won! Miss! Miss! I've won!"

I looked down into a pale excited little face and smiled as the girl beamed up at me . . . That was all a long time ago now. Everything was a long time ago now.

I took one of the cheap pens down from the shelf, and checking that no one was watching, I slipped it into the little girl's pocket. Then I handed her a teddy bear. I put my finger over my lips to show her that the two prizes were our secret.

"Edward's here, Mummy!"

I looked up as Charlotte ran over to the stall. She gave the girl with the teddy bear a shy smile, and watched her walk away. "Edward's in the trailer," she said, turning back to me and trying to sweep the thick black curls from her eyes.

"Is he?" I said, smiling as I lifted her up over the counter. "And don't tell me—he bought you a cotton candy."

Her grey eyes rounded with amazement. "It's all over your face," I laughed, and as she hugged me I felt my heart swell.

"Ouch, you're hurting me," she complained, struggling to get away, and putting her down again, I watched her skip off through the fair. "Come on," she called, peeping back round the lucky dip, "he's waiting."

My hand tightened around the scrap of newspaper in my pocket, and taking it out, I read it one last time. A year. He'd been married for a whole year and I hadn't even known.

There was no point in fooling myself any longer. I'd waited, I'd never stopped loving him, but now, just like when my parents had died, I knew that it was time for me to move on.

It was Violet May who had introduced me to Edward Walters, the tycoon art dealer. They'd first met more than twenty years before, when Edward's wife started to visit the fair to have her fortune told. And after Edward's wife died, Violet May had continued visiting him.

That was until Charlotte was born. Since then it was Edward who came to visit us, traveling the country as often as his business would allow—all because he was besotted with a baby girl. I knew he was lonely, it was what had drawn us together, even though he had a brother and sister who lived with him at their country estate in Kent. He tried to persuade me to take Charlotte down there, but I wouldn't go. His elegant city suits and expensive tweeds, his easy composure and the distinction of his greying hair and wise blue eyes, all reminded me that I had already proved I didn't belong to his world.

But I was always pleased when he came to the fair—though no one could be quite as pleased as Charlotte. It was odd, watching this distinguished-looking man take such time and trouble with my daughter. He radiated warmth and kindness. It was rare that I spoke about Alexander, but Edward sensed that I still loved him, and even though he knew it might mean that he would have to say good-bye to Charlotte and me, he had offered to find him for me. I suppose it was because I was afraid that I wouldn't let him. Alexander had been little more than a boy when we'd been in love; by now he would have changed, probably forgotten all about me. No, I didn't want to find him, I told Edward, I just wanted to stop loving him.

As time passed and my confidence started to come back, I grew more and more attached to Edward. I looked forward to seeing his tall figure stride through the crowds, to hearing his jocular voice when he crept up behind me and asked if he could buy a ticket. I laughed when he was sad, because he was only sad when he remembered his age. He was old, he kept telling me, too old for me. What could I possibly want with someone who was fifty, past his prime, and ready to fall apart at the seams?

"Then I'll just have to stitch you back together, won't I?" I said. That was after the first time we made love.

Though I had been determined not to make comparisons, it was impossible not to. But Edward was here, and Edward loved me. Alexander was no more than a dream now. So why did I keep on believing that if only I waited just a little bit longer, he would come?

"But he won't, child," Violet May said, on the night Edward asked me to marry him. I'd told him no, as gently as I could, but the hurt I saw in his eyes almost tore me apart. He held me in his arms, and I despised myself for what I was doing to him, but he only wiped away my tears and told me he understood. In the end, not knowing what else to do, I had run to Violet May and asked her to look into the crystal ball for me.

I sat before her in the warm dimness of her caravan and searched her fleshy face, trying to get her to meet my eyes as she spoke, but she wouldn't, and I knew she was lying.

"You've got to tell me," I whispered. "Please, I want to know."

"I told you child, he won't come."

"Look, I know you want me to marry Edward, but if there is any chance, any chance at all . . . Please, Violet May, tell me the truth."

She peered into her crystal ball again, then with a gesture of impatience, pushed it to one side. "Give me your hand," she wheezed.

She studied it for a long time, until finally she looked up and I saw that her eyes were swimming with tears. She shook her head, slowly.

"Violet May!" I cried. "Tell me!"

Then she smiled, and the icy hand that had been pushing my heart into my throat seemed to draw back. "Did you see him, Violet May? In the future, was he there?"

She nodded. "Yes, child, he was there."

"Does that mean . . .?" I swallowed. "Does that mean I will see him again?" I stammered.

"Yes, you will see him again."

"When? Violet May, tell me when? Is it soon?"

She shook her head. "It is a mysterious thing, this love you share with him. It has a power beyond my understanding, but the seeds of fate have already been sown. There are still long roads to be traveled before you see him again. When you do, Elizabeth . . . Don't do it, child. It will only bring pain. There is death and hatred, such hatred. And foreign lands . . ." But I wasn't listening. All that mattered was that one day, it didn't matter when, we would be together again . . .

Leaning against the side of my stall remembering the confidence I'd felt then, how happy I'd been as I left Violet May's trailer I could hardly hold back the tears. Like a fool I had waited, believing in my heart that he had meant it when he'd said he would always love me. But he was married now, and I was nothing more than a memory.

"We got tired of waiting."

I jumped—and Edward laughed as he held his hand out for mine. Charlotte was bouncing up and down beside him, wearing his hat and pleading with him to play her new game. As I looked at them I knew in my heart it was time now to get on with my life. I put my basket down and let myself out of the stall.

Edward's eyes were searching my face, and as the wind swept up my hair he brushed it back. "Why do I get the feeling you want to tell me something?" he said.

"Because I do," I whispered. "I'd like us to get married, Edward, if you still want me, that is." And seeing the way his mouth trembled, I wondered how I could have been so blind as not to have realized a long time ago how very much I loved him.

15

SLIPPING THE RING onto my third finger I turned my hand to the chandelier and nearly gasped as tiny splinters of light shot between my diamond and the crystal above me. Edward was standing beside me, watching my face, waiting for me to speak. I put my arms around him and hugged him. "Darling, it's beautiful," I said. I looked at the diamond again, then laughing, I threw out my hands. "I just don't know what to say."

"Then don't say anything," he said. "Just as long as I know you like it, that's all that matters."

Like it? I could hardly believe what was happening to me. After all, less than two years ago I had been just the girl from the fair. I'd always read about people who were wealthy then, though I'd seen them often enough, at the fair, and at Foxton's too, but it was as if they belonged to another world. And now here I was living in that world, Edward's world. He did everything he could to make me a part of it, but still at times I couldn't help feeling like an intruder, as if I had borrowed someone else's life and at any time it might be snatched back again. Violet May would tolerate none of that talk, though, and told me to grow up and mind when I was well off. It did me good to go and visit her from time to time, it brought me back to earth. I had no regrets at leaving the fair; once again my uncle had been glad to see the back of me. As for the others, I had always been "too hoity-toity" for them anyway.

David clapped his hands. "Champagne!" he called, and on cue the double doors that opened out into the West Hall were thrown wide and Christine, outrageously overdressed in her new Zandra Rhodes and a tiara, wheeled in a trolley laden with two bottles of Dom Perignon and four glasses.

Edward rolled his eyes, and Christine stuck out her tongue. "Mmm, very ladylike," he grunted, then laughed as she blew him a kiss.

"Well, come along, David." She thrust a bottle of champagne at him. "What are you waiting for?"

Edward slipped his arm around my shoulders and waited until everyone was holding a glass. "It's not often a man gets engaged two years after his wedding," he said, "but it was a good idea for an anniversary present, even if I say so myself." He gave me a gentle squeeze and as I looked up into his face I could see that his sister and his brother were, for the moment, part of another world. "To you," he whispered.

"To Elizabeth," Christine and David echoed, and the moment was broken.

After we had drunk the toast, and another to Edward, we sat down. Wanting to remain close to him, I curled up on the floor at his feet. He always sat in the same chair, the one on the left-hand side of the hearth. David's was the chair on the right, and many was the night I had sat just like this, at Edward's feet, studying the intricacies of the eighteenth-century fireplace, while the two of them discussed Edward's next trip to Paris or Rome, a forthcoming auction or the needs of one of their many collector clients. I felt comfortable and safe, and smiled as I hugged my knees to my chest. I was almost happy.

The last thought slipped into my mind before I could stop it, and I tossed my head back, as if trying to shake off the introspection. It had come, not as a spontaneous, pleasurable thought, but as if it were struggling to establish its presence while at the same time denying me its sentiment. Feeling guilty, I rested my head against Edward's knee and reached up for his hand.

Christine and David were arguing gently. "Oh do be quiet,"

Christine said, as she flicked David on the shoulder.

"Your problem, young lady," he retorted, "is that you go looking for trouble." He was referring to the fracas Christine had become involved in at the village store that morning, and since Edward had been in London, it was David, the younger of the two brothers, who had had to go and smooth Mr. Russell's feathers. They were always dragging Christine out of one scrape or another. She had been only a child when their parents died, so the brothers had brought her up. She was devoted to them both, but we all knew Edward had a special place in her heart.

"More champagne anyone?" she said, holding up the bottle.

I held out my glass. "What time is Rupert arriving?" I asked. Rupert was yet another in the long line of Christine's escorts.

"I didn't invite him in the end, thought it might be nicer if it was just family." At the slight emphasis on the word family, I looked round, but no one else seemed to have noticed.

"Quite right too," Edward said. "Not, of course, that I have anything against Rupert," he added quickly.

Christine laughed and dropped a kiss on his head. "*You* don't have anything against anyone," she said.

"What time are you setting off tomorrow?" David asked, turning to me.

I looked at Christine. "We thought about nine-thirty, didn't we?"

"About that." She went to sit down again, and as she crossed one leg over the other I saw her looking at mine. "We all know you've got wonderful legs, Elizabeth, but please stop showing them off. Envy-green clashes with my dress."

"There's nothing wrong with your legs, Christine," David remarked, "which is more than I can say for your navigation, incidentally. Are you sure you're leaving yourselves enough time tomorrow?"

"My legs are fat, I'm fat," said Christine—and David rolled his eyes in a here-we-go-again pantomime as Christine launched into another bout of destructive self-criticism. According to her she looked like a roundhead, with her mousey club-cut hair and circular face, but in fact she was rather beautiful, and her short bangs and round blue eyes made her look much younger than thirty. That was a compliment she had no time for, however. What really obsessed her were her freckles, and she spent hours soaking her face in lemon juice in the hope of getting rid of them. And if anyone dared to tell her that what she lacked in height she made up for in personality, they were sorry for it, especially David, since he was the one she resembled. Why couldn't I have been tall and slim like Edward? she would ask pathetically.

"You know," Edward said suddenly, "I think I might come along to the auction tomorrow after all."

"Oh no!" Christine protested. "You said you were going to leave it all to us. Besides, it'll be Elizabeth's first auction without you—how's she ever going to learn if you're always there?" She looked at me. "You're mad, you know. Why you should want to get involved in all this wheeler-dealering when you can have a nice easy life at home here, I don't know. Anyway," she said to Edward, "I shall be there if she comes unstuck—which she won't."

"Then don't forget, if you feel you don't want to go through with it all you have to do is place your bid with the auctioneer before the sale begins, he'll do the rest."

I smiled at the way he was trying to protect me, but Christine snorted. "As if she's going to do that."

"We all know you wouldn't," David said, "but you've had a lot more experience at this than Elizabeth has."

The argument continued as Edward told us yet again how much he was prepared to go up to in order to secure the neo-classical Bullock sofa, one of the items being auctioned at a country house sale over in Sussex the following day.

I was becoming a little more used to this new world of mine now, but it had taken time. I had had no idea of just how wealthy Edward was, and at first I was overwhelmed by the lavishness of his generosity. My wardrobes were brimming with clothes flown in from the best couturiers in the world—and with alarming frequency they were packed into a fifteen-piece set of Hermès luggage as we flew off to distant, exotic places where Edward conducted his business and I explored and socialized. We both attended every royal function that Edward was invited to—and there were many—and were constantly entertaining clients, either in West End restaurants or our London home—businessmen, film stars, celebrities of all kinds. There were charity balls at least twice a month, some in London but most of them in New York, Dallas or Hong Kong. At these functions, Edward hardly ever left my side. He advised me, because I insisted, on how I should dress, how I should speak and how I should eat. He loved me, almost to the point of idolizing me, and was never happy unless I was with him. He still couldn't believe that I really did love him, when he was so "old and decrepit," as he put it, and I was so young. His devoted attendance on me was his way of trying to hide this insecurity, and it was because of his insecurity that I loved him.

The pomposities and eccentricities of the people who belonged to Edward's world of art and antiques also took me some time to get used to. But with time, and again a great deal of patience on Edward's part, my knowledge of the business increased, and even in that most difficult of worlds I began to feel more at ease. Walters & Sons was one of the largest art dealers in the country. Nevertheless I was relieved that we rarely invited people down to our house in Kent. It was the family home, and David's particular refuge. Since the accident had killed Edward's first wife and left David's face badly scarred he'd given up his post as a university professor and now lived in virtual seclusion.

Soon after Edward and I were married I had taken over the running of the household while Christine concentrated on carving herself a niche in the family business and joined the board of directors. She was almost as passionate about antique furniture and old masters as David was. Not that Edward wasn't too, but anyone who really knew him knew that his heart had been captured long ago by the mysterious works of ancient Egypt. There was a room on the second floor of Westmoor—the Kent house—filled with limestone reliefs, faience bowls, broken grey granite faces and schist and marble statues. It was known simply as the Egyptian Room.

I often teased Edward about his passion for all things Egyptian, knowing that he was, in a way, made vulnerable by his obsession. Whenever he had spent some time in the Egyptian Room he would emerge looking disheveled and childlike, almost as though he had been playing with a forbidden toy. I was reminded of my days at Foxton's, when I caught one of the younger boys up to no good— and Edward was so like a boy, especially in the way he tried so hard to please me. It was impossible not to love him. His great passion was King Tutankhamun and his excavated tomb. On that he could wax lyrical for hours.

I couldn't help wondering what Alexander would make of my new life—wondering, too, if he ever thought about me. To be thinking of him so frequently after all this time, and when my life was now so complete, was madness, I knew. But how could I help it, with Charlotte there, looking more like him every day? What would I do if he were to walk into my life now?

"Elizabeth! Elizabeth! Where are you?"

I blinked, wondering how long they had been calling my name. "Sorry," I laughed. "I was miles away."

"We could see that," said Christine. "We want to know where?" Sometimes her manner of asking questions was hard, accusatory even, and I felt Edward's hand move through my hair as if to take away the edge of her sharpness.

At that moment the double doors were thrown open and Jeffrey, the butler-cum-chauffeur-cum-part-time chef, walked stiffly into the room. "Mesdames et messieurs, dinner is now being served in the Baroque Room," he announced.

Everyone burst out laughing, and as if someone had removed his backbone, Jeffrey fell against the door and laughed too. "Honestly," he complained, as we filed out of the room, "no one ever takes me seriously. By the way, love the rock, Mrs. Walters."

"Thank you, Jeffrey," I said, and offered up my hand for him to have a better look. As he gushed his delight and Edward looked on with pride, I couldn't help remembering the ring Alexander had given me, the one that had cost a fraction of this, and sat untouched now in a little box upstairs. I swallowed hard against the unexpected nostalgia. Why, tonight of all nights, was I thinking about Alexander?

Over dinner I noticed that Christine seemed agitated, but when I asked if there was anything on her mind she smiled brightly and said no. David and Edward smiled indulgently; they were used to her erratic moods and had learned to ignore them. I listened as she talked about the furniture she had taken to the restorers that day, then abruptly changed the subject to discuss a board meeting called for the following week. I tried to fight back the niggardly envy. It was ironic; she envied me my looks and figure, and I envied her the respect she had earned through her knowledge of antiques. It seemed to me that Christine always had something of value to say, while I could only engage in the kind of affected small talk favored by art dealers' wives. I hated myself for minding. I was luckier than any woman deserved to be, and would be grateful to Edward for the rest of my life. But still, I couldn't stop myself from being envious of Christine, not only for her intelligence but also for the freedom she had to be herself. She didn't have to hide what she was really thinking, or bear the guilt of not loving her brother enough . . .

I caught her grinning in my direction, and smiled back. She really was much more striking than she realized. I'd asked her once why she had never married. "What, and give up all this?" she'd cried. "Why should I do that? And now I've got you and little Charlotte too, what more could I want?"

I was to find out.

Charlotte dipped her head and stared at the floor. Her hands were clasped in a knot behind her back and I could see her little shoulders heaving up and down as she struggled valiantly to accept her un-deserved fate. "I do understand, Mother," she said, her eyes still riveted to the carpet. She shifted her weight onto one leg and a little knee poked out from under the rags of her skirt. "Will there be some mending for me to do while you are gone?"

I caught David's eye across the room, and had to turn away so that she wouldn't see I was laughing. Ever since David had taken her to see Cinderella, the entire household had been both wittingly and unwittingly playing the roles she cast them in. Needless to say, she was Cinderella; I was the wicked stepmother, and Christine and Jeffrey the ugly sisters. I suspected that Canary, her nanny—called after her bright yellow uniform—was expected to appear at any moment as the fairy godmother, and deliver her to Prince Charming—Edward. David was a less than enthusiastic Buttons.

She was waiting for an answer, so putting on my best haughty face I glared down at her. "You mean you haven't already scrubbed the grates today, you lazy child? What do you think you're about? Off to the kitchens with you."

"Yes, Mother," she murmured, and keeping her head lowered she sidled past me and let herself out through the door.

"Charlotte!" I called, just before the door closed. Her face peeped back in. "Did you call, Mother?" she said. "Have I done something wrong? Oh, please don't beat me, Mother."

That was too much, and I burst out laughing. "Come and give me a kiss before I go," I said.

"Oh, Mummy! You've spoilt it all now." Then seeing I was laughing, her face turned pink and she ran into my arms. "Can't I come too?" she said.

"Not today, darling. I have to do something for Edward. I thought you were doing something for him too. Weren't you making him a cushion to put your glass slipper on?"

Her face brightened immediately. "Oh yes," she said. Then hugging me tightly, she pressed her mouth to my ear. "Canary's making it really, but don't tell."

"No, of course I won't," I whispered. "Now, how about that kiss?"

It was wet and slobbery, and very long. She had walked in on Edward and me a few nights ago and caught us kissing—not that she hadn't seen us kissing before, but this time she had wanted to know why we took so long over it. Edward had done the explaining, and it was now her mission in life to perfect the art of long kissing. She practiced on anyone who would allow her close enough, which was all of us—but not on Edward; he was Prince Charming, and destined to be the recipient of the final, perfect version.

"Hey, how about one of those for me?" David said.

She slid out of my arms and ran across the room. David, stooping to catch her, was knocked off his feet as she bowled into his arms.

"I think I'll leave you two to it," I said, laughing as they rolled across the carpet.

I found Christine organizing Jeffrey into the van, listing the errands he needed to run before he drove over to Rowe House to collect the sofa. It made me both pleased and nervous to think that Edward was so sure I would succeed in obtaining it. It had been quite a battle to get him to let me go to this auction, but I had explained as gently as I could that, like so many other women these days, I needed to prove that I could be more than just a wife.

"But darling," he had said when I'd first suggested I might take a more active role in the business, "I love you being 'just a wife,' as you put it. I want you and Charlotte to be happy and not to have to worry about anything. You are happy, aren't you?"

"Of course I am," I answered. "It's just that I want to share more with you."

By the time I had persuaded him to see it my way, he actually seemed to like the idea of his wife being a working woman. "Who knows, you might have a seat on the board before long, and then there'll be no stopping us, will there?"

And provided I pulled it off at this auction, then who could tell, he might well be right.

"All set?" Christine said as we got into her Volkswagen Beetle.

"I think so."

"Good God, Elizabeth, you sound like a lamb going to the slaughter. It's only an auction, you know."

At eleven-thirty we hurtled up the drive of Rowe House and lurched to a stop at the front door. I say lurched because Christine had very little regard for a clutch. I was so relieved that we had survived the ordeal of her driving and arrived in one piece—albeit late—that the auction seemed as nothing in comparison.

The house was somber, even menacing inside, but I refused to be daunted. Christie's had set up an office in the library, so I went off to register, and Christine, spotting someone she knew, wandered off in the direction of the stables. I wasn't unduly worried by her disappearance for it was some time before Lot 137 was to be auctioned, so I sat and watched the other dealers as they made their bids for the various items of Queen Anne and Regency furniture. There were several paintings too, one of which fetched the staggering sum of one hundred and eighty-five thousand pounds. I was beginning to feel a little sorry that Edward had set a limit on what he was prepared to pay for the Bullock sofa—the idea of bidding and winning, whatever the cost, held a certain appeal. But there would be time enough for that sort of thing in the future; what was important now was to show Edward that I had the confidence to carry out his instructions. I knew the American collector who wanted the sofa was important to him, and I sent up a silent prayer that no one would outbid me. I looked at my catalogue for the hundredth time and the neat figures written beside Lot 137: fifteen thousand pounds. I felt comforted as I looked at the picture beside it. Surely no one would want to pay so much for such an ugly piece. I might even get it for less.

In what seemed no time at all Lot 135 went under the hammer, and I looked round for Christine. A Minton porcelain and brass lamp was Lot 136 and I heaved a sigh of relief as she appeared in the doorway.

"Ready?" she said, sitting down in the chair next to me.

"Of course," I answered, despising my stomach for calling me a liar.

The auctioneer was speaking. "I offer you Lot 137. Who will start the bidding? Ten thousand pounds. I have ten thousand pounds. Ten thousand five hundred. You sir, you at the back, eleven thousand? Yes, eleven thousand."

Within seconds I was overwhelmed by the certain knowledge that I was invisible. I looked at Christine in panic. She must have sensed my fear because instead of turning to look at me, she fixed her eyes on the auctioneer and nodded her head.

"Eleven thousand five hundred," he said. "Twelve thousand. A new bidder in the middle there. Twelve thousand five hundred." Had it really been me who had pushed it up another five hundred?

"Twelve thousand five hundred. Your bid at the moment, madam. Twelve thousand five hundred. Thirteen thousand."

I nodded. "Thirteen thousand five hundred."

I felt a movement beside me but was too tense to look round. "Are you bidding, madam? Yes. Fourteen thousand." The woman beside me had entered the bidding, and calmly folded one leg over the other as I raised my card.

"Fourteen thousand five hundred. Fifteen thousand." Suddenly it occurred to me that the woman next to me must have seen my catalogue and would know what I was prepared to go to.

"Fifteen thousand five hundred." I hadn't moved, and the woman beside me would not be bidding against herself, so there must be someone else in the arena. I leaned to one side, peering between the backs of heads to see if I could spot who it was.

"Sixteen thousand." I caught my breath. Had the auctioneer thought I made a bid?

"Sixteen thousand five hundred." It was the woman again. I looked at her, hating her and wanting to shout that she had cheated. How had everything got beyond my reach so quickly?

"Seventeen thousand."

My head swung round and I felt as though I were caught in a nightmare. All around me people were bidding, and I had lost. Didn't they know my husband wanted that piece of furniture? Didn't they understand that I couldn't let him down? Why didn't they stop?

"Eighteen thousand."

My hand shot to my head.

"Eighteen thousand five hundred."

Christine turned to look at me, her smile triumphant, and I knew that had she been in my shoes, she too would have carried on.

"Nineteen thousand. Nineteen thousand five hundred." I wouldn't allow myself to look at the figure on my catalogue. What would Edward have done? He would go on, I knew he would. The woman beside me was slumped in her chair, now intent on watching me, and whoever it was at the front of the room who was bidding against me.

"Twenty thousand pounds."

Would no one make the auctioneer stop? I couldn't go any higher.

"Twenty-one thousand pounds. Twenty-two thousand pounds." People were stirring in their seats and turning round to see who was bidding against the man at the front.

"Twenty-six thousand pounds."

To hell with everyone. I was going to win that sofa. No matter what it cost, that sofa was going back to Westmoor.

"Twenty-seven. Twenty-eight. Twenty-nine. Thirty thousand pounds."

Suddenly I stopped. Thirty thousand pounds. Twice the figure Edward had set down. There had been no let-up in the bidding, no hesitancy from the man in the front row. He wanted that sofa too. He was going to have it.

"Thirty-one. Thirty-two. Thirty-three. Any advance on thirty-three? Are you going on, madam?" The auctioneer's gaze was fixed on me. The room was silent. Everyone was waiting for me. Christine's eyes were gleaming and I noticed the moisture on her forehead. Had I done wrong? She had said she wouldn't interfere, that she was only there to lend me moral support. But surely if I had gone too far she would have stopped me. Gone too far? Was I mad?

I had more than doubled what Edward had said he was prepared to pay. I couldn't go on. Feeling slightly sick, I slumped back in my chair.

"The George Bullock sofa, sold for thirty-three thousand pounds." The hammer went down, tearing through my nerves like a sweeping scythe.

"Damn!" Christine muttered.

My eyes stung as I looked at her. "Oh my God, should I have gone on?" I gasped.

She shook her head irritably. "No. No, it's just that he didn't say who bought it." She craned her neck to get a better view of the front row. "Who is it?" she hissed.

I could only see the back of his head. I was feeling nauseous, all I wanted to do was to get out. I stood up and began to clamber my way along the row, to the door. I stumbled as I got to the end, and a doorman caught me and supported me by the elbow into the hall.

A few seconds later Christine followed. "Take me home," I breathed. She put her arm around my shoulder. "Come on, don't take it so hard. Someone has to lose and let's face it, you put up a hell of a fight. I would have lost my nerve long before that. Just wait 'til I tell Edward, he'll be so proud of you he'll probably . . ."

"No!" I cried. "You mustn't tell him. Please, Christine. He was so clear about the fifteen thousand pounds. He mustn't know, he'll never trust me again."

"Stop being so dramatic, he'll have a good laugh about it, you'll see."

I caught both her hands in mine and begged her not to tell him. To her it might seem unimportant, but she didn't understand.

"Honestly, Elizabeth," Christine said later, as we were driving back to Westmoor. "I don't know why you're so afraid to tell Edward, you must know he'll forgive you anything."

Which was precisely the reason I didn't want him to know. I didn't want him to forgive me. Just for once, I wanted him to be angry. I wanted him to rant and rave at my obstinacy, shout that I'd almost cost him eighteen thousand pounds. I wanted to have to beg his forgiveness, suffer his silent anger—anything that would instil a passionate emotion in us both. But I could see already in my mind's eye his kind and patient face, the look of sorrow in his eyes as he blamed himself for putting me in a situation that had caused me so much distress. Already I could feel his suffocating arms around me.

Christine dropped me at Westmoor, then went on to meet Rupert. Edward was still in London, Charlotte was in the nursery playing with a schoolfriend, and David had gone to the village. The house was quiet; it smelt of polish, and the silver gleamed in the sunlight that streamed in through the windows. I couldn't think of anything to do. I toyed with the idea of taking one of the horses out across the common, but it didn't really appeal. The latest editions of *Vogue* and *Harper's* were on the coffee table, I might find some new menus, we were giving three dinners in London the following week. But who cared about menus? The past week I had had the auction to look forward to. Now it was over, and those brief minutes of excitement had only intensified my restlessness.

I flopped down on the sofa and stared, unseeing, at the porcelain and the paintings that adorned the room. I must have dozed off because it was past five when Edward touched my cheek, and taking my hands, pulled me to my feet.

"Congratulations, darling," he whispered. "And thank you."

I blinked, trying to pull myself from sleep. "Thank you? What for?"

He laughed. "For the sofa, of course. Well done."

"But . . ."

"Edward!" I looked up as Christine came into the room. "Ah, there you are," she said. She turned to me, her face incredulous. "Elizabeth! What happened? How did it get here?"

"Jeffrey brought it, of course," Edward answered.

We both turned to stare at him. "Jeffrey?" I repeated.

"Yes. Why are you both so surprised? He'll be taking it on to the warehouse later. It's in the library now."

"The sofa?" I said. "But how?"

Edward laughed. "What on earth has got into you two? Did you or did you not go to the auction this morning and acquire one sofa?"

"We did—it seems," said Christine.

"Well then, shall we go and take a look at it?"

As soon as I clapped eyes on it my heart began to thump. What on earth had happened? The man in the front row had made the final bid, so how had it arrived here? And in God's name, how much had we paid for it?

Edward voiced the question. I looked at Christine, but her voice seemed as far from her throat as my own. "Well?" Edward prompted.

"Uh, I think we'd better take a look inside the envelope," Christine suggested, picking it up from the seat.

My worst fears were confirmed as she read out the total. "Thirty-three thousand pounds?" Edward echoed. He turned to me. "I thought . . ."

"Why don't we all go and sit down," Christine interrupted. "I've no idea how this has happened but I'm sure we can get to the bottom of it."

Edward listened patiently as Christine explained. By the time she had reached the end of the story Edward was laughing. "My poor darling," he said. "And all for me. Well, there's obviously been some confusion at Christie's end, I'll get on to them and find out who the rightful owner is." He dropped a kiss on the top of my head before he left the room.

When he returned a few minutes later, with David, he was no longer smiling. "I'm still not sure how it happened, Christie's are looking into it. But the sofa is ours." He paused as David handed him a drink. "For thirty-three thousand pounds."

I closed my eyes and groaned. "I'm sorry, Edward, what can I say? I don't know . . ."

He came and put his arms around me. "Sssh. It wasn't your fault. It seems that someone contacted one of Christie's staff, asking him to act on my behalf." He turned to Christine. "Do you know anything about it? Who it might have been?"

Christine shook her head. "Shall I check with the office, see if anyone there placed it?"

"They'll have gone home now. We'll try in the morning." His arms tightened around my shoulders. "Don't blame yourself, darling. It was just some stupid muddle." But his voice held no conviction.

I pushed him away, "Edward, how can you sit there and take it so calmly? OK, you'll get some of the money back, but whichever way you look at it this has cost you personally something in the region of eighteen thousand pounds. And I am responsible. Me! *I* have messed it up."

"Elizabeth."

I looked at him, and for one blinding instant I wanted to slap him. I realized then that in a perverse way I was almost glad at what had happened. It had shaken him. He hadn't got angry, nothing ever made him angry, but he had not been completely unmoved. Someone's head would roll for this—not mine, of course—but Edward would fire whoever had placed the bid. I wanted to be there when he did it. I wanted to watch him be unkind to someone.

I stared at him, shocked by my thoughts. "I'm going upstairs," I said.

"I'll come with you." He was already on his feet.

"No, Edward! Don't you understand? It was my fault! If I'd stopped at fifteen, as you told me to, this would never have happened. At least let me feel guilty about it." I swept out of the room, aware that I had hurt him deeply and feeling more wretched than ever.

An hour later there was a knock on the door and Edward let himself into the bedroom. One look at his face was enough to send me running into his arms. He forgave me my outburst, and in his calm, gentle voice he explained that this was what he had been afraid of all along—afraid that if he did allow me to become part of the business we would end up fighting with each other. Didn't I understand that, as his wife, I was far more important to him than any old sofa or painting could ever be?

Yes, I understood that. I understood too that it wasn't my failure at the auction that had really upset me, but the way I had hurt Edward by suggesting that just being his wife wasn't enough to make me happy. Edward wanted above all things to make me happy. He loved me, and I owed him so much—all the fun, the laughter and the loving of a proper family life. I had to get a grip on myself, and put a stop to whatever it was that was driving me to try and ruin it all.

Edward never did get to the bottom of what happened at Rowe House. I often wondered how hard he tried. Though he fought to hide it, I was never in any doubt that my decision to take no further part in the business was a great relief to him. I had made the decision—but it didn't stop me from feeling unnerved by the way all the doors to his professional life seemed closed to me after that. It was only many years later that the truth of what happened at the auction came to light—years during which Alexander returned to my life more than once, and was, in the end, to take control of events that very nearly destroyed my life.

A week or so after the auction we were all once again in the drawing room at Westmoor. I was beginning to hate that room. Like Edward's adoration, its portraits and its statues seemed to stifle me—no matter how often I tried to tell myself how fortunate I was. I stood at the window, watching the rain outside. Edward looked up from the *Times* and asked me if I was feeling all right.

My reply must have sounded irritable because he put aside his paper and came to stand beside me. I turned away. How could I tell him that I didn't want to fly to Paris that night? That I was bored by Paris, bored by Rome, bored by New York? I longed to do something different, something unplanned, impulsive. I felt as if my whole body were on the point of exploding, with frustration.

"Isn't he simply divine!" Christine exclaimed, giving me the diversion I needed.

David caught my eye and winked. "And just who are we gushing about this time?" he asked.

"Alexander Belmayne, of course, who else?"

I froze in Edward's arms. Had Christine found out somehow, and was this her way of tormenting me? No. I was being paranoid. How could she possibly know? I didn't dare look at Edward—but he couldn't know either; I'd told him about Alexander, but I'd never once mentioned his surname, and everyone thought Charlotte looked like me.

Edward shook his head and went back to his chair. "He's not in the papers again, is he?" he said. "What's he done this time?"

"It says here that his father has bailed him out."

"Bailed him out of what?" David was only half listening.

"The debt he got himself into through gambling. There's a picture of him here coming out of Annabel's with some woman. God, he's beautiful. It says here that 'the Belmayne marriage is on the rocks and according to close friends his wife has moved out.'

Mmm, sounds hopeful. I don't suppose we could invite him for drinks when we're next in London, could we, Edward? Elizabeth, are you all right, you look positively pale today."

Edward dropped his newspaper immediately. "Christine's right, you know, darling. Come and sit down. Call Mary, David, get her to bring in some tea."

I allowed Edward to lead me to a chair. He was talking to me, rubbing my hands. It wasn't the first time Christine had read aloud articles about Alexander, but this time her words rang in my ears with terrifying clarity. Now I knew why I had been behaving so badly, and what it was that was forcing me to reject Edward. Did I really still love Alexander as much as my reaction said I did? Wasn't it all buried somewhere in the past? Why had it come back now to haunt me. I looked into Edward's face. What was I doing here with this man? Everything around me was alien—and somewhere out there Alexander was alone, alone as I was here, in this room. Then, for one wild moment, I was back in Bayswater, sitting on the bed, looking at him and listening as he swore that he loved me, that I would never be able to shut him out of my life, because no matter what happened in the future, it would always be me he loved.

I clutched at Edward's hand. I loved Edward. I would never do anything to hurt him. He had to save me from this . . .

I turned abruptly as the door opened. Canary came in, brandishing a long stick with a star glued to one end. Jeffrey followed her, miming the blowing of a royal trumpet, then bowed and swept his arm to usher someone in through the door. And there was Charlotte, her black hair curled round her face, her satin dress sprinkled with stardust and a glass slipper balanced on the cushion she held out to Edward. Her face was beaming as she looked round the room and her eyes—his eyes—pleaded with mine for approval.

Too late I stifled a sob, and before anyone could stop me I ran from the room.

Alexander

16

JESSICA AND I were reunited the day Henry married Lizzie. She'd been living with her parents at their house in Holland Park and we'd neither seen nor spoken to each other for over six weeks. I hadn't really cared much when she went—at least it meant no more of those macabre paintings would find their way onto the walls. Lizzie had remained at the house with me, a situation that, amazingly, seemed to cause no speculation. In fact, Henry all but lived with us, so it was only when he was out that Lizzie turned her insatiable appetite on me. I didn't like myself too well for my weakness in giving in to her, but she blackmailed me by threatening to tell Henry. I didn't know whether or not she would actually have carried out the threat, though I rather suspected she wouldn't—which only went to show what an altogether contemptible character I was.

Henry and Lizzie tied the knot at Chelsea Register Office, with a reception afterwards at the Ritz. Jessica was there. I was surprised at my feelings when I saw her. She'd lost weight and her eyes seemed larger in her pale face. Watching her, as she mingled with the other guests, brought back all the shame I felt at the things I had done to her. One way or another she had suffered at my hands ever since we'd met.

At first we were uncomfortable with each other, but the readiness with which she turned her back on the rest of the party told me she was as keen as I was that we should at least make an effort. She put up a good show of enjoying her freedom, laughing and chattering as if she hadn't a care in the world. But I knew her too well. Every time a waiter passed she helped herself to a drink, and as the day wore on I could see how close she was to the breaking point. In the end I took her home and put her to bed. The following day we drove round to her parents' house and collected her things.

In the weeks that followed our reconciliation we did something we should have done years before—we talked about our relationship, and our feelings for each other. I was shocked to discover that for the past year, up until the time she left me, she had been taking drugs. It was the only way, she said, she could cope with the fact that I didn't love her. And the morbid paintings on the walls of our home had been intended to represent her womb as time passed and it shriveled and discolored in infecundity.

"But it was all my fault really," she said. "I was so confused about you, and because I was suffering, I wanted to make you suffer too. I was afraid that if I couldn't give you children, you would use it as a weapon against me, and because I was afraid of you, afraid to talk to you, the only way I had of expressing myself was through my paintings . . . I've always thought that you still loved Elizabeth, you see, and I suppose that's what it's all been about really. I wonder if you know how it feels to live with someone, and love them, knowing all the time that they love someone else."

I was appalled to think that I could have lived with Jessica for so long and not known anything of the pain she was suffering. In fact, I probably *had* known, the trouble was I hadn't really cared. Now I was simply grateful for the opportunity to try, in whatever way I could, to make it up to her.

I saw to it that we spent every possible minute together. One of my favorite ways of relaxing was to sit in the corner of her muddled studio, now once again filled with bright and vivid colors, and watch as, naked—and it had to be naked, she assured me—she tied a paint brush to each hand and rotated so that the tips of the brushes swept over the canvas. I was no more au fait with her peculiar form of art than I had been before, but it reminded me of our days at Oxford, and that touch of nostalgia drew us even closer together.

I noticed quite early on how much she was drinking, but if I ever mentioned it she became defensive. "I'm just having a bit of fun," she hiccoughed, when I came home early one afternoon and found her sprawled on the sofa, the best part of the way through a bottle of gin.

"But Jess, darling, that bottle was full last night."

"Are you having a go at me, oh Godalmighty Alexander? Why are you home early, anyway?"

"I live here, remember? Now come along, let's get some coffee inside you."

"Not one of your little babies?" She giggled as she saw me flinch. "Still haven't got me pregnant, have you, Alexander?"

"Jess, stop before you say something you regret."

Suddenly she burst into tears. "I'm sorry. I didn't mean it. I don't know what I'm saying. I don't know what I'm doing anymore. You confuse me. You've never loved me before, and now that you do, I don't know how to handle it. What shall we do? Shall we go and see someone? I know you want to have a baby. *Well, I'm not damned well giving you one!*"

I walked out of the room, knowing it was pointless to stay. When she sobered up we'd talk again. And maybe she was right, we should go and see a specialist—after all, we'd been trying long enough with no results. But how could we even think about having a baby with Jess in this state?

So we muddled on from row to row, each more acrimonious than the last. But I was certain that once she was pregnant, everything would change; then at last she would allow herself to believe how much I cared for her. To have something in our lives that we could share and love together was what we both needed.

It was on the day Jessica and I finally plucked up the courage to go for our fertility tests that I received instructions in the Pinto case. No one—with the possible exception of Raddish, the clerk at chambers—was more surprised than I was. It was a case that had been in and out of the press for some time and I came across it when I had to attend a Section I at the magistrates' court. The committal proceedings were brief, and I barely met Ruth Pinto. However, I succeeded in getting her bail, and it was because of this, her solicitor told me, that she later insisted I should be the one to continue with her case. He was determined to make it abundantly clear that the decision had nothing to do with him.

The British Government, or more precisely, the Ministry of Defence, had accused Ruth Pinto of stealing top-secret defense documents and selling them to one of the hundred and five Russian diplomats who were subsequently expelled from Britain. These documents, I was told—I never got to see them—outlined certain key details of Royal Naval maneuvers in the Baltic.

The case, with much press coverage, lasted four days, and the interaction between myself and prosecuting counsel was bitter, amusing and, for me, increasingly exhilarating as my certain, and public, victory drew closer.

The night before the final day of the trial Jessica and I dined at home. I was edgy because of an unexpected turn in court that day, when Pinto's boyfriend took the stand and all but handed the prosecution their case on a plate. I'd have my work cut out preparing my summing up before I went into court the following morning, so I was even more depressed than usual when I realized that Jessica was drunk.

I watched her across the table as she helped herself to minestrone. She slapped the ladle back into the bowl and I stared pointedly at the mess she had made. She glared back at me, then picking up the ladle, she emptied it over the salt and pepper.

Swallowing hard on my anger, I held out my hand for the ladle. "I'd like some of that soup, please." For a moment I thought she was going to throw it at me. Instead she burst out laughing, and soon I found that I was laughing too.

She stopped. "Why are you laughing?"

"I was laughing because you were."

"But you don't know why I was laughing, do you? I was laughing at you, Alexander, so you were laughing at yourself. The great Alexander Belmayne, he who knows everything. I suppose you think you know what's wrong with me tonight, don't you? Yes, of course you do, because you know everything. But even if you did know, which you don't, what would you care? What do you care about anything, except yourself?"

"For Christ's sake, don't you think I've got enough on my mind tonight of all nights, without having you and your childish tantrums to contend with. Either tell me what's on your mind, or shut up. Frankly I don't care which."

We glared at each other, the air between us simmering. In the end I put my napkin on the table and stood up. "I'm going to do some work. Why don't you do yourself a favor and go upstairs and fiddle around with your paintbrushes. It might improve your temper."

I saw a dangerous gleam leap into her eyes and her fingers tightened on the knife beside her. I turned away, and as I walked into the hall the telephone began to ring, drowning the string of obscenities she was screaming after me. Suddenly I felt all the old antipathy surging back into my veins. I'd tried, I kept on trying, but there was no point; I didn't know what she wanted, or what I had to do to make her happy. She couldn't accept my love, and now she had me so confused I didn't know which way to turn.

"*Answer that bloody phone!*" she screamed.

I picked up the receiver. "Someone sounds out of sorts."

"Father."

"Haven't rung at a bad time, have I?"

"No, as a matter of fact, you've rung just *in* time. How are you?"

We chatted for a while until I realized that he was actually saying nothing at all. It wasn't in my father's nature to indulge in idle chat—here was someone else who wouldn't come right out and say what they were thinking. Trying to keep the irritation out of my voice, I asked him if there was something on his mind.

"No, nothing really. Just wanted to know how you were feeling about the Pinto case. The jury goes out tomorrow, doesn't it?"

"That's right."

"Mind if I offer a word of advice?"

I did, but nevertheless told him to go ahead.

"Go easy on the summing up," he said.

I looked at the receiver, uncertain whether I had heard him right. "I beg your pardon."

"You heard me. In your own and your client's interest, go easy on the defense. That's all. Goodnight, son. Love to Jessica." And he'd gone.

I slammed the receiver down and spun round to find Jessica standing in the doorway. "What did he want?" she asked.

"Good question. He's someone else who's talking in riddles tonight. Now, if you don't mind I'm going to my study and I don't want to be disturbed. By anyone!"

"In that case, I'll go and fiddle with some paintbrushes," she spat, and flounced off up the stairs.

My summing up speech would have been difficult enough to prepare without my father's words ringing in my ears. "In your own interest," he had said. But just how could it be in my interest deliberately to lose the case which is what I supposed him to mean and see the girl go to prison? With the sort of press coverage the case was receiving I'd be on the map if I won, and there weren't many barristers who could say that at the age of twenty-four.

Then it dawned on me: I was being subjected to government pressure . . . Outraged, I picked up the phone, ready to demand that my father—more accurately described, under the circumstances, as the Lord Chancellor—should explain exactly what he was after. I didn't even finish dialing; it wouldn't be any use, he wouldn't tell me anything. I must simply ignore him. The girl was clearly innocent, and it was my job to see that justice was done.

But the doubt had been planted, and the question that until then I had refused to ask myself—why had the government decided to proceed with the prosecution at all when the defense case was so strong?—danced about in my mind until I couldn't see the papers in front of me. I dropped my pen and rubbed my fingers over my eyes. Something was wrong with this case, something fundamental that I must have overlooked. And I was convinced that whatever it was, was staring me full in the face—which only added to my frustration.

"In a better mood, are we?"

I turned to see Jessica leaning against the door. "I told you I didn't want to be interrupted," I said.

"I was bored upstairs alone, and you know how you getting angry always turns me on. I thought you might like to play." She ran a hand over the thin white silk of her blouse, pulling it tightly against her skin. The pink nipple stood out enticingly.

I looked at it for a moment, then sighed as I turned away. "Jessica, I'm not in the mood."

The ice clinked against the glass as she finished her gin and tonic. For a second or two there was silence, and then the glass smashed against the wall in front of me. The ice cubes melted across the pages on my desk, turning the ink to an illegible blur.

"Actually, darling, it wouldn't make a lot of difference to me if you were in the mood. What I need right now is a *real* man."

I made no answer. I could neither trust myself to speak nor move.

"Got any suggestions? How about one of the husbands of the hundred wives you've fucked?"

"Jessica, just get out of here."

"At least there's one thing you can be sure of, there won't be any little Belmayne bastards running around anywhere, will there?" And she swept out of the room.

I was behind her like a shot. "What the hell was that supposed to mean?"

She stopped, and staggered against the wall as I turned her round. "What do you think it means, Alexander darling?"

Blood was pounding through my ears and my hands were sweating, but I forced myself to remain calm. "You've had the results?" I said.

"To the little testie-westies we had? Yes." She started to laugh.

I caught her by the wrists and pinned her against the wall. "Well?" She gave a nervous giggle and looked away. I shook her, and twisted her arms painfully behind her back. "Well?"

She giggled again, but couldn't meet my eyes as she spoke. "Well," she sighed, "it would seem that your little testie-westies simply don't work, Alexander. It had to be one of us, didn't it? And it's you! Defunct, I·think the word is. But don't worry, I'll stick by you, darling."

"Are you trying to tell me . . .?" I looked at her, and felt myself physically recoil.

"That you're infertile? Yes, that's exactly what I'm telling you. You can't have babies, Alexander. You can't have heirs, because what's coming out of you is nothing."

I let go of her. She was lying. She had to be lying.

"What's the matter? Not going to cry, are you? Not Alexander, the big man. It's not the end of the world, you know, and as I said, your loving wife is prepared to take on your deficient manhood. Now how's that for devotion?"

I walked slowly down to the sitting room and sank into a chair. Several minutes later she followed me in, another drink in her hand. She stood in front of me, smiling, waiting for me to speak.

"Why, Jessica? Why did you have to tell me like that?"

"You mean, with the contempt you always treat me to? Hurts, doesn't it, Alexander? And after all you've put me through, all you've done to me, at last you've got what you deserve." She gave a sickening laugh. "Just look at you, all white and shaking. I wonder what your darling Elizabeth would say if she could see you now. Well, I'll tell you something, she wouldn't stay with you, no woman would, because you're a sexual cripple. You're pathetic, do you know that? Pathetic!"

Looking at her then, her bright blue eyes bloodshot and puffy, her skin mottled, I felt myself drowning in the sorrow of our lives. "Shall I tell you something, Jessica?" I said quietly. "Shall I tell you the truth about me? The truth is, you were right. I've only ever loved one woman, and that was Elizabeth. She was everything to me. I begged her to marry me, but she said I was too young. I asked her again and again, because I thought if she left me I'd die—and that's just what I have been doing, all these years, dying. But it's my fault, because I turned my back on her at a time when she needed me. I'll never forgive myself for that, never. But I'm paying for it. And you, Jessica, are the price."

17

_A_FTER THAT NIGHT I could no longer be in any doubt about our marriage. The way I had used the one weapon I knew would wound Jessica more than any other was unforgivable, but the shock of hearing I was sterile, and the way she'd told me, had pushed me over the edge. "Defunct," she had called me, "a sexual cripple," and I would never forget the look on her face when she'd said it. It haunted me, persecuted me, and I started to see that same look on the face of every woman I met. Triumph and contempt. I understood it—they saw it as their just revenge—and I felt everything they meant me to feel; inadequate, futile and sick.

Somehow I dragged myself through the days that followed. Ruth Pinto was acquitted—despite the judge's summing up, which I have to say was shamelessly biased. However, she was free to go, and as she shook me by the hand she said something that was only to make sense to me later.

"I don't know what will happen to my life now, Mr. Belmayne. I was convinced my stupidity, coupled with your inexperience, would put me in prison."

That evening the papers led on the case. Triumph was mine, and Henry held a party to celebrate at his flat in Eaton Square.

"Oh come on now, no false modesty," he protested when I tried to tell him that it had been an open-and-shut case from the beginning. "You wait 'til the morning, you won't be able to see old Raddish for the pile of briefs he'll be carrying into your office."

I laughed, and promised to pass my overload in his direction. Robert Lyttleton was the next to congratulate me. We saw very little of him these days, as he slogged it out at the Foreign Office, working his way towards that elusive overseas posting. Whenever we did meet, we neither of us referred to his affair with my wife, nor mine with his mother. I was glad that these near-incestuous involvements, and my jealousy, had not affected our friendship—even though I had no idea at that time just how valuable a friend Robert would turn out to be.

Now he nudged my arm and nodded towards Lizzie as she slid past us with a tray of hors d'oeuvres. "She's not wearing any panties, you know."

"And how would you know that?" I enquired.

"She showed me."

I shook my head, not in the least surprised. "I take it Henry was nowhere in sight?"

"Then you take it wrong, old chap. Henry was right there with me. In fact, he told her to do it. No, Scout's honor," he said as I started to protest. "Henry, old chap." He grabbed Henry's arm as he sailed past with Caroline. "Did you or did you not instruct your wife to display her private parts to me?"

"Guilty." He looked at me. "Don't tell me you want to see them too? I'm sure she'll oblige if you ask. Or would you like me to make the request on your behalf?"

It wasn't until much later that I was able to get Henry alone and ask him just what was going on between him and Lizzie. "Apart from a series of orgies, you mean? Very little," he said.

"I assumed you were happy together."

"I fuck her, that's all she wants. She's happy." He was smiling as he spoke, but I knew him too well.

"Are you seeing Caroline again?" I asked.

"As often as possible." The smile faded. "I should never have given her up."

"Then why don't you leave Lizzie?"

"Why don't you leave Jessica?"

We looked at each other for several minutes before he spoke again. "Well, we sure made one hell of a mistake when we got into bed with those two, didn't we? The question is, which of us is going to be the first to do something about it?"

The following morning when I arrived at chambers I found a stack of newspapers on my desk. Perhaps Henry was right, I would see a few more briefs coming my way now, and God knew I needed something to take my mind off the situation at home.

I sorted through the mail first, then picked up the papers to read them again. There was still something that unsettled me about the Pinto case, not that I seriously expected to find the answer in the press.

"Telegram for you, sir." I waited for the junior clerk to go before I tore it open. You didn't have to have lived through the war to experience a certain trepidation at the delivery of a telegram.

There were only two words to the message—two words so unexpected that my legs gave way beneath me. I was stunned, transfixed, feeling my heart slow and somersault. I tore my eyes away and turned to the window, as if expecting to find an explanation there. The distant noise of the city faded even further as I heard her voice speaking those two words. All these years had passed, and now, suddenly, today . . . I gazed down at the telegram again, my eyes hungry, wanting there to be more. Still there were just the two words: *Congratulations, Elizabeth.*

I must have sat there at my desk for almost an hour, staring into space, as slowly I unlocked the doors of my memory. I could see Foxton's so clearly that I might have been there yesterday. I heard the stampede of feet and the babel of young male voices as boys descended from dormitories. I saw the old building slumbering amid its lawns, the clearly marked sports fields. I saw the classrooms, the dining room, the Head's study. Then the cottage, the surgery and the railwayman's hut. And almost, just fleetingly . . . I jerked my head up, half expecting to see her eyes laughing back at me. But there were only the blank walls of my office in front of me, and I dropped my head in my hands. I had shut it all out for so long now, so much had happened since, and with the pain of the last few days . . .

I met Henry that evening at El Vino's. As the day wore on and the telegram worked its way into my subconscious as well as my conscious mind, I had ground myself into a near catatonic state of frustration and resentment.

"Two words! Two lousy words! Why doesn't she say where she is, for Christ's sake?"

Henry handed the telegram back. "So I take it you want to know where she is?"

"Of course I do! I'm surprised you even need to ask."

He shrugged, and let a long silence elapse before he spoke again. "You don't need me to tell you how much you hurt her, Alexander. Maybe she's afraid you'll do it again."

"Then why the telegram?"

"I think you can answer that for yourself." He held up his hand as I started to speak. "As far apart as your worlds were, you two were right for each other, you knew it, she knew it, we all knew it. Even Old Anger tried to make you face it, didn't she, when she came up to Oxford? I suppose this is Elizabeth's way of letting you know she still thinks about you, perhaps even that she wants to see you again. And if you want my advice, then go and find her. With everything that's happening to you at the moment, well . . . find her before you hurt anyone else, because I think quite enough people have suffered as a consequence of your bleeding heart."

My immediate impulse was to get up from the table and tell him just what I thought of his agony aunt routine, but he caught hold of my arm and pulled me back down again.

"I'll tell you this for nothing, Alexander. You weren't the only one who missed her after she'd gone. I think about her too. And I've never understood why you refused to talk about her, especially to me. I'm supposed to be your best friend, for God's sake! So, you can talk now, and you can start by telling me—because I've always wanted to know—why the hell you let her go so easily."

I felt my anger diminish, only to be replaced by the onset of that burning misery I had thought never to feel again. "I wish I could answer that. All I know is that my father sounded so convincing. I think he even told me he had proof to connect her with those damned gypsies. I believed him when he said she'd made a fool of me, somehow at the time it all added up. But I tried to find her afterwards. You must remember that."

Henry nodded. "I also remember the pride that made you give up. The same pride that has hurt so many people since. So what are you going to do now?"

"What the hell can I do? It's as if she's some sort of a ghost come back to haunt me. She's there, but I can't touch her. Why now, after all these years, and like this?"

We neither of us had the answer to that, and the next two weeks dragged painfully by. I couldn't concentrate on anything as visions of the past flooded my mind to drown the present. My eyes strained across busy streets, trying to pick her out among the crowd. Every time the phone rang, the door opened, the postman knocked . . . The agony of waiting seemed endless. My relationship with Jessica deteriorated even further. Ever since the night she had told me I was incapable of fathering children, I had taken to sleeping in another room. Jessica, I soon discovered, was seeking solace in the arms of her new mentor, Thomas Street. I didn't care. If anything, I was glad. Jessica embodied all that was wrong with my life, and all I wanted was to get as far away from her as I could.

Then one morning I received a telephone call from my father. He wanted me to meet him at his club; there was a matter of great importance he needed to discuss with me.

My heart leapt into my throat. Had he found Elizabeth? Was he going to tell me that he had made a mistake all those years ago? My obsession was such that it didn't occur to me that my father might want to see me on an entirely different matter.

True to form, he wasted no time in coming to the point. The Pinto case. As I listened to what he was saying, I remembered all too vividly the hollow feeling I had had when I won. Now here it was again, this time stripped of its pretense, and revealed in all its horror. Ruth Pinto had been a British agent, not a Soviet one. The information she had been "acquiring" for the Eastern Bloc had in fact been given her by the Ministry of Defence—and her communist masters were beginning to suspect her. The court case had been staged to allay their suspicions and to save Ruth; for once justice had been seen to be done and after a reasonable lapse of time she would have been quietly released from prison, whisked away somewhere and given a new identity. The bottom line, my father told me, was that the pseudo-trial had been engineered to save her life. As it was, due to my "brilliant defense," she had been acquitted. Her body had been found the night before on an East Berlin street.

The whole thing seemed incredible. If my father hadn't been the Lord Chancellor I would have accused him of reading too many spy thrillers. What I wanted to know most of all was why I had not been told the truth from the beginning.

"That's simple," my father answered. "There were agents from the KGB in court. If you had known what was going on, it would have been bound to show in your defense. These people aren't stupid, Alexander. The whole thing had to be conducted as a bona fide case."

"Then why the hell didn't the prosecution make a better job of things? They practically handed it to me on a plate."

"You do yourself an injustice. What no one was prepared for was just how cleverly you would conduct the defense. Now don't flare up. You're still an inexperienced barrister. The brief could have gone to anyone, it just so happened that you were the one who attended the Section I at Clerkenwell. You became the obvious choice."

"So I was set up?"

"No need to dramatize, Alexander."

"I said, I was set up."

"In a manner of speaking, yes."

I drew breath to deliver my outrage, but he held up his hand to stop me. "The case is closed now. But there is one other thing I wanted to tell you before you read it in the press. I shall be retiring at the end of this session."

"Retiring!" I echoed. "But you're only sixty-four." Alarm bells began ringing in my head.

"And your mother is not far past fifty." I was touched by his loyalty in not revealing her actual age. "She's still young, Alexander, and I want to spend some time with her before it's too late. Nothing wrong in that, is there? You should try it some time, good for the old heart."

"Heart? Have you had more warnings?"

"There's plenty of life left in this old dog yet. But yes—" and I saw the veil drop from his eyes—"the doctors are insisting. And what with your mother nagging away at me too, she'll probably do for me long before the old heart goes! I've given in. She's won—but then women always do." He smiled as he spoke of my mother; they were still very much in love, even after all these years.

I swallowed hard. Though we had had our differences over the years, I loved my father.

"Come along, old chap," he laughed, reaching out and clasping my arm, "enough of the long face, can't have you weeping into your soup, now can we? Besides, I shan't be going anywhere yet awhile, that I can promise you. And as for you, well, you'd better brace yourself for the public humiliation that is very likely on its way."

Never one to pull punches was my father.

The only good thing about finding myself back in the newspapers was that it might prompt Elizabeth to get in touch with me. But the days passed, and I heard nothing.

From time to time I took the telegram out of my pocket and looked at it, vainly searching for the telephone number that wasn't there. Henry and I met in El Vino's every evening, ostensibly to mull over the day's events in court, but in reality to commiserate with one another over our unfortunate marriages. Steeped in self-pity, I wasn't backward in pointing out to him that at least he saw Caroline.

"Not the same," he slurred. "I want her there all the time. Do you know, for the first time in my life someone else's happiness is more important than my own. Isn't that amazing?"

"Isn't that love?"

"Don't let's get shlushy, old chap." And he got up to get more drinks.

"Do you think Elizabeth's happy?" I asked him when he returned.

"Can't be. Wouldn't have sent the telegram if she was."

I knew I hadn't wanted him to reply in the affirmative, but thinking of her, maybe alone somewhere, and unhappy, was unbearable. "I'm going to find her, Henry. If it kills me, I'm going to find her."

18

JESSICA WAS PREPARING the house for the big send-off we were giving Robert Lyttleton. At last he had attained his overseas posting, and would be flying to Baghdad at the beginning of the following week. It had been Jessica's idea that we hold the party—as much, I guessed, to avail herself of another opportunity of flaunting a "real man" in my face, as to say good-bye to Robert.

At various intervals during the morning she bumped open the door of my study to regale me with yet another problem that had cropped up, and enquire whether I didn't think I should do something about it. My refusal was unvarying, and she would slam out again, hissing obscenities—under her breath so the hired help wouldn't hear. After lunch, which was a sandwich behind the now locked door of my study, Lizzie and the florist arrived. Unable to think why it hadn't occurred to me before, I snatched up my coat and went off to play a round of golf with Henry.

Later, when we returned to Belgrave Square with Henry boasting of his victory, Jessica and Lizzie were nowhere to be found. "Gone shopping," Mrs. Dixon informed us. So Henry and I decided to make a start on the champagne. By five o'clock they still weren't back, and Henry sauntered off to Eaton Square to put his head down for an hour.

I was in my study when I heard Jessica and Lizzie come in, but didn't bother to get up. I was going over a file that a private investigator had delivered to my chambers the day before. Not that there was anything much to read—all I'd been able to give him to go on was the telegram, and that, he discovered, had been sent from a post office in Chelsea. It heightened my frustration no end to think that she could be so close. I picked up the telegram and read it again. Then angrily I crumpled it into a tiny ball. Damn her! Why was she doing this to me?"

A snigger from the doorway brought me round sharp. Jessica was holding two glasses while Lizzie filled them with champagne. "Poor Alexander," she sighed. "Is he dreaming about his long lost lover again, do you think?"

Lizzie tutted and giggled. "Would you like some champagne, Alexander darling?" She held the bottle towards me, but I ignored it and glared at Jessica.

"I don't think Alexander wants any champagne, Jess."

"No, I guess not." Jessica clinked her glass against Lizzie's. "Let's drink to my darling husband. Should we tell him our little secret, Lizzie? What do you think?"

"I don't know. Shall we?"

Jessica looked at me. "No, I don't think so. He'll only get cross." And, giggling, they started to walk out of the room.

"Tell me what?" I demanded.

"Nothing," Jessica threw over her shoulder. "Come along, Lizzie, let's go and see how Mrs. Dixon is getting on in the kitchen."

"Have you been holding something back from me, you bitch! What is it? A letter? Where have you hidden it?"

"Oh, he thinks he's had a letter," Jessica said. She turned back to me. "No, darling, not a letter."

"Then what?"

"I'll tell him, Jess, shall I?" said Lizzie.

"Yes, you tell him."

"Alexander. What's my name?" She smiled and nodded her head. "I think he's beginning to get it already, Jess. That's right, Alexander, my name's Lizzie. And what is Lizzie a derivative of?

That's right, Elizabeth. Congratulations, Alexander." And shrieking with laughter, they walked out of the room. After they'd left my
study I sat staring into space, not daring to move, afraid of what I
might do if I did. Eventually I picked up the phone and rang Henry.
Briefly I told him what had happened. He swore he would beat
Lizzie to within an inch of her life, but by that time my temper had
abated, and a feeling of defeat had set in. I told him not to mention
it, saying that it would be better if from now on we just forgot it
had ever happened.

The evening didn't go with the swing we had hoped it would.
Jessica and I could barely be civil to each other, and matters weren't
helped by the presence of Robert's mother. Naturally, neither Jessica nor Lizzie could resist the odd oblique, barbed reference to our
affair. I was past caring, but there were twelve others present, mostly
old friends of Robert's; they, and Rachel, were clearly embarrassed.
Robert got roaring drunk, so did Lizzie. Jessica disappeared for half
an hour at one stage, and then I noticed Robert was missing too. I
felt sick. My only hope was that she would get pregnant. It would
be good enough grounds for a quick and uncomplicated divorce.

Around eleven several people drifted off, and I walked Rachel
to the door.

"I couldn't help but notice how bad things are between you and
Jessica," she remarked, as I held out her coat for her.

"An understatement, Rachel."

"You look tired, and you've lost weight."

"That's what a bad marriage does for you."

"Then get out of it. You're young, you don't have any children
to consider. Get out now, while you still can."

"I'm seriously thinking about it."

"Do it. I know things didn't work out well for us in the end,
but I cared about you, Alexander. I still do. And despite everything
I said that day, I know that behind that handsome façade of yours
there's a good and decent man. The trouble is, between you, you
and Jessica are suffocating him."

I gave a sad smile, and drew her into my arms. "Did I really
treat you so badly, Rachel?"

"One way or another you've treated everyone badly. Time to
stop, eh?" She opened the door.

"Excuse me, sir. I'm looking for Lizzie Roseman."

Rachel and I turned to find a tall blonde man standing on the pavement outside, shuffling uncomfortably from one foot to the other as if he were more than ready to move on. The collar of a purplish check shirt appeared above the neck of his fur-lined leather jacket, and his jeans, which had seen better days, were stuffed inside the legs of what looked like size fourteen cowboy boots. All he needed to complete his appearance was a cork-dangled hat and a can of lager.

"Er, maybe you know her better as Lizzie Poynter," he said, when neither Rachel nor I answered him. "I'm told her sister, Jessica, lives here."

"I think I'll be on my way," Rachel said. She leaned over and kissed me on the cheek. "Think about what I said." And she ran off down the steps. The man smiled pleasantly as she passed him, and doffed the invisible hat. I followed her down the steps and asked what he might want with Lizzie. He hooked his thumbs through his jean loops, as if trying to give himself a confidence he was clearly far from feeling, and leaned against the pillar of the porch. I listened in stupefied silence as this stranger, who had appeared out of the darkness on a cold and windy March night, told me who he was, and why he was looking for my sister-in-law. In the end I asked him to wait, and went inside to fetch Henry.

I let him take a good look at the man standing at the door before I made the introduction. "Henry Clive, meet John Roseman. Or should I put it another way? Henry, meet Lizzie's husband."

After the shock had worn off, a rather cosy little party developed. Lizzie had been horrified when John followed Henry and me in through the drawing-room door, but her horror soon changed to delight as the Australian turned on all the charm that had probably made her marry him in the first place. Henry, I noticed, sat back and watched the proceedings with detached interest.

We learned that Lizzie had married John some four years ago, while she had been traveling round Australia. By all accounts it had been something of a whirlwind romance; they'd known each other a total of three months before she walked out and left him. Quite why she walked out we were never told, but I suppose that was their business. She seemed wholly unconcerned that she had committed bigamy, and so too did Henry and John. Jessica, I noticed, said nothing, and I soon realized that she had known about John all along. It was decided that as Henry was a lawyer he should sort the whole thing out—John would do anything he had to do to help—and with that, Lizzie and her newfound husband left. To go where? Heaven only knew, and Henry didn't care.

I was dumbfounded. Between the time of John's arrival and his departure, I don't think I'd uttered more than a dozen words.

"Always did like the Aussie," Henry said, putting on his overcoat to go. "Get in touch with their embassy, old chap. See if they can't rustle up a little something for you too."

"I might just do that," I laughed. "Something's got to be done. Robert Lyttleton had her tonight. D'you think he could be persuaded to take her with him?"

"Not a chance."

As I turned back inside I saw Jessica standing at the drawing-room door. From the look on her face there was no doubt she had heard every word. I walked towards her, heading for my study, and as I brushed past, her voice snaked over me.

"I'll never let you go, Alexander, so don't even think it."

In the early hours of the morning she crept into my bed and cried as though her heart might break. Understanding her pain, I held her in my arms and wondered what the hell was to become of us.

When Henry and Caroline announced the date of their wedding it was impossible not to share in their long-delayed happiness, though I had to admit to more than an occasional stab of envy. After that one night of tenderness Jessica and I had, yet again, talked long and hard about our relationship, but this time there was no point in fooling myself: I would never be able to trust her again, and whatever love I'd had for her had been killed the day I found out about the telegram. I was as faithful to her now as she could have wished but my fidelity was born of my impotency, not of love, and she knew it. She tormented and ridiculed me for what she called my "defective organ," but if I threatened to leave her, she threatened in return to tell the world how "the great Alexander Belmayne couldn't get it up." She even went so far as to hang a plaque over my bed quoting William Congreve's words: *Heav'n has no rage, like love to hatred turn'd, Nor Hell a fury, like a woman scorn'd.* These two lines epitomized our relationship so perfectly it would have been laughable had it not been so tragic.

No longer able to prove myself in the bedroom, I threw myself into work. My professional reputation was growing, and I took on more than it was humanly possible to cope with. In the end Henry took me to task and tried to persuade me to seek psychiatric help before I killed myself with overwork. I told him to mind his own business, and that I was perfectly capable of sorting out my own life. But the dilemma grew. I wanted children, now more than ever. I wanted them so badly, I would find myself smiling at them in shops, or walking the parks in order to watch them play. I felt sick at myself for such a display of weakness, but my yearning was too strong to be denied.

It was on one such day, while I was walking in Hyde Park, that I felt something knock against my legs. I looked down to see a girl's small face gazing up at me—she was laughing despite her fall. She had been running away from a hot air balloon that had rolled towards her while someone was trying to inflate it. I bent down to put her back on her feet, expecting her to run away, but she lingered, looking me over in the curious way children have, until a woman appeared beside us.

"There you are, I thought I'd lost you under the balloon."

I could see the woman was nervous at finding the child with a stranger, so I stood up and smiled, wanting to reassure her. "No harm done," I said, and ruffled the girl's hair. "Definitely all in one piece."

The girl's face broke into a smile that turned my heart over, then allowing the woman to take her by the hand, she walked off. I watched them go, the thin legs of the girl skipping along beside the elegant, though stiff, figure in canary yellow.

That night was one of the rare occasions on which Jessica and I sat down for dinner together. I was relieved to see that she was moderately sober and in a better mood than usual—the following week she was to have an exhibition of her own in a Bayswater gallery. She chattered gaily on in her excitement, not really interested in what

I might have to say, but obviously glad to have someone to talk to. After a time I found myself telling her about the little girl, and how I often walked alone in the park. To my surprise she seemed genuinely touched. Despite the turbulence of our relationship, there were still rare moments of tenderness between us, and when she came to sit beside me I slipped an arm around her and sighed wearily.

"What are we going to do about us, Jess? We can't go on hurting each other the way we do."

She turned to face me, and brushed the hair away from my face. "Do you want a divorce, is that what you're saying?"

Was that what I was saying? The truth was, I didn't think I did want a divorce. If Jessica so despised me for my infertility, how could I be sure that that wasn't the way all women felt about men like me? And despite all she said, Jessica still stayed with me. Perhaps that counted for something. In the end I said, "I don't know, Jess. I just don't know. But you've got to admit we do seem to bring out the worst in each other."

"Not all of the time. Sometimes we're good together. And I've been thinking."

"What have you been thinking?" I asked, when she didn't go on. "Come on, you're cooking something."

"Let's just say it's something that's going to surprise you, and make you very happy."

"And what might that be?"

"I'm not telling. Not yet anyway. But what I will tell you is that despite the way we hurt each other, despite everything I say, I do still lo—"

I put my fingers over her lips. "No, don't say it."

The light went from her eyes and I heard her swallow. "If I can't say it, Alexander, then maybe . . . Well, I know it's been a long time, but maybe you'll let me show you?"

"Oh, Jess, it won't change anything. You know that."

But it did. It changed everything.

It was May 4th. I will always remember the date because it was Jessica's birthday. Fortunately her mother rang me the day before to remind me, thus avoiding what would inevitably have been yet another showdown between us. Her mother was also good enough to suggest what I could buy her.

I was at the Old Bailey all day, engaged in legal arguments for a fraud case. I had thought we might finish in plenty of time for me to get to Christie's, where I was going to bid for a plique-à-jour pendant, but the judge wanted to know far more than a judge normally did in these cases, and it was past four-thirty when we came out. The auction wasn't until six, but I had to call in at chambers on the way to see if there were any returns for the following week. There were, so it was another three quarters of an hour before I got away. I dashed out to Fleet Street and flagged down a passing taxi. The traffic was especially bad, as it always was when it had been raining, and I was already racking my brains for an alternative plan if I didn't get to Christie's on time. However, after a few neat back-doubles and even more near-misses, the driver got me there.

"Hope it's worth it," he said, as I jumped out.

"So do I," I laughed, as I delved into my pocket for the fare. I was on the point of handing it over when my eyes were drawn to someone standing further along the pavement, outside Spinks.

The cab driver leaned over and took the money. "Something the matter, guv?" he called.

When I didn't answer he must have driven off, because I was standing alone, people pushing past me, hurrying to get out of the rain. My briefcase fell against my legs, and still I stood there.

And then I started to run. I wasn't thinking, I wasn't aware of what I was doing or what I intended, I just ran. As I turned into St. James' Square I saw her disappear into Duke of York Street. I think I called out her name, but she couldn't have heard because she didn't turn round. I ran faster, until there was no more than ten yards between us. Then she stopped, took down her umbrella and ran up the steps to Jules' Bar in Jermyn Street.

The bar was crowded, and when I looked round I couldn't see her. Someone behind me vacated a chair, so I sat down. The waitress came and I ordered a Scotch. Five minutes passed, then ten. I looked down at my glass and told myself I had been a fool. I'd been so sure it was her, but even if it had been, what then? Damn it! What kind of idiot was I, running down the street after strange women? My hand curled tightly around the glass, my eyes searching every face that passed.

I finished my drink and got to my feet. My mind, shamed by my foolish behavior, was already turning to Jessica, trying to concoct some excuse for having missed the auction. If I hadn't stood back to let a group of people through from the bar, I might never have seen her.

I could say that at that moment the room seemed to go quiet, but of course it didn't. I could say that my heartbeat changed, but I don't know if that would be true. All I knew was that Elizabeth was there, at the bar, talking to another woman and laughing as she stirred her drink.

I tried to move and found that my feet were like lead weights. Ever since that telegram I'd thought of little else but what I'd do if I saw her again. Now that the moment had come, all I could do was slump back into my chair and order another Scotch.

After a while she picked up her bag and started to walk towards me. She would have walked straight past, but I was on my feet. Feeling my hand on her arm she turned round, and the moment she saw me the blood drained from her face.

"Alexander?"

I tried to smile. "Hello, Elizabeth."

We looked at each other for some time as if unsure whether there might be some mistake, until, suddenly agitated, she turned to see if the woman at the bar was watching us.

"How are you?" I asked.

"Oh, I'm fine. Fine. How are you?"

She wasn't looking at me, and I felt my control beginning to slip away. "Can we talk?" She seemed uncertain and glanced round again, nervously. "Elizabeth."

She must have seen the anguish on my face, because for an instant her eyes softened. "Not now. Christine will recognize you."

"When?"

I could see the indecision reeling through her mind. "Can you wait here? I can come back in half an hour. Christine has to meet someone then."

My heart soared. It was more than I could have hoped for. "I'll wait."

Almost an hour passed before she returned, and in that time I experienced such dread as I have never known before or since. The crowd had thinned out a bit by then, and I had managed to get a table in the corner. I stood up and waved as I saw her come in.

"A white wine, please." She smiled at the waitress as she took the order.

My eyes scanned her face, and it was some time before either of us said anything. In the end she was the first to speak.

"I hardly recognized you." Her hand trembled on the glass as she lifted it to her mouth. "You're um . . . well, you're . . . older."

"Twenty-four."

"Of course. Four years younger than me."

"Almost five," I corrected her with a grin.

She laughed, and I can barely describe the joy I felt. Seven years had passed, seven years in which she had become more beautiful, more contained, somehow more aloof. Her hair was pulled back from her face, showing small amber studs in her ears. Her skin looked smooth and olive, and her dark eyes slanted as she smiled. Everything about her was stylish, from the way she moved her hands and folded one leg neatly over the other, down to the tan suede purse that matched the suede insets of the leather jodhpur suit she wore. She had a sophistication that was almost too perfect, yet when she laughed I saw the Elizabeth I'd known—the Elizabeth I'd loved.

"I've often wondered what happened to you, after . . ." I looked up and saw that she was watching me. "I tried to find you."

"I went back to my family." She was still watching me, the challenge clear in her eyes.

"I was wrong . . . my father, we were wrong about you, weren't we?"

She nodded. "It doesn't matter now, though. It's all in the past."

"Nevertheless . . ."

"How about another glass of wine? My treat."

I laughed. "The answer is, OK, we'll change the subject."

After the waitress had brought the wine we talked for a time about Miss Angrid, united in our guilt that we never wrote to her now. We talked about the weather, about my father becoming Lord Chancellor, and about the lines for the Tutankhamun exhibition that had just opened at the British Museum.

She leaned forward, resting her hands on the table, and our knees touched. She jerked hers away so quickly that for a moment there was an embarrassed silence between us. Then we laughed. I picked up her hand from the table, half expecting her to pull it away, but she didn't. Twisting the wedding band round her finger I asked her how long she'd been married, trying to keep the pain from my voice.

"Almost three years."

"Tell me about him."

She did. As she talked I began to feel as though it had been weeks since we'd last seen each other, rather than years. She sounded bright—too bright—as she told me about Edward and David, and I knew there was something she was hiding. I didn't ask her about it, but a sixth sense told me that whatever it was was causing her pain. Then she made me laugh by telling me about Christine's crush on me.

"Christine? The woman you were with at the bar?"

She nodded. "Quite besotted with you. A good job she didn't see you."

I shrugged. "Not my type. Too round. Besides, women with severe faces frighten the life out of me."

She threw me a look, then went on to tell me about Violet May, who had gazed into a crystal ball and told her that we would meet again. When I raised my eyebrows, she kicked me. And as I gazed into the eyes that I had tried so hard to forget, I could see so clearly how empty my life had been.

She looked away, trying to hide the color that had crept into her cheeks.

"Why did you never get in touch with me again?" I asked.

"For lots of reasons. You were so young, Alexander. You had your whole life ahead of . . ."

"A life I wanted to spend with you. You knew that."

"You could have changed your mind."

I looked down at our hands entwined on the table. "There are a host of platitudes that either one of us might come out with now," I said, "but let's take them as read. Don't let's lie to each other. Yes, perhaps we are different people now, but that doesn't change the past. What I'm trying to say, Elizabeth, is that I want to see you again, that we can't just walk out of here as if nothing has happened."

"No, I don't want that either. But—"

"If we could turn back the clocks, which moment would you choose?" I was half teasing her, and she laughed, but it sounded sad.

"We were on our way to Sark. And I was going to tell you . . ." She shrugged.

Putting my finger under her chin, I tilted her face up to look at me. "What were you going to tell me?"

She smiled and shook her head. "Nothing."

"Will you come there with me now?"

She stared at me.

"Will you?"

She pulled her hands away then, and tucked them into her pockets. Her eyes scanned the room, then fell to her wine. I knew she was going to look anywhere but at me, and I could feel her slipping away.

"Elizabeth. Please, Elizabeth, just listen to me. I probably have no right to say this, but I'm going to say it anyway. I still love you, at least I think I do, but I've got to find out for certain. And if the past seven years have been as much hell for you as they have for me, then for God's sake don't you think we owe it to ourselves to try again?"

She didn't speak for a long time, and when she did she covered her face with her hands. "You don't know how I've dreamed that one day I would hear you say that. How many times I—" She looked up, and through her tears she was laughing. "Seeing you now, touching you, hearing you, I don't need to find out, Alexander, I already know."

I reached up to wipe the tears from her face, and she turned to kiss my hand. "The answer is yes," she whispered. "Yes, I'll come with you."

19

THE INITIAL AWKWARDNESS of meeting again, this time in the cold light of morning, was augmented by Elizabeth's guilt at leaving her daughter. Throughout the short flight to Guernsey she tried hard not to let me see how she was fretting, but by the time we stepped off the plane I could tell she was near tears. Unable to bear her anguish, I took her in my arms and told her I would book us seats on the next flight back to London.

"I want to be with you, Alexander," she said.

"You will be. We can always see each other in London, as often as you like. I just don't want you to be unhappy."

"I'm not. I won't be. I know in my heart that Charlotte will be all right. She's with people who love her, she probably won't even miss me." She tried to laugh and I watched her face as she fought with her emotions. "I can't seem to think. I've wanted this for so long, but now . . ."

"These yours, squire?"

We looked round to see a baggage handler hauling our suitcases off the conveyor belt. It wasn't a particularly educated guess he'd made as everyone else had long since departed. I thanked him, took our cases, and turned back to Elizabeth.

"I'm afraid, Alexander. I'm afraid of the way I feel. And afraid to go back again in case I lose you."

"You won't lose me, darling. I promise, you'll never lose me again. If you want to go home then all you have to do is say so."

For a long time she stared down at our luggage, her hands now firmly stuffed inside her coat pockets, her hair falling around her face. When at last she looked up her eyes were swimming with tears. "I think we'd better hurry if we don't want to miss the boat, don't you?"

I felt such a rush of relief that I dropped the bags and gathered her into my arms.

"Do you suppose we're being dreadfully selfish?" she asked, when we were aboard the ferry.

"Dreadfully," I replied, without a moment's hesitation. "Not to mention irresponsible, self-indulgent . . ."

"You're beginning to remind me of that awful schoolboy I used to know."

"And if you remember, I was always at my very worst when I was with you." She laughed and looked away, but not before I saw the color that had come to her cheeks. "Almost," I added, "as bad as you."

By the time we docked at Creux Harbour the barrier that had risen between us that morning had disappeared. A horse and carriage carried us up over the steep hill towards our hotel, and Elizabeth was almost childlike in her enthusiasm for the rugged beauty that greeted us. Wild spring flowers spread between the trees and hedgerows, creating a carpet of violet blue that swayed in the breeze, and the winding pathways that eased into the long grass promised even more celebrations of undisturbed nature. On either side of the crumbling road, primroses peeped out of the banks, smiling into the face of the sun. I watched Elizabeth as she looked all about her, absorbing her surroundings, her eyes sparkling with joy.

"Oh, Alexander!" she cried, "it's so beautiful!" And I pulled her into my arms . . . As I kissed her it was as if all the knots inside me were unraveling. As if some secret place inside me that had always belonged to her and had lain cold and deserted for seven years was opening up to her. I felt so alive. When finally I let her go, her cheeks were flushed, and I was embarrassed to see that several of the locals were standing at the side of the road, watching us, each one of them sporting a grin that practically hooked onto their ears.

The seventeenth-century hotel was at the top of the wooded hill that led down to Dixcart Bay. The porch was bright with hanging flower baskets, and an old bassett hound lay across the front step, slumbering peacefully in the afternoon sun.

After checking in we followed someone who turned out to be the chef up the rickety stairs to our room. I hadn't missed Elizabeth's quick look as she heard me announce us as Mr. and Mrs. Belmayne.

When the chef finally departed, after proudly pointing out every eccentric nook and cranny of our room, which was made even more bewildering by the oddness of decor, Elizabeth went to the windows and pulled back the curtains. I went to stand beside her, and it was as I slipped my arms around her waist that I realized how very nervous she was now that we were alone. I let her go, but kept her hand in mine as we stood looking together over the gardens that sloped down to the bluebell woods beyond.

I sensed her relief when I suggested we take a walk, and once outside in the crisp May sunshine, her lighthearted mood returned. We wandered down the steep, tree-lined path to the bay where we stood for a long time, watching the tide as it roared against the cliffs. Five or six yachts bobbed on the horizon but otherwise there was no sign of human life; we could have been the only people in the world.

Feeling her hand slip into mine I looked down at her and smiled.

"Are you really here?" she whispered.

I brushed the hair from her face and touched my lips against her nose. "Yes, my love, I'm really here."

By the time we returned to the hotel, night was drawing in. I carried our drinks outside and we sat in the darkening courtyard huddled into our coats, watching the shifting shadows, listening to the stirrings of invisible night sounds.

We talked long into the evening, telling each other about our lives. I told her how Lizzie had sent the telegram that I had thought was from her; "I wish it had been," she said, and I saw tears fill her eyes.

"You haven't said up until now, and maybe it's none of my

business, but where did you tell Jessica you were going?" she asked, after a while.

"Just, away."

"But wasn't she curious to know where?"

I shrugged. "If she was, she didn't ask." I didn't add that we had had a blazing row when I had arrived home late, without her birthday pendant. In fact, it was because of the fight that I hadn't had to elaborate on where I was going. I merely packed a bag and told her I'd be back in a week. Her parting words, screamed from the top of her lungs, had been: "Don't bother!"

"And you?" I asked. "What did you tell your husband?"

"I didn't have to. He's in New York at the moment." At the mention of her husband, she seemed to close herself off. I said nothing, understanding that this was a part of her life that was hers alone. Then, as the moment passed, she was smiling again, and asking me about Henry.

She laughed when I told her the incredible story of his bigamous marriage. "But now it's all worked out perfectly," she sighed wistfully, when I'd finished. "And when will he be marrying Caroline?"

"Sooner than they intended. She's pregnant, or so he told me when I called him last night."

"You spoke to him last night? Did you tell him about . . ."

"Yes."

She sighed again. "So Henry Clive is going to become a father. It hardly seems credible. I still think of him as the boy I used to know. I'm glad he's happy." She turned in her seat. "And you, Alexander, are you happy?"

I picked her hand up from the table. "Now I am. Yes."

"Me too."

I lifted her hand to my lips. "What are you thinking?" I asked, when she had remained silent for several minutes.

She shook her head. "I'm sorry, but I can't help it. I was thinking about Charlotte, wishing she was here, wondering if she's all right. I suppose it's thinking about Henry, and oh . . . I don't know . . ."

I squeezed her hand. "Don't be sorry. Tell me about her. How old is she?"

Slowly she entwined her hands round mine and stared down

at them for a long time. "She's beautiful, she's naughty, she's every-thing in the world to me, just like . . ." She looked up with a quick smile. "Was that your stomach telling us it's time for dinner?"

I laughed and tweaked her nose, and at the same time was ashamed of my relief that she had gone no further. I didn't want to confront my feelings about Charlotte. It seemed ludicrous to be jealous of a child, but I knew I was. Even worse were the feelings I experienced whenever I thought of Charlotte's father. Unbidden images of the three of them, and their togetherness, were already eating away at me like a cancer. And the fact that he had been able to give Elizabeth something I could never give her razored my mind.

When we got upstairs Elizabeth threw her coat on the bed and went to close the curtains. When she turned round she stopped as she saw me standing against the door, watching her in the semidark-ness; she started to speak, then stopped, and I held her gaze with my own. All I wanted just then was to look at her, and in the silence neither of us moved.

"Standing there like that you remind me of the Alexander I knew when he was seventeen." There was a slight catch in her voice.

When I didn't answer she gave an uncertain laugh, then cov-ered her face with her hands. "Oh God, I can't believe this is happening. Tell me I'm not dreaming, Alexander. Hold me, please hold me."

At the note of desperation in her voice my heart twisted, and taking her in my arms I held her close. "My darling, oh my darling. God, how I've needed you. How I've wanted you."

I drew back to look at her. "Don't let me go," she whispered. "Don't ever let me go." She lifted her mouth and as I covered her lips with my own I felt her begin to tremble.

Wave after wave of longing swept through my body, and when, minutes later, she stepped naked into my arms, my fear of impotency was over. I ran my hands over her back, and through her heavy hair, piling it onto her head; I pulled her face to mine, mold-ing my lips and my tongue into her mouth. She stood against me, pressing the length of her body against mine, until gently I lifted her into my arms and laid her on the bed.

Slowly our bodies began to move together. She whispered as

she kissed me and I whispered too, making up for all the years I had been unable to tell her how much I loved her. Her skin was so soft and I held her close, as if afraid she might slip away. I had forgotten what it was truly to make love with a woman, when passion was born of love, not lust; when the mouth you were kissing was the only mouth you would ever want to kiss, and the body that molded into yours was the one without which yours would never be complete. "Elizabeth, Elizabeth." I said her name, over and over, never moving my lips from hers.

The hazy light of dawn was beginning to penetrate the windows when finally, exhausted by the depth of our love, we fell asleep.

Running away, expecting everything to be the same after so long, was madness of course. But madness or not, it was not the present that seemed unreal to us, but the years we had been apart. To have the chance to tell each other at last how we'd felt when we parted, and how we'd thought of each other in the years that followed, was like a gift from heaven. Elizabeth had changed, so had I, and the changes sometimes delighted us, sometimes saddened us. But there was no awkwardness between us, everything we did felt as natural and as easy as if we had always been together. It wasn't that either of us had forgotten what we had left behind, it was simply that it didn't seem to matter. This time belonged to us. I watched her, the slant of her eyes, the slow curl of her smile and the gentle rise and fall of her breasts. The sense of recognition I had as she flicked her hair from her face, as she used her elegant fingers to emphasize what she was saying, as I watched the easy movements of her long legs when we walked about the island—was mesmerizing. Just listening to her as she laughed and talked, or watching her eyes darken with love, rushed warmth through my veins.

The sea spread like wings on either side of us as we cycled north to Greve de la Ville, La Banquette and Eperquerie Landing. The road—which was no more than a cart track—was rough, and Elizabeth, not one of the world's greatest cyclists, swore as she plowed into one pothole after another. I yelled with laughter when she threw her bike into a hedge, declaring she would be more comfortable on a three-legged camel. I managed to catch her as she started to stomp off up the road, and spun her round. Then, making sure no one was in sight, I rubbed my hands soothingly over her buttocks and thighs, asking if that felt any better. Her eyes were bright as she answered.

The only sounds were those of the birds and the sea. As we rode on, a sweet fragrance of coconut wafted gently by on the breeze and the occasional cow favored us with a lazy glance. Now and again we stopped, on the pretext of looking at something unusual or resting our legs, but really all we wanted to do was touch each other, and kiss.

We climbed down to the Boutiques Caves, where we sat for a while watching the waves. Elizabeth got up and strolled to the mouth of a cave to look inside. All around us there was an air of mystical romance. If you close your eyes long enough, I told her, you can hear the ghosts of smugglers hauling their booty into the bay. She stood quietly for several minutes, straining her ears for the sounds. With one eye partially open I watched her and tried not to laugh.

"Aar Haar! And what sort of contraband 'ave we 'ere?" It was my best smuggler's voice, and scooping her up in my arms I ran with her into the cave.

"Oh help! Put me down, put me down, you beast."

I did, and she threw herself against the wall of the cave. "Oh no, please don't ravish me, I beg you!"

"All right." I doffed an invisible cap. "If you don't wish to be ravished, my lady, then far be it from me to press my attentions."

"Alexander!"

"You called, my lady?" I sighed wearily and turned back. "Do I take it you want to be ravished, my lady?"

She nodded, and fell into my arms, almost speechless with laughter.

We roamed beaches I have now forgotten the names of, carrying our shoes and gasping as the icy sea washed over our toes. So often I felt her eyes on me, and when I turned to her she would laugh and throw her arms round my neck. And then I would watch her—laughing, frowning, running away from me, gasping for breath as she looked back to find that I was nowhere in sight. And when she came looking I would spring out from behind my rock and topple her to the ground, drowning her shrieks with kisses.

Later we rode horses out onto the cliffs that overlooked Dixcart
Bay. Far beneath us the sun sparkled across the sea, and behind,
keeping a lonely vigil, was Jespillière House. We walked round it,
peering in through the windows. It looked as if it had been deserted
for many years. We decided we would buy it, and began a game of
what we would do when it was ours. We would buy two rocking
chairs for the veranda, where we could sit on balmy nights watching
the sun go down over the sea. And facing the middle window
upstairs we would set our bed, so that each morning we could look
out and watch the day stirring into life. Elizabeth wanted chintz
curtains, I wanted plain. She wanted oak panels, I wanted walnut.
She wanted grey carpet, I wanted green. She wanted four children,
I wanted . . .

I smiled, then taking the reins of my horse, I led it to the edge
of the meadow. There was a gap in the gorse, so letting my horse
go to graze freely, I dropped down onto a ledge in the cliff. To one
side I found an old stone seat that had been carved into the rocks,
and sat down.

Our little game of plans for the future, which had started so
innocently, had ended by serving as a bitter reminder to me. I asked
myself what I was doing here. Hadn't I hurt Elizabeth enough
before, without needing to do it all over again? Perhaps I should tell
her now, before her dreams became so real that she believed them.
But how could I? What we had together, here, so far from the harsh
realities of our everyday lives, was too perfect to shatter. And, just
like her, I wanted to imagine our children playing on the veranda,
riding their ponies in the meadow, calling to us to watch them. I
needed my dreams too. What did it matter if they could never be?
For now they were all we had, and I couldn't take them away from
her. And though I hated myself for the lies, I would deal with them
later, when we were far away from here.

I ran my tongue over my lips, tasting the bitter salt that had
carried on the wind from the sea. I could hear her picking her way
through the undergrowth towards me, and I dashed my hand across
my eyes. I hated this weakness—this curse of infertility that made
a grown man cry tears of self-pity.

She came to sit beside me and linked her fingers through mine.
Somewhere in the distance a dog began to bark, discordant against
the background sough of the waves. Seagulls cawed, and somewhere

the engine of a speedboat roared into life. Then all was still again.

"Alexander? Is everything all right?"

"All right? Of course it is." Down in the bay two people were rowing out to their trimaran and I leaned forward to watch them boarding.

"You're very quiet suddenly."

"Just soaking up the atmosphere."

She waited. "Alexander, you're not being honest with me."

I sat back. How could I have thought that I would be able to fob her off with inanities? I lifted a lock of her hair and wound it round my finger, looking into her face and seeing bewilderment and fear where earlier there had been only love. I smiled.

"I know there's something," she said, her eyes searching mine. "Darling, please tell me."

I slipped an arm around her. "There's nothing. Only the fact that I love you so much it frightens me."

For a long time she looked into my eyes. I met her gaze, willing myself not to look away. Then slowly she lifted her hands, and placing them on either side of my face, she kissed me, slowly, and with the greatest tenderness I had ever known.

On the second day I took her to Little Sark. It was a steep and difficult climb down the cliffs, but when we finally reached the bottom, I knew I had been right to come. This would be our special place, this tiny pool—Venus Pool—that was scooped deep into the rocks, hiding away beneath a hanging boulder. The water was clear and blue so that we could see the pebbles at the bottom. And behind us the sea roared onto the surrounding cliffs, growling as if to protect its young. The sun was hot and we lay down beside the pool, holding hands and feeling the breeze sweep gently over our faces. Every sense was touched by nature.

After a while I opened my eyes. I could tell from her steady breathing that Elizabeth was sleeping. I turned onto my side to look at her, and as my eyes roamed slowly over her face I felt my heart swell. Her olive skin was smooth beneath my fingers as I lightly touched her cheeks. She was the most beautiful woman I had ever known. But it wasn't only her physical beauty, there was another kind of beauty too; it was what made her the woman she was. I thought of Jessica then. She would never understand why I loved Elizabeth so much. I wondered if she would be looking for me now. Would she care at all where I was? My marriage had been a lie from the start, and I knew now what a fool I had been to think I could use it to forget Elizabeth. What a mess I had made of all our lives!

"Alexander, come down from there." I had climbed the rocks while she slept, and was lying on the boulder that overhung the pool, looking up at the sky.

"No." I smiled to myself as I heard her laugh.

"Please come down."

"I can't. The tide's practically in, there's no way through. I'm afraid you're stranded."

"What!"

"I tried to wake you but you were snoring so loudly it drowned out my voice."

Her voice was bubbling with laughter as she answered. "I don't snore! And I'm not stranded either."

"How do you know?"

"Because if the tide really was coming in, which it's not, you wouldn't have left me here."

"I wouldn't?" I raised myself on one elbow. "And what makes you so sure of that?"

"You love me too much, that's what."

"Do I?"

She nodded. "Yep. In fact, I bet if I asked you to prove it by jumping into the pool right now, fully clothed, you'd do it."

"Ask me."

She asked.

"No," I said, and she burst out laughing. I got to my feet and descended by the dry route.

"I missed you," she said, as I put my arms around her.

I lifted my hand to her chin and stroked my thumb over her face. "Shall I tell you ten reasons why Miss Sorrill is the best?" I whispered. "One, because she looks lovely when she smiles. Two, because she says outrageous things. Three . . ."

I laughed as I saw the look on her face. "You—you know about that?"

I nodded. "I should, I wrote it."

"*You* wrote it! But I always thought it was Mark Devenish! Why didn't you ever . . ."

"Sssh," I whispered. "Just kiss me."

When I let her go she began to unbutton her dress, her eyes holding mine. I watched her until, naked, she walked to the edge of the pool. All around her shapeless formations of rock pushed against the horizon, and set against that harsh and uncompromising background the silhouette of her body appeared infinitely vulnerable. She glanced over her shoulder and smiled at me, but I was holding my breath at the vision of incomparable beauty. Then she was gone. The water parted and I waited for her to resurface. When she did, her hair floated round her and she smiled and waved. Then she drifted onto her back, presenting her body to me, the full breasts caressed by ripples, the thatch of black pubic hair silky at the join of her long legs. She was watching me watching her. Then taking off my clothes, I slipped into the pool and we swam together.

Looking back now, I think we both knew how selfish we were being, but at the time we were so much in love that nothing else seemed to matter. I listened for hours while she told me about the fairground and Violet May. Then I basked in her admiration as I told her about the cases I had been involved in, shamelessly exaggerating my successes. I'm sure she knew what I was doing, but nevertheless allowed me to wander on in my own fantasy world— until, with an ear-shattering snore, she brought me back to earth again.

Every day we strolled along the narrow high street, watching the women as they shopped and chatted. Elizabeth often stopped to talk to them, and the way she could make them flush with pleasure, or laugh, made me want to burst with pride. She was interested in them all; it was plain to see that people were a joy to her.

"She told me it's her anniversary so she's going to try out a new recipe tonight," she said, as she waved a dumpy, smiling woman off on her bicycle.

"I heard," I remarked dryly.

"Oh, you weren't bored, were you?" she teased.

"Stiff."

She laughed, and ran on ahead. When I caught up with her she was sitting on a wall, waiting, so I sat down beside her. "Were you really bored?" she said.

"No. But I was wondering. Is it enough, do you think?"

"Enough?"

"For these women. Do you think they're happy, you know, living here on this island. Or do you think they want more out of life? More than just looking after a man?"

She turned to face me. "Alexander, don't tell me that on top of everything else, you're a feminist too?"

I laughed. "If I am, then I'm definitely still in the closet! But tell me, you're a wife and mother. Is it enough for you?"

"What you really want to know is, am I one of the lesbian brigade, as you so chauvinistically call it, that Jessica belongs to?"

"Yes."

"No, I'm not one of them. But that doesn't mean I don't agree with a lot of what they say. I just think they go about things in the wrong way, that's all."

"So how would you go about it?"

"Me! My darling, I have neither the education nor the rhetoric to be a leader of women, but I can tell you this: they're missing the point. OK, what they're achieving materially and socially is right, admirable. But the aggression they use only makes people hostile to their cause—women included. It's a bit like the old fable about the wind and sun, isn't it? It was the sun and the warmth that made the man take his coat off."

"And who says she doesn't have the education or the rhetoric?"

She pinched me. "But there's another reason why I wouldn't do for them. You see, I'm hopelessly and incurably in love with a man, and that's simply not allowed."

Though I knew I had never been so happy, dark thoughts were never far from my mind. I knew I should tell her, I even tried to persuade myself that she would understand, but I was a coward. I kept remembering Jessica's face when she told me, and I knew I wouldn't be able to bear it if my infertility was the reason Elizabeth and I said good-bye. I hated myself for the plans I allowed us to make, our undying promises that we would never be parted again, when I knew that as soon as we left the island it would all be over. Sometimes when I made love to her I was violent, but I couldn't help myself—my frustration at the futility of our lovemaking overwhelmed me. I knew there were times when she sensed that things weren't as they should be between us, but whenever she tried to talk about it, I would laugh and tell her she was imagining it. But as the days passed I felt my love for her turning to a pain so excruciating that I thought it would choke me.

And then there was only one more day, one more night, before fantasy must give way to reality. Elizabeth didn't want to go to Venus Pool again, she said the pain of leaving it would be too great to bear.

Dixcart Bay was deserted, and we sat down on the pebbles to watch the yachts sail in over the skyline. Later other people wandered onto the beach, an old couple walking their dog, teenagers strolling hand in hand, boys in a boat, rowing out of the bay and disappearing from sight. Neither of us spoke, we were both too aware of our looming departure. A man about my own age walked to the edge of the sea. His jeans were rolled up to the knees, and he tested the temperature with a bare foot, then turning, he waved to somebody behind us. A boy and a girl, neither of them older than six, sped towards him, and their mother followed, laughing as her husband gathered the children into his arms and swung them round. Tentatively, they ventured into the waves, the children shrieking at first, then gaining enough courage to plunge their bodies into the surf, and finally trying to splash their parents. For a long time the four of them played, oblivious to the rest of the world, and Elizabeth and I watched. Then the little boy fell. I felt my body stiffen and jerked myself up. But his father was there, ready to pick him up and comfort him. I relaxed and lay back again. It was several minutes before I realized that Elizabeth had turned her attention to me.

"Alexander, what is it that's making you so unhappy?"

"You have to ask?"

"No, there's more. I've sensed it ever since we arrived here."

I started to get to my feet, but she pulled me back. "Alexander, please. Don't shut me out. If there's to be any future for us, you must tell me what's troubling you."

I already knew the truth of what she was saying. Tears were gathering in her eyes and I felt my own stinging too. Then I looked round me again and knew that if we were to say good-bye anywhere, then it must be here. Here, where we had known love again.

"Darling," I faltered. She said nothing, only took my hand and waited. For a time I was afraid to speak, afraid to tell her how I had cheated her by making promises I could never keep. And I was afraid to lose her—which I would in the end, no matter what she said, because my inability to have children, together with my jealousy of the child she already had by another man, would tear us apart. "Elizabeth." The family were moving away from the sea, chasing one another to the smugglers' arch. Gently she turned my face back to hers, and waited for me to go on. "I should have told you the truth from the beginning, Elizabeth, but I was a coward. I wanted you so badly that I told myself it would be all right in the end. But it can't be. We can't be together, it's just not possible."

I felt her fingers tense as I spoke, but couldn't bring myself to look at her.

"Is it because of Jessica?" she said, after a while.

I shook my head.

"Because I'm married?"

"No. Though God knows, that should be enough."

"Then what is it, Alexander? Tell me." There was desperation in her voice.

I took her face between my hands and for an instant I saw Jessica's mouth laughing back at me, ridiculing me. I let her go and leaned forward. "I'm infertile, Elizabeth. It's why Jessica has never conceived. I am sterile, empty, useless, call it what you like, but I can't give you any children. I know you'll say it doesn't matter, but it will. Living with you day after day, watching you and knowing that I . . ."

"Alexander! Stop! Stop! How can you think that would ever make a difference? How little you must think of me to believe that I would be capable of turning away from you over something like that. Something that's not even . . ."

"Please, Elizabeth, don't make this any harder. I know what you're going to say next, that I will come to love your daughter as my own. Well, I can't live with your daughter, Elizabeth, knowing she is the child of another man. I know I'm a coward, but I can't do it."

"Alexander, look at me."

When I didn't, she pulled me round to face her. "No, stop," she said, as I tried to speak. "Stop and listen to me. You're not infertile, Alexander, do you hear me? You can't be."

"There's no point in denying it. Jessica . . . there were tests . . ." I didn't want to go on.

She started to speak, then stopped. She tried again, then threw herself away from me and ran off across the beach.

I let her go, as again I saw Jessica, heard her laughing even, but this time Elizabeth was there too. She had turned away from me, as I'd known she would. But God, how I had prayed she wouldn't.

She was sitting beside a rock not far away, her head buried in her hands. She looked up as my shadow fell over her. I was surprised to see that she wasn't crying, though her face looked ravaged. I sat down beside her and held out my hand for hers. She took it.

Staring straight ahead I started to speak. I told her then about Jessica, about the bitter fights we had, and the cruel way I had tormented her during the first years of our marriage. And I told her how, when Jessica found I was infertile, she had taken her revenge in the scorn and contempt she threw at me, knowing that I wanted a child more than anything else.

When I had finished I raised her hand to my mouth and kissed it softly. "So, my darling, you can see now what my infertility has done to me and Jessica. I couldn't bear that to happen to us."

I turned to look at her and saw that tears were streaming silently down her face. "Oh my God, what have I done?" she whispered. "What have I done to you?" She put her hand over my mouth as I started to speak. "There's something you must know, Alexander. Something I should have told you a long time ago. I could have saved you all this pain. But I didn't know what to do, please believe me, I was so young then, and so were you, and I didn't know what to do for the best. I'm sorry, my darling . . ."

"Elizabeth . . . ?"

"It's Charlotte, Alexander, she's . . . Charlotte is six years old."

At first I didn't move. The sounds of everyday life continued, but all I could hear was the echo of Elizabeth's words. I was too stunned to speak or to think, and feeling myself go weak, I leaned back against the rock and closed my eyes.

How hurt she must have been to shield herself from me like that. And Jessica, how I must have hurt her too, for her to lie to me the way she had. I looked at Elizabeth and for a moment I didn't understand her. All the times she could have told me in the past week, and hadn't. I had a daughter. I closed my eyes again as tears slid unchecked over my face. I felt her arms go round me, cradling me like a child. But I couldn't respond, my heart was numb. "I'm sorry," she said, over and over. "I should have told you before. I'm sorry, my darling."

It was a long time later, when the tears had dried on my cheeks and the sun was sinking towards the horizon, that I was finally able to speak. "Tell me about her, Elizabeth. Tell me everything about her."

The following morning dawned dull and grey. It was the first miserable weather there had been, and Elizabeth sat at the window looking out at the rain.

The night before we had been closer than I had ever dreamed possible. This morning we were quiet. In less than an hour Jack Serle would come with his horse and carriage to take us to the ferry. Already Elizabeth was wrapped up against the weather.

The clock ticked monotonously in the corner. Elizabeth got up and said she was going for a walk. She wanted to go alone.

I waited for her in the lounge, thinking about her and wondering what the future would bring. When it was almost time to leave I went to the window and looked out, but there was no sign of her. The door opened and Jack Serle came in. He was early, and went off to the kitchen for a cup of tea.

I started to pace the room, looking at my watch. Where was she? Had something happened to her? The wind was vicious this morning, and the sea. Had she slipped and . . . ?

I went outside. The rain was heavier now, and the sound of the wind, raging through the trees that cloistered the hotel, seemed sinister. I listened, straining my ears, as if expecting to hear her.

And then suddenly I knew where she was, and I knew that I must go to her. Circling the hotel, I strode quickly through the garden behind, oblivious of the driving rain, only knowing that I had to get to her. Then I was running, through the orchard, over the stile, past Jespillière House and across the meadow. There was the barely hidden gap in the yellow gorse. I pushed through and out on to the cliff edge.

She was a small figure huddled into the stone seat, her hair plastered to her face, alone in her grief. I held her close.

"We will come back, Alexander, won't we? Promise me that one day we will come back."

"I promise you, my darling. With all my heart, I promise you."

How could either of us known then what was to come?

Elizabeth

20

I WAS TRYING very hard not to look at my watch. Every muscle in my body was tensed to the point of breaking, and my heart thumped more rapidly as each minute passed. One o'clock on Friday at Jules' Bar, he had said.

I looked around at the lunchtime drinkers. A party in the corner that had sung "Happy Birthday" a moment ago; a group of men standing at the bar, talking too loudly; office girls, businessmen. I turned back to my drink. He's not going to come, I know he's not going to come. The words beat a tattoo on my brain.

A shadow fell over me, and the moment I saw Henry's face I felt the blood drain from my own."

"Elizabeth."

I tried to smile, but my heart was in my throat and I dug my fingers deep into the palms of my hands in an effort to keep calm.

He sat down. "How are you?"

"Oh, I'm fine. How are you?"

"Yes, I'm fine."

I rushed on. "Alexander told me all about Caroline. I'm very happy for you, Henry. When's it to be?" I gave him a big smile, as if by doing so I could stop him from delivering the news that was written in every line of his face.

"Next week, actually."

Neither of us said anything after that, as the waitress took our order then came back with the drinks.

"He's not coming, is he?" I whispered.

He looked down at his hands, bunched together on the table in front of him. Slowly, he shook his head.

The denial rushed at me with such force that it snatched my breath. It couldn't be true. This wasn't happening. Any minute now I would wake up and Alexander would be walking through the door. All I had to do was open my eyes.

When I did, Henry was still sitting beside me and I wanted to die. "Is it Jessica? Is he going back to her?"

"He has to, Elizabeth."

I didn't want to hear the compassion in his voice, I only wanted this to stop.

"There was an accident. While you were away. Lady Bel, Alexander's mother, was killed." I closed my eyes. "Jessica was driving. She's in the hospital. The doctors say she'll be all right, but it'll be some time." He waited a moment, then went on. "There's something else, Elizabeth." I looked up. "After the accident, Jessica had a miscarriage."

Again I closed my eyes. The bitter irony, after all the lies she had told him, was too much to bear.

"Did you know Alexander thought he was . . . ?"

I nodded. "Why did she lie to him like that?"

He didn't answer and I could feel the pain dragging me down, swirling through me in relentless waves.

"He told me about Charlotte."

"Where is he now?"

"With his father."

"She's very like him, you know, Henry. She's got his curly black hair, it even falls over her face the way his does. And her eyes. They're grey, but she has tiny specks of blue in them. She knows how to use them, of course, just like he does. You know, she even laughs like . . . Henry, I don't know if I can bear this."

He reached out for my hand. "Come along, let's get you out of here."

He took me back to his flat in Eaton Square where we talked until it was dark outside. I had stopped crying by then, but I knew that in the months that stretched emptily and endlessly ahead there would be many more tears. I had lost him once, and survived, but I didn't know if I could do it again. I didn't know if I even wanted to.

Henry handed me my coat and tried again to persuade me to let him drive me home. I shook my head. I needed some time alone before I could face Charlotte.

"He wants to see you, when all this is over. He's asked me to find out where you live."

I looked into Henry's face, and felt the years slip away. It was as if we were all back at Foxton's and Henry had come to tell me that Alexander wanted me to be in their play. I shook my head. "No, Henry. It'll only mean more pain for those who love us." For the first time I was thinking about Edward.

"What about Charlotte?"

"One day I will tell her about him. She'll come to find him, I know she will. Just ask him to be patient."

He walked with me to the door. "Henry, please tell him . . ." I stopped and looked into his face. His eyes were clouded and I guessed, in his own way, he was suffering too. "Nothing, it doesn't matter, he'll know anyway."

I can't describe the way I felt in the weeks that followed, I only knew that the pain was more intense, more agonizing than I had known anything could be. I thought about him day and night, reliving every moment we'd spent together, and asked myself a thousand times why God was punishing us like this. But even as I asked the question, I still refused to believe that this was the end.

It was this denial of the truth that proved to be my downfall.

As I carried out the daily tasks that were expected of me, the certainty that Alexander and I would be reunited grew in my mind until everything I did was in preparation for his coming. I stocked the library with law books and had the Renaissance paintings in the long gallery replaced with Impressionists—Christine scoured the auction rooms, armed with lists of what to look out for. Westmoor was suddenly buzzing with builders, decorators, gardeners. I bullied them along, they must be finished by the time Alexander came . . .

"But it's got to be done," I said, when Edward told me I was going to wear myself out if I didn't slow down.

He smiled. "I'm going to Florence at the weekend. How about taking a break and coming with me?"

I looked at him, aghast. Couldn't he see I was far too busy to go to Florence, why didn't he take Charlotte instead?

But Charlotte didn't want to go, either. At least, she did want to go, it was just that she didn't want to leave me behind.

"Leave me behind?" I laughed. "If nothing else, it'll be good to have you out from under my feet. Why aren't you playing with your friends?"

She looked up at me with her big eyes and I felt a surge of impatience. "Honestly, Charlotte, I just don't know what . . ."

"Why are you always getting at me? What have I done?"

"Done? You haven't done anything. Oh Charlotte, you're impossible. Why don't you take the horses out over the downs, they could do with the exercise, and so could you."

"We took them this morning."

"Did you?" I laughed. "I don't know, there seems to be so much on my mind lately . . ."

"Can we do something together, Mum? Just me and you? You know, like we used to."

"Can't you see I'm busy, Charlotte? He'll be here soon and I . . ."

"Who'll be here soon? You keep saying that."

I stared at her.

"Who, Mum? Who's coming?"

"Why don't you run along and find Edward if you're going to Florence?"

I found her later, sitting on her bed combing her doll's hair. She looked as if she'd been crying and turned away when she saw it was me. I had to swallow my irritation. "How would you like to come up to London with me at the weekend? We'll go to the theater." Alexander lived in Belgrave Square. I'd go there, tell him everything would be ready soon.

"But what about Edward? He wants us to go to Florence."

"We won't tell him. We'll wait until he's gone, then sneak off to London without telling anyone. Well, I suppose we'd better tell Canary. In fact, why don't we take her with us? Run along and ask her, darling, I've got a lot to finish off here, and the designer will be coming back again this evening."

We saw an unmemorable matinée at the Savoy, drove out to Hampton Court, tore round the zoo and went to hamburger bars and cinemas. I didn't go to Belgrave Square, it wasn't time yet. But I'd go soon.

When we got back to Westmoor Edward was still away, and the delivery men were waiting to install the apparatus in the gym. I supervised them as they unpacked, making sure everything I had ordered for Alexander was there. At four o'clock I dragged Charlotte along to visit Miss Barsby who lived in a cottage just outside the estate. Charlotte loathed the old woman and did very little to hide it. I watched with mounting annoyance as she delivered her monosyllabic replies to Miss Barsby's questions. I stood it for half an hour then, making my apologies to Miss Barsby, I took Charlotte by the hand and led her out to the car.

"You're a nasty, spoiled little girl," I said, once Miss Barsby had gone back inside. "She's a lonely old lady who looks forward to your visits, and all you can do is sulk. Next week you'll spend the whole afternoon with her, and talk to her properly. Do you hear me?"

Charlotte sustained a mutinous silence until we pulled up outside the house. I leaned across and threw open her door. "Go to your room. I'll deal with you later."

"You're always picking on me these days. I wish I'd gone to Florence with Edward, he's much nicer than you. You're horrible."

She'd run into the house before I could catch her, and as the decorator was bearing down on me with yet more curtain samples for the new bathroom, I had to let it go for the moment. But it wasn't forgotten, and the next day, although I had promised her she could go with Jeffrey to collect Edward from the airport, I made her stay in her room.

The new tennis courts were ready, so I challenged David to a game before lunch.

"You mean you've got the time?" he teased.

"Don't say it like that. It's hard work getting this house together."

As we strolled down to the courts Charlotte was watching us

from her window. David waved out, but when I turned round she shrank back. The sun was already beating down, it was no day for a child to be cooped up in a bedroom, but when David started to plead on her behalf I shoved a racket into his hand and told him to play.

I wasn't sure whether it was the heat, or the fact that I hadn't had any breakfast that morning, but after four games I started to feel dizzy. And when I missed a fourth service David asked if anything was the matter.

After that I didn't remember anything until I woke up in my bed with the doctor gazing down at me. I tried to struggle up, but he pushed me back. Then I heard Charlotte, sobbing outside the door. The doctor let her in and she ran into my arms.

"Are you going to be all right, Mum?" she said.

"Of course I am, darling. I fainted, that's all. And it serves me right, I shouldn't have been so awful to you. Will you forgive me?"

She nodded and I started to get out of bed, reminding her that we had the summer fête to organize. At that moment the doctor came back, and when he saw me hunting round for my dressing-gown he started to shake his head. "Back to bed for you, young lady," he said. "Your brother-in-law has been filling me in on all you've been doing lately and—"

"Oh doctor, honestly. It's an extremely hot day, and you know what they say, a little hard work never killed anyone. So I'd like to get up now, if you don't mind."

The doctor put his hand on Charlotte's head. "How about going downstairs and asking Mary to bring us up a nice cup of tea?"

Once she'd gone the doctor pulled back the bedclothes and pointed to the bed. "In you go," he said, "it's about time you and I had a bit of a talk."

I didn't get up again until early September. During those weeks I couldn't bear anyone near me except Charlotte, but even when she was there all I could do was stare at her and stroke her hair. I knew I was frightening her, but I couldn't bring myself to tell her what the doctor had told me. I couldn't even think of it myself. I had sworn him to secrecy, telling him I wanted to deal with this in my own time and in my own way.

Despite my breakdown, during this time I noticed that Edward was changing towards me. It was as if he had put a barrier between us. He was still as kind and solicitous as ever, but there was a ring to his voice I didn't recognize. How much he understood about the reason for my breakdown, I didn't know, but he was away more often than he was at home, and as far as I could tell Christine had all but taken over the daily running of his life. He talked only about her when he came to my room, and wouldn't allow me to speak at all. It was breaking my heart to see how much he was suffering, but there was nothing I could do.

Then, for no accountable reason, I woke up one September morning feeling I couldn't wait to face the world again.

Everyone looked up as I walked into the breakfast room, and the sunny smile I beamed at them so took them by surprise that Jeffrey, who was pouring the tea, allowed it to overflow into Christine's saucer.

Edward stood up and put his arms round me. His kind face looked down into mine, and I saw the lines deepen around his eyes as he smiled. They were more pronounced now than they had been and I knew I was to blame. I reached up to touch his face, then pulling him closer, lifted my mouth for him to kiss me.

"We must all go out for dinner," I announced, pulling up a chair. "Tonight. It will be a belated celebration of Edward's birthday. What do you say?"

Still looking somewhat bemused, they nodded. "Yes," Charlotte echoed, giving her egg a bashing. "Can I come too?"

"You have to be up for school in the morning, darling."

"Oh, Mum!" she groaned.

"Let her come," Edward said, tousling her hair. "We can always make it an early dinner."

"Yippee! Will you let me choose the wine, David?"

I looked at her aghast. "The wine?"

"I'm afraid it's her latest hobby," David admitted. "She heard Edward discussing it with someone on the phone, and insisted he teach her. The happy task befell me. No, no, don't worry, we haven't got around to the tasting bit yet."

I shook my head and laughed. What would Alexander make of her? But I mustn't allow myself to think of that.

‡

203

We arrived home just before ten that night, after going to the French restaurant in the village. Charlotte fell asleep in the car on the way back, and drowsily insisted that Edward take her up to bed. David poured the brandy while we waited for Edward to join us. He was a long time in coming.

"I had to tell her the story of Osiris and Isis again," he explained, as he came to sit beside me.

"Who?"

"The great Egyptian love story of an ancient god and his goddess."

"You must tell it to me sometime," I said.

"Don't, or he will," Christine warned. "But if he does, get him to tell you all the bits I'll bet he leaves out with Charlotte, like how Osiris' body was cut into fourteen pieces, and the only bit missing when they put him together again was the phallus."

"I don't leave those bits out at all," Edward objected.

"Don't you?" I laughed. "Didn't she want to know what a phallus was?"

"She most certainly did, so I told her. Then she asked me if I had one, and then she wanted to know if she could see it. So I explained that it was a part of the body people didn't show each other until they got married."

"Oh God, Edward, you're the limit," Christine said.

"You haven't heard the best part yet. After complaining bitterly at how long she'd have to wait for that, she went off to inspect her dolls. Canary caught her. I tell you the whole thing was worth it just to see Canary's face when Charlotte said 'phallus.' "

I waited for the laughter to subside, then clutching my glass nervously and trying hard to sound casual, I said, "If Charlotte was to have a little brother, she wouldn't have to wait quite so long, would she?"

I should have sensed the mood change then, but I didn't. I looked from Edward to Christine to David, not seeing the emptiness of their smiles. "That's why I wanted us all to go out to dinner," I went on, "but I didn't want to say anything with Charlotte there—I thought I would tell her on our own."

"Tell her what, darling?" There was an edge to Edward's voice that in my excitement I chose to ignore.

"That I'm going to have a baby."

I heard Christine gasp, but she was looking at Edward. So was David. Their faces were white.

"It's due in February," I added lamely.

There was a long silence. I turned to Edward and saw he was staring into his drink. Then David got up and said he was going to bed. Christine followed.

I went to pour Edward some more brandy. When I handed it to him he ignored me, so I put it on the table beside him.

"Come and sit down, Elizabeth," he said eventually.

He took my hands between his and as he looked up I saw how sad his face was. That night had been the first time in months he had relaxed with me, but now, despite the love that shone in his eyes, I sensed him pushing me away. "Darling, I should have told you this a long time ago, but you always swore that Charlotte was enough and you never wanted any more children. You see, my first wife gave birth to a stillborn child. It was a girl, and I sometimes wonder if that's why I love Charlotte so much." He smiled. "But who could help loving Charlotte? Anyway, the birth was difficult and my wife almost died. Afterwards she was advised not to try again, so I had a vasectomy to save her from any more pain."

Until that moment I don't think I'd realized the insanity of what I had tried to do. I stared at him, struck dumb by the sheer horror of it.

It was some time before he spoke again. "You don't have to tell me anything, darling, but it might help if you did."

I buried my face in my hands. My self-loathing was so complete I couldn't speak.

"Is it Charlotte's father?"

I nodded.

"You were with him when you went away?"

I looked up into his face. I thought he had aged since I'd been ill, but now he looked almost haggard. "Edward," I sobbed, "I don't know what made me say it. I don't . . ."

"Hush, hush. People often say or do things they don't mean when they are hurting badly. I know how much you love him, Elizabeth, I've always known."

Hearing him say that, I wanted to get up and run and never stop. I wished he would hit me or shout at me, his kindness and understanding were tearing me apart.

"Does he know about the baby?"

"No."

"Will you tell him?"

I shook my head. "I can't. There's nothing he can . . . I'm sorry, Edward. Please forgive me. No, don't forgive me. I'll go. I'll go as far away from your life as I can. You can divorce me, I won't make any claim on you. I'm sorry, Edward, I'm . . ."

"Hush now, you're not going anywhere. I know you don't love me in the way you love him, Elizabeth, but I love you, and I love Charlotte too. I don't want to lose you."

"But what about the baby?" I looked at him, suddenly stricken with panic. "I couldn't have an abortion."

He put his hand over my mouth. "Of course not. The baby will be mine—if you allow it to be. No one need know, only the family."

"No, Edward, I can't let you do it."

"I want to do it, Elizabeth. But I have one condition, and I suppose even that's not a condition, I would want you to stay anyway. But if you can, I want you to promise me you will never see him again."

For an instant I thought I heard Alexander's voice telling me to deny him, warning me not to listen. But I had to ignore it. Alexander was again a part of my past, and this man here, my husband, who loved me more than any woman ever deserved to be loved, was waiting for my answer. I made him the promise.

In the early hours of the morning I woke to find the bed empty beside me. When I went to find Edward I saw lights in the Egyptian Room and tried the door, but it was locked. I listened, and after a while I could hear him sobbing.

21

EDWARD DIDN'T COME BACK to bed at all that night. The following morning he joined Christine on an early flight to Cairo, leaving me a note to say he would call when he got there. After what had happened it was a relief not to have to face them, and when David left a message with Jeffrey to say he'd gone up to London for a few days, I guessed he too was anxious to avoid seeing me.

When Charlotte arrived home from school, she came up to my room and we sat on the window seat for a long time, drawing patterns on the steamy windows. As she chattered, I tried so many times to tell her about the baby, but every time I opened my mouth the words wouldn't come.

Life was so cruel, and yet in other ways so kind. While it allowed me to have Alexander's children, it would not allow me to be with him. I put my arms round Charlotte and hugged her tight. At least I would always have a part of him, but what did Alexander have? I couldn't bear to think of how unhappy he might be. I never once doubted his love, nor how much he must want to be with Charlotte and me.

But what about Edward? Last night had served to remind me

just how much he loved me. Often I sensed the struggle he had to keep his feelings under control and always knew when he was losing the battle because he would go away. His love was so overpowering, at times I could almost see the way it threatened to engulf him. It was as if I wasn't real but an object to be treasured, revered almost. But it was the complexity of his sophistication and almost childlike adoration that made me want to protect him.

When he came back from Cairo three days later, I could see how relieved he was that I was still there, that I hadn't run away, and my heart twisted with pity and guilt. He talked excitedly about the deal he had in hand, but wouldn't go into detail because he wanted it to be a surprise. He asked about Charlotte, wanting to know everything we'd done while he was away. Then he laid his hand on my stomach and told me he loved me. I turned away before I could stop myself, but he didn't notice. His eyes were almost glazed as he seemed to drift into a world of his own. It was at moments like that, when he appeared so remote, that I wondered how well I really knew him.

Christine stayed in Cairo much longer than was originally planned. She rang Edward daily, but he took the calls in his study and she never asked to speak to me. After the calls he always seemed distracted, irritable almost, but when I asked him why he just said that the man they were dealing with in Cairo had an absurd passion for riddles. After one such phone call he got his secretary to book him on a flight to Istanbul and was gone for five days, during which he didn't ring home once.

Christine returned four weeks later. Edward and I were at an art dealer's party in London. He hadn't told me Christine was flying back that night, so I was surprised when she walked in around eleven. She greeted the host and his wife, throwing her arms around them in the ostentatious manner they all affected. Everyone wanted to know how she had got on in Cairo. She exchanged a quick glance with Edward—then declared loudly that they were all a very poor bunch, bombarding her with questions the minute she walked through the door and not even offering her a drink. Then she went off into a corner with Edward, and they talked quietly but heatedly for several minutes, before separating and mingling with the other guests again.

I waited, watching her from the corner of my eye as she

worked her way round the room. Eventually she was standing behind me, talking to Edward's secretary. I'd been dreading seeing her, and now she was so pointedly ignoring me I didn't know what to do. Suddenly I felt a thump on my back.

"Oh Elizabeth, I'm so sorry." Her voice was thick with sarcasm.

I smiled. "No harm done. How are you?"

"Very well." She looked me up and down. "No need to ask how you are."

I tried again. "You've been gone ages, I missed you."

"Did you, sister-in-law darling? And what about when you were off wherever it was with your lover? Did you miss me then? Or were you too busy to think about anyone else? You know, like the people who were left looking after your daughter?"

I stared at her.

"Oh, so you didn't miss me then. How about Edward? Did you miss him while you were away screwing another man? You know, the man whose child you tried to push onto my brother?" She was shouting now, and I looked round wildly to see if anyone had heard her.

"What's the matter, Elizabeth, afraid everyone will find out what a sly, conniving little bitch you are?"

"Christine, please . . ."

" 'Christine please!' I could kill you for what you've done to Edward. He's never hurt anyone in his whole life—but you've hurt him all right, haven't you, you slut! You're not fit to bear his name, you never were. Why don't you do us all a favor and take your bastards back to the gutter where you belong!"

I felt myself being dragged backwards and there was a loud crack as Edward's hand flew across Christine's face. "Go home, now!" he hissed, then without uttering another word he took my arm and marched me out of the room.

When we arrived home Edward told me to go upstairs. He caught Christine's arm as she made to follow me, and pulled her into his study. Once the door had closed I went back to the landing. Even though their voices were raised it was difficult to make out what they were saying, but I did hear Christine telling Edward to pull himself together and "see the little slut for what she really is."

The door opened then, and as Edward came out I drew back into the shadows.

"You're doing this because of her!" Christine yelled. "She's not worth it!"

Edward turned back. His voice was too low for me to hear, but when Christine answered I knew they were no longer talking about me.

"You've got to be insane even to think of it! How the hell are they going to get in? Have you thought about that?"

"Yes, I've thought about it. All we have to do is talk to the . . ." I couldn't make out what Edward said after that because the door closed again.

It was the early hours of the morning when I finally heard Christine come upstairs. When Edward didn't follow I tiptoed down to his study. He wasn't there, but I was shocked when I saw the chaos on his desk; catalogues and leaflets were strewn all over it, and on top of the pile was a blown-up color photograph of the Tutankhamun death mask. I closed the door quickly, feeling, for no earthly reason, that I had intruded upon something I hadn't been meant to see.

At the bottom of the west stairs I hesitated and looked up at the silent landing. There was only one light at the end of the gallery, casting long shadows across the walls. A sixth sense warned me not to go to the Egyptian Room. I remembered the way Christine had looked at Edward when she'd arrived at the party, and the oddness of Edward's manner after the phone calls from Cairo. I thought of the curious exchange I had heard only a few hours ago in Edward's study. I stood there in the half-darkness, and as my skin prickled with sentience I was suddenly engulfed by a premonition that something very sinister was going on at Westmoor.

Jonathan was born the following February, only three days after Alexander's birthday. It was a difficult birth and Edward was there throughout. Afterwards I couldn't bring myself to hold the baby, and the more Edward fussed and cuddled him, the worse I became. I was in the hospital for four days, then Edward, David and Charlotte came to take us home. Christine wasn't there, nor had she come to visit.

Since the night of the party there had been an uneasy truce between Christine and me, though I knew the only reason she made any effort at all was to keep Edward happy. She was unkind to Charlotte, which caused bitter scenes between her and David. Edward sent her off more and more frequently to far-flung places in search of paintings or antique furniture; she always came back with something, and always, no matter where she was, managed to make a stop in Cairo.

One night David teased her that she was hiding a lover there. Her denial was so vehement that the two brothers raised their eyebrows, and Edward wondered if David hadn't hit on something.

Charlotte was all ears. "Oh do tell us about him, Christine," she begged. "What's he like? Do you kiss him?"

"For God's sake, Charlotte, I've already told you . . ."

"What's his name?" Charlotte persisted.

Christine glared at me. I took hold of Charlotte's hand and pulled her onto my lap. "That's enough, darling," I said.

" 'That's enough, darling,' " Christine mimicked. "God, it makes me sick the way everyone round here hangs on that kid's every word. I suppose it's going to be the same with Jonathan. No darling, yes darling, that's enough, darling . . ."

"And that *is* enough." Edward got to his feet. "We've got guests arriving in less than two hours and there are some things I want to discuss with you before you go to New York tomorrow, Christine. Now Charlotte, how about a nice big kiss before you go up to bed?"

An hour later Edward came upstairs to our room. I was sitting on the bed, holding the baby. I turned sharply as I heard the door close, and my arms tightened around Jonathan. He was three months old now and I couldn't forgive myself for the way I had rejected him when he was born. He started to bounce around as Edward came to sit beside us, and to stop him holding out his arms for Edward, I stood up.

"It's all right, darling, I'm not going to take him away from you."

I nuzzled my face into Jonathan's and didn't answer.

Gently Edward took hold of my elbows and sat me back on

the bed. "You've got to stop blaming yourself. A lot of mothers react the way you did after a difficult birth. As long as you love him . . ."

"It's not that," I interrupted.

"Then what is it?"

"It's Christine. She hates me being here. I can't stand all this pretense."

Immediately, Jonathan started to cry, and Edward took him from me. I made to snatch him back, but stopped myself just in time. Then, afraid of what I was feeling, I jerked myself from the bed and went to close the curtains, while Edward put Jonathan in his cradle. Jonathan had slept in our room since we'd come home from the hospital. He'll have to go to the nursery soon, I thought, and was ashamed at how pleased I was at creating just that little distance between him and Edward.

Edward put his arms around me and I leaned my head against his shoulder. "I've had an idea that I think just might sort everything out once and for all," he said. "Meanwhile, just try and be patient with Christine, darling. Despite everything, I know she loves you very much."

I wrenched myself away and went to stand over Jonathan. I could feel Edward beside me, smiling down into the cradle, and I was suddenly possessed by the conviction that I had to get Alexander's son away from him.

A month or so later I was busy with the organization of the charity bazaar in the village hall. Edward had been in London for days, but on the morning of the bazaar he returned, proudly announcing that he was sending Jeffrey back up to London to collect a truckload of saleable bits and pieces he'd managed to wheedle out of friends in the art world.

Christine went into action to help with the last minute arrangements. By now we were all convinced she was conducting a secret love affair, for she flew off to Cairo as regularly as the rest of us went up to London. At the same time I had noticed that David was becoming very friendly with a neighbor, Jenifer Illingworth, whose husband had run off a year ago with another woman.

"Why don't we invite Jenifer up to the house for dinner tonight?" Christine whispered in my ear. I was so startled that she had actually spoken to me by choice that, for a moment, I could only stare at her.

It was settled. Jenifer said she would love to come, and I laughed as I saw the pained expression on David's face. He knew two matchmaking women when he saw them.

The bazaar was an unprecedented success, for which Edward accepted the credit with outrageous immodesty. "And things seem to be better between you and Christine," he said, as we were dressing for dinner later.

"I think you could be right," I admitted. I was still cautious, though.

"Good. I hoped it would work out once . . ." He didn't finish, and when I looked up he seemed intent on trying to cover the bald spot at the back of his head. I took the brush from him, and he leaned back in the chair and watched his reflection as I pampered him. "Aaah, Elizabeth," he sighed, after a while, "what kind of life is it for you, cooped up here with two crusty old men, trying to hide their bald spots and matching them up with abandoned women?"

Despite the lightness of his tone I could tell he was troubled about something. Putting my arms round his neck I met his eyes in the mirror. "It's a wonderful life," I said. "And you're two wonderful, crusty old men. Now what is it, Edward? What's on your mind?"

He turned round in his chair, and taking the hairbrush from me, he put it on the dressing table. I knelt down in front of him and slipped my hands in his.

"You always could read me so well," he said.

I felt a flash of irritation at the pride in his voice that we knew each other so well.

"I wasn't going to tell you now," he began, "but I suppose it's as good a time as any. It'll give you a chance to think it over, anyway." He seemed reluctant to go on.

"Is it something to do with Christine?" I prompted.

"Not really. Well, in a way I suppose it is. It's got something to do with all of us, but mainly the children."

My heart gave a sickening lurch.

"No, don't worry," he patted my hand, "it's nothing awful. I've talked it over with Christine and David, and they agree it would be for the best, too. Well, Christine was against it at first, but once I'd assured her it wouldn't change anything as far as she was concerned—in my will, that is—she saw the sense of it. And now, just as I'd hoped, things are getting better between the two of you because of it. So you see, it could be a good thing."

"What could be a good thing, Edward?"

He looked at me blankly, then laughed as he realized he'd told me nothing. "I'm sorry. And I hope you won't mind that I talked to David and Christine first, but I suppose I needed to know if I was doing the right thing. Well, I always thought it was the right thing, but I didn't know how you would take it."

I smiled. "And you still won't, if you don't tell me what it is."

"It's Charlotte and Jonathan. I want to adopt them, Elizabeth."

I stared at him, feeling myself go suddenly cold.

He rushed on. "I think it would be best all round. You know, if legally they were mine. I have no heirs, and when the time comes I'd like to provide for them properly. I want to be their father, Elizabeth. Their real father."

I still couldn't speak. I looked down at my hands and saw that they were still entwined in his. I pulled them away and suddenly I wanted to scream at him. How could he be so stupid! How could he even think I would let him have Alexander's children?

"I waited 'til now to see if you would change your mind and decide to go back to their father. God, Elizabeth, if you only knew what I've . . ." He swallowed hard. "It doesn't matter. All that matters is that you're still here, and that you seem happier. I think you want to stay. And if you do, then I want us to be a real family. Can we be that, darling? Can I be their father?"

I stood up slowly, not trusting myself to speak—and Edward talked on and on, his words hitting me like stones.

I didn't go down to dinner that night. I sat in my room, holding myself, sure that if I let go I would fall apart. I needed Alexander then as I had never needed him before. I wanted him to tell me that I didn't have to do it, that they were his children, and that nothing and no one should ever divide us. But he wasn't there, and Edward was asking, and how could I deny him when he had done so much for me? How could I find the words to say no, he couldn't have Alexander's children? And then, with a tremendous sense of relief, it occurred to me that I wouldn't have to. As they were Alexander's children, surely Alexander would have to give his permission for the adoption to go ahead, and I knew that was something he would never do.

It was then that I started upon a mindless exercise of self-torture. I told Edward I needed some time to think, and went to stay at our London house, alone.

It was a bitterly cold March night. The taxi dropped me at the corner of Belgrave Square, and through the drizzling rain I searched the imposing houses for the right number. When I found it my courage failed. Crossing the road quickly, I tucked myself in tightly against the railings and pulled my fur hat down over my eyes. The lights were on in Alexander's house, but there was no sign of life. It looked warm and comfortable, and I wondered what he would do if he knew I was standing outside. The hours slipped by until, chilled to the bone, I hailed a taxi and returned home.

The following night I did the same. And again, night after night. I never saw him, though I guessed the Mercedes parked outside the house was his. At first I got a grim comfort from the pain of being so near him, but as the nights wore on I began to despise myself for my weakness.

Then one night, when I was sickened by the knowledge that again I was going to walk away, and when my feet were so numb with cold I could hardly move, the door opened and an elegant woman, wrapped, as I was, against the wind, ran down the steps, got into the car and drove off. My heart was thumping unnaturally. Though I'd never met her, I knew it was Jessica.

Now I had only to cross the street and knock on the door. And then . . . Dear God, what would happen then? Would I really beg him to help me? Would I really tell him about Jonathan? I must. I knew that no matter what happened afterwards, no matter who got hurt, Alexander must know what Edward was planning.

But as I started to cross the road the Mercedes came back round the square and Jessica, leaving the engine running and the door open, ran up the steps to the front door. As she reached the top Alexander came out. He was laughing, and reached out to grab her. She shrieked and cried out that she had only been teasing. He wrapped his arms round her and squeezed her until she cried out again. Then he ran to the car, closed the door and drove off. Jessica stood on the pavement watching the car disappear around the corner. I could hear her laughing as she turned towards the other end of the square, waiting for him to drive round. Instead, he reversed the car back and drew up beside her. As they drove away together I could see he was still laughing, and I shrank back into the shadows as they passed.

David came to sit beside me on the sofa. "Jeffrey told me you were back," he said. I was in the Blue Sitting Room, a room we rarely used, that adjoined the dining room.

I smiled. "I got bored, entertaining myself," I said. "Where's Edward?"

"He's taken the children to see Violet May. The fair's only a couple of miles away, did you know?"

Mary came in with a tray of tea which David poured and we sat quietly watching the flames shoot up into the chimney.

"Have you decided what your answer's going to be?" he asked, gently.

I shook my head. "I just don't know what to do." He slipped an arm round me, pulling me onto his shoulder. "I've seen him, David, it's why I went to London."

"I guessed as much. What did he say?"

"Nothing. I didn't speak to him."

"Why?"

"It doesn't matter."

"If he knew about the children, would he want them?"

I sobbed. "Yes, he would want them. He would want them very much."

"Then maybe you should let Edward adopt them. That way, if their father ever found out about them he would never be able to take them away."

"No. I don't know. If Al . . . if he knew that I was even thinking about it, then . . ."

"He won't know."

"But I'd have to get his permission."

"You wouldn't. He's what's called the putative father. As such he doesn't have to know about the adoption."

A dreadful buzzing began in my ears. That couldn't be true. It was the only hope I had left. "Doesn't he?" I whispered.

David shook his head. "Edward's already consulted a lawyer. He wants this very much, Elizabeth."

I sat up and turned to look at his poor, scarred face. He loved his brother and knew how terribly I had hurt Edward when I had tried to tell him he was Jonathan's father. I owed Edward the adoption—that was what David was really saying.

So the adoption went ahead, and Charlotte and Jonathan were no longer Alexander's.

22

NONE OF US WOULD EVER forget Charlotte's first day at St. Paul's Girls' School. The honor of driving her fell to Edward, and as she was ten now, he allowed her to sit in the front seat; Jonathan, who didn't start kindergarten until the following week, insisted on accompanying them. Christine and I stood at the door, with Canary, Jeffrey and Mary, and all four of us had to wipe away a tear or two as we waved her off, her big grey eyes peering up over the top of the door frame of the Rolls Royce, bright with anticipation. That afternoon, as a very special treat to mark the occasion, David was going to come up to London with Jenifer Illingworth. The first Charlotte would know of it was when she came out of school to find David waiting.

The telephone call came at just after half-past three. No one was to blame. Who could have foreseen that an over-excited ten-year-old would go dashing out into the road to greet her uncle just as a motorcyclist came round the corner?

When we got to the hospital David was waiting on a bench outside the operating room. Sitting beside him was a young boy wearing leather and holding a crash helmet. I stared at him. Christine led me away, while Edward and David stayed to talk to him.

Much later the doctor came to find us and showed us into a side ward. I think I must have cried out as I saw her little body lying on the bed, because the doctor turned abruptly and Christine put her arms round me. I pushed her away and ran over to the bed. There were tubes fixed into Charlotte's wrists, mouth and nose. Her eyes were closed and her face was as white as the pillow beneath it.

I turned back to the doctor. "Will she . . . ? Is she . . ."

He stared at me for a moment, then with a grim face turned back to Charlotte. He didn't know.

Edward went outside with him where he learned the full extent of her injuries. I wasn't ready to hear yet. All I knew was that she might die and that, whatever happened, I mustn't leave her. I prayed then, as I had never prayed before. David prayed too. He was in a state of shock, and the doctor had tried to make him lie down in a room along the corridor. He blamed himself. If he'd been a few minutes earlier, he would have been on the right side of the road, and there would have been no need for her to run out . . . If that taxi driver hadn't blocked the one-way street, he wouldn't have been late . . . Christine tried to soothe him. Edward held my hand, but didn't speak. The only sound was the bleep of the machine beside us, monitoring the unsteady rhythm of Charlotte's life . . .

It was dark in the room. Edward was still sitting beside me. His eyes were closed, but I knew instinctively that he wasn't sleeping. Christine was there too. Her head had fallen to one side and her mouth was open. David was nowhere to be seen, and then I dimly recollected him giving in to the doctor and going to lie down.

I felt utterly exhausted. Someone had once told me that if you concentrated hard enough, you could penetrate another person's mind; lives had been saved that way, they told me. And for the past seven hours that was what I had been trying to do with Charlotte. Every ounce of energy I possessed I had poured into trying to reach her. Somewhere, deep down in the dark recesses between life and death, I had tried to grasp her and bring her back to me. Her breathing was so shallow now that her tiny rib cage barely moved. I lifted my eyes to her face. She seemed so lonely. If only it could have been me lying there. I picked up a stray curl that was stretched across the pillow and wound it gently round my finger.

"Charlotte, please," I whispered, "please, my darling, don't go away."

She didn't move. I looked at the black curl, and for the first time since I'd learned of the accident I thought of Alexander.

Edward opened his eyes. "What is it?" And when he saw I was on my feet, he got up too. "Where are you going?"

"I'm sorry, Edward," I croaked, "please try and understand. He's her father."

Christine caught me at the door. "No, Elizabeth!" she hissed. "No! Edward's her father now. You can't do this to him."

"My daughter is dying and you tell me what I can and can't do? I'm telling you, he's got to see her. Christine, get out of the way." We struggled in the doorway. Christine was stronger than me and managed to grip me by the shoulders and turn me round.

"Look! Just look!"

Edward was slumped forward, his elbows resting on his knees, his face buried in his hands. "Don't do it to him, Elizabeth. Please, don't do it to him."

"I'm sorry, Christine. Edward, I'm sorry." I tore open the door and started to run down the corridor. I was getting into the elevator as I heard Christine scream my name. "Elizabeth! It's Charlotte! Come quick!"

With my heart in my mouth I flew back along the corridor. As I burst into the room I saw that my daughter's eyes were wide open, dark pools in her pale face.

"Charlotte," I breathed. Edward stood aside as I ran to the bed. "Charlotte, my darling. It's Mummy. I'm here, angel. I'm here."

The nurse came in and turned on the overhead light. She tried to push past me and I all but threw her out of the way. Now I was closer I could see that Charlotte's eyes were dilated and wondered whether she could see me.

"Mummy?" she croaked.

"Yes, darling. Mummy's here."

"Mummy?"

I looked at Edward in panic. She couldn't hear me.

Two huge tears rolled from the corners of her eyes. "It's dark. Where's my Mummy? I want my Mummy."

Alexander

23

ENRY GAVE A LOW WHISTLE as his ball sailed into the sky and came to land only a few feet from the eighteenth green. "Damn good shot, if I say so myself." He stood back to make room for me. "So, how much did you win?"

"Ten quid."

"Ten! Is that all?"

"It was twenty," I said, selecting a number one wood, "but Froggo refused to cough up the other ten. He claimed I hadn't said the exact words."

"So let's hear how you managed to slip in this little nugget of blasphemy."

I placed my ball on the tee, then leaning on my club, recounted my summing up of the day before, when Froggo, the barrister originally briefed to prosecute in the Saxony case, had bet me twenty pounds that I couldn't slip the phrase "Take up thy bed and walk" somewhere into my speech. As the case had concerned an armed wages snatch at a bedding warehouse in the East End, when I delivered the line, "And so, members of the jury, I ask you to consider the evidence put before you very carefully, because to allow any of the accused to take up their beds and walk from this courtroom, free men, would be tantamount to inviting them to put more lives in jeopardy . . ." I'd had the gratification of a rare wince from the normally impassive Judge Burr.

Henry grunted. "You're not normally as corny as that, old chap. Losing your flair."

I shrugged and took up my stance to hit the ball. We both watched in disgust as it sliced off the end of my wood and rocketed towards a clump of trees, to land God only knew where, probably in the lake behind.

"Jesus, Alexander, that's the third time you've done that today. What the hell's got into you?"

"Fellow can have an off day, can't he?"

We picked up our clubs and started off down the fairway.

"Everything all right at home, is it? Jessica's OK?"

"Henry, you're not going to start an amateur analysis on me because I've hit three bad ones, are you?"

"Just asking. Tell me, how did you fare with fair Rosalind what's-her-name?"

"Rosalind who?"

"Don't play dumb with me, old chap, this is Henry you're talking to. You know, the solicitor in the Godwin case.

"Rosalind Blake."

"Well, anything doing?"

"Henry, ever since you've become a respectable married man you seem to think every other man in the world is leaping in and out of bed with any woman he can lay his hands on. The fact is that I've given up that sort of behavior for good. It's all in the past for me now, I've told you. Why won't you believe me?"

"Because it's against your nature."

"Not when I've got a crippled wife who might not be crippled if I hadn't . . ."

"I wouldn't say the loss of three fingers on her right hand makes her a cripple, Alexander. And you hardly notice the limp these days."

"When you live with her, I can tell you you're required to notice her limp, and every other blemish, and do penance for them several times a day."

We parted company then as I went off to find my ball.

Life with Jessica was, indeed, even worse than it had been

before the accident. Her self-confidence had been destroyed, and even though I never stopped trying, nothing I said or did seemed capable of restoring it. I couldn't blame her for not trusting me, but during her bad weeks things were so unbearable that all I wanted to do was walk away and never come back. I couldn't do it, of course, my conscience would never permit it. And should I ever be in danger of forgetting my conscience, Jessica would be at hand to remind me of the way I had disappeared with my "slut," leaving her to tear round the countryside trying to find me.

"*I* was the one driving that car when the truck hit us! The truck that killed *your* mother! And my baby! You might just as well have been the driver of that truck!"

I knew now why she had lied to me about my infertility. As it so often was, her reasoning had been convoluted and perverse: she'd wanted there to be something in my life I couldn't have; she'd wanted to see me suffer in the way I'd made her suffer all the years of our marriage. My desire to have children had been like a gift to her, she told me, because nothing hurts a man more than to have doubt cast on his manhood. When I explained that the kind of lie she'd told me could come close to destroying a man, she answered, quite calmly, that I deserved to be destroyed . . . But once she had sensed she was losing me, getting pregnant had been the only thing she could think of that might make me stay. I made the insensitive mistake of asking if the child had been mine and she flew at me, hissing and spitting like a wild cat.

All this was while she was in the clinic recovering from the breakdown that had followed her accident. The doctor insisted that her mental condition was caused as much by the fear that she might never paint again as by the trauma of the accident—and my infidelity. The fear that she might not paint again had vanished now. She painted every day, and the centerpiece of her first exhibition after leaving the clinic had been a macabre impression of the accident. It was gruesome, and made even more so, I felt, by its dedication to me.

The affection that had grown between her and my father since he had withdrawn his resignation from the Cabinet and moved into Belgrave Square both surprised and annoyed me. They talked endlessly about my mother and how special she had been to them both. In fact Jessica and my mother had never hit it off, and though I knew this was her way of trying to cope with what had happened, I despised her hypocrisy.

Her moods were so erratic that I took to working late into the night at chambers—anything to avoid going home. Only the week before she had presented me with a portrait of myself. She was touchingly shy about it, but the following evening I arrived home to find ugly scars daubed across it and a dagger plunged into the throat. A thin trickle of blood ran from the wound down over the frame. As I stood transfixed by the sheer horror of it, Jessica walked into the room, smiling pleasantly and waving a large brown envelope at me. "I've been waiting for you," she said. "Can you give me the address of your girlfriend, I thought she might like the painting. As a memento."

It was three years since I had gone to Sark, and still she was making me pay. At least I had never told her about Charlotte. But hardly a minute of the day passed when I didn't think about my daughter—and the longing that swept over me for Elizabeth, for the uncomplicated way she had loved me, was at times almost unbearable . . .

"Hey!" Henry shouted. "Are we playing a round of golf or aren't we? You're miles away, old chap. Come on, let's get it over with. I'm freezing, and in sore need of a drink."

We finished the round in double-quick time, and sauntered back in the direction of the clubhouse. "Henry," I said, as we walked down the hill past the seventeenth hole, "I want to tell you something, but I don't want you to make a big deal out of it."

"Fire away."

"It's about Elizabeth."

He stopped. "What about her?"

"You're going to think I've lost my marbles, but I think she needs me."

When he didn't answer I went on, "I don't know what it is, it's not something I can put into words, but I have this feeling that she . . ." I shrugged. "Probably just my imagination."

He turned slowly and walked on down the hill. "Are you going to do anything about it?" he asked eventually.

"What can I do? I tried to find her once before, remember? I don't even know her married name."

We were at the clubhouse now and Henry was bending down

to take off his shoes. "I suppose you could always try mental telepathy," he said.

"What kind of answer's that, for God's sake?"

"Just a suggestion, old chap." And slapping me on the back, he went inside to order the drinks.

I saw a lot of Rosalind Blake during the buildup to the Godwin trial. She was an unusual woman with chaotic red hair and bright blue eyes that sat oddly with her somewhat aloof and efficient manner. I enjoyed her company and was rather proud that I had managed to establish a friendship with a woman in which neither of us was trying to get the other into bed.

The niggling feeling that Elizabeth needed me had disappeared, and if I thought about it at all, I put it down to a lack of sleep and tricks of the subconscious. After all, reason told me, if she had needed me, she would have found a way to contact me.

After the first day in court, with opening speeches completed and the first witnesses called, Rosalind and I went for a drink. I wasn't happy with the way things were going, and was angry at Godwin's apparent failure to appreciate the seriousness of the case. Euthanasia might be his word for what he had done, but murder or manslaughter was the way the law termed it. Rosalind tried to calm me down, saying things would be better the next day, and I snapped at her for patronizing me.

We wound up at her flat. By that time, although I had drunk enough to sink a battleship, I still felt sober—though extremely morose. We'd talked all evening about Godwin and what he and his wife must have been through before he helped her out of her misery. Enough to make anyone depressed.

Rosalind's flat was a surprise. With her pre-Raphaelite looks I had expected to find her home furnished with antiques. However, hi-tech modernity seemed to suit her quite well, too. Her heels clicked across white tiles as she walked down the hall, kicking a rug into place as she went, and I followed her into a kitchen that seemed to have every gadget imaginable.

"I know what you're thinking," she said. "How does anyone on my salary afford such luxuries."

"Well, I must admit . . ."

"My husband. Ex-husband. It's all his, or would be if he came back to claim it."

"Where is he now?"

She shrugged. "Haven't a clue. He went off to work one morning three years ago, and I haven't seen him since."

"But didn't he tell you . . . ?"

"Oh yes. I had a phone call a week later, telling me he didn't want to be married any longer and he was going off to do his own thing. I was devastated at the time, but more for my son than myself."

"I didn't know you had a son."

"He's at boarding school. Charterhouse, down in Surrey. He'll be thirteen next week. I'll go down to see him, but the best present he could have would be his father turning up. At least the bastard left enough money for me to educate his son. Be thankful for small mercies, eh?"

I sighed. "Do any marriages work out these days, I wonder?"

"Some must." She turned to look at me, her eyebrows raised. "Don't tell me yours . . . ?"

"Don't let's even speak about mine."

We took our coffee and moved into the sitting room. "She's a feminist, your wife, isn't she?" Rosalind said, curling her feet under her at the other end of the white leather sofa. "She did a lot of good work back in the late sixties, early seventies. I remember her name was always in the papers. How did you cope with all that? Did it annoy you?"

"Like hell. Don't get me wrong, I've got nothing against equality of the sexes. What I objected to were Jessica's motives—not that I think she knew what they were herself. But she used the cause as some sort of weapon against me."

"Weapon? Or shield?"

I looked into her blue eyes. "Do I look like the kind of man you need to shield yourself from?"

"You are exactly that kind of man. And I can just imagine what you were like at university. If you ask me, Jessica was a brave woman to take you on."

"Especially when she knew I was in love with someone else."

"You were?"

"Still am."

"Poor Jessica. It must have been very difficult for her." She paused. "And the other woman? Does Jessica know you're still in love with her?"

"Oh yes. She knows."

"I'd like to meet her. Jessica, I mean."

"Then you'll have to get someone else to introduce you." I looked at my watch. "I suppose I ought to be getting along."

"Do you have to? You could always stay here tonight."

I was surprised but assumed she was offering me the spare room. Only when I looked at her face did I realize she wasn't.

"Are you shocked?" she said.

"I suppose I am, a bit. I mean, I didn't come here expecting . . ."

"I know you didn't." She put her coffee cup back on the table. I moved along the sofa, took her in my arms and kissed her, waiting for the stirrings of desire to begin. After a while she led me through the dark hallway to the bedroom at the end. As she started to undress I watched, still waiting for my own response, but not until she was lying naked between the sheets did I realize that I couldn't go through with it.

I begged her to forgive me. It wasn't because I didn't find her attractive, I told her, it was just . . . I couldn't meet her eyes, and like a petulant schoolboy I hammered my fist against the doorframe in frustration. Then, to my horror, I was sobbing in her arms.

I pulled myself together quickly, fumbling out some lame excuse about too much to drink, a lot on my mind—and bolted before I could disgrace myself further.

It was past one in the morning when I finally arrived home, to find that Jessica had packed her bags and left. It was, I knew, another empty gesture. I went upstairs, threw a few things into a suitcase and made an early start for Suffolk, where I was going to have to spend the weekend sorting out the aftermath of the heaviest snowfall for years. I left a note for Jessica, knowing she would follow—she always did.

The following Monday, when I saw Rosalind again, she made no reference to what had happened. Embarrassed as I was, I still felt great warmth for her. I was so accustomed to Jessica's sneering if

I made any show of weakness that Rosalind's kindness touched me in a way that reminded me of Elizabeth.

Godwin was found guilty and received a two-year suspended sentence. Rosalind and I took him and his daughter for a quiet drink later.

When they'd gone, on impulse I invited Rosalind to come to the gallery where Jessica's latest exhibition was opening that evening. I called Henry and arranged for Rosalind to go with him and Caroline—if she turned up with me, Jessica would throw a fit.

Jessica was in good spirits when I arrived, and busy sorting out last minute details. My father was already there, giving the benefit of his advice as usual, so I helped myself to a glass of wine and stood back to watch.

Jessica's exhibitions were always well attended, and little red stickers found their way quickly onto frames. The theme for this latest one was rather sober for her, in view of her past excursions into surrealism and the abstract. We had spent a month in Tuscany that spring, and she had made the Italian hills and valleys the background for a series of paintings entitled "Child Lost in Tuscany." The child, which had to be searched for in every painting, bore a striking resemblance to Jessica herself, though in one or two pictures it appeared only as a fetus. She'd taken me through the paintings some weeks before, in the belief that I would otherwise never understand their hidden message. The use of the fetus was pointed enough, I thought, without her having to add, "I like to think our child is somewhere beautiful, don't you, darling?"

As I watched her now, excited, moving with ease among the guests, I was suddenly gripped by an overpowering desire to walk out. I didn't belong in this world of hers, I never had. I hated the farce we staged every time she had an opening. People talked about us, even wrote about us, as a loving couple, when nothing could be further from the truth. It was only guilt that bound me to her now; all I really wanted was to get as far away from her as I could . . . But she was coming towards me now, smiling and holding out her hand for mine. She whispered something in my ear that I didn't catch, then planted a kiss on my cheek.

"I've been neglecting you," she said. "But you must blame your father. He's invited so many people and wants me to meet them all. Did you have a good day?"

I nodded absently, then looked down into her eyes. Successful Jessica might be, but I knew how fragile she was, too. There was still a long way to go before her shattered confidence could be completely restored. She needed me now in a way she never had before. It was as if she were afraid to do anything without me, even though she couldn't stop herself hurting and resenting me.

"Jess! There you are!" My father clapped his hand on her shoulder. "The chap from *The Times* has arrived, come and say hello. Henry's looking for you," he added to me, as he led her away.

I found Henry and Caroline—Caroline was more than halfway through her third pregnancy—standing next to the table that had been set up as a bar. I looked around for Rosalind. "Gone to the ladies," Henry whispered. "She tells me she's dying to meet Jessica. Do you think that's wise, old chap?"

"I've got nothing to hide. Besides, I don't think Rosalind is going to let on we already know one another."

"Got you. So who is she?"

"A friend of yours, of course . . ."

Half an hour later I noticed Rosalind standing in a corner with Jessica. They were looking at one of the paintings, and I could almost hear Jessica as she explained to Rosalind what she was trying to convey. I watched them for a while, touched by the similarity of their lives. One way or another both had suffered at the hands of the men they loved. I hoped they would become friends, they would be good for each other.

After the exhibition the six of us—Henry, Caroline, Rosalind, Jessica, my father and I—went to Langan's. Jessica and Rosalind paid scant attention to the conversation going on round the table, they were too engrossed in one another.

Rosalind became a frequent visitor to Belgrave Square after that. She and Jessica hit it off so well that they sometimes made me feel like an outsider. Occasionally Rosalind and I would lunch together but she rarely talked about Jessica, except to say that she thought she was regaining her confidence. I had to agree. To start with, Rosalind had rekindled Jessica's interest in the Women's Movement. I was never sure which rally they were attending when, but each time Jessica returned from a march or a meeting, she was a different person. There was no bitterness in her fight for equality now; there was a new gentleness about her, which found its way into her paintings too.

Jessica's part-independence, and part-dependence on someone else, had a strange effect on me. On the one hand I felt free and able to breathe again, on the other hand I missed her. I missed the arguments and the acrimony. I missed her being there when I got home at the end of a day. I missed the way she coped with my father. Most of all, perhaps, I missed the shock of her sudden, sadistic gestures—the cruel tricks, the drunken malice, the bizarre practical jokes. So often when I arrived home now, I would find a scribbled note saying "Back in a few days," or she'd phone from Rosalind's and say she was staying over. As she began to stand on her own feet, so I began to feel unimportant, unnecessary; in fact I must have been feeling something of what Jessica had felt during the years of our marriage. Of course, she had not left me. We still slept in the same bed, dined together occasionally, even went away for weekends together. But it was as if she had somehow outgrown our marriage, was learning to stand free of it.

"I think things between us are better than they've ever been, don't you?" she said one day. "I mean, we don't fight anymore. I don't hate you anymore, and I don't mind so much that you don't love me."

"Don't you?"

"OK, I'm lying. I mind a lot, but I can handle it better these days. Rosalind's been a marvelous influence on me, don't you think? She's helped me to come to terms with things. To think of myself as an individual; you know, as Jessica, rather than as Jessica-and-Alexander."

"Do I figure anywhere in the picture?"

"Oh, don't start getting sentimental on me, not now. I've fallen for that too often in the past. You'll only end up hurting me again."

"I never meant to hurt you."

"I know."

"Do you love me, Jess?"

"You know I do. And what about you? Do you think you might be able to start loving me now?"

"I always did love you. Just not in the way . . ."

"No. Don't say any more."

"I miss you. When you're not here, I miss you, you know."

"I miss you too. But it's best this way."

It was after that conversation, when she had flown off to Rome for the weekend with Rosalind that I realized I had been kidding myself. I didn't miss her at all. It was Elizabeth I missed. I had deluded myself into thinking it was Jessica because for the past three years I had rarely allowed myself to think of Elizabeth—the memory and the longing were too painful. Now there was nothing to fill the hours of loneliness, no one demanding my attention, no one constantly reminding me how I had ruined her life. At last I was free to think, and all I could think about was Elizabeth.

My father picked up Jessica and Rosalind from the airport when they got back from Rome, and took them to Henry's where we were all dining that night. But by the time I arrived Rosalind had left; she'd had a phone message to say that her son had been rushed into the hospital with appendicitis. Jessica had offered to go with her, Henry told me, "but then she changed her mind. Wait 'til you see her, she looks gorgeous. If you ask me she's fancying a bit of jig-a-jig later."

"You've got sex on the brain," I told him.

"Me!"

"Three children in three years, I rest my case."

"Two," Caroline corrected, as she waddled in through the door. "The third can't make up its mind when to arrive. I wish it bloody well would, it's no fun being this shape. Have you been up to say goodnight to your godson, Alexander?"

Two Rupert Bear stories later, I came down to find the table laid for dinner. After Sarah, Henry's second child was born, Caroline and Henry had moved out of Eaton Square to a house in Chelsea, and my father, Jessica and I spent a lot of time there.

Henry was right, Jessica did look gorgeous. She'd had her hair cut in Rome, and it looked blonder, too. It was the first time I'd seen her with short hair; it made her eyes look bigger and her mouth fuller. She was wearing her normal jeans and sweater, but somehow tonight even they looked different.

When I kissed her she put her arms around me. "You look tired," she said. "Not been having too many late nights while I've been in Rome, I hope?"

I pushed her away. "Let's eat."

Her face darkened, but my father was already asking her to go on with what she'd been saying before I arrived. It seemed she and Rosalind were going to join a march the next day to Aldermaston, the headquarters of the Atomic Weapons Research Establishment. "A lot of women from our group are going, and we've arranged a meeting for Thursday to report back. In fact, Rosalind and I are thinking of joining CND on a permanent basis. Well, a girl's got to protect the next generation and all that." She looked at me, but I didn't react.

When dinner was over Henry asked me to go to his study with him, there was a brief he wanted my thoughts on. I saw him exchange looks with Caroline before we left the room.

Once in his study he took a bottle of brandy from his filing cabinet. He seemed in no hurry, and chatted for some time about Nicholas and what he was doing at kindergarten. "Well," I said eventually, "where's this brief?"

"There isn't one," he answered shortly. "It's something else, Alexander. I don't know whether I should tell you this or not, but I'm going to. It's about Elizabeth."

I froze. "What about her?"

"I've got her address. It's written there, inside that envelope." When I made no move to pick it up, he handed it to me.

The skin felt so tight over my face it was difficult to speak. "How did you find it? Did she telephone you?"

"No. I was picking Nicholas up from kindergarten a couple of days ago, I saw her then. She didn't see me. She got into the car in front of mine and drove off. Nicholas and I followed."

I stared down at the envelope.

"There's something else you should know, Alexander. The child she collected from kindergarten. It was a little boy, same age as Nicholas. His name's Jonathan. I've seen him, Alexander . . ."

"Go on." My voice was hoarse.

"There's no doubt in my mind, and well, with his age as well . . ."

There was no need for him to elaborate. We looked at each other for a long time without speaking. In the end it was Henry who broke the silence.

"It's up to you now, Alexander."

"Why up to me? She's always known where she could find me."

"For Christ's sake, Alexander, you were the one who broke it off. You were the one who told her you couldn't leave Jessica after the accident . . ."

"She could have told me. If he's my son . . ."

"And since then you've done nothing, have you? You could have gone to her once everything had calmed down, but you didn't. You've done nothing . . ."

"But things never did calm down, did they? Jessica's still a mess. Am I supposed to walk out on her now, on top of everything else I've done to her?"

"You've got two children out there. Don't you think you owe them something too? Your marriage is a bigger farce now than it ever was. You make me laugh, you two, the way you go about pretending you're over your difficulties . . . If you ask me, it's about time you stopped wallowing in guilt and got on with your life."

I was out of my chair like a shot—but the door burst open before I could speak. It was Jessica. "Henry! It's Caroline. The pains have started."

Henry glared at me. "Just think about it, Alexander," he growled, then raced out of the door.

"Don't tell me you two were having a lovers' tiff?" Jessica scoffed. She stepped back as my eyes blazed into her.

"I'm sick of you, Jessica! I'm sick of the damned sight of you. I thought you'd changed, but even tonight you couldn't resist twisting a knife in my guilt, could you? Well, you've done it long enough, so do us both a favor and get out of my life before I do something we might both regret!"

"Oh it's too late for that, Alexander. You did it three years ago."

Elizabeth

24

I WATCHED EDWARD STALK OFF through the crowds. "It will be a most wonderful book Mr. Walters is writing." Kamel was standing at my elbow—he seemed to have been standing beside me all the time we'd been in Egypt. Next to him was one of the museum's curators, his round brown eyes dilated with something akin to worship as they followed Edward.

The Cairo Museum was seething with tourists. I'd known nothing about a book until we returned from Aswan to Cairo—Kamel had told me. Kamel was with us to protect us, though Edward had never told me from what. His presence unsettled me, as did the crowded streets and anonymous, staring eyes that seemed to follow me everywhere. From the moment we'd arrived the city had appalled me with its frightening pandemonium of noise and disorder; Cairo was a jungle of pungent, decaying streets and crowded alleys where modern hotels and ancient crumbling houses stood cheek by jowl. It was a bizarre, amorphous place that vibrated with an almost sinister extremism. As I got to know it better, the poverty and ignorance horrified me. I talked to Edward about it but he just patted my hand and told me there was nothing to be done. I know he didn't mean to but he made me feel as if Cairo were his particular territory, and he was sorry he'd brought me.

Every day he went to the Museum to study the people and their reaction to the Tutankhamun collection. His fascination with it bordered on obsession. We'd come here for a holiday for Charlotte to recuperate, but ever since we'd arrived Edward had spent his time here. As well as doing his research, he was advising the museum authorities on the installation of an intricate alarm system. He was treated like a royal visitor, and behaved like one too. He wore his galibaya as if he had been born to it, ate nothing but Egyptian food, read Egyptian newspapers, and unless speaking to the children or me, always spoke Egyptian. He even had the heavy, musky smell of an Egyptian.

The curator fiddled with his collar. His brown, Western suit didn't fit him well. His bad teeth were exposed in a grin, and turning, I found Kamel had hoisted Jonathan up onto his shoulder. The curator looked at Jonathan just as he looked at Edward—with admiration verging on reverence. It was a look I was getting used to, but I didn't like it. Almost everyone we'd met, especially on our cruise down the Nile when we had stopped in remote villages, looked at Edward and Jonathan like that. I wondered if it had anything to do with the vast amounts of money Edward dished out to the poverty-stricken villagers, who rushed out of their mountain-side homes to greet him, their galibayas billowing behind them. What Edward talked about with these men, closeted away in dark, sunbaked houses while they sucked on hookahs and drew diagrams in the sand, I didn't know. Whatever it was, though, it seemed to have a profound effect on him.

Wherever we went, Kamel went too. Sometimes he entered the huts with Edward, but usually he stayed outside with the children and me. I knew he carried a gun even though Edward denied it. And the way Kamel watched the slow movements of the villagers while listening to the distant, guttural sounds of Nubian drums, I knew he was waiting for something. Always in the distance was the Nile, a shimmery blue ribbon parting the desert. The conferences continued through the heat of the day while, forgotten by Edward, Charlotte, Jonathan and I sought refuge from the sun. The only break in the proceedings came when the cry of the Muezzin beckoned the Egyptians to prayer. Then Edward would emerge, his galibaya and turban coated in dust, and wait while a woman, her face shrouded in a tarha, wiped the sand from his face. He seemed then like a man I didn't know. Until we went to Egypt I'd all but forgotten the sinister premonition I'd had that night at Westmoor when I'd heard Christine and Edward arguing. But while I was in Egypt my fears increased like a swelling black cloud. A sixth sense told me the storm was almost ready to break—and all I wanted was to go home.

Jeffrey was at Heathrow to meet us when we flew in from Cairo. Edward was returning with Christine the next day. We drove straight to the London house in Priory Walk, where Canary was so overjoyed to see the children that I thought she was going to break down and cry. In the Scots lilt we had all missed she clucked her delight at the gifts Charlotte and Jonathan had brought for her, and listened with wide eyes while they talked of pyramids and camels and the trips they had made in a felucca.

The following day I was in the kitchen with Mary when Canary came in. "Would you mind coming to the nursery, Mrs. Walters? There's a wee matter I'd like to discuss with you." And without waiting for an answer she left.

She was sitting in her wicker chair when I walked into the nursery, her hands folded in her lap, her papery eyelids blinking rapidly.

She got up and closed the door behind me. As she passed I could smell jasmine. "I think it would be better if no one overheard this conversation," she said. I perched on the edge of the wicker sofa beneath the window and waited. I could see she was uncomfortable so I smiled to try and help her relax.

"Somebody came to call while you were in Egypt," she began. Her face remained somber, and though she had told me nothing yet, I felt my smile begin to freeze. "He asked to see you but I told him you had gone on holiday."

Her words hung in the air while I tried to control the thoughts that were suddenly careering about inside my head. "Did he leave his name?" I asked finally.

"No." Her face softened. "He didn't have to."

I knew instinctively that there would be no point in trying to deceive Canary. Alexander wouldn't have told her anything, but I could tell from those few short words that she had read the situation perfectly. "Did he say anything at all?" I asked.

"Not then, no. But he came back again the next day." She pulled a letter out of her pocket and handed it to me. "He asked me to give you this."

I stared down at the envelope, recognizing his untidy scrawl. All the time Charlotte had been recovering in the hospital, I'd thought about him. When I was in Egypt, watching the sun set over the Nile, I'd wished he could be there. All the times I'd felt afraid and alone—and had almost cried out for him. And now he had come. My heart was beating so hard I thought Canary must be able to hear it.

I got up. My body felt stiff and it was an effort to put one foot in front of the other. When I got to the door, I stopped. "Canary . . . ?" She was still watching me. "Thank you for not telling anyone about this."

In the privacy of my own room I peeled back the flap of the envelope. My hands were shaking so badly I could hardly pull the letter free.

After I'd read it I lay back on my bed. He'd given me a phone number where I could reach him. He wanted to see me, he wanted to see his children. *His* children. Oh God, what was I going to do?

He said if he didn't hear from me by the tenth he would call again. Today was the eighth.

I lived through the next twenty-four hours in a daze. I had to stop him from coming here—but I knew that as soon as I heard his voice on the phone my courage would fail me. In the end I felt I had no choice. Edward was back from Cairo so I asked Canary if I could use the telephone in the nursery. She folded her sewing away and left the room.

A man answered, and when I asked if I could speak to Alexander Belmayne, he said, "I'm afraid he's in court at the moment. If you call again about five he should be here then."

At five o'clock the children were in the nursery and Edward had gone out, so I used the phone in my bedroom. This time I was put through. As I heard Alexander's voice come over the line, my fingers gripped the phone and my mouth was suddenly so dry I couldn't speak.

"Hello? Hello? Is anyone there?"

"Alexander."

There was a brief silence at the end of the line. "Elizabeth." His voice was soft and I felt tears rush to my eyes. "I was afraid you wouldn't call."

I didn't answer. "Are you still there?" he said.

"Yes."

"You read my letter." He stopped, and I could feel his presence so strongly it was as if he were in the room with me. "Can I see you?"

The tears spilled from my eyes and my whole body began to shake.

"Elizabeth! Are you all right? I'm sorry, I shouldn't have done this to you. But I have to see you, I'll go out of my mind if I don't. Please, for God's sake, say you'll meet me."

"No, Alexander," I sobbed. "No, I can't. Please don't ask me to explain."

"Elizabeth! Don't hang up! Elizab . . ."

I pressed the phone back on the hook and sank to my knees, whispering under my breath for him to forgive me.

At that moment the door swung open and Charlotte came skipping in. "Look at this, Mum, what do you . . . ?" She stopped as she saw me kneeling on the floor, then ran into my arms, frightened tears starting from her eyes. "Why are you crying, Mummy? What is it? What's happened?"

"Hush, hush, darling. It's nothing. Nothing for you to worry about." I smoothed my hand over her hair and felt myself being crushed from within. "Oh Charlotte, Charlotte, what have I done? What am I going to do?"

"I don't know, Mum, but it'll be all right, I promise you. We'll make it all right, Please stop crying, Mummy."

Jonathan let out a loud wail as he came in and saw us sitting on the floor wiping tears from each other's eyes. I held out my arms to him.

"I'm sorry," he sobbed. "I didn't mean to do it. Honest, Mum, I didn't mean it."

"Didn't mean to do what, darling?"

"Whatever it was that made you cry. I didn't mean it, Mum. I'm sorry."

I met Charlotte's eyes and through our tears we started to laugh. "Oh Jonathan," I hugged him fiercely, "I love you so very much." I reached out for Charlotte. "I love you both so much."

We were still sitting on the floor an hour later when the smell of Canary's jasmine perfume made me look up. She stood there for a moment, looking at me, then turned and walked away. When I reached the landing she was waiting in the hall below, holding the door to the sitting room. Her face was grim as she watched me descend the stairs.

"It's all right," I said as I passed her.

"I'll be getting back to the children," she answered.

I didn't look up until she had closed the door behind me, and when I did it was as if I was being carried away on the current of my own longing. Alexander was standing there, in my drawing room, his dark overcoat unbuttoned to reveal the somber grey suit beneath. He could have been anyone—except for the power that drew my eyes to his face, unleashing the blood that, for a moment, had seemed to stop in my veins. He was thinner, and his handsome face looked drawn and tired. I knew I should be angry with him for coming, but when he smiled and I saw the crooked tooth my heart turned over. It was as if a magnet had suddenly drawn together the fragmented pieces of my life.

"I had to come, you know that, don't you?"

I nodded, then suddenly I was in his arms. "Oh, Alexander, I've needed you so much."

He held me close, crushing me, telling me he was sorry, that he should never have left me. I looked up into his eyes and touched his lips with my fingers. "Why do our lives have to be like this?"

He cupped my face in his hands. Suddenly a door slammed upstairs and someone ran down the stairs.

"What are we going to do? You can't stay, Edward will be back soon."

"Tell me about Jonathan, Elizabeth. Is he my son?"

Unable to meet his eyes, I turned away and went to sit beside the fire. "What do you intend to do?" I asked, after a while.

He came to stand beside me and reaching out for my hand turned me round to face him. "I think that rather depends on you."

I pulled my hand away, but still his grey eyes held me. "Please, Alexander, please go now, before anyone gets hurt."

"Elizabeth, you've given birth to two children, my children, whom I've never even met. Now isn't it about time it all got sorted out?"

"It's too late, Alexander, there's nothing to be sorted out anymore."

His face paled. "What do you mean? Either I am their father or I'm not. Which is it, Elizabeth?"

"I think I'm in the best position to answer that." The door closed, and we spun round to find Edward standing there watching us. He walked towards us. "Are you going to make the introductions, Elizabeth?" he said, never taking his eyes from Alexander.

I mumbled their names and turned away as they shook hands.

"I think what Elizabeth is trying to tell you is that Charlotte and Jonathan—those are their names, by the way, in case you didn't know—that Charlotte and Jonathan are no longer . . ."

"*No!*" I screamed. "No, Edward. Please!"

Edward turned to me. "But he has to know, my dear, otherwise he'll think he can come here whenever he pleases."

I saw Alexander bristle and stepped in quickly. "Please, Edward, let me deal with it."

"Shut up!" I had never known Edward to shout at me before. I must have recoiled—and Alexander took a step forward as if to defend me. Edward visibly shrank away from him, but his resolve remained firm. "What I'm trying to tell you, young man, is that the children you so arrogantly assume to be yours are, in fact, mine. Three years ago I adopted both Charlotte and Jonathan."

"Edward, stop!" I ran to Alexander's side. "You've gone too far, Edward!"

Alexander snatched his arm from me. "Tell me this isn't true, Elizabeth. Tell me he is lying."

I hung my head but he caught me by the shoulders and wrenched me round to face him. "You let this man adopt *my* children!" he spat. "After all we meant to each other, you let *him* . . ."

"Alexander, it wasn't like that. You don't understand. I had no choice . . ."

Edward pulled me away and shoved me behind him. His eyes bored into Alexander's. "You have no right to come here, upsetting my wife . . ."

"Your *wife?* And just what kind of wife is it who runs off and gets herself pregnant by another man? And what kind of man are you who steals another man's children?"

"Get out of here!" Edward snarled.

I tore myself away from Edward and ran to Alexander. "Please, listen to me. Please . . ." But Alexander wrenched himself free. His eyes were like ice as he looked back at me. "I'll never understand how you could have done this, Elizabeth. You, above anyone else, knew . . ."

"Enough!" Edward's voice cut between us.

"Alexander! No! Don't go!" I cried, as he started to turn away. "Edward, let me go after him. He mustn't leave like this."

"Stay where you are, Elizabeth. He's out of your life now."

"How can he be? For God's sake, he's their father!"

The blow to my cheek stunned me to silence. And then, before I knew what was happening, Alexander had knocked Edward to the floor. I threw myself down beside him, but he flung me away and dragged himself to his feet. He was breathing heavily and reached out for the back of a chair to steady himself. "Get out!" he growled. His face was grey and menacing and I felt a sudden stab of fear.

Alexander reached out for my hand and pulled me to my feet. "Take me with you," I begged. "Please, take me with you."

"Go with him now and you'll never see your children again," Edward gasped.

"She's not coming with me."

I spun round and my blood turned cold as Alexander's pitiless eyes swept over my face.

"No, Elizabeth. You made your decision the day you let him adopt our children." He shook his head slowly, and at last his eyes began to thaw. "Jesus Christ, why did you do it?" His voice was quiet now. "They were my children, Elizabeth. My children." Then he turned and walked out the door.

I went slowly over to Edward. He was wiping the blood from his nose, his hands shaking badly. For several minutes neither of us moved. He was still holding on to the chair, his body sagging against it. Then suddenly he slumped awkwardly to his knees and his voice slurred from the back of his throat as he tried to say my name. I looked at him in horror as he slowly rolled to the floor.

‡

When we reached the hospital Edward was wheeled away and I was left alone. I paced the corridor, going over and over all that had happened. I detested myself, knowing that I was to blame. If I hadn't married Edward, I could have saved him all this and he wouldn't be lying here in the hospital, maybe dying.

But even then I was thinking about Alexander and the pain I had caused him too. Everything was my fault. If I hadn't seen Alexander and Jessica looking so happy together that night as I stood in the dark at the edge of Belgrave Square, I would never have agreed to let Edward adopt the children. And now he was the one who was paying the price for that unforgivable act of revenge.

David and Christine arrived. Christine's face was white with anxiety and I couldn't bring myself to meet her eyes. If she knew what had brought this on she would never forgive me. I was saved from any immediate explanations by the doctor.

"Mrs. Walters?" He smiled. "Don't look so worried, your husband's going to be fine."

My knees buckled with relief. David caught me before I fell and led me to a chair. "But . . . what was . . . ? Is he . . . ?"

"Your husband's suffered what we call a transient ischaemic attack," the doctor explained. "In plain language, he's had a very mild stroke. Ah, no," he said, as I tried to speak, "it's nothing to worry about, he'll be ready to leave in the morning."

"In the morning?" I echoed, hardly daring to believe it.

"Indeed. I suggest he takes it easy for a while, but there's no reason whatever why he shouldn't continue a completely normal life."

"But what brought it on?" Christine asked.

I felt myself tense, but the doctor was still smiling. "It can be brought on by a number of things—in this case, it appears to have been the spasm of a blood vessel in the brain."

When we reached Westmoor late the following afternoon, Edward and I went straight upstairs. It was cold in our room, so neither of us took off our coats. Out of habit Edward went to sit on the sofa beside the empty fireplace, and motioned for me to sit beside him. We sat quietly for a long time, both of us understanding that he must be the first to speak.

Finally, long after it had grown dark and I had turned on the lamps on either side of the bed, Edward spoke. His face was still grey, though a tiny spot of color highlighted his left cheek where he had been resting it on his hand. His hair, normally immaculate, was ruffled, and automatically I ran my fingers through it, smoothing it into place.

"I was afraid," he said, simply. "It is the only excuse I have for the way I behaved. No, please, hear me out. The moment I saw him I knew who he was, and I was afraid. I could see I was losing you, that I had probably already lost you. I was thinking only of myself and what my life would be like without you and the children, and the loneliness and emptiness I saw stretching before me robbed me of reason. He was so young and handsome, and there was I . . . I realized then what I had done to your life by marrying you." He lifted his hand and wiped the tears from my face, then he sighed and smiled, looking out through the window into the black night. "I can't keep you here any longer, my darling. I know now that I have to let you go to him. I've decided to fly to Cairo with Christine on Sunday, so that it will be easier for you when you go. But I want you to know how sorry I am, Elizabeth. Sorry for the years I've held you to me, and sorry for everything that happened yesterday."

I was crying so hard my voice jerked from my body. "Oh, Edward, Edward. What have I done to you?" He rocked me gently in his arms, stroked my hair and my face as if I were a child. "I'm not going to leave you, Edward."

He squeezed me. "But I shall still go to Cairo. If you change your mind while I'm there, or even before . . ." The breath caught in his throat and he buried his face in my hair.

Edward flew off as planned on Sunday, but Christine didn't go with him. Instead she came up to London to spend the night with me and the children before catching a flight to Hong Kong the next day. She would be joining Edward in Cairo the following Friday.

Canary was waiting when we arrived at Priory Walk, and ushered the children upstairs to prepare their things for school the next day. Jeffrey carried the luggage up after them, and Christine and I followed Mary into the drawing room.

"Now," said Christine, as the door closed behind Mary, "perhaps you'd like to tell me what's been happening." I looked up from the tea tray. "I'm talking about the mild stroke, the pregnant silences, your red eyes, and most of all what Edward said to you in the drive at Westmoor before he left. 'If you do want to leave . . .' Isn't that what he said? So what the hell's going on?" The skin was drawn tight across her cheekbones, and her lips were white.

I put the teapot down slowly, then drew myself up to face her. "I don't wish to be rude, Christine," I said, trying to keep the edge out of my voice, "and I know how much you care for Edward, but what goes on between us doesn't concern you."

The color flooded up from her neck into her face, turning it an ugly puce. "It damned well concerns me when my brother is rushed to the hospital with a stroke!"

"I don't think we should continue this conversation. As I said before . . ."

"Don't patronize me, you bitch! You nearly broke his heart once before, and this time you almost killed him." She was advancing across the room towards me, her fists clenching and unclenching at her sides. "You and your two bastards have caused him more pain than any man deserves, but let me tell you this, Elizabeth, you hurt him once more, just once more, and so help me God, I'll kill you." I thought she was going to strike me—but suddenly, as if she couldn't bear to look at me a moment longer, she turned on her heel and walked out of the room.

I didn't see her again that day, and she had already left for the airport by the time I came down the following morning.

I resolved not to tell Edward anything about it, I knew it would upset him, and cause more arguments between him and Christine. When they returned from Cairo two weeks later Christine greeted me with a sisterly kiss as if nothing had happened, and I decided to follow her lead and keep up appearances. But from then on I was wary of her. If only I'd known how wary I needed to be.

Life resumed its normal pattern after that. Edward and I still entertained a great deal, and Westmoor became an art dealer's Mecca. On the rare occasions when we had no guests, Edward spent his time going over the plans he was still drawing up for a security system in the Cairo museum. His constant complaint was that with such a lack of security there, the Tutankhamun mask was in real danger. I did wonder why it was taking him so long to finalize the museum's security plans, but it was obviously a complex job, and Edward was nothing if not a perfectionist.

In June David returned from Gstaad with Jenifer Illingworth and gave us all the good news we'd been waiting for: they were to be married.

But as the months passed and the dreadful shock of that day in spring wore off, I found myself thinking more and more about Alexander. I even got as far as picking up the phone, though I never called him. Much as I wanted him, I couldn't risk causing Edward a moment's more pain. In the end it was neither Alexander nor I who made the move towards a reconciliation, but Henry.

He made no mention of why he had chosen to call when he did, but I gathered that it was something he had been thinking of doing for some time. He spoke briefly and to the point. He didn't know why I had let Edward adopt the children, but he was sure I had had my reasons, and what he asked of me now was simply that I should explain those reasons to Alexander. He felt—and he was sure I would agree with him—that I owed Alexander at least that.

So, with a complete disregard for all the promises I had made Edward, I waited only as long as it took for Henry to ring off before I called Alexander at his chambers and arranged to meet him the following day.

After that we met at least once a month, sometimes more often, on the bridge over the Serpentine. We would walk for hours, talking and laughing, as I told him about his children. He was hungry for every detail, all the little anecdotes I had stored away in my memory over the years, in the hope that one day I could tell them to him. Sometimes he came with me to collect them from school, watching from a distance, until we drove away. I can't imagine what it must have been like for him, but he never asked for more.

I had dreadful feelings of guilt about what I was doing, but although I was terrified of Edward finding out, I couldn't stop. Edward, though, seemed more preoccupied than ever lately. I sensed a distance creeping between us, and though I couldn't explain it, I knew it was of his making. On the rare evenings when we were at home together, I felt his mind was elsewhere. But if I asked him what he was thinking he'd only smile and hug me, all the time staring abstractedly into some other world.

Then, through the developing friendship between Jonathan and Henry's son, Nicholas, it became possible for Alexander to get to know Jonathan. We spent many hours at Henry's house in Chelsea, and Caroline became a good friend to me. Occasionally Caroline would bring her children round to Priory Walk; it was her idea to do that—she thought it would appear less suspicious if she were to let Edward meet her children.

Alexander and I, no matter what the weather, continued to meet in Hyde Park. Neither of us ever suggested meeting anywhere else; I think we were afraid of what might happen if we did. In all that time we had been careful never to touch one another, though sometimes his smile was so like a caress that it was all I could do not to throw myself into his arms and beg him to hold me. I can't explain how it felt to know that each time I left my car and walked towards the bridge over the Serpentine, he would be waiting there for me. And he only had to turn and look at me—the relief in his eyes at seeing me, then the slow, teasing smile of appreciation as he took in my appearance—for the laughter to well up inside me, making me feel like the happiest and most beautiful woman alive.

Then one day, when we were sitting in the little cafeteria on the edge of the Serpentine, sheltering from the rain, he started to talk about his father. "He was very upset when I told him about you, so we now have another person riddled with guilt on our hands. He blames himself, as you and I do; he thinks he should have tried to understand us more when we were young. He'd like to make up for it, Elizabeth. What do you say? Will you come to meet him?"

"What about Jessica?"

"When she's not on a march she's at the studio she and Rosalind have rented in Windsor. She's designing publicity material for CND, and Rosalind gives free legal advice if anyone falls foul of the police. I imagine they're quite a force to be reckoned with. Anyway, she hasn't been home in weeks."

"How was she, the last time you saw her?"

"The same old Jessica. Charming and sweet when she arrived, at my throat by the time she left. But at least she starts off with good intentions. I don't suppose I help much."

"Why?"

"Well, for one thing I've moved all my things into another room."

The following week I met Lord Belmayne at their home in Belgrave Square. It went off better than either Alexander or I could have hoped. Alexander teased his father because it was clear he had been expecting to see the gauche twenty-one-year-old he'd last confronted at Foxton's. I showed him photographs of his grandchildren while Alexander boasted about how closely they resembled him. I was having such a good time I didn't want the afternoon to end.

At the Lord Chancellor's invitation I went again the following week. He was waiting for me at the door; he had his coat on, and there was a car outside with its engine running. He had to rush off to a meeting, some crisis had erupted.

"Alexander's inside feeling extremely sorry for himself," he said. "He lost a case on Friday after locking horns with someone who's better than he is—but don't tell him I said so."

Alexander was standing in front of the fire beneath the portrait of his mother when I walked in. His hands were clasped behind his back, and with his long legs set slightly apart he looked every bit the viscount he would one day be.

"How are you?" he smiled.

"Cold." And I went to stand beside him at the fire. "Your father tells me you lost a case on Friday."

"After locking horns with someone better than I am. I heard!" He walked over to the record player in the corner. "He was getting his own back because I told him he had a meeting to attend."

I turned to look at him. "You told him . . ."

"I can't take any more of this, Elizabeth."

I stood very still, feeling the color seep into my face. "Remember this?" he said, as "Sealed with a Kiss" began to play.

His eyes held mine, and I was dimly aware of my heartbeat beginning to race. The fire crackled in the grate. And then he was reaching out for me, pulling me into his arms. We danced slowly, until the music had finished. His mouth was so close to mine I could feel his breath on my face. He waited, then as I closed my eyes he gathered me into his arms and carried me up the stairs.

25

THE SCREAM SHRILLED THROUGH the house, waking me with a jolt. Groping frantically in the dark for my dressing-gown, I ran to the door. David was on the landing in his pyjamas and Canary was running down the hall, tucking her curlers into a hairnet.

"What's happened? What is it?"

"It sounded like Christine." David crossed the landing and threw open her door. The room was in darkness, the bed hadn't been slept in.

"Where's Edward?" David asked.

"I'm here," Edward answered. We all turned to see him coming up the stairs and I noted, with surprise—for we had gone to bed at the same time that night—that he was fully dressed. "Everything's all right, you can all go back to bed now."

"But the scream," I protested. "What was it?"

"It was Christine. She had a bit of a shock. Nothing to worry about." His face was haggard and as his eyes moved from mine, I saw him exchange a meaningful look with David.

Canary offered to go downstairs and make a hot drink for everyone, but David put his arm round her and ushered her back to the nursery, leaving Edward and me on the landing.

"Where's Christine now?" I asked. "Is there anything I can do?"

"I think not." He looked over the banister into the hall. "David will go down to her in a moment."

We were all at Westmoor for the summer holidays, except for Charlotte, who was now fourteen and had gone to spend a week in the south of France with a schoolfriend and her family.

At breakfast the following morning no mention was made of the night's incident, and when Christine emerged from her room, much later in the day, there were no visible signs of damage. So I shrugged the whole thing off and started devising an excuse for going up to London the following week.

In fact excuses were hardly necessary these days. Edward spent so much time in his study, or flying backwards and forwards between Cairo and London that he barely noticed whether I was there or not. I knew he was about to pull off some big deal he had been working on for years, but he never discussed such things with me and I had to confess to being guilty of complete indifference now that Alexander was back in my life.

I was in the Blue Sitting Room that afternoon when I heard voices in the dining room. As far as I knew Edward and Christine had gone to the warehouse for a stock check, so I was surprised when I identified the voices as theirs, and was on the verge of opening the adjoining doors when something Christine said stopped me in my tracks.

". . . but for Christ's sake, Edward, they killed him."

"Well, what was he doing there in the first place?"

"They said he'd fallen asleep."

"And what about the . . . ?" I couldn't make out what Edward said after that, but Christine's answer chilled me.

"Is that all you can think about? A man's lying dead, and all you care about . . ."

Edward interrupted. "I've been waiting too long for this to let anything get in the way now. Now, what else did they say? When are they getting it out?"

They left the dining room then. And when I went to look for Edward later, Jeffrey told me he'd gone out and didn't know when he would be back.

I waited for the rest of the day, but there was no sign of him and neither did he call. Christine had disappeared too, though she hadn't gone with Edward, Jeffrey said. Once or twice a foreign-sounding man telephoned, asking for her, but he wouldn't leave a message or give his name.

I drove up to London and found Alexander waiting in the flat we now rented in Chelsea. We'd been living our double lives for over three years now; it was easier for him as Jessica had all but moved in with Rosalind. Our own flat was small, cluttered with things we had bought together in antique markets and junk shops. The children's school drawings were pasted all over the kitchen walls, and photographs of them were scattered about the sitting room and bedroom. When I arrived Alexander was in the kitchen, an apron round his waist, starting the evening meal. I was too distracted by all that was going on at Westmoor to eat much, and as Alexander talked about his day in court the feeling of depression that had been lingering about me for so long seemed to reach him too. We snapped at one another, then yelled over the washing up, broke a few plates and drenched one another in dishwater. We made up later, in bed, but the following morning I drove back to West-moor early.

Edward was in such a good mood I ventured to ask him about the conversation I had overheard. He didn't even flinch.

"Oh that!" he laughed. "It was all a misunderstanding. You know what the Egyptians are like, they make a drama out of every-thing."

"But I thought I heard Christine say someone had been killed," I insisted. "How can that be a misunderstanding?"

"Easily. As far as I can make out there was a fight and one of them fell and hit his head against something. The other one assumed he had killed him, panicked and ran. So apart from one Arab with a large bump on the head, no one's any the worse for wear."

"But what were they fighting about in the first place?"

"Money."

"That you were paying them?"

"Yes. But as I said, there's nothing to worry about now, every-thing has been sorted out, and within a few days the deal will be finalized and your husband will have pulled off one of the greatest coups the art world has ever known."

And that was as far as I got—until Charlotte told me something she had overheard the day after she arrived home from France.

She came in from the garden to find me in her room, sorting out clothes for jumble. She sat down on the edge of her bed. "Mum, I've just heard the strangest thing."

"What was that, darling?"

She giggled. "Well, it was like something out of a movie, except it happened right here, in our garden."

It seemed she had been sitting against the wall under the parterre when Christine and David had walked out of the French windows. She hadn't taken much notice of what they were saying until Edward joined them and David said, "I don't want to know any more than I already do, I'm going in." Edward had laughed, and said to Christine: "So you've spoken to your husband, and I take it you're satisfied it wasn't him?"

I interrupted Charlotte. "Husband?"

"That's what he said."

"But Christine's not married."

"I know."

"You must have misheard, darling. Is that all?"

"No. Then Edward asked Christine where the plane was coming in, and Christine said it was landing at Greg Dunne's airfield, the same as before, and that she'd given him the money."

I put my arm round Charlotte's shoulders and tried not to laugh. "Edward's always having things flown in from all over the world, you know that."

"I know, it's just that, I don't know, somehow this sounded different."

"In what way?"

"Well, David wouldn't listen, for one thing."

I thought about this for a moment. "Tell you what," I said, "why don't we ask Edward what he's expecting? I'm sure he'll be only too glad to tell you."

And sure enough, he was. He was expecting a cargo from Hong Kong the following week, and Greg Dunne was going to call him when it had been cleared by Customs. No mention was made of the "husband," as it was absurd to think Christine would want to hide something like that, so we just assumed Charlotte had misheard.

Over the next few days I noticed a distinct change in Edward. He almost skipped around the house, his eyes brimming with excitement; he looked younger—in the last week he seemed to have lost ten or fifteen years. There was a great deal of activity in the Egyptian Room, painters going in and out, the old treasures being removed and carefully transported by truck to the warehouse. At night Edward tossed and turned, keeping me awake, even though we now had separate beds. In direct contrast to Edward's ebullience, Christine seemed annoyed all the time, and kept telling him to pull himself together. Then David announced abruptly that he and Jenifer were going to the house in Gstaad, and wouldn't be back for at least a month.

After David's departure Edward's behavior changed again. Now he veered from melancholy to downright bad temper and seemed constantly on edge. On one occasion, when Jonathan answered the phone, Edward actually pushed him out of the way. It was his secretary, obviously asking him when he next intended coming to London as work was piling up. Edward barked that he would inform her of his movements when he knew what they were and slammed the receiver down. Then Charlotte came into the room, and the next thing I knew, Edward was shouting at her too.

All this was quite untypical of our normal family life, and I found it so upsetting that I decided to go to London. Jonathan was all for going, but Charlotte wasn't keen. I guessed this had something to do with Colin Newman, who was playing Romeo to her Juliet in the village play, so I said she could stay behind, but Edward declared he was too busy to look after a lovesick teenager and she had to come. And so, with an eager son and a sulking daughter, I arrived at Priory Walk late one hot Wednesday night in August.

It was these small details I had to remember later, when I was giving evidence at my own trial.

Alexander called me from his chambers the following afternoon. By the time we hung up, arranging to meet in the flat at seven thirty, he'd got me so aroused I could have torn off my clothes and raped the milkman. I was still feeling flushed when the phone rang again twenty minutes later. It was Edward.

"Elizabeth, I want you to get back here as soon as you can.

Leave the children in London, Jeffrey can pick them up tomorrow."

"Edward, I can't . . ."

"For Christ's sake, Elizabeth, this is an emergency!"

"What do you mean, an emergency?" But he had already hung up. I dialed the Westmoor number immediately, but the line was busy, and it remained busy. Suddenly all the warmth had gone out of the day and that cold feeling of dread was creeping over me again.

Alexander was in a conference, so I drove round to the flat and left him a note.

I arrived at Westmoor just after seven. Edward was waiting in the drive. As I pulled up beside the Rolls Royce, he tore open the door of my car. "Thank God you're here." He gulped, as if he was trying to catch his breath. "Christine's hurt her foot, I need you to drive the car. We haven't much time."

He ushered me behind the wheel of the Rolls. "Where are we going?" I said.

"Just head for Dover, I'll tell you when to turn off."

By the time we reached the A2 he had calmed down a little. I glanced at him, trying to gauge his mood, then asked again where we were going. He smiled. His eyes were too bright. "Just wait and see, my darling. Just wait and see."

There was a gnawing sensation in the pit of my stomach. I wanted to stop the car, demand that he tell me what was going on—but there was something about him that stopped me.

Just after we passed the Aylesham turning we turned right, down a one-track road. The sun was sinking into the trees by this time, though it was still light enough to see without headlights. After several very rough miles, Edward told me to pull in beside a gate. As we came to a halt he looked at his watch. "We're too early. We'll have to wait."

"Too early for what?"

"Don't ask any more questions, Elizabeth, you'll know everything soon enough."

His eyes were fixed rigidly ahead. This was so unlike any situation I had ever been in before that I couldn't begin to imagine what was happening. What were we doing here, parked miles from anywhere, waiting for a rendezvous with God-only-knew-who? I started to tell him I was afraid, but the words dried on my lips as I realized it was Edward I was afraid of . . .

The sound of a light aircraft droned overhead. It came into view. Edward never took his eyes off it, but he didn't say a word, and even when the plane landed about a mile away, the malignant silence continued. From time to time he looked at his watch, then at the horizon. Finally, when night was a black, solid mass around us, he told me to start the car.

It was a hazardous journey, he made me drive in the all but useless beam of sidelights. I was amazed at how well he knew the road, every twist and turn. At last he told me to pull in through an opening in a hedge, and the road became smooth and straight—it was some time before I realized that I was driving along a runway.

I was so shocked by what happened next that I could only sit in appalled silence and watch.

A man stole out of the darkness and Edward, yanking the keys from the ignition, got out of the car. They spoke for a few minutes, pointing towards the aircraft that I could now make out in the dim moonlight, then back at the car. I watched them walk away until their figures dissolved into the shadows. I was alone.

My ears strained into the silence, half expecting to hear a scream, a gunshot, feet running . . . I looked about me, trying to fight down the nausea of fear. The bushes were great black clumps in the semi-distance and as I looked I thought I saw something move in the darkness. My nerve ends pricked, I could hear my heart thumping. Was there someone there, waiting to leap out of the shadows? Suddenly something moved in the back of the car. I spun round, my mouth open to scream.

It was Edward. He took a small package from the backseat, then got out again. The man was still there; he took the package, then waited while Edward opened the trunk. I heard something being lifted and placed inside, then the trunk closed. The man walked away, and Edward got back into the car. He handed me the keys and, still mute, I started the engine.

"Take it slowly," he said. "No lights until we reach the main road."

All the way back in the car I kept my eyes fixed on the road. I didn't ask what we were carrying, I didn't want to know.

It was almost midnight when we pulled into the drive at West-moor. Christine was waiting at the front door. Edward jumped out, again snatching the keys from the ignition. I followed him, standing back as he opened the trunk and he and Christine eased the packing case out. I looked down at Christine's foot.

"Put the car away, Elizabeth," Edward snapped.

As I walked back from the garage I looked up at the house, knowing already that the lights would be on in the Egyptian Room. And suddenly I understood that whatever it was I had been afraid of for so long was here.

I was in the front hall when Edward came down the stairs. His face was flushed, and he was trembling. "Elizabeth," he sighed, as if one of us had just returned from a long journey. Then walking towards me, he opened his arms and pulled me into them. "Oh, Elizabeth, today is the greatest day of my life." He took me by the shoulders, but when I looked up he was staring past me. "Today I have achieved what no other man will ever achieve." And then the insane, glazed look retreated and his kind blue eyes were shimmering, threatening any moment to spill tears onto his cheeks.

He turned round as he heard Christine on the stairs. She nodded to him, then walked past us into the drawing room.

I pulled back as he took my hand, but he only smiled, and like a father coaxing a child into doing something it was afraid of, he led me up the stairs.

The lights were off in the Egyptian Room, but he didn't turn them on. I could hear him panting as he positioned me at the door, and only then did he flick the switch, flooding the room with light.

My breath caught in my throat. Gone were the ancient stone and alabaster treasures of Egypt, gone were the mummies, the reliefs, the hideous carved faces. In their place, its slanted ebony eyes staring straight into mine, while the headdress fenced blades of pure gold and turquoise which reflected like lasers from the same colored walls and ceiling, was Egypt's—the world's—most priceless treasure: the Tutankhamun death mask.

26

MY SKIN BEGAN TO PRICKLE and I shivered. It was as if evil were a real presence in the room's chill air. I tore my eyes away from the mask and looked at Edward. His face was beatific; I half expected him to fall to his knees in worship.

"My God," I breathed, "what have you done?"

"Hush, hush," he soothed.

"But for God's sake . . ."

He gripped my hand and pulled me outside onto the landing. "Wait, we'll speak downstairs." Then turning away, he switched off the lights and locked the door.

He was right, no one would ever know that the Tutankhamun death mask was here, because in its place in the Cairo museum was another death mask, a brilliant forgery. And no one would suspect, because who in their wildest dreams could ever have imagined that for the past five years a small team of expert forgers had been taking advantage of the deplorable security at the museum to enter the building by day as tourists, hide in the storeroom until the museum closed, then come out of hiding at night and begin their work. It seemed the only problem they had faced was the one of getting the mask out of the museum. But in the end, even that hadn't proved too difficult. The forgers had simply added the case containing the mask to a truckload of packing cases being transported to Luxor, then hijacked the truck on the outskirts of Cairo; later in the day the truck was found with its cargo intact—except for the one crucial packing case that no one had known was there in the first place.

When Edward had finished his recital I got up to pour myself another brandy. I didn't normally drink a lot, but that night I needed it. It was incredible, the two of us sitting in our own drawing room like any other married couple, talking and drinking brandy, while my husband told me calmly and quietly how he had master-minded a crime of theft and forgery unparalleled in the art world's history.

I slept in Charlotte's room that night. Edward frightened me. All these years I'd thought I knew him, and now he was a stranger.

When Jeffrey and Canary brought the children back the next day I was terrified that Edward was going to invite them into the Egyptian Room. He didn't, nor did he go there himself. Instead he drove Charlotte to the village hall where she was needed for a *Romeo and Juliet* rehearsal, and took Jonathan on to see one of his clients in Tunbridge Wells. Business was continuing as normal.

I found Christine in her office and asked her the reason for the lie about her foot.

"Edward didn't want to wait to unpack the mask when he got back, so everything that still remained in the Egyptian Room had to be moved out to make way for it. Jeffrey and I took it all to the warehouse; you were the only one left who could drive."

"But why couldn't he drive himself?"

"You saw him," she answered. "He wasn't in any state to drive."

How I wished David was there!—I so badly needed to talk to someone. I thought of ringing him in Gstaad, but realized that the reason he had gone there in the first place was so that he shouldn't have to have anything to do with this business . . .

Knowing Alexander would be worried about me, I rang him at chambers and for once found him there. I told him some story about Edward being ill. The night before, as I'd tossed and turned in bed, my one thought had been to ask him for help, but in the cold light of day I realized I couldn't involve him. He was a lawyer. If it should ever come out that he had known what was going on at Westmoor, his career would be finished.

On the weekend an absurd normality prevailed. Though Edward was ludicrously happy, and showered us all with gifts, no one seemed to sense that things weren't as they should be. The strangest thing of all was that Edward never went near the Egyptian Room.

The day Edward died began like any other—the children shouting to each other across the landing, breakfast in the dining room, Christine on the telephone to the London office, and Edward lounging with the newspaper in the Blue Sitting Room. I went to find him. I knew I didn't stand any hope of persuading him to return the mask, but I had to try before I decided what I should do next.

I suggested we go into the garden where we couldn't be overheard. As we walked he pulled my arm through his, smiling the half-crazy smile he had worn ever since the night the mask arrived. Again I was struck by the insane unreality of it all: here were a husband and wife apparently taking an innocent stroll round their garden, while all the time they were discussing the presence in their home of the world's greatest treasure.

"Superstitious nonsense," he laughed, when I told him how I had sensed something evil the moment I'd set eyes on it. "Now put all that sort of thing out of your mind. All we need to think about is that I've finally got the very thing I've wanted all my life. And look at it in this way, it's safe here—infinitely safer than it was at the Cairo museum with that appalling security system. They don't deserve . . ." He stopped, and I could see he was trying to get himself under control. "I'm sorry," he said, "it's just that it makes my blood boil to think that anyone, at any time, can break in there and take anything they want. They've no security cameras, no alarms, no . . ."

"But Edward, don't you see, you're one of the people you're talking about. You, or someone you've paid, has breached that security system and taken the most valuable piece in the museum's entire collection. Isn't there some way you can get it back there, darling? That's where it belongs, you know it is."

"You're wrong, Elizabeth. It belongs here, with me."

"But how can it? I mean, you're not even Egyptian."

263

"Who knows who or what I was in a past life?" he smiled. "Perhaps I should tell you about the affinity I've always . . ."

"No, Edward, I won't listen. It's madness. What's happened to you? You've always been an honest man. Why have you done this? What's going to happen to you if anyone finds out?"

"But I've already told you, my darling, no one will find out. There's no reason for anyone to examine the mask that is in the museum now, and only an expert would be able to tell the difference."

"Then now you've got it, why don't you ever go and look at it? You've never been near it since the night it arrived. Oh please, Edward, get it out of the house. Even if you have to keep it, please, just take it somewhere else. I can't bear it being under the same roof as Charlotte and Jonathan."

"We could ask them what they think about it," said Edward. "Here's Charlotte coming now. Shall we ask her?"

"*No!*"

"I was only teasing," he whispered, and kissed my forehead. Turning to Charlotte who was walking across the lawn with Christine, he cried, "And to what do we owe this pleasure? I thought you were dashing off to a rehearsal?"

"I am," she answered, "but there's something I want to ask you first." She seemed reluctant, and I guessed immediately it was something to do with her new boyfriend. "It's just that Colin and some of the others are going to Devon camping next weekend," she said, "and they've invited me."

"I'm sorry, darling," I said, "it's out of the question. All those boys and girls are at least sixteen, aren't they, and you're only fourteen and a half. It's too young to be going away for a weekend like that. And besides, Colin's not exactly the type of boy you should be mixing with, is he now?"

"You mean, because he's not the same class as us. Because his father's only a baker. Well, you're a fine one to talk!"

"I didn't mean that at all. I was referring to . . ."

"You did! You're a snob, Mother. Well, his father may be a baker, but what about yours? You grew up on a fairground! You were little more than a gypsy before . . ."

"Charlotte!" Edward's voice cut across hers. "That's enough! I don't ever want to hear you talk to your mother like that again.

Now, you heard the answer, you can't go, and that's final."

"Who asked you?"

"Charlotte!" I cried.

"No one asked me," Edward snapped, "but I'm telling you. I've had just about enough of you these past few weeks. You're rude and insolent, and it's about time someone taught you a lesson. Now go to your room, I'll speak to you later."

"You can't tell me what to do, you're not even my real father."

Edward's face turned ashen. "What did you say?" he breathed.

"I said you're not my real father."

"Charlotte, come back here," I cried, grabbing hold of her arm.

"Let go of me!" she yelled.

Suddenly Christine caught her by the shoulder and dealt her a stinging blow across the face. "You little bitch!" she snarled. "How dare you speak to your father like that?"

"He's not my father!" Charlotte cried. "He's not! He's not! I hate him!"

"Take her inside, Christine," Edward said.

Charlotte tried to fight her off, but Christine was too strong. Edward and I watched them cross the lawn until they disappeared inside the house.

"I suppose we always knew that one day this would happen," Edward said. "I never thought it would be quite like this, though." He turned to face me. "Does she know him?"

I shook my head.

"But you've been seeing him? No, don't lie to me, Elizabeth, I saw your face just now. How long has it been going on?"

"Four years, maybe longer."

He seemed to crumple then. "All that time," he whispered. "I told you you could have your freedom, but you said you wanted to stay. And all the time . . ."

When I didn't say anything, he covered his face with his hands. "I've tried so hard to understand you. I've done everything I could do to make things easier for you, but in the end you always go back to him. What is it about him, Elizabeth? Why is it that you can't let go?"

To have tried to explain my love for Alexander would only have added to his pain. I stayed silent.

"You've held your love back from me all these years. Charlotte's sensed it. It's what's turned her against me."

"I didn't turn her against you, Edward. I don't know why she behaved as she did, but I swear to you, she knows nothing about her father."

He tried to smile through his tears. "Her father." He turned away and started to walk slowly towards the house. His shoulders were hunched, as if trying to shield himself against any more hurt.

I followed him inside. I thought at first he was going to Charlotte's room, but as he reached the landing he turned in the opposite direction towards the Egyptian Room, and I stayed close behind him—for some reason I felt he wanted me to.

When he opened the Egyptian Room door, I gasped. The walls and ceiling of the room had been painted in turquoise and gold stripes, and with the sun streaming in through the slats in the blind, it was as if the entire room was filled by the mask.

Edward turned to me. "Beautiful, isn't it?" And it was. We stood at the door, letting the light fall over us, absorbing us into the unholy pattern of gold and blue. Again I was aware of the ebony eyes watching me from the center of the room.

Edward went to stand beside it. The serene face, supported by the plaited beard and resting on the magnificent collar of lapis lazuli, quartz and amazonite, gazed up at him with youth and innocence.

Suddenly my blood turned cold. Edward was touching the mask, his fingers trembling so hard they were banging against the side of the golden head.

I caught him as he collapsed, falling to my knees with him.

"The years!" The words gurgled at the back of his throat. "Years," he said again.

"Years?" I said. "What about them? What is it? Oh Edward, please." I screamed for help, but it was already too late.

Over the next few days my most difficult task was trying to console Charlotte. Nothing would persuade her that Edward had died of a stroke, she was convinced she had brought about his death herself. I didn't ask her why she had chosen to mention her real father when she did—she was suffering enough already.

Christine confined herself to her room.

It wasn't until after the funeral that I told David what had happened when Edward died. He was as baffled as I was about why, in his last moments, Edward should have been trying to say something about "years." None of us talked about what was to happen to the mask now, though we were all acutely aware of its presence.

The day after the funeral, Alexander rang. He had heard about Edward. I knew from the sound of his voice that he was genuinely sorry. It was so good to hear him, to speak to someone who was not connected in any way with the whole dreadful business of the mask, that I broke down and cried. They were the first tears I'd shed since that terrible morning in the Egyptian Room.

Alexander listened as I explained that I would never be able to forgive myself for the way in which Edward had found out about us. I told him that we had both lied and cheated for long enough, that it was time to say good-bye before we brought more pain into other people's lives—including the lives of our children.

His parting words echoed my own thoughts and descended over me like a dark cloak. "God only knows why things have to be like this for us, Elizabeth. Our only crime has been to love one another. But this time I know there is something you're not telling me. So I want you to know, when you feel you can trust me, that I'll be here. Until then, please remember that I love you with all my heart."

I was dumbfounded when I learned that Edward had left everything to me. There was, of course, a sizeable sum for Christine, but for reasons known only to Edward, it was tied up in trusts. There was a codicil to the will, to the effect that, should I die before Christine, she was to hold the money in trust for Charlotte and Jonathan. From the tight expression on Christine's face as we left the lawyer's office, it was obvious that this was not the will she had been expecting, and I knew that life from here on was going to be difficult . . .

It started when she came to me a week later and asked for money. I was shocked—not because I would have refused her anything she wanted, but because of the amount she asked for, and the reason she gave for wanting it.

"You're asking me to pay for the forging of that mask? I'm sorry, Christine, but I want nothing to do with it. You'll have to sort it out yourself."

"For God's sake, grow up! Don't you realize you're as deeply implicated in this as I am? You've known all along the mask was here, and haven't told anyone. You even drove Edward down to pick it up that night. You went to Egypt with him, you even went to the museum with him. In fact, if it weren't for you the bloody thing might not be here at all."

"Me! It's got nothing to do with me!"

"It's got everything to do with you. Before you came along, the mask was just an object to him, a beautiful object that he admired. It was because of the way you treated him that the obsession started. He was crazy about you, Elizabeth, so crazy that when you abused his love, kicked him in the face time after time, the only way he could survive was to clutch at something that wouldn't turn on him, wouldn't keep reminding him that he wasn't good enough. It was all a substitute for you. So, like it or not, you're involved right up to your neck." She paused. "Now, fifty thousand pounds is what the forgers want. It's the first instalment of what Edward promised them. And it would be better for both of us if you paid because, as I'm sure you realize, they have it in their power to send us to prison for a very long time."

"But I didn't know anything about what Edward was doing! Oh God, this is all too ridiculous for words. Why didn't he ever talk to me about it? I *did* love him, he must have known that. You must have know what was happening all along—why didn't you stop him?"

"Stop him! I could no more have stopped him than I could have forged the damned thing myself. He had to have it. As far as he was concerned, he was the only person in the world who could protect it. But he wouldn't have needed to protect it if he hadn't been afraid he couldn't hold on to you. He had to have something he could cherish—Edward was like that." There was a cruel smile on her mouth as she continued. "And you ask why he didn't talk to you about it. He didn't tell you about it because you didn't want to know. You were only interested in your lover. All you ever wanted from Edward was his money and his status. Well, you've got them—and now you're going to have to pay for them."

"But I'm not going to pay, Christine. Do you hear me, I'm not! I'll give the mask back!"

She threw her hands in the air, then slapped them against her thighs. "This is the Tutankhamun death mask we're talking about, not some bloody hamper from Harrods! Don't be naive! They want money, Elizabeth. Money! They've given us five days in which to pay, or they'll start leaking what they know—and that includes the murder of a museum security guard, whose body is even now hidden in one of the sarcophagi."

"What!" It was all too much for me to take in.

"You heard me." Her voice was quiet, but the bitterness that coated her words sent shivers down my spine. "He was murdered, Elizabeth, because he found the forgers at work. You heard me scream that night, didn't you? That's what it was all about. I thought it was someone else who'd been killed at the time, but that doesn't matter now. Are you getting the picture? These people aren't to be messed around with. Pay—or I'm telling you, you'll live to regret it. And so will those bastards of yours, too."

I had been sitting at Edward's desk when she'd come into the study, but now I was beside the sofa, gripping the back of it. "I'll need time to think," I said. "I have to go up to London tomorrow, the children are starting back to school."

"You can think all you like, Elizabeth, but there's only one answer, and the sooner you come to terms with it, the better. I'll telephone you tomorrow night. What time are you seeing your lover? I'll make sure I call before you leave. Or perhaps you'd like to give me the number of your flat in Chelsea?"

I walked out of the room, telling her to call me by seven. I refused to give her the satisfaction of asking her how she knew about our flat.

Long before she rang the next day I had made up my mind what I was going to do. She was mad to think I would allow myself to be blackmailed by the forgers. I would go to Edward's solicitor and tell him the whole story. Then at least the mask would be taken away, even if there were dire consequences to be faced.

Christine was furious when I told her what I'd decided. "Don't you care about your bloody children, for Christ's sake!" she screamed down the phone. "These people have no scruples, Elizabeth, they'll stop at nothing."

I told myself she was only trying to frighten me. The truth of the matter was that she had far more reason to be frightened than I did—there was evidence of her involvement in the crime scattered all over the world. So I remained firm, and ended up by putting the phone down on her.

Stupidly, I thought that would be the end of the matter—that I had only to piece together the facts before I went to Edward's lawyer and got everything straightened out. I had no idea what would happen to Christine then, but I would warn her before I made my move so that she could decide what she wanted to do.

David called me later that evening to say that he and Jenifer were returning to Gstaad. He hated to admit it, he said, but neither of them like being in the same house as the mask. I wished I had the courage to ask *him* to sort the whole thing out, after all he was Edward's brother, but I knew the problem was mine—David had washed his hands of it before it had even entered our lives.

The resolve that had carried me through so far was shaken when I called Edward's lawyer, Oscar Renfrew, and found he would be out of town until the following week. I had assumed he would take control of everything; now I wasn't sure what to do next. I left a message for him to call me the moment he got back.

That weekend I took the children down to Westmoor. I would have avoided it if I could, but it was the weekend that Charlotte was opening in *Romeo and Juliet*.

Christine had already gone out by the time we got there on Saturday morning, but she had left me a note attached to the previous day's newspaper. The headline on the page she had directed me to read: "Tutankhamun Death Mask Under Scrutiny." My heart skipped a beat, and I turned to her note before I read on. "Dear Elizabeth, perhaps now you will believe me when I tell you that these people mean business. It won't be long before the experts discover the mask's a fake, but that is the least of our problems. Britain has no extradition treaty with Egypt, but *we* will still have to face charges of illegal import and God only knows what else this end. This leak of information to the Egyptian authorities is just a warning from the people Edward and I have been dealing with. As I told you, they couldn't care less about the mask, what they want is money. I suggest you start saying your prayers, and keep an eye out for those children of yours. Be a good girl and destroy this note when you've read it."

At long last it got through to me that I was in danger. Christine was right, these people would stop at nothing to get the money that was owed to them.

My first concern was the children. Charlotte was at the village hall with the rest of the theater group, where she would be staying until after their first performance tonight. Jeffrey was with Jonathan in the garden. For the moment they were safe.

Next I called Oscar Renfrew's home. His wife answered, but said Oscar wouldn't be there until Tuesday.

"Can I contact him wherever he is?"

"I'm afraid not. He's walking somewhere in the Pennines."

Almost sick with fear, I paced the room, not knowing what to do next. Every now and again I glanced at the newspaper article. It was an innocuous enough piece, but in my agitation I read all manner of threats into it.

At two o'clock the phone rang. It was Christine. "Oh, thank God," I gasped, "where are you?"

"I'm at the warehouse. Now, listen to me carefully. Things have moved faster than I expected. Someone is on their way to see you."

"Who?" I almost screamed.

"Customs and Excise, the Foreign Office, I don't know. What I do know is that someone here has had a tip-off from the Egyptians that Edward is in some way involved in the investigation going on in Cairo. The security guard's body has been found and the Egyptians want an investigation on this end."

"How do you know all this?"

"I just do. Now listen. The mask is still in the house and somehow or another we're going to have to get rid of it. But that's not our only problem. It'll only be a matter of time now before it's discovered that Edward's entire Egyptian collection was acquired as illegally as the mask—and that's enough to create an incident on its own. There's more. It's about time you knew everything, then perhaps you'll realize just how serious this is. You remember all those visits we made to the villages along the Nile? The purpose of those little trips was to grease the palms of the villagers—who, my dear sister-in-law, are sitting on wealth such as you've never dreamed of. All those houses are built on ancient tombs you see, full of priceless antiquities—and while the Egyptian authorities try to buy the householders off, people like Edward give them money to keep them there. In return the householders do a little excavation . . . The bulk of the money goes to Cairo. It's used to buy arms for the PLO, or the Libyans—the Israelis even, it doesn't matter; all that matters is who's paying the right price that day. It was there, Elizabeth, going on right under your nose, and you were too stupid to see it." She paused, and I thought I could hear her laughing softly. "Now, just get yourself out of the house and meet me here. Make it look as though you've gone shopping, and don't for God's sake tell anyone where you're going."

When I didn't answer she spoke again. "Elizabeth," she breathed, and the coldness of her voice curled my insides into a knot of terror. "You were his wife, you have inherited everything. And I mean everything."

I tried not to rush as I gathered my things together, to make it look as though I was going into Tunbridge Wells. As I drove into the village I saw Miss Barsby giving directions to someone, and then I suddenly remembered I'd left Christine's note lying on Edward's desk. Quickly I reversed the car back round the bend, praying I would get to it before anyone else did.

When I finally arrived at the warehouse Dan, the warehouse-keeper was waiting at the door. I rushed past him and up to the second floor. I looked round for Christine. There was no sign of her. Because it was Saturday the place was eerily silent. I flinched at the sound of my own footsteps as I walked to the storeroom at the other end of the building.

When I pushed open the door, I cried out in horror. The entire contents of the storeroom had been smashed to fragments; all Edward's lovingly cherished artifacts were now no more than piles of dust and rubble. His desk had been overturned and the contents strewn over the floor. On top of everything lay torn canvases, all that remained of Edward's collection of old masters, and broken pieces of antique furniture.

I spun round as I heard a noise behind me, then recoiled in terror as I found myself looking into a pair of manic, staring eyes.

Alexander

27

T WAS THE FIRST TIME I'd been to Westmoor. On any other occasion I might have been impressed by its grandeur; as it was I was driving too fast to notice the beauty of the gardens or the breathtaking views over the countryside. I skidded to a stop outside and rapped hard on the front door.

Canary answered, but I pushed past her and was on the point of calling out when suddenly Elizabeth appeared at the top of the stairs. I looked at her, my heart somewhere near my throat. She was dressed in black. Her face was stark, and her hair, her beautiful raven hair, had gone.

She stared back at me, and then I saw the terrible fear in her eyes. Slowly I lifted my arms and held them out towards her.

She clung to me. I could feel her bones jutting through her skin. "I didn't do it," she whispered. "I didn't kill them."

"I know, it's why I'm here."

Behind Elizabeth I could see Charlotte standing at the top of the stairs, as beautiful and tragic as her mother. Canary went to her and led her back along the landing.

It was all too bizarre to be real. In an attempt to cover up what looked as if it might turn out to be one of the biggest and most complex art crimes in history, someone had set fire to a warehouse on the outskirts of London. Daniel Davison, the warehouse keeper, had died in the fire. Two days later Elizabeth had been arrested for murder, then released on bail. Police were still searching the warehouse debris for Christine's remains.

I spent the next three days with Elizabeth, going over all that had happened. She was still in a state of shock, and so distressed that I felt callous in the way I coaxed and cross-examined her. But I had to find out the truth. Of course she was innocent, I never doubted that, but how was I to defend her if I didn't know exactly what had happened?

I knew the Bar Council would never condone my taking the case, so when Henry told my father that this was precisely what I intended to do, I wasn't surprised that he summoned me to his office.

I leapt up from my chair. "For God's sake, father, she's been charged with murder."

"And arson."

I glared at Henry.

"Whatever she's been charged with, Alexander, you cannot defend her. It's simply not ethical."

I rounded on him. "Ethical! Who the hell gives a fuck about ethics! This is Elizabeth we're talking about. She wants me to defend her, and I'm damned well going to."

"Freddie Rees has offered to take her on," Henry said. "He's about the best."

"She doesn't want Freddie Rees. What the hell are you doing here anyway?"

"I asked him to come," my father answered. I hoped he might be able to talk some sense into you. Does Elizabeth know what it could do to your career if you take her case?"

"Of course she doesn't know. And no one's going to tell her. She's frightened half out of her mind as it is."

"Do *you* realize what it could do, Alexander?"

"Do you think I care a damn about that? I've told you, I'm going to defend her." I couldn't tell them how, when I had suggested someone else should defend her, Elizabeth had begged me not to hand the case over. She didn't understand, didn't even know, how the bar would view it, and it would have been selfish and insensitive of me to have told her. I couldn't explain that I loved her too much to let her down, and that, as far as I was concerned, what she wanted and how she felt came before my career—before anything else.

"You don't have the experience to take on something like this," Henry said.

"Especially," my father interrupted, "if they find the remains of her sister-in-law."

"They won't. She's out there somewhere, alive and well, all we have to do is find her."

"But you don't know that for sure. Look, son, can't you see you could be jeopardizing her chances by taking this case? I know how you feel, we both do, but . . ."

"Where in the rule book does it say I can't take this case? Eh? Show me!"

"It doesn't, you know that. But there is a code of practice we all follow, Alexander. It would be wiser all round if you stuck to it."

"How d'you think you're going to keep yourself under control when the going gets rough?" my father said. "Just look at the way you're behaving now."

"Of course I'm emotional now, what else would you expect? By the time it comes to the trial I'll be as detached as you like."

"And if you lose," my father said, "how are you going to live with that?"

"I won't lose."

Finally my father stood up. "I am not giving this my blessing. You have said nothing to convince me that you're pursuing the right course. You will take the case as a junior. Freddie Rees, if he agrees, will lead. It is up to him whether or not he lets you conduct the defense. If you do, then on your head be it."

It was four months before the case came to trial. During that time I all but moved into Priory Walk with Elizabeth and the children, and we tried to carry on our lives as normally as possible. Jessica came to see me from time to time, but our meetings always ended in bitterness. Though she professed to be leading a perfectly happy and fulfilling life on her own, she still behaved like the jealous wife as far as Elizabeth was concerned. It was no surprise when she said she thought Elizabeth was guilty.

"The trouble with you, Alexander, is that your precious Elizabeth can do no wrong. She's guilty, all right, you wait and see. I hope she gets what she deserves—and the irony of it is, it'll be you that gets it for her. You can't win this case, never in a million years."

Rosalind wasn't with her on that occasion and I was sorry for it. At least when Rosalind was around our meetings were a little more civilized.

But as time went on and Freddie Rees agreed to take the case—Freddie who, unlike my father, thought there might be something to be gained from my presenting it—Jessica mellowed, and even took to telephoning me from time to time to see how we were getting on. Freddie monitored my research every step of the way and gave endless advice and encouragement. But our real problem was Christine's disappearance. I even flew to Gstaad to speak to David about her but he had no idea where she might be. He and Elizabeth were both convinced she wouldn't have gone to Cairo as she didn't have the money to pay whoever was blackmailing her. When David refused to come to court and testify on Elizabeth's behalf, I was shaken. Elizabeth had been so certain he would. Nevertheless I took a signed statement from him, detailing everything he knew about the theft of the death mask.

And that was something else that had delivered its own staggering surprise. The mask was a fake.

"You can tell," one of the experts from the British Museum told me, when I went down to Westmoor to see how they were getting on. "You can tell by the holes in the ears."

"What holes?" I asked.

"Precisely. There are no holes. The real mask has pierced ears. And what's more, the holes are quite large. Whoever made this copy deliberately set out to have his work recognized as a fake."

"Why would he do that?"

The specialist shrugged. "Search me. It's such an obvious mistake, and one Walters couldn't have failed to notice. Apart from that, the workmanship is incomparable."

So that was what Edward had been saying in his dying moments—"ears."

I was speechless. Knowing that both Elizabeth and Charlotte

blamed themselves for Edward's death, when all the time it had been this fake that had caused it, sent me into a blinding rage. The only good thing to come out of it was that Customs and Excise were suitably baffled by the expert's findings and decided that, providing the relevant import taxes were paid on the precious metals, the charge of illegal import would be dropped.

Elizabeth could hardly believe it when I told her. "You know, Christine told me that Edward developed this obsession when he realized I would never love him the way he wanted me to. Now it seems he was cheated even over the mask. Poor Edward. All those years, Alexander. All those years I lived with him and hardly knew him. What is it that makes someone do the things he did? It can't just be love."

"The important thing is that you don't blame yourself. There was nothing you could have done. As you said, he was cheated. And by the time he found out he had already lost his mind." I paused. "The person we have to worry about now, Elizabeth, is Christine, not Edward. Christine tried to kill you, and she's likely to try again."

Her face turned white. "You've got to face it, Elizabeth. Under the terms of Edward's will, if anything happens to you Christine gets everything. At least, until Charlotte and Jonathan are old enough to take over their inheritance."

"By which time she will have made sure there is no inheritance to take over," Caroline said.

I had called at Henry's on my way home. Elizabeth was staying there now, until the trial was over; with Christine's whereabouts still not known I didn't like her staying at Priory Walk alone. Henry's house was bursting at the seams with children, for he and Caroline now had four, and Charlotte and Jonathan were staying there too.

Henry walked to the door with me. "Why haven't you told her yet?" he said.

"I will. I'll come back later and take her to the flat. I think she'll need to be alone with me when she finds out."

The trial was set for the following Monday at the Old Bailey. What I hadn't told Elizabeth was that Michael Samuelson was prosecuting. I had seen Samuelson cross swords with barristers far more experienced than I was, but I'd never seen anyone beat him yet. Not even Freddie Rees.

28

THE CLERK OF THE COURT stood. Only his bespectacled eyes and the dome of his balding head were visible above the sheet of paper that bore the indictment. Behind him was Justice McKee, dwarfed by his wig and red robes, though still managing to look his usual irritated self. He cast a glance at the full public gallery. It had come as a blow to us to find ourselves in Number One Court; the oppressive dark wood and claustrophobic air were menacing. I looked up at Elizabeth. Her face was drawn, evidence of the sleepless night she had passed. The royal blue of her dress seemed to cast a bluish tinge over her skin too, and with the weight she had lost during the past months she looked almost skeletal. Behind her in the dock was a prison officer. I looked away quickly, before emotion got the better of me. For a fleeting moment I saw the court as Elizabeth must see it: strange and familiar faces, black gowns and white curled wigs. A macabre theater.

"Prisoner at the bar, you are charged upon an indictment containing five counts. Count one. Murder. In that, you, on the fifth day of September, 1981, did murder Daniel Raymond Davison. How say you? Guilty or not guilty?"

"Not guilty." Her voice was small but firm, and she looked at the judge as she spoke. He didn't return the compliment, and though she didn't move she seemed to shrink back into the dock.

"Count two. Arson. In that on the fifth day of September, 1981, contrary to the Criminal Damage Act 1971, section one, paragraph two, subsection . . ." The clerk's voice droned on as he related each and every word of the subsection, until he asked, "How say you? Guilty or not guilty?"

"Not guilty."

Three more times we went through the same performance as the counts for theft, forgery, and receiving stolen goods were read out. Then there was a hush over the room as the jury was sworn in. Eventually Michael Samuelson got to his feet. The trial had begun.

For two days prosecution witnesses filed into the court. The main focus of attention was on the murder and the fire, but since no one had actually witnessed the start of the fire there was very little evidence to be heard on that score. Finally, on the third morning, Elizabeth took the stand. For the moment, as so much of the evidence so far had been based on hearsay and conjecture, I wasn't unduly worried and felt confident that things were going our way. Nevertheless, as she took the oath Elizabeth's voice shook. Every member of the jury had his eyes fixed on her. This was their first and only opportunity of hearing firsthand what had happened that day at the warehouse.

We began by going over the details of Edward's will, something I would have preferred to avoid, but I knew that if I didn't bring it out first Samuelson would be sure to do so later.

When I was satisfied that the jury understood that the will gave Christine a motive for killing Elizabeth, I moved on to the day of the fire.

I smiled encouragingly and asked Elizabeth to begin by telling us at what time she had arrived at Westmoor on the morning of the fire, and what had happened after she found the note from Christine. She spoke quietly, but coherently, going over the details of the telephone conversation with Christine. She confirmed Canary's testimony that she had said she was going shopping, then told how she had driven her car into the village before returning to Westmoor to make sure Christine's note was not left around for anyone else to find.

"Is this note available to the court?" Justice McKee interrupted.

"I'm afraid it isn't, my lord," I answered. We had searched everywhere for it but in the end had come to the conclusion that it must have been destroyed in the fire.

"Oh," was all McKee said, but it was enough to throw the existence of the note into question, and add credibility to Miss Barsby's testimony that she had been directing Customs officers to Westmoor when she saw Elizabeth reverse out of the village; her implication—that Elizabeth had been trying to hide from the Customs officers—was clear.

I turned back to Elizabeth. "After you collected the note, what did you do next?"

"I drove straight to the warehouse. When I got there, Dan, the warehouse keeper, was at the door. I ran past him up to the second floor where my husband had a large storage area. I looked for Christine, but there was no sign of her. I had only been to the warehouse once before, but I remembered that there was a smaller storeroom at the end of the corridor, which Edward used as an office. As I walked towards it I checked all the units to see if Christine was in any of them. Then, as I pushed open the door at the end, I remember screaming out for Dan."

"Can you tell the court why you screamed out for Dan?"

"Because everything in the room had been smashed to pieces. I couldn't believe my eyes. Even the wreckage must have been worth a fortune."

Out of the corner of my eye I saw Samuelson scribbling. "And what happened next?" I asked.

"I heard a noise behind me. I turned round, but before I knew what was happening I was being pushed into the room."

"Can you identify the person who pushed you into the room?"

"No. I only know it was a man."

"A man. But it was your sister-in-law who had asked you to go to the warehouse?"

"Yes."

"Did you, at any time on that Saturday afternoon, see your sister-in-law?"

"No."

I nodded. "And what happened after you were pushed into the room?"

"I fell into the debris. It reeked of kerosene. Then a lighted newspaper was thrown into the room and the door was closed."

"What happened after that?"

"The whole room went up in flames. I managed to get to the door, but it was locked. I tried to find something to break it down with, but then I slipped and fell and my clothes caught fire. I tried to scream but nothing came out. The room was filled with smoke and I could hardly breathe.

"I threw myself at the door. Then it was as if I was being pushed back into the fire. I didn't realize at first that someone was trying to open the door from outside, so I tried to resist. Then I heard shouting above the roar of the flames and I was dragged out onto the landing.

"It was Dan. He was beating me with his overall to smother the flames and asking me what had happened, but all I could say was Christine's name.

"He must have assumed she was in the fire because he covered his face and hands with the overall and ran into the room. It must have been only seconds after that that a dresser fell and crashed on top of him. He screamed, and I tried to drag myself towards him. He was still screaming when something else fell, and then . . . he didn't scream any more."

She was sobbing, and the judge nodded to the usher to bring her a chair. I waited, letting the silence hang over the court. Eventually she indicated that she was ready to go on.

"Did you assume Dan was dead at that point, Mrs. Walters?"

She raised her hand to her eyes, rubbing away the tiredness. "I don't know what I thought. Yes, I suppose I must have thought he was dead."

"What did you do?"

"I was still lying on the floor. The fire was spreading fast and I knew I had to get help. I managed to drag myself to my feet, then I started to choke again. I realized I had to get outside."

"Did you not consider using the telephone in Dan's office at the warehouse entrance?"

"I only thought of it when I got downstairs, but by then I could hear sirens in the distance and I knew help was on the way."

"And can you tell the jury why you were no longer at the warehouse when the police and fire brigade arrived?"

She started to shake her head, and wiped the back of her hand across her eyes again. "I panicked. I was a coward, and I panicked."

"Why did you panic?"

"My thoughts were so confused . . . I didn't know who had started the fire, but I kept thinking about the people Christine had been dealing with, and how she had said they were capable of anything. And then all I could think of was my children, and that I had to get to them."

"When you got home, what happened then?"

"Canary—our nanny—was coming down the stairs as I let myself in. I told her to get me upstairs before the children saw me. When we got to the bedroom she tried to call the doctor but I wouldn't let her. I knew my burns were severe, but both Canary and I are trained nurses. I think I passed out then, because it was half an hour or so later . . ."

"What time would that be?"

"Four-thirty. Canary helped me to the mirror. I told her to cut away the burnt hair. Then I sent her to the hairdressers to get some hairpieces. While she was gone I changed my clothes and put on some trousers and a long-sleeved shirt. I was trying to hide my burns because I didn't want to frighten the children."

"Why, at that point, did you not call the police?"

She lifted her face, as if to sink the tears back into her eyes. "I don't know," she sobbed. "But I wish to God I had."

"You say here in your statement that you didn't call the police because you were trying to protect your children."

"I was, but I was afraid, too, that if I went to the police, whoever had pushed me into the fire would try to kill me again. I wasn't thinking straight, I did everything wrong, but I knew that eventually the police would come to me."

I turned to the jury for emphasis. "And we have already heard from the police how helpful you were when they did. And your sister-in-law, Mrs. Walters, did she contact you again?"

"No."

"Did you have any other visitors?"

"Only the police. They came to interview me several times, then two days after the fire, they came to arrest me."

She looked drained, and I asked the judge if we might break

for lunch. He agreed immediately, knowing she would need her strength to face the cross-examination.

Samuelson started by taking her back over the terms of Edward's will.

I saw immediately what he was implying—that over a period of years Elizabeth had managed to cajole her husband into leaving her everything, and had then been determined to remove the only obstacle—Christine—that stood in the way of her children inheriting. He didn't belabor the point, but he made sure the jury appreciated it.

He moved quickly to her arrival at the warehouse. "You tell us that on arrival at the warehouse you were accosted by a man. In your statement you say you looked fully into this man's face before he grabbed you and pushed you into the fire—and yet you would have us believe that you are unable to identify him, or give any description of him."

"That's right."

"You are left with absolutely no impression of what this man looked like?"

"No."

Samuelson looked at the jury, his eyebrows raised. "Who are you trying to shield, Mrs. Walters?"

She looked at me. "No one. I'm not shielding anyone. It was as I said . . ." She stopped as I looked away—"Just answer the questions," I had told her.

"Please correct me if I am wrong, Mrs. Walters, but it is your intention, is it not, that the court should believe your sister-in-law wasn't at the warehouse?"

"I didn't see her."

"So she might have been there?"

"I don't know."

"I put it to you, Mrs. Walters, that she was there. Why else should Daniel Davison have thought she was in the fire? After all, it was a Saturday afternoon, a quiet day. Davison would have seen her enter the warehouse."

"No. She wasn't there."

"You claim your sister-in-law had threatened your children. Is that why you fought with her and pushed her into the fire, Mrs. Walters?"

Elizabeth was staring at him in horror, as if she couldn't register the fact that he, or anyone, might really believe she was capable of doing what he suggested.

"Was that why you asked her to meet you at the warehouse? So you could kill two birds with one stone? By setting light to what was stored in the warehouse, and pushing your sister-in-law into the fire, perhaps you thought you would put your children and yourself out of danger?"

"No! No, it wasn't like that. I didn't . . ."

"You didn't what, Mrs. Walters?"

"I didn't see her."

"The jury may think you did, Mrs. Walters. The jury may also think she's in hiding now because she's afraid of you. It is clear she escaped the fire, but perhaps she was a witness to Daniel Davison's murder? The murder you committed with the man you are trying to shield. Is your sister-in-law still alive, Mrs. Walters?"

"No. Yes. No."

"Yes or no, Mrs. Walters?"

"Yes."

"She's still alive? But you say she hasn't contacted you since the fire, so how can you know?"

"I don't . . ."

"If she's alive, as you claim, Mrs. Walters, then where is she?"

I could see Elizabeth was close to the breaking point. Samuelson was just waiting for the moment of her greatest confusion and vulnerability to trick her into confessing. I stood up. "My lord, I think it has been fully established that Mrs. Walters has no knowledge of the whereabouts of her sister-in-law. Perhaps we could proceed . . ."

"Please sit down, Mr. Belmayne."

Samuelson smiled and left a long pause before continuing. "We have heard Mrs. Daniel Davison testify that her husband knew the goods stored on the second floor of the warehouse—the goods that belonged to the deceased Edward Walters, and now belong to you—were either illegally obtained or stolen, and that Davison had been wondering for some time whether he should report this. Is that why he had to die, Mrs. Walters? To shut him up?"

"He didn't have to . . . I didn't . . ."

"And the man you met at the warehouse, was he your accomplice? After all, Davison was a big man; you would need help."

"You're wrong! I hardly knew Dan. I didn't even know myself that the goods were stolen until I read my sister-in-law's note."

"Note? But there is no note, Mrs. Walters."

Elizabeth looked at me, but all I could do was shake my head.

"The kerosene can, found half a mile from the warehouse in some bushes. We have already heard your chauffeur testify that it is the can normally found in your car. How did it get into the bushes?"

"I don't know."

"How did you get your burns, Mrs. Walters? Why did you try to hide them? Why didn't you go to the police after the fire? What were you afraid of?"

"I don't know. I didn't kill him!"

"You are a liar, madam!" His voice boomed through the court and Elizabeth shrank back in terror.

I leapt to my feet. "My lord! My learned friend has gone . . ."

"Yes, quite, Mr. Belmayne." He turned to Samuelson. "I do not approve of theatrics in my court, Mr. Samuelson, as well you know. Please return to a direct line of questioning and refrain from harassing the defendant."

"I have no further questions, my lord." Samuelson was still smiling pleasantly as he sat down.

I did a short re-examination. I would have spared her the distress of answering any more questions, but for the fact that it was important to establish fully in the jury's minds that Elizabeth had been the intended victim of a premeditated murder, arranged by Christine, to be carried out by a person or persons unknown, probably the people who were blackmailing her. Again I got her to demonstrate the obvious grief she felt at Davison's losing his life just after saving hers.

When we left court that day I was unnerved by the way things were going. Although he tried to hide it, I knew Freddie was too.

In the robing room Samuelson congratulated me on the way I had handled the case so far, subtly reminding me of how inexperienced I was. But we both knew our guns were empty of any real ammunition. The lack of facts meant the outcome now rested on our skill as barristers—whichever one of us succeeded in getting the jury on our side would win. And Samuelson had had years of practice.

At ten o'clock the following morning Samuelson rose to his feet to begin his summing up. His notes were spread out in front of him—but over the next hour he hardly needed to refer to them at all. His speech was every bit as powerful as I'd expected and I listened carefully as, step by step, he took the jury through the evidence. He did it succinctly, and in an easy language that no one could fail to follow.

"We now have no choice, members of the jury, but to conclude that the accused is an arsonist." His voice was trembling with indignation. "Why did she try to hide the fact that she had been in a fire, if not because she herself had started that fire? It was only when the police came to question her, and she could no longer conceal the burns, that she admitted to having been there. And where is her sister-in-law now? Afraid to come out of hiding, or . . . Well, I wonder where she is, members of the jury. It is convenient, is it not, that there are no witnesses to this crime? The only certain survivor of the fire is the woman before you, the woman who stood to benefit more than anyone from the destruction of the Bridlington warehouse. Daniel Davison had known for some time that the antiques and antiquities on the second floor were either fraudulently obtained or stolen, and it was because he was on the point of doing his duty as a law-abiding citizen that he died the worst kind of death there is—death by fire."

He stopped suddenly, leaving the courtroom empty of sound. In the electric silence, the full horror of Davison's death came home to everyone.

Samuelson hitched his gown over his shoulders and after a few seconds looked up. "And for what? To disguise a lifetime of cheating, stealing and lying. Remember the accused's own words when she claimed to have found the destruction in the warehouse? 'Even the wreckage must have been worth a fortune.' Her first observation, and one that has come with her into the courtroom. It gives us some indication, perhaps, of the way this woman thinks. Members of the jury, I'm sure you will agree that the few facts we have in this case speak for themselves. There in only one verdict, is there not? Guilty."

Despite his pleasant smile, Samuelson couldn't have looked more like an executioner as he retook his seat.

As I got to my feet there was a shuffling in the public gallery.

The Old Bailey regulars were there, the modern equivalent of the hags who knitted their way through the French Revolution, beside the guillotine. Like leeches, they sated their gruesome appetites on other people's misfortune.

After Samuelson's speech, the jury now presented to me two rows of uniformly hostile faces. Freddie and I had been right to assume, when we put the finishing touches to my speech the night before, that they would not want another detailed review of the events of the case.

"May it please your lordship, members of the jury. It is never an easy task to present the case for the defense, and it is especially difficult for me today, when my learned friend has put such a convincing argument before you. But there is one fundamental flaw in his argument. That is, that he has no proof whatsoever to substantiate his claims.

"As he himself has pointed out, there are no witnesses to the events at the warehouse, and therefore all the evidence on that score is either hearsay or conjecture. In legal terminology, it is circumstantial evidence only. It is on circumstantial evidence only, members of the jury, that you must decide the defendant's fate. And remember too that she is innocent until proved, beyond all reasonable doubt, to be guilty.

"Miss Barsby claims she saw Mrs. Walters drive into the village at two-thirty on the afternoon of the fire. Miss Roberts, the Walters' nanny, has testified that Mrs. Walters returned to Westmoor just after four o'clock. According to Mr. Samuelson, in that one and a half hours Mrs. Walters accomplished the following: a thirty-minute journey to the warehouse, where she started the fire, argued and perhaps fought with her sister-in-law, then—after suffering extensive burns—called Daniel Davison from his post and, together with a man so far unidentified, thrust Davison into the flames; she then ran half a mile down the road to dispense with the kerosene can, ran the half mile back again, and then returned to Westmoor after another thirty-minute drive. Is this likely, members of the jury? Is it even possible?

"Miss Roberts has also testified that she had overheard Christine Walters threatening the defendant. And the evidence presented by British Airways, Pan Am and Singapore Airlines makes it clear that Christine Walters was likely involved over many years in what have turned out to be extremely dubious international transactions. It was the threatened exposure of those transactions, and the defendant's refusal to bow to blackmail, that drove Christine Walters to hire someone to—in the words of my learned friend—'kill two birds with one stone' by setting fire to the warehouse and depriving Mrs. Walters of her life. That, members of the jury, is why Christine Walters has gone into hiding and is not present in this courtroom.

"During this trial my client has never denied her presence at the fire, nor has she sought to deny the evidence of the prosecution witnesses. I ask you to take a look at her, members of the jury. Does she really look like the gorgon of Mr. Samuelson's conjectures? Of course not. She is a decent, law-abiding citizen who has become embroiled in a series of events almost too fantastic to credit.

"There are a great many more things I could say about my client's sister-in-law, but we are not here to try Christine Walters, we are here to see that justice is done in the case of Elizabeth Walters. Justice—British justice—dictates that she is innocent until proved, beyond all reasonable doubt, to be guilty." I smiled and looked up at Elizabeth. Her eyes were lowered, and when I turned back to the jury every one of them was watching her. "There is so much doubt in this case that I am sure you are as surprised as I am that we are here at all. It is physically impossible for Mrs. Walters to have committed these crimes; on the contrary, she was the intended victim. I leave it to you, then, members of the jury, to see that justice is done by returning a verdict of not guilty."

As I sat down I felt a tap on my shoulder, and Oscar Renfrew, Elizabeth's solicitor, passed me a note. "Holy Shit! You've done it!" I read, and I allowed myself a smile. Freddie's face was expressionless, but when I caught his eye he winked. Every face in the jury box showed a confusion of doubt and sympathy. Oscar Renfrew was right, I felt it in my bones.

The judge decided to adjourn until ten-thirty the next morning, when he would deliver his summing up before sending the jury to consider their verdict.

That night Jessica left a message at chambers asking me to see her. On my way home I called in on Henry and Caroline to speak to Elizabeth and tease her for not having faith in me from the beginning. She looked better than she had over the past few days, but the strain was still evident. I didn't feel the time was right to tell her that the next step was to find Christine—before Christine came to find her.

Jessica and I went out for dinner. We talked mainly about the trial, and I was surprised at how sympathetically she listened. I must confess it was good to have someone I could confide in after keeping my feelings under such tight control, and when Jessica told me that my father had grudgingly praised my performance, I couldn't help being pleased. Yet I had to admit to myself that his reservations about the case hadn't been entirely unjustified; defending Elizabeth wasn't the easiest thing I'd ever done, and I still wasn't sure it would turn out to have been the wisest, either.

Jessica smiled at that. "You were so confident a moment ago."

"I still am. Well, I suppose there's always a chance the jury could have some sort of mass aberration . . . No, what I meant was that maybe I behaved immaturely over the whole thing. Because it was Elizabeth, I wouldn't hear of anyone else taking the case. I didn't even know if it would be the best thing for her, I just felt I had to do it." I shrugged. "Too late for all this now, eh? Just thank God it worked out."

After that we talked about Jessica, and what she and Rosalind were doing—but all the same, by the time dinner was over we were on the point of snapping at each other. It was probably as much to do with my intolerance as with Jessica's incurable jealousy of Elizabeth. When we got home we went to our separate rooms, and she was still in bed when I left for court in the morning.

Justice McKee's summing up wasn't exactly biased, but with his reiteration of all I had said about doubt and the lack of hard evidence to tie up the loose ends of the prosecution case, I could see that Samuelson knew he had lost.

The jury returned at two. As they filed in, Henry, who was sitting behind me, directed my attention to the public gallery. Charlotte was there, and my heart gave a flutter as she waved to me. Later that day we were going to tell her and Jonathan that I was their father.

The clerk of the court was speaking. "Members of the jury, have you reached your verdict?"

The foreman stood up. "We have, sir." He looked at me—and in that instant I knew.

"Members of the jury, on the first count of murder, do you find the defendant guilty or not guilty?"

"Guilty."

"Members of the jury, on the second count of arson, do you find the defendant guilty or not guilty?"

"Guilty."

The blood pounded in my ears as I sat rooted in shock. I had been so certain. Henry grabbed my arm, and I swung round to see that Elizabeth had collapsed.

The clerk's voice droned on as verdicts were given on the three other counts. All I could do was stand and watch as the court ushers picked Elizabeth up and held her on her feet.

"Members of the jury, on all counts you find the defendant guilty?"

"Yes."

"And that is the verdict of you all?"

"Yes."

"Thank you. You may sit down."

The judge called for order. "I know you will wish to mitigate on your client's behalf, Mr. Belmayne, so perhaps we should continue."

Freddie stood up. I barely heard his mitigation, but when I looked up I could see that the judge was sympathetic, and indeed before he passed sentence he expressed his surprise at the verdict.

Life imprisonment. Seven years, and three terms of five years, to run concurrently.

I caught up with her as she was led from court, pushing the prison officer to one side and holding on to her, trying to keep her upright.

"The children," she mumbled, "what will happen to the children? Oh Alexander, you will take care of them, won't you?"

"Yes, of course, I—"

Before I could say anymore, she was snatched from me and taken away to prison. It was the worst moment of my life.

When I got to the robing room Henry was waiting with Caroline and Charlotte. Until that moment I had forgotten Charlotte had been in court. Seeing her face, white with terror, I took her in my arms and swore that I would do whatever I had to do, to see that her mother was freed from a prison sentence she should not be serving.

29

THE FOLLOWING MORNING I went into chambers. I knew that for the children's sake, as much as my own, I must carry on as normal. Jessica had been in court for the verdict. She had called Rosalind and the two of them had sat up with me through half the night. There was a certain irony about her support, since she herself had predicted that Elizabeth would be found guilty. Before she left that morning I hugged her, and even had to swallow a few tears as she told me how sorry she was things had turned out so badly. Whether she meant between us or for Elizabeth, I didn't know, but either way I sensed her sincerity and sadness.

Raddish was coming out of my room as I walked in. "We're going to appeal, Raddish," I said. "Get on to Oscar Renfrew and fix a meeting."

"Will do, sir. There's a gentleman to see you, sir. Says he's been to your home first, and your father sent him here."

"To my home? Did he give his name?"

"Yes, sir, Mr. Walters."

My immediate thought was of Edward, but that was absurd. David stood up as I walked in, and extended his hand. Reluctantly,

I took it; I couldn't forgive him for refusing to testify on Elizabeth's behalf.

"Mr. Walters," I said, "I'm afraid you're too late. Didn't you hear?"

"Yes, I heard. It's why I'm here."

"Oh?" I took off my coat and hooked it onto the coat stand behind the door.

"I've heard from Christine."

The name hung like poison in the air between us, and the hatred I felt toward this woman—whom I'd never even met—began to churn in my stomach. "When? Where is she?"

"She called me yesterday, after she'd heard the verdict. She's in Cairo."

I picked up the telephone. "What are you doing?" David asked.

"Informing Interpol."

He shook his head. There wouldn't be any point in doing that, he told me. "The people she's with are at least three steps ahead of anyone in Interpol."

"How did she hear the verdict?"

"Simple. She called someone in Fleet Street." He paused, and looked down at his shoes. "She was at the warehouse, Mr. Belmayne."

"I was never in any doubt of it."

"I think you should go to Cairo and find her."

I looked at him levelly, noticing that the scar on his face seemed to have deepened since the last time I'd seen him, in Gstaad. His thin hair looked as if he'd just come in out of a high wind, and I realized he'd been running his fingers through it nervously ever since I'd come into the room.

"She's your sister, why should you want her found?"

His face was sad as he smiled. "Because, contrary to what you might think, I care very much for Elizabeth. I knew she wasn't capable of setting fire to that warehouse, and I knew too that my sister was. But you see, Mr. Belmayne, Christine *is* my sister, and despite everything I love her very much. When she disappeared—and I swear to you I had no idea where she was—I assumed Cairo was the last place she'd go, given that she didn't have the money to pay the Pasha . . ."

"The Pasha?"

"It means 'lord.' He's the one Edward and Christine have been dealing with all these years. A nasty piece of work. Anyway, after she disappeared and Elizabeth was arrested, well, I suppose my faith in British justice was misplaced, because I never dreamed Elizabeth would go to prison. I just assumed there wouldn't be enough evidence."

"Your sister is cleverer than you think, Mr. Walters. Go on."

"That's it, really. All I know is that this Pasha character has some sort of hold over Christine. I want her out of it, and if it means facing up to what she has done, then so be it, she must stand trial."

I was surprised by that. "Not just a signed confession?"

He shook his head. "But that's probably all you'll get—and you'll only get that if you can find her."

"Oh, I'll find her, Mr. Walters, that I can promise you."

To my relief, the first class area of the British Airways flight to Cairo was almost empty, so I settled back to watch the outlying suburbs of London recede into the distance, and wondered how I was going to endure the five-hour journey.

I willed myself not to think of Elizabeth, but it was impossible. I had seen her the night before, and her face, bloodless and bewildered, was etched on my memory. It was obvious she was still in a state of shock. That worried me more than anything else: how would she cope when she came out of it and fully understood what had happened to her, and worse, what was to come? My heart sank when I thought of the abuse, even violence, she might have to suffer from her fellow prisoners. How would she find the strength to cope, after the ordeal of the last four months and the trial itself? As it was, after just two days she looked ill and couldn't meet my eyes when she spoke. If a door clanged somewhere in the distance, she flinched, and once, as footsteps approached the room we were in, she tensed so hard her nails left deep red weals across her palms.

When I told her I was going to Cairo, she mumbled that she didn't want me to go, that it wouldn't help anything. I knew she wasn't in any state to discuss it, so I tried to change the subject, but she kept muttering over and over again that I didn't know what kind of people I would meet there, that they were evil and I mustn't get mixed up with them or my life would be in danger. I tried to make her understand that this was the only real chance we stood of getting her out, but her only answer was to say she didn't want me to find Christine.

When the time came for me to leave, a prison officer was waiting to escort her back to her cell. Elizabeth followed her down the corridor, her head bowed and her hands clenched at her sides. I waited, but she didn't look back . . .

My head began to throb until it forced me from my seat. Maybe I was in some sort of shock too, for all I seemed able to feel was blinding rage at what so-called British justice had done to her. And I knew already that, once this was over, I wouldn't have to be asked to leave the bar, I would go anyway.

Ten minutes later I was back in my seat and signaled for the stewardess to bring me a drink. She'd been openly flirtatious when I boarded the plane, but after she realized I didn't want company she'd treated me with thinly disguised contempt.

"Alexander."

I turned in my seat and at first I couldn't believe my eyes, "Charlotte!"

She tried to force her smile wider. "I knew you'd never agree to me coming," she said, "so, well . . ." She shrugged.

Fighting to pull myself together, I got to my feet. "How did you get here?"

"I thought I might be able to help. There might be something or someone I remember when we get there. I know Cairo."

I knew she had been to Cairo only once, when she was eleven. Now here she was at sixteen, her hair scooped under her beret and her eyes red and swollen, wanting desperately to do something to help her mother. I smiled and swallowed hard, then I kissed her on the head and sat her down in the seat beside me.

"You're not angry, are you?" she whispered.

"No. I'm not angry, but once we land I'm going to have to put you on the first plane back to London."

Tears welled in her eyes. "Don't send me back. Please! I'll go mad if I can't do something. I'll stay in the hotel, I won't even move from my room if you insist, but please, let me stay with you."

My heart contracted as I watched her face. With her slanted dark eyes and fresh young skin she looked so like Elizabeth. I considered her a child, but she was the same age I had been when I fell in love with her mother.

"Alexander?" Her eyes were imploring as she waited for my answer. I ran my fingers over her cheek and tucked a stray curl behind her ear. "Alexander," her voice was soft, and shaking. "I know you're my father."

To hear her say those words was almost too poignant to bear.

"It is true, isn't it? You are my father. And Jonathan's too?"

"Yes," I whispered, "and Jonathan's too."

She rested her head on my shoulder, her hand tightly gripping mine.

"How did you know?" I said, after a while.

She giggled. "Because Mum was always nuts about my smile. And then when I saw her looking at you, well, I've got a crooked tooth too, see?"

I burst out laughing and hugged her before she could see the tears in my eyes.

"When all this is over," she said, "when we're back in London and Mother is free, can I change my name to yours?"

"It'll be the first thing we do, as a family," I promised, and felt both bitter and sad that Elizabeth wasn't with us to share the moment.

It was past ten o'clock when we got off the plane. Robert Lyttleton was there to meet us. His career with the Foreign Office had flourished, and he was now the Military Attaché at the British Embassy in Cairo, something that until two days ago I had been unaware of. Henry had rung him to fill him in on everything that had happened, and straightaway Robert had offered his help.

I watched his face as he shook hands with Charlotte, and was somewhat bewildered by his lack of surprise at seeing her. "There's a car waiting outside," he said. "I've made your reservations at the Marriott." He smiled at Charlotte, who was busily wrapping herself in a voluminous coat. "I've booked a two-room suite, so you'll be sharing with your . . ."

"You mean you were expecting her?"

"I certainly was. Henry rang to warn me she was on her way, and, I might add, to give me her instructions."

I turned to Charlotte, who was now pulling a woollen hat down over her ears. "Henry knew you were coming?"

She nodded. I shook my head and laughed. I'd have a few words to say to him when I got back.

On the way into town Robert filled me in on what he had managed to find out so far. It seemed that Kamel—I wracked my brains for any previous mention of the name but couldn't recollect one—had been arrested. Robert was uncertain what for, though he was pretty sure it had something to do with the running of an import-export racket somewhere in the Valley of the Kings.

"But what I do know," he went on, "is that the police are trying to find some way of linking all this—the forgery, the alleged drugs and arms offenses, and of course the murder of the security guard—to the Pasha."

"The Pasha? David Walters mentioned him. He thinks Christine is with him."

"He could well be right, but that doesn't help us much. The Pasha practically owns Cairo, she could be anywhere." He waved his hand for me to look out of the window.

Little as I could see in the dark, I understood at once what he meant. Cairo looked as if it were the sort of place you could hide in forever without being found. By the light of madly winking neon signs I could see that behind the modern buildings that lined the main thoroughfare the city became immediately a maze of little streets and alleys, a warren of decaying houses and tenements, all of it seething with human life and activity. To my foreign eyes, it looked like a vision of chaos. Even the main road wasn't much better. Death-defying drivers honked their horns and jammed their accelerators with a recklessness bordering on lunacy. We ground to a halt at the base of the Sixth of October bridge, where ahead of us a policeman was yelling at a man whose body was half out of his car window. Somewhere in the distance loud yet haunting music wailed its contribution to the city concert.

As we crossed the bridge, heading for Zamalik, Robert laughed. "Cheer up! It's not as bad as it looks."

The Marriott Hotel was the most welcoming sight so far: white marble fountains and a golden web of cast-iron arches, it was like an island of civilization quietly resisting the encroaching chaos. As it was nearing midnight I insisted Charlotte go to bed. Robert and

I ordered drinks from room service and sat up talking late into the night.

The following morning at eight o'clock, breakfast arrived, and Charlotte and I sat on our balcony chewing rubbery toast. We overlooked the palm trees, fountains and waterfalls that surrounded the hotel pool. The air was still cold, but the sun was struggling up through a grey, low-lying mist. From the corner of my eye I watched Charlotte as she stretched out her long legs and reached for her tea. She flicked her hair out of her eyes, in just the same manner as Elizabeth always did. I felt a stabbing sense of loss. I had missed so much of her childhood. I had never allowed myself to think too long or too hard about the way I felt about her before, but seeing her now, I could hardly believe the ridiculous surge of pride I felt that she was mine.

She didn't turn her head as she spoke, but continued to look out over the gardens. "I know you're pretending not to, but you're watching me," she said. "What are you thinking?"

I found I had to swallow before I could answer, and then I laughed. "I was wondering how I came to be lucky enough to have a daughter as beautiful as you."

She thought about that for a moment, then turned to look at me with a mischievous gleam in her eyes. "Do you think Mum might have had something to do with it?"

"I think she had everything to do with it. After all, apart from you, she's just about the most beautiful woman alive."

"And you're not biased, of course?"

I laughed. "If I remember rightly, she once accused me of the same thing herself." I sighed. "God, that all seems such a long time ago now, probably about the time you ceased being just a twinkle in my eye."

"Tell me about it. Tell me how you first met, and why it was you didn't marry her when I was born. I'd really like to know."

The phone rang then and I got up to answer it. It was Robert saying he wouldn't be able to get away from the Embassy until two. I didn't relish the idea of waiting so long, but I knew that without his help there was very little I could do. On the other hand I was glad to be able to spend some time with Charlotte. She was right, it was time for her to know the truth about Elizabeth and me.

We were sitting by the pool when Robert arrived, an hour earlier than he'd said. With him was a short, scruffy-looking Egyptian dressed in what had once been a rather smart Western suit. The man grinned, showing more gaps than teeth. His name was Mohammed Abu el-Shami. We were to call him Shami, he said.

Robert explained that Shami had returned to Cairo that morning, and seemed to think that his arrival heralded an end to our problems. I regarded the weaselish little man sceptically—but I had only to listen to his broken English for half an hour to realize that he knew everyone and everything to do with the city's covert world. Favors was the currency used, and I was soon persuaded that half of Cairo owed Shami a favor—I didn't ask about the other half. Robert had already explained to him why I was there, and he would go away now, he said, and "begin the ball turning."

His round face beamed with pleasure as he added, "You have no cause to worry, Meester Belmayne. There is nothing Shami cannot do." And he dragged a tobacco-stained hand from his pocket which he held under my nose, rubbing thumb against fingers and leaving me in no doubt as to the magic ingredient required for the performance of Shami miracles.

That evening Charlotte and I attended a cocktail party at the British Embassy. The Ambassador, David told me, had taken a particular interest in our case, and had expressed a desire to meet us. I guessed immediately that my father had been on the phone to him.

It was a strange feeling, turning up at an official function with my daughter on my arm and I had to hide a smile as she took a compact from the beaded purse Robert's wife Susie had lent her, and checked her lipstick before we went in. She looked beautiful. Her dark hair curled loosely round her shoulders, and the long white jacket and pleated grey-and-white linen skirt—"by Calvin Klein," she'd informed me—highlighted perfectly the slight tan she'd already acquired. I felt ridiculously proud when heads turned as she walked in, and almost choked when she winked at me and asked if I'd feel happier introducing her as my girlfriend.

When we got back to the hotel there was a message from Shami. It told me that if I wanted to find out where Christine was,

I should go straightaway to the supine statue of Rameses II at Memphis.

Robert was still at the Embassy, so—since I didn't know how long I would be—Susie offered to take Charlotte home with her. The minute the Embassy car turned the corner, heading for Aguza, I asked the doorman to call me a taxi.

"You go to Memphis?" the driver said, as he pulled away from the hotel. I caught his eye in the mirror. I hadn't told the doorman where I wanted to go.

It was a long drive, and once out of the glare of the city lights we were driving into a dark unknown, with a cluster of black bushes to our right and an expanse of dry, barren land to the left. Neither of us spoke. Finally, after about half an hour, we pulled off the road and the driver switched off his headlights. In the dim glow of the moon I saw no more than a sandy wasteland.

"Rameses." The driver was pointing. "You wait."

I got out of the car and started to walk in the direction he had indicated. I heard the car turn round. Then, to my alarm, it drove off.

About ten yards in front of me I could make out a building. Then the moon slid behind a cloud. I had never known such darkness. The wind whined over the desert and strange night creatures twittered and squalled. My skin prickled.

I trod carefully through the sand. Coming up against the building, I ran my hands along the smooth concrete until I found an opening. I called out, but the only answer was my own voice, echoing eerily around an open chamber. I decided to wait at the door—there was no point in going inside when it was too dark to see.

Time ticked by. Once I saw a car approaching in the distance, but it turned off before it reached me. The wind picked up. Something ran across my foot. I stepped back and it scuttled off into the night. Then I heard a noise and spun around. There was only the looming shadow of a tree, bending and creaking in the wind.

As quickly as the wind had risen, it dropped. The silence it left was eerie, and I was beginning to wonder how the hell I would get back when suddenly the chamber was flooded with light. I waited a moment, expecting someone to come out. When no one did, I made my way tentatively inside. The only sound was the flutter of a bird, disturbed by the sudden blaze of light. That, and my footsteps.

I looked round. In front of me, lying on its back in the center of the room, was a colossal statue. I froze. The slanting, stone eyes were as sinister as the insane serenity of the limestone smile. Pugnacious arms with clenched fists pressed against the skirted torso, and below the powerful thighs and knees the right shin bore the jagged edge of amputation.

"Mr. Belmayne?"

I spun round as the owner of the voice stepped out of the shadows. He was as tall as me, but slighter. His black hair was combed neatly back from his face, and greased into place. His suit was dark, his shirt a dazzling white against his brown skin. He held out his hand to me. I looked at it, but didn't take it.

"Are you the Pasha?" I asked, knowing instinctively that he wasn't.

He smiled, and the gold in his mouth glinted. "You are very formal, Mr. Belmayne," he said, eyeing my dinner suit. "I saw you earlier, leaving the Embassy with your daughter. A very beautiful girl."

He shrugged when I didn't answer, and took out a cigarette. "Shami tells us you are looking for someone."

"Do you know where that someone is?"

He laughed. "Maybe she does not want to be found."

"Then why are you here?"

"I am here to show you it would be wise to return to your own country."

"I'll leave when I've found her."

"It is unlikely, Mr. Belmayne, that you will have the chance to find her. She has asked me to deliver a message to you. It is a very short one." He took a long draw on his cigarette, then ground it into the dust.

I waited. Our eyes locked. He was smiling, mockingly. Not for one second did I doubt that he meant to use the gun he was now taking out of his pocket.

His finger tightened on the trigger and there was a dull click. He laughed, and I felt myself breaking into a cold sweat. Again his finger moved. I didn't have time to pray for a distraction before it was upon us. I looked up at the bird, and so did he. The gun flew from his grasp as my foot connected with his wrist and my fist smashed into his face. I swung round, searching frantically for the gun. As I made a dive for it, his foot exploded into my groin and I dropped to the ground in agony. Within seconds he was holding the gun to my head. I heard footsteps, then, as something crashed into my skull, I lost consciousness.

30

I WAS WOKEN BY a party of Japanese tourists peering down at me. Dazed and disoriented, I blinked hard as I tried to focus on the ceiling of bewildered faces. Seeing my eyes open, one of them helped me to my feet while another, somewhat robustly, dusted me down.

Fortunately the Japanese tour guide spoke English, so I was able to ask for the nearest phone. He laughed loudly, and translated my request to his party who, slapping me fondly on the back, joined in the joke. However, after much toing and froing I managed to hitch a ride on a horse and cart. The driver, an elderly, toothless peasant who spoke not a word of English, dropped me off at a run-down hotel somewhere on the road to Sakkara.

Once he had established where I was Robert came to collect me.

"Do you know who it was?" he asked. We were nearing the outskirts of Cairo, and I saw his hands tighten on the wheel as he prepared to do battle with the city drivers.

"No. He didn't leave his calling card. All he said was that he had a message from Christine."

"And the message was your hasty despatch?"

"You know, what beats me," I said, as we bumped our way through uncordoned roadworks, "is why he didn't kill me."

"Well, don't sound so put out. My guess is they were just putting the frighteners on. If they'd wanted to kill you they'd have done it, be in no doubt of that."

When we got back to the hotel Robert came in and waited while I showered and changed. The hotel manager called to check that everything was all right, as the security guard he'd posted outside my door, at the Ambassador's request, had told him my room hadn't been slept in all night.

It was probably because of the manager's call that I noticed, when we left half an hour later to go and collect Charlotte, that there was no guard outside. I asked Robert if he remembered there being one when we'd come in. He frowned. He thought there had been, but he wouldn't swear to it.

I went back into the room to call the manager, leaving Robert outside, searching the corridor for the guard. But before I could pick up the phone it rang.

"Mr. Belmayne?"

"Speaking."

"You don't know me, Mr. Belmayne, but I am calling for the Pasha." The voice was Oxford smooth. "It was *inshallah,* was it not, Mr. Belmayne, that you came to no harm last night in Memphis. Allah smiles upon you. However, the gun was merely a means of communicating to you Miss Walters' reluctance to be found. The Pasha feels certain that you will now be willing to do as he asks so that we can avoid any further unpleasantness. All you have to do is go to the Suez Canal Bank, where the Shari el-Giza meets the Shari el-Nil. Somebody will be waiting for you there. You will be given an account number. Please place into this account one hundred and fifty thousand Egyptian pounds—roughly fifty thousand pounds sterling. When you have done this, you are to take the next flight back to London. Your seat is booked, courtesy of the Pasha. I thought you would prefer to fly British Airways. You will find your ticket waiting for you at the . . ."

"And Christine Walters?"

"I think you misunderstood me, Mr. Belmayne. The money is not for the deliverance of Miss Walters. The money is merely the first installment of what Mrs. Walters owes the Pasha. And in re-

turn, because the Pasha is a generous man, he will endeavor
to . . ."

"I will pay the amount you ask, not as an installment of any
deal *Mr. Walters* set up with the Pasha, but for Christine Walters."

"Mr. Belmayne, you *will* pay the money. But, I am sorry to say,
on the Pasha's terms, not your own."

"I am in this country to locate Christine Walters. Until I do,
then please tell the Pasha I shall not be leaving."

"Perhaps, Mr. Belmayne, you will reconsider when I tell you
that your daughter, even as we speak . . ."

My mouth went dry. "Charlotte! Where is she? What the
hell . . ."

"She is safe, Mr. Belmayne. Please, just do as I ask and she will
remain so." And the line went dead.

"*Jesus Christ!*" I spun round as Robert came running in. "Charlotte! Where is she? I thought she was with your wife."

"She is. What's going on?"

"That phone call . . ." I snatched up the receiver and started
to dial. The phone rang at the other end, and almost straightaway
Susie answered.

"Alexander. At last. What happened? Where . . .?"

"Where's Charlotte?" I barked.

"Isn't she with you?"

I felt the bottom drop out of the world. "No, she's not with me.
When did you last see her?"

"About an hour ago. I dropped her off at the hotel."

"Then where is she now?" The question was futile, of course.

I slammed the phone down and caught Robert by the throat.
"They've got her. Do you hear me?"

Robert wrenched himself free and snatched up the phone. "I'm
going to ring the Ambassador. What did the man say exactly?"

I told him. "Have you got the money?" he asked.

"Of course I've got the fucking money. The money's nothing."

"Then I suggest you do as they say."

"Robert, you'd better get this into your head now. I am not
leaving this country until I've got my daughter, so don't let's even
discuss it."

"Robert Lyttleton here," he said into the phone, "put me on
to the Ambassador. I don't care if he's in a meeting, put me on now!"

He waited as the operator put him through, and I paced the room, berating myself over and over for not sending Charlotte straight back to England.

"What did he say?" I asked, as Robert replaced the receiver.

"He's getting on to London."

"London! What fucking good will that do?"

"We'll see," he answered. "Meanwhile I suggest we get ourselves over to the Suez Canal Bank."

We stopped off at the hotel manager's office. Thank God he wasn't like his fellow countrymen. Instead of the million apologies I had been expecting, he merely picked up the telephone. I had no idea what he was saying, but when he'd finished he told me to go to the National Arab Bank by the lobby where one hundred and fifty thousand Egyptian pounds would be waiting for me.

When we got to the Suez Canal Bank we didn't have to wait long before I was approached by an old woman, huddled darkly behind her gilbab and khimara.

'Eengleesh?" she hissed.

I nodded, and she handed me a scrap of paper, then turned and disappeared into the crowd. I made to go after her, but Robert pulled me back. "She'll have been paid to deliver the note. It'll have passed through too many hands before hers for us to be able to find out where it came from." He took the piece of paper from me and unfolded it. The only thing written on it was a bank account number.

The transaction went smoothly and I was outside the bank again in less than ten minutes. Robert was waiting in a taxi. "I think we'd better go to the Embassy," he said.

"Drop me at the hotel. If anyone wants to contact me, that's where they'll try."

But for the rest of that day we heard nothing.

The first call came the next morning. It was the Ambassador to say the tracing of the bank account had led nowhere. However, his instructions had come through from Whitehall. He was to inform President Mubarak that Her Majesty's Government would be greatly obliged if every effort would be made by the People's Assembly to ensure the safe return of the Lord Chancellor's granddaughter, forthwith.

I looked at Robert, dumbfounded.

"I don't think you realize, Alexander, just what . . ."

"*You don't think I realize?* This is my daughter we're talking about. She's been kidnapped. *Kidnapped!* Given the lunatics we're dealing with, she could be lying out there dead for all I know—and all you lot can come up with is a polite request that she should be returned! What bloody good do you think *that's* going to do?"

"You'll see," he answered calmly. And within the hour I did.

The Cairo Chief of Police came to my room at the Marriott. With him was the British Ambassador and two henchmen. The Chief questioned me for over an hour, during which time an emergency police headquarters was set up in the Verdi Salon downstairs.

"The Pasha is being questioned," the Chief said, as he pulled back the curtains and looked down into the garden.

My heart thumped adrenalin into my veins. "You know where he is?"

"We have him at headquarters. I'm afraid so far this is all we have to go on." He took a scrap of paper from his pocket and laid it on the table. "It is all the Pasha will say."

We all looked at it, but it was written in Arabic. I didn't bother to disguise my irritation. "So, what does it say?"

"It says, Mr. Belmayne, the French earl curses into double figures."

"And what the hell is that supposed to mean?"

"As it stands, nothing. We have to work it out. It is the way the Pasha works."

The Ambassador looked bemused. "You mean it's a riddle?"

"I suppose, yes. But it is more than that, I'm sure. I believe it will give us the clue to where your daughter is being held, Mr. Belmayne." I glared at him, certain he had taken leave of his senses. He turned to the Ambassador. "Your intelligence agents, sir, I think they should join forces with the police in order to break this code. We have very little time."

I snatched up the piece of paper. "For God's sake, it's a riddle. The way you're behaving, anyone would think it held the answer to the Middle East crisis. A French earl is a count! Curses. Oaths, spells, scourges, plagues . . . Double figures. Anything from ten."

"The ten plagues," Robert said.

"Incidentally," the Ambassador said, "I have just learned . . . What is it, Mr. Belmayne? Has something . . .?"

"The tenth plague," I whispered, and when I realized they were all staring at me, I almost yelled, "If you knew your Bible . . . The tenth plague was the death of the first-born."

The Ambassador looked at me, appalled, and I stared back at him. *She's dead! She's dead!* The words thumped with my heartbeat. Her face swam before my eyes, and I felt the knife of terror rip through my body.

The Chief was speaking. "Please, don't be alarmed," he was saying, "it is early days yet. And now you, Mr. Belmayne, you have given us a beginning." Despite his words he looked defeated.

I exploded. "Didn't you hear what I said? Isn't the message loud and clear? Isn't that what the tenth plague means? It's your damned country, your damned history!"

"Oh yes, that is without a doubt what it means. But that is only the surface meaning. The Pasha, he will never make anything so simple as that. You see, you break the code in minutes, or so you think. But what we do now is solve the riddle of the tenth plague."

Observing my reaction, the Chief obviously felt it best he withdraw at that point. I had been living on my nerves ever since Charlotte's abduction, and now, with this new, implausible turn of events it was highly probable I might go over the edge at any moment.

After a sleepless night the police were still no closer to finding her. The Verdi Salon was in chaos; just about every cryptographer in the Middle East had been sectioned off to help decipher the "conundrum," as they were now calling it. The only people keeping a reasonably cool head seemed to be the Chief of Police and the hotel manager.

Another day went by, and still we heard nothing. My father telephoned but I cut him short, wanting to keep the line free. Henry rang later, but again I terminated the call before he could get started.

On the third day, just before lunch, Robert arrived with a handful of telegrams. He passed them to me just as the telephone, which had been silent all morning, burst into life.

"Mr. Belmayne? Claude de Rousse here, from *Le Monde.*"

"*Le Monde?*"

Robert pressed his fingers on the connectors and ended the call. "I should read the telegrams if I were you. Somehow the story has leaked out. What you have there are messages from the great British public, expressing their support."

"What!"

"Some clever hack has pieced together your story, Alexander, old chum. It's all over the press back home, so I'm told. Front page stuff. The great love story of the century, I think one of them called it. You and Elizabeth."

"Me and Elizabeth? But what . . .?"

"You'll find it goes right back to Foxton's, I'm afraid. The gypsy and the aristocrat. It's caught everyone's imagination. How you've loved each other secretly all these years, even that you're the father of her two children. Everything's there. Haven't read it myself, of course, Henry told me. He called me last night. Said he called you first, but got cut off."

I was listening to him in stupefied silence, while all the time a volcanic rage was rumbling through my gut. When he finished I exploded. "This isn't a bloody soap opera!" I yelled. "Don't they realize . . ."

The phone cut me short. Robert picked it up. "I'm afraid Mr. Belmayne isn't available for comment at the moment," he said, and hung up. He rang through to the manager then, and asked him to instruct the operators to divert all calls from the press to the Verdi Salon.

"Now calm down," he said, turning back to me. "Don't you see, with the British public and the press on your side, it puts all the more pressure on the Egyptians to find her. And they will."

"I wish I had your confidence. And where the hell is Shami?"

Robert looked at his watch. "He should be arriving any minute. He says he knows where Christine is."

"What! Why didn't you tell me this before?"

He shrugged. "Thought I ought to warn you about the paparazzi. They all flew in this morning, so we're going to have to sneak out the back way."

"And the police? Have you told them you might know where Christine is?"

"The Chief is on his way up. Incidentally, the telegram on the top is from your wife."

He grinned at my look of dismay. "I'd read it, if I were you. I don't think you'll be disappointed."

It was very short. "Good luck, darling," I read, "try and stay in one piece for our divorce. Love, Jess."

I looked at Robert and saw he was laughing. For the first time in days I laughed too. "She certainly knows how to pick her moment," I said. "Cable her back for me, will you?"

"The message?"

" 'It's a promise.' "

The moment Shami walked in and saw the Chief of Police, his eyes sank back in their sockets. He mumbled his apologies for bursting into the wrong room and started to close the door. The Chief was too quick for him and hauled him back inside.

He looked more shifty than ever as he admitted that it wasn't he who had seen Christine, but his brother. He shrugged. "But is the same thing, no?"

The Chief shook his head, and Shami looked crestfallen. "But I explain, my brother, he know wife of second cousin of Pasha, she take my brother to a place where they see your Christine. It is in Khan-el-Khalili, where the men they make the gold. The gold they use for King Tutankhamun mask, no?"

The Chief was eyeing Shami. "What Tutankhamun mask, Shami?"

Shami looked round the room helplessly. "I dunno, sir. Shami, he know very little." He turned his eyes to me. "But my brother, he say to be at Fishawi today. Someone will lead us to the men, and maybe they tell you where is your Christine. We hurry there now, yes?"

"Yes," said the Chief.

Shami's face was gloomy as he said his brother would not be pleased if he arrived with the police. "Not that he no like the police," he hastily assured us.

The Chief tossed us a wry smile and picked up the telephone. He spoke hurriedly in Egyptian, then asked us to wait a few minutes while his men arranged a decoy out of the hotel, to mislead the press.

A fleet of cars was waiting, none of them marked with police insignia. As we sped away from the hotel I noticed several of them break away from the convoy and fall anonymously into the traffic.

When we reached the bazaar the Chief disappeared inside the

Sayyidna el-Hussein Mosque. Two of his men followed, and when they emerged several minutes later, they were all three dressed in traditional Egyptian garb. A police officer I recognized from the Verdi Salon approached us. He spoke to the Chief, waving his arms in the direction of the bazaar. The Chief listened gravely, nodded his head, then turned to us.

"My men are in position. They are covering the Khan el-Khalili at every strategic point. I must instruct you, Mr. Belmayne, that should we encounter any danger you are to leave everything to them. Please, no heroics. You do not understand the kind of people we are dealing with here. To them everything is *inshallah*— God's will. If a man stands in their way and they have to kill him to get what they want, it is *inshallah,* they do not think twice." He turned to Shami. "Go ahead to the Fishawi, and no tricks, Shami, you will be being watched."

When Shami had blended into the crowd the Chief turned again to Robert and me. "Now, please, follow me. I will lead you to the Fishawi—it is a coffee bar a few streets from here. When you see me sit down, please go no farther than a nearby stall where you should inspect the merchandise. Do not, under any circumstances, move from there unless I say so. We will be in Shami's hands. And again I stress, please, no heroics."

A few minutes later we plunged into the pandemonium of the Khan el-Khalili. The Fishawi wasn't far, but I knew that if I tried to find my way there again I would undoubtedly fail. The Chief, in his striped galibaya and turban, blended perfectly into the coffee bar crowd. Robert and I stood innocuously by, hustled and jostled as we inspected a display of brass and copper pots. Within seconds the owner of the stall was asking us to name a price, and so as not to call unnecessary attention to ourselves, Robert entered into a long-drawn-out haggle. I made a pretense of watching them, but all the time my eyes were fixed on Shami, who was seated a few tables from the Chief of Police.

Through the hanging haze of smoke and steam I could see blank faces sucking peacefully on their hookahs, while excited traders bellowed for turbid mint tea and Turkish coffee. The Fishawi was a strange place. Though decaying and filthy, it had a unique sepia-like charm; battered tables spilled out into the covered alleyway, and waiters scuttled back and forth hoisting hookahs and trays from kitchen to table.

Robert bought a copper tray.

To my dismay I watched Shami remove his shoes and hand them to a shiner. The Chief called for a hookah, and Robert bought an urn. Time dragged on.

Eventually the Chief set aside his hookah and wandered over to us. He made a pretense of admiring the brass pots while saying he could only assume that either Shami had been lying, or he himself had been recognized.

My heart sank. I moved to one side to let a woman and her baby pass, thrusting my hands in my pockets before I hammered my fists against the nearest object.

I felt a sharp kick on the leg and Robert—now so laden with purchases he could barely move—nodded towards Shami. The woman who had just passed us was standing over him, speaking to him hurriedly. Shami listened, stroking the baby's head. When the woman had finished, she tucked the baby back into its blanket and started to move away. Shami got to his feet.

I started towards him but the Chief pulled me back. "Wait," he hissed.

The woman and Shami disappeared round a corner and we moved across the Fishawi. As we rounded the curve of the building I spotted the woman, pressing determinedly through the crowd. Shami was behind her. Following him, we pushed steadily on through the maze of passageways, past stalls selling carpets, jellabas, jewelry . . . Traders dived into my path, thrusting their wares in my face, and motorcycles roared through the crowds, but I never took my eyes from the woman ahead. Suddenly somebody screamed, there was the crash of a stall falling, and a motorcycle skidded into a shop front. I looked up, and the woman had disappeared.

I started to run, tearing through the people, thrusting them ruthlessly aside. My eyes darted from left to right, searching the alleys. A man grabbed me by the arm, spinning me round to show me the damage I'd done to his stall, but I shook him off and charged on. A sea of startled faces loomed towards me as I pressed through the crowds. And there was the woman with the baby again, but no Shami. She was standing on a corner, looking to her right. I forced my way towards her, but as she saw me she ran on. I let her go and turned into the dark alley. It was thronged with sheep, but at the other end I saw Shami's scrawny figure disappear into a doorway.

The animals huddled round my knees in a knot of bleating, lice-ridden bodies. I grabbed at them, throwing them one on top of another as I forced my way through. There was no sign now of either Robert or the Chief.

The doorway opened into a blackened passage. I almost drew back as the acrid stench kicked at my gut. The walls were slimed with mildew and the dingy linoleum floor was coated with filth. I strained my eyes to see into the shadows. Several feet to the right was a staircase. I took it, two steps at a time. When I reached the top, I could see daylight at the end of a corridor. I rushed towards it, and as I pushed out into the fresh air I found myself faced with a maze of roofless gangways and stairwells. Turning into the near-est, I felt my foot hit something heavy and soft. I looked down into a face covered in blood. Shami groaned. I bent down to help him, and as I did so a foot crashed into the side of my head.

Then there was mayhem. I fell onto Shami, blood cascading from my mouth and nose, as my attackers trampled over me and ran back the way I had come. I dragged myself to my feet and down the stairs after them. A gun was fired and I dodged back into the shadows. Then there was the sound of running feet and voices yelling. More gunfire—and I dashed out into the street. The police were swarming in as my attackers—four of them—fled in all direc-tions. I saw one of them dive into a twisting alley and made after him. We broke out at the other end into the very heart of the bazaar. I paused and looked round. Someone screamed, and a black Peugeot sprang out of the crowd.

Quick as a flash, I heaved a driver out of his taxi. As I started the engine the passenger door flew open and Shami, his face bat-tered and still bleeding, leapt in beside me. "Let's go, Meester Bel-mayne!" he cried.

I roared out into the traffic. Shami hung out of the window, screaming at everyone to get out of the way. Minarets and domes sped by in a blur. Behind me I could hear the wail of police sirens, while in front the black Peugeot tore through the streets until eventually it screeched into the Pyramids Road. I turned in after it, then slammed my foot on the brake as I skidded round a pack of

meandering camels. The Peugeot was surrounded. I leapt out of my
car. Then suddenly the camels parted and the Peugeot was speeding
off into the distance. Back behind the wheel, I pressed my hand on
the horn, yelling at the camel drivers to clear the way. The police
came round the corner, managed to skirt the mêlée, and roared off
towards the Pyramids, after the Peugeot.

By the time I was clear there was no sign of the chase. About
two miles farther on, where the road stretched endlessly out in front
of me, I knew it was pointless to carry on. I turned round and drove
slowly back. Then a police car came speeding up behind me and
screeched to a halt as I waved. The Chief clambered out of the back
seat.

"We've got him! Turn your car round and follow us. If you
get lost Shami knows where the Alexandria Road is. And you,
Shami . . ." He said something in Egyptian and went back to his car.

A few minutes later we pulled up outside a palatial villa. The
gates were locked but a police officer got out of the Chief's car and
spoke for some time on the intercom. Eventually the Chief joined
him, listened for a while, then went back to his car and opened the
back door. Robert got out and the two of them came over to me.

"The Pasha is inside," the Chief said. "He wants to speak to
you. I have agreed to wait outside, but Mr. Lyttleton will go in with
you. I think you know by now that the Pasha is a dangerous man.
Please, just listen and don't do anything foolish."

I nodded and waited while the Chief went back to the intercom. A few seconds later the villa gates slid slowly open. As I drove
in I saw the Chief and two police officers creep in behind me and
disappear into the bushes of the garden.

Robert followed me over to the door. Tentatively I tried the
handle, and to my surprise the door opened. The entrance hall,
carpeted in tiger skins and ornamented with elaborate gilt mirrors,
was empty. I turned back to Robert and suddenly the double doors
at the end of the hall swung open.

"Mr. Belmayne."

The first thing I noticed about the Pasha was the almost overpowering beauty of his smile. The second was his height. His forehead was masked by the doorframe, but his eyes gazed down into
mine as he lifted a gold-laden hand. With a long, clawlike finger he
stroked his lips. His movements were almost feminine and yet his

every gesture exuded menace—a sinister combination that made me shudder with revulsion.

"We will not waste words, Mr. Belmayne," he drawled. "If you want your daughter returned, then you will ask the police to leave my premises immediately."

Suddenly my control shattered and I lunged at him, grabbing him by the throat. "Tell me where she is now, or so help me, I'll kill you."

He squealed like a rabbit, his limbs thrashing about in all directions.

"Let him go!"

I wheeled round to see a woman standing at the bottom of the stairs. She was pointing a gun at Robert. Her hair and part of her face were covered by a spangled scarf, and her eyes were heavily ringed with kohl. She was looking at me and I sensed rather than saw the triumphant smile.

I let the Pasha go. He held his hand out for the gun, then casually looked Robert and me over. "It would seem, Christine," he said, "that they have not yet solved my little riddle. So what we have in the child is our passport out of the country."

Christine looked up at him, and I saw a strange, almost hypnotic adoration shine from her face. The Pasha nodded for us to go into the room behind him. Robert and I exchanged glances, but there was very little we could do with a gun at our heads.

I was already inside the room when I heard the shout. The front door crashed open and suddenly the place was filled with police. Two shots were fired, almost simultaneously. I swung round—and the Pasha's eyes seemed to bore into mine. Before he fell I saw more evil in that one look than I had ever seen before in my life. Christine screamed and ran towards him, then before any of us had time to move, she had seized his gun and was pointing it at me.

"You!" she spat. "You! Everything that's happened is because of you and your slut! You killed my brother, and now you've killed my husband." And before anyone could stop her she had pulled the trigger.

The bullet tore through my shoulder. Within seconds the police had seized her. Robert was hanging on to me, keeping me from falling. It must have been only minutes later that I lost consciousness.

I passed the night at the Embassy, drugged with painkillers, and my left arm supported by a sling. Robert came to see how I was the next morning, and after taking my temperature and checking my wound, the nurse told him I was fit enough to leave the room. On the way to the Ambassador's office he filled me in on what had been happening throughout the night.

The Pasha wasn't dead. While Robert brought me back to the Embassy doctor, where I would be safe from the press, the Pasha had been rushed to the hospital under police escort.

"And Christine?"

"She's being held at El Knater—the women's prison." He stopped to let someone pass, but made no move to walk on again. "I don't suppose you knew she'd married the Pasha, did you?" he asked.

I shook my head. "No, but I suppose that's what her brother meant by the Pasha having some kind of hold over her. She's going to live to regret that marriage."

We started to walk on. "Why do you say that?"

"Under the laws of Islam isn't a woman her husband's property? I take it the Pasha is a Moslem?" Robert nodded. "Then she'll have to face the rigors of Egyptian law. With the murder of the security guard, the forging of the mask, illegal import and export, kidnapping and God only knows what else they've been up to, she could be facing a death sentence." I steeled myself before asking the next question, even though I already knew the answer. "Has either of them told you where Charlotte is?"

Robert shook his head. "She wasn't in the villa, the police searched it from top to bottom. But there is some good news. They've called in some egghead from the Cairo Museum who thinks he's cracked the conundrum."

We were at the Ambassador's office now. Inside were the Ambassador, the Chief of Police and the professor. The professor was seated at a table by the window, surrounded by bibles and history books.

"It was necessary to channel thoughts in a new direction," the

Chief said, once the introductions were over. "My friend here has done that, and now, after a long process of elimination, we have the answer." The professor sat by, smiling benignly, as the Chief explained how the professor had come up with the solution. It was, like almost everything else I had encountered since I'd arrived in Egypt, bizarre in the extreme.

"We merely used hieroglyphs," the professor explained, as if one might use hieroglyphs to solve any old problem. "First, we took the rod. Do you remember? Moses' rod changed to a snake. It was God's way of showing Moses he had the power of God within him. Here," he held up a piece of paper, "the hieroglyph snake. Do you see?"

Robert, the Ambassador and I looked blankly at a squiggle that vaguely resembled a snake. The professor merely shrugged at our lack of appreciation. "Then we considered the plague and how the children died. They were visited by the angel of death, yes? Flying like a bird by night over Egypt, yes? And the bird that flies by night? An owl. And the hieratic script for owl, see here?"

Again he showed us a piece of paper. On it was scribbled what looked to be the figure three.

"This is the sign for the owl. And now see, if you put them together, the sign of the snake and the sign of the owl, this is what you have."

He waited while we passed round the results of his efforts, then taking it back from Robert, and, hardly able to contain his excitement, he said. "This is the sign which is inscribed over a door in El Khalifa—the City of the Dead. It is the door of the Pasha's mother's house. I have no doubt in my mind that your daughter is there, so if you are ready, Mr. Belmayne, we will go."

I was too stunned by the tortured logic to do more than smile stupidly.

It was a long journey to the southeastern outskirts of the city, and one I can barely remember now, for I spent the time praying that the Chief's confidence was not ill-placed. As we drove into the City of the Dead Robert wound up the windows to block out the stench. We remained in the Chief's car with the Ambassador while, surrounded by his men, the Chief made his way into the macabre town.

I could hardly believe what I was seeing as they stepped

through the dust among emaciated animals, mud-fronted tombs and wretched, tired-looking old men. But it wasn't that that shocked me, it was the brand new Mercedes, Jaguars and most incredible of all, Rolls Royces. Robert explained that even if they became rich, some people preferred to stay with their neighbors among the ancient tombs, where they had become used to living side by side with the dead. If I hadn't already, then it was at that point that I gave up any hope of ever understanding this nation.

We had been waiting for ten minutes, maybe less, when the haunting cry of the muezzin drifted from distant minarets. Hunched and shrouded figures shuffled past on their way to prayer, and round brown eyes glanced furtively in our direction. A few minutes later the Chief came striding towards the car. Behind him an old lady, wailing loudly, was being escorted by two police officers. They bundled her into a car, and the Chief got back into his. There was no sign of Charlotte.

"She is gone," the Chief said. "They took her away this morning."

"They? Who are you talking about?" I demanded, failing to keep the desperation from my voice.

The Chief nodded to his driver, then turned to face us. "I'm sorry, Mr. Belmayne, I cannot say. All I know is that she was alive when they took her. My men are taking the Pasha's mother away to be questioned, but I think she was speaking the truth when she said she didn't know the people who came for your daughter."

I slumped back in my seat, unsure if I could take any more. None of us spoke as we were driven back to the Embassy. None of us wanted to admit that we could be right back at square one.

"Ah, Meester Ambassador, Meester Belmayne," Shami said as we walked into the Ambassador's office. He was grinning like a pumpkin. "The secretary she say I can wait here for you. You find your daughter, no?"

"No!"

The smile fell from his face. "You no find her? But was my . . ." He threw up his hands in exasperation. "He drink again," he said, mysteriously. "You come with me, Meester Belmayne, I take you to your daughter. Very fine, very beautiful girl, your daughter. I take you there now. She wait for you."

"You mean you know where she is?"

"Sure. She with my brother. I take her from El Khalifa in this morning. She no like it there. Come, she wait for you."

I was aware of my whole body turning rigid as grim suspicion flowered into certainty. "Have you known all the time where she is, Shami?"

Shami nodded brightly. "For sure I know, Meester Belmayne. Shami know everything."

I lunged at him but Robert and the Ambassador pulled me back. "If you knew, then why have you let us go through all this?" I yelled.

Shami shrugged. "To say mean no money, Meester Belmayne. Like everyone in the world, Shami need money." He grinned. "And the chase, aaah, the chase, he was good, no?"

For the moment, robbed of the power of speech, all I could do was stare at him. While my daughter had suffered in God only knew what kind of hell, with God only knew what kind of people, this man had thought no further than the money he could make and the sport to be had in making it. He shuffled his feet and grinned sheepishly from me to Robert. Then the Chief of Police ushered him out of the room before I could regain control of my faculties . . .

Elizabeth

31

I HAD BEEN IN HOLLOWAY Prison for exactly sixteen days when Alexander brought Charlotte back to England; already it felt like a lifetime. Henry came to see me that day to tell me Alexander had taken Charlotte straight to the hospital. I can't explain what it was like living with the frustration of such helplessness.

The day after he flew in, Alexander, together with Oscar Renfrew, came to see me. As I was led up to the visiting hall my heart was in my throat and I felt sick with the humiliation of him seeing me like this. The first time he had come, the day before he went to Cairo, I was still too dazed to think straight. But now, as I walked soundlessly along the corridors, avoiding the eyes of the officers we passed, I was all too aware of the living hell my life had become. When I'd been told he was coming I'd brushed my hair and left it loose, but I knew it wouldn't hide the dark rings round my eyes or the dullness of my skin. Of the three outfits I'd been allowed to take into prison I'd chosen a black Chanel suit as the one I would wear for visiting days. I no longer had it. The other women, resenting the open display of wealth, had ripped it to pieces and were using it as dusters to clean their cells. Very few of them spoke to me except to sneer and hiss and catcall across the landings. I was terrified of them. I stood at mealtimes—unable to sit down because no one would let me. I ate very little, as they spat in my food or knocked it from my tray. Most of the time I was dirty because I was too afraid to go to the washrooms. It wasn't until Isabelle, my cell mate, decided to befriend me that I managed to utter more than a few words to anyone. Without Isabelle I don't know how I'd have got through. After days of silently watching the way I was treated, she took it upon herself to protect me from the constant threats of violence and sexual abuse, and pulled strings to get me a job in the library with her. It was my only respite from the nightmare.

Just past the visiting hall, the prison officer stopped and opened the door to an interview room. There was brown carpet on the floor and the walls were bare. In the middle was a table. I went in and she closed the door behind me. A few minutes later I heard footsteps, then the door opened and Alexander was there. I had promised myself I would be strong, that I wouldn't let him know how awful things really were, but when I saw the look in his eyes my control fell apart. I had never seen a man's face so filled with love and anguish.

With one arm he held me, burying his face in my hair and whispering for me to be calm. Oscar nodded to the prison officer and she left us alone. It was some time before I could pull myself together. Throughout the time Alexander and Charlotte had been in Cairo, Henry had kept me informed of what was happening, and now, knowing they were both home and safe, all the torment and terror I had somehow managed to bottle up came pouring out. Alexander waited while I reminded him that I'd told him not to go, that I had warned him about the kind of people he was dealing with; I called him irresponsible, selfish and stupid, I even lashed out at his wounded arm. In the end he caught hold of me and turned me to face him.

"It's good to see you too," he said.

He sat me down then and, perched on the edge of the table, he laughed as he told me how Jonathan was green with envy that he hadn't been kidnapped too, and couldn't wait for Charlotte to come home from the hospital so he could hear all the gory details.

"Don't worry," he smiled as he saw my look of alarm, "my father's taking Jonathan off to the country this afternoon, so Charlotte will be spared. Canary and Caroline will be looking after her. And me, of course."

I looked away, my heart aching. They would be together now—Alexander, Charlotte and Jonathan, and here was I . . .

He must have sensed how I was feeling because he slipped his arm out of its sling and hugged me. "We'll have you out of here, darling," he promised. "I know it's difficult, but please, try and be patient."

But I knew from the way his eyes met Oscar's that something was troubling him, and when I challenged him, he admitted it. It was the way the Egyptians had gone about interrogating Christine. Although he had no actual details of what they had done to extract the confession from her, he knew that when it came to appeal the prosecution would make a great deal of their methods and perhaps succeed in invalidating the confession altogether.

"Our only hope is for her to be present at the appeal," Oscar said. "Even then, there's no way of knowing if she will admit to the crime."

But she did. Exerting every ounce of influence they had, between them the British Ambassador in Cairo and Alexander's father managed to get Christine, under heavy guard, flown to London for the appeal. It was only later I found out, that, had she not been there, there would have been no appeal.

It was almost nine months since I had last seen her, and four of those she had spent in an Egyptian prison. She was forty-three now, but looked closer to sixty. Her hair, what was left of it, clung to her skull, and as she looked up from her bony hands and shifted her weight stiffly from one leg to the other, I saw the strange pallor in her eyes. Her small, heavy-lipped mouth was drawn into sharp, parallel lines of rancor. She held herself erect, but I could see that beneath the brown serge that almost engulfed her, her emaciated body was beginning to sag with the effort.

Mesmerized, horrified, I watched her as she took the oath, almost choking on the pity and sadness I felt at seeing her like that. Then, as she looked out across the courtroom, a triumphant gleam lighting her yellowed eyes, I knew the time for reckoning between us had come.

"I am in no doubt," she said. "I know that by the end of this year I shall be dead. The crimes my husband and I have committed in Egypt are sufficient to earn us not one but two death sentences. I welcome them. There is nothing left to live for. My husband and my brother were my life. I am under no illusions about the way they manipulated me, the way I became a pawn in their dangerous games, the way I was used as an exchange of favors between them, but it doesn't matter. I got what I wanted. I got Salah—the Pasha. He married me because my brother requested it. He never did and never will love me, I know that, but I can accept it. For me it was enough to be his wife. He was a man who wielded immense power; he could be ruthless and tyrannical, he was malevolent, corrupt and cruel—yet he only ever treated me with kindness.

"I am telling you all this because I want you to understand why I did what I did for my brother. You see, I knew what it was to love someone who was in love with another man. My brother lived with that hell for more than twelve years. Every day was torture to him—to be with her, yet not to be loved by her. It drove him out of his mind, in fact it killed him. Salah too loved a man, but I shall be the one who is with him at the end, in a way my sister-in-law was never with my brother."

As she continued to speak, trying to explain her blinding passion for the Pasha, it was as if she were reliving it all again, oblivious of the courtroom and everyone in it. Until Alexander told me I'd had no knowledge of her marriage, and now, together with everyone else in the court, I sat spellbound as she spoke of the obsessional and unrequited love she had for Salah—a love that, time after time, she likened to Edward's love for me.

Finally she lowered her eyes. "Maybe now you will understand why I set fire to the Bridlington warehouse with the intention of killing my sister-in-law." I felt my body go rigid and everything around me started to swim. "I hated her. She brought her bastard daughter into our home, that man's bastard—" her hand was trembling as she pointed towards Alexander, though she had not raised her voice—"and my brother treated the child as his own. He gave them both everything they could want. And how did she repay him? She ran off with her lover again, returned to us when he had finished with her, and tried to palm her second bastard off as my brother's child. And even after lying to him and cheating him in the way she had, he forgave her, because he loved her. He even adopted her children as his own. He changed his will for them. And all the time

I was the one helping him to realize an ambition that would save him from the final ignominy of her faithlessness. The need for the mask burned in him with all the might of his love. If he couldn't have it, there was nothing left for him. And while I helped him, *she* was back in her lover's bed. This time when my brother found out, it killed him. My sister-in-law deserved to die, and she would have died if Daniel Davison had not saved her life." Her eyes rested fleetingly on me before she looked away again. "If it were left to me she would not go to prison, she would rot in hell." She paused again, and a gruesome smile dawned on her face. "But my brother loved her. He would have forgiven her anything, and it is because of him that I am prepared to absolve her from her sentence. She is innocent."

My hands bit into the rail in front of me as she turned and fixed her yellow eyes on mine. Her smile had widened now, and there was something so sinister about it that my mind went numb with terror. Why was she doing this? Why, when she hated me so much, was she setting me free? My whole body trembled with horror as she hissed the answer:

"Now live with the guilt."

Her eyes were still boring into mine as a barely audible chuckle escaped her lips. She had won.

After my release, as the weeks passed I saw less and less of Alexander. I couldn't look at him and love him without seeing Christine's face and the way she had looked that last day. He tried everything he could to persuade me to pull myself together, but the more he yelled or cajoled, the more I withdrew.

Then, on the day Christine was sentenced to die—September 14th—a messenger arrived with a special delivery. Even now I find it difficult to put into words the way I felt when I opened the envelope. There was nothing to say who had torn the page from Christine's diary and sent it to me, I even wondered if she had done it herself. The entry was for September 12th and as I read, my heart was filled with the terrible loneliness and confusion she must have suffered, not only during her final hours, but ever since I had come into her life.

From the moment I met her there was never any doubt in my mind that one day I would have to kill her. Perhaps it was a genuine vision of the future, though I recall no images, not even the vividness of the fire that was to consume so much. I felt only the overwhelming need to protect myself, and all that was mine.

Elizabeth Sorrill. She was blessed with the kind of beauty I had only ever dreamed about, bringing love and laughter to my brothers, while all the time she nursed the pain of a love she had lost—a love she would never give up.

And what right had she to that love? I am a woman, I have known love, I have known the pain of loss. Have I spent my life making others suffer for it?

But I know now that I have never experienced anything like the love that bound Elizabeth and Alexander. It was a love that not only bridged the gulf of class, but survived years of parting, the agony of rejection, and that most destructive of emotions, guilt. Do I envy her that love? No, I pity her. A love of that depth, that strength, exacts its own price. I was the one to call in the debt, and I have no regrets. Why should she have had it all? What was her suffering compared to mine? My brother gave her the world—but it was my world too, and I lied, cheated and murdered to get it back. Yet all the time my enemy—my invincible enemy—was not Elizabeth, not Alexander, but the love they shared.

Why was their love so indestructible?

I rest my head against the wall now. There is nothing to see here, only darkness, but my nostrils flare at the cloying stench of my surroundings. Among the few, almost indistinguishable sounds, I can hear myself laughing. Laughing and laughing. The bitter irony of it is, if anyone could answer me that last question, then here, at the end, they would hand me the key to life itself.

As it is, it is they who hold the key—Elizabeth and Alexander.

As I finished reading there was no longer any doubt in my mind that it was Christine who had sent it. I could almost see her smile, the smile she had aimed at me across the courtroom. By giving me my freedom she had sentenced me to a prison from which there could be no escape—a prison of guilt. She had known what she was doing then, and this was a final reminder. Her way of letting me know that, with her death, the door was locked on me and the key taken away for ever.

As I continued to grieve for us both I withdrew further into myself, unable to speak to anyone about it and unable to pick up my life and start again.

Sometimes, from an upstairs window, I would watch Alexander as he left the house with Charlotte or Jonathan. He had left the bar and would be taking up a consultancy in the city at the beginning of the following year. He'd wanted it to be a new start for us both, but every time I saw him I was reminded of the people who had suffered because of us. If he saw me looking, I let the curtain fall back into place, unable to meet his eyes. I longed for him so much that sometimes I thought I might go mad. And the more I tried to stop loving him, the stronger my love became, so that I wanted to die rather than carry on without him. But my guilt was always there, ready to deny me even the luxury of a final release.

It was one Saturday afternoon towards the end of September when Jessica telephoned. I stared at Canary as she held out the receiver; just the mention of Jessica's name was enough to make my conscience flare. Another victim, another accuser. She was asking if she could come to see me. I refused, but she was insistent.

She arrived around four o'clock in her silver Volkswagen. My heart lurched painfully as I saw the car pull up outside. It was the same car as Christine had driven, the same color even. I heard her talking to Canary in the hall, then the door opened and, bracing myself, I turned to face her.

Her blonde hair, silky and smooth, glinted in the afternoon sunlight. Her face was bronzed, and though I had seen her once before, she was much more beautiful than I remembered. Her eyes widened as she took in my neglected appearance. "Well," she said, "I don't suppose you always look such a mess, but I have to admit you're not at all what I expected."

I stared at her, but her eyes had begun an assessment of the room. "Would you like some tea?" I offered.

"I think Canary—that is her name, isn't it?—is getting some."

I gestured for her to sit down, and slipping her jacket from her shoulders she sat in Edward's chair, folding one leg over the other, looking small and elegant and relaxed. She seemed in no hurry to start a conversation, and the frank way in which she studied my face unsettled me. Then she laughed. "You look like him," she said. "My God, you actually look like him."

I stood up as Canary came into the room. She put the tea on the table between us, then left.

"I don't imagine you've come just to look at me," I said, as I handed Jessica a cup. "So why are you here?" I hadn't meant to sound so abrupt but I'd been on edge ever since she'd phoned.

"I'm here to find out just what you are playing at."

"Playing at?" I put my cup down, spilling tea in the saucer. "I don't think you've got any right . . ."

Her voice was smooth as she interrupted. "Elizabeth, I have lived with your ghost for more years than I care to remember. That alone gives me the right."

I looked at her, aware of the animosity between us growing. "OK, if you've got the right, then say what you've come to say. I'm listening."

She fumbled in her bag and brought out a pack of cigarettes. "I hate the gutter press, do you know that? Week after week these hacks ridicule what Rosalind and I are doing at Greenham Common, just for the fun of it—they've no conscience, no morals, and no compassion. But it's not the first time I've been one of their victims, is it? Because along with you and Alexander, Edward and Christine, I've been reaping the rewards of their mucky little exposé ever since they chose to blow your and Alexander's life to smithereens at Foxton's. They had nothing to gain by doing it, except momentarily to discredit Lord Belmayne. A few paragraphs of sensationalism with never a thought for the people whose lives they're destroying, and before you can even say 'repercussion' they've moved on to their next victim. The gutter press, that's where it all began. So are you really going to sit up there in that bedroom of yours for the rest of your life, taking all the blame for everything that happened? It must be quite something to think you've got the same sort of power as God Almighty."

She laughed. "I mean, three people are dead and no one else shares the blame. That is what you think, isn't it? Tell you what, why not give me a bit of it? I mean, if I hadn't married Alexander then you would never have married Edward, would you?"

I felt the blood drain from my face. For a fleeting moment I thought I saw Christine, smiling back at me.

Her voice was filled with derision. "You're pathetic. You're hurting Alexander, you're hurting yourself, and you're hurting your children—all because you can't come to terms with the fact that a lying, cheating, murdering bitch was sentenced to death in a foreign country for crimes she alone committed. Do you hear what I'm saying? *She alone!* She didn't need any help from you. You couldn't have stopped her doing it, you didn't even know what she was up to. So why are you making everyone suffer now?"

"How can you sit there and say that? Did Alexander tell you what Christine said in court? Did he tell you how I had cheated on Edward and lied to him all those years, while Alexander was cheating on you? How we took what we wanted, not caring what we might do to other people? Did he tell . . .?"

"Alexander's told me everything. And yes, I knew he was cheating on me. He was cheating on me from the day we got married—before, even. He loved you then, and he loves you now. That's why I'm here, though God only knows why I'm bothering. Look, for heaven's sake, Elizabeth, you can't have gone through all you have to throw it away now. Pull yourself together. You're behaving . . ."

"Edward and Christine are dead, Jessica! Nothing you say . . ."

"Edward died because he was a thief and a forger who played his hand too far and was double-crossed. That bloody mask was what brought on his stroke. You know it and Christine knew it too. So how the hell can you sit there letting Alexander, Charlotte and Jonathan pay for it? What's past is past, Elizabeth. You've got to put it behind you, and carry on."

I looked down as the button I had been twisting broke from my cardigan and rolled onto the floor. Jessica looked too, and laughed as she got up to help herself to more tea. "Well, now that we've dispensed with Edward and Christine, let's get back to you. I'm sure you won't mind me saying so—and too bad if you do—but you're spineless, Elizabeth. An out-and-out coward. Alexander's out of his mind, letting you get away with what you're doing to him."

"If you knew the truth, the real truth . . ."

"Elizabeth, believe it or not I do understand how you feel. No one could have come through the ordeal you have suffered and not be scarred by it. But think about Alexander. He gave up on his marriage, he threw away his career and then risked his life—all for you. What more do you want from him? I'll be honest, I don't much care about you, but don't hurt him any longer, please."

It was several minutes before I could speak. I was too crushed by her sudden compassion even to look at her. "Does he know you're here?" I asked.

"No." She downed her tea, then picked up her jacket. "I came because I think you should know; Alexander and I were divorced yesterday."

I watched her walk to the door. As she reached it she turned back, stared at me for a few seconds, then said, "I'm glad I came. I never knew Edward but I feel . . . Well, we had a lot in common, didn't we? He with his obsession, me with my search for a meaning to life. The cross we shared was loving you two. We've all paid the price, Elizabeth, every one of us. Don't let it be for nothing."

Long after she'd gone I sat in the chair going over everything Jessica had said. The fact was, she had been more accurate than she could possibly have known when she called me a coward. I was a lot worse even than that. But now I knew that I had to do something I should have done from the start. I had to tell Alexander the truth, so he would know why there could never be any future for us. I had to tell him how, on that Saturday afternoon in September, I had set light to the Bridlington warehouse and killed Daniel Davison . . .

I hadn't intended to kill him, I had intended to kill Christine. From the moment I turned from the chaos and destruction in the store-room and looked into Kamel's eyes, all I knew was unadulterated terror. He laughed when he saw how frightened I was, and turned to Christine, who was standing behind him.

It was her idea to set fire to all the evidence against us, hers and Dan's. Kamel sent me to get the kerosene from my car. He was the one to pour the contents over the wreckage, but it was I who set light to it. Within seconds the whole room was ablaze. Kamel started to run and yelled to us to get back. But Christine stood at the door, staring into the flames. And suddenly I felt myself blind to reason, so that all I could see was that here was a way out of the blackmail, an end to the threats to my children. I lifted my hands and slammed them against Christine's back. As she staggered forward, I pushed her again. She fell into the fire, but as I turned to run she wrenched herself from the flames and caught my foot, so that I crashed to the ground. We fought, trying to force each other into the blaze. My hair was burning and her dress was alight. She was on top of me and pain seared through my hands as I grabbed her. Then with all my strength I threw her off, and she screamed out as she landed on her back in the heart of the fire. Then I watched, unmoving, as she struggled to get up. She was screaming and I could see the terror in her eyes. But still I didn't move.

Then I was knocked out of the way and Dan rushed in to drag her out. He called out for me to help, yelling that I was a murdering bitch, but all I could do was watch, paralyzed by what I had done, unable to take my eyes from Christine. Before the dresser fell on Dan I saw him pull her free, but once it had fallen I could no longer see either of them. It was then that I ran away.

So I was a coward. I was a murderer and an arsonist too. And all the time he was defending me, while Michael Samuelson so nearly put together the pieces of what had really happened, Alexander's belief in my innocence never wavered. He had put his life at risk, and Charlotte's too, all to get me out of prison when I was guilty of the crime that had put me there. I had lied to him, and had gone on lying to him. And I knew it was that he would never be able to forgive.

32

B Y ELEVEN THE NEXT morning my bag was packed and standing in the hall. I told Jeffrey he could take it out to the car, then turned back to the stairs.

I used the telephone in my bedroom. My heartbeat was steady now, but still my fingers shook as I dialed the number. After the seventh ring I started to replace the receiver, but as I did so I heard a voice answer.

Now the moment had arrived, my voice died in my throat.

I could hear him breathing. And then very quietly he said, "Elizabeth? Is that you?"

I swallowed hard, willing myself to go through with it. "Alexander, we have to talk," I said finally.

"I'll come over."

"No!" I took a deep breath. "I want to tell you now. I don't want to see you, and when you've heard what I've got to say you'll understand that it's for the best that we don't meet."

He listened in silence as I told him. Sometimes I paused, thinking that now he would speak, but he didn't. So I went on, telling him everything, exactly the way it had happened, until I got to the end.

I waited, but still he didn't speak.

"Alexander, I'm sorry," I whispered. "I know it's too late now, and it won't change anything, but I want you to know I love you with all my heart. There are no excuses, nothing I say can change what happened, but I just . . ."

"Why didn't you trust me, Elizabeth?"

The silence drew out until, unable to stand it any longer, I replaced the receiver and left the room.

I stayed in Sark for three days. It was cold and wintry, and not at all as it had been the last time I was there, with Alexander.

I visited all the places we had been together—the smugglers' caves, Dixcart Bay, Venus Pool. I even stayed at the same hotel. I tried and tried to recapture what we had had, to remember how much in love we had been before I lied to him, before Christine had died, before I deceived Edward . . . but my memories were drowned by the sound of his voice asking me why I hadn't trusted him.

It was late in the afternoon, the clouds were thickening overhead and the rain drizzled miserably from the sky, as I walked along the path to Jespillière House.

I had been afraid to come. Afraid because, of all the places on the island, it was Jespillière, the meadow and the cliffs around it, that held the most precious of my memories. The house was still there, dignified in its neglect, and I remembered how we had dreamed that one day it would be ours. I turned and walked on, out across the tiny meadow and down through the gorse, on to the cliff edge. My breath caught in my throat and threatened to choke me as the memories came flooding back. It was here, at the end of that week, when I thought the pain of leaving him would crush me, that he had come to find me. It was here, on this island, that Jonathan had been conceived, and where I first told Alexander he had a daughter. And now, looking back, I couldn't help wondering what would have happened if we had come here the first time he'd asked me, when he was still only seventeen and I was twenty-two. Things might have turned out very differently. Would our love, given time, have burned itself out? Had it been the separation and the desperate need for something we couldn't have that had bound us to each other all these years? But no, it was more than that, it was something I couldn't put into words.

The wind howled round the cliffs, biting my face and penetrating my clothes with its cold breath, and suddenly I knew I had been right to come. At last I was remembering him as he had been the first time we were here, when he held me in his arms and promised me that one day we would return. He would never keep that promise now, but I would always remember how in love we had been.

I looked up to the sky, letting the rain wash away my tears. It was all over now. I would always love him, nothing would ever change that.

Pulling my coat tightly round me, I took one last look across the sunless seascape. My eyes followed the tide, moving ever and steadily inwards to the shoreline below. I stood for a long time, looking down into the bay, until the darkness gathered shadows—as if trying to draw together the fractured pieces of my heart. I buried my face in my hands, drowning in the bottomless gulf of grief.

And then, even before he spoke my name, I knew. Lifting my head, my eyes blinded by tears, I turned and walked slowly into his arms.

BY SUSAN LEWIS

A Class Apart